No Enemy But Time

'What are you saying to yourself?' she asked him. She was feeling sleepy and reassured. She yawned.

'Nothing for you to know,' her brother said. 'Come on, Clarry, go to your bed.'

'All right. Kiss goodnight?' It was their ritual, ever since she'd been able to string words together.

'Kiss goodnight,' he said, wanting her to go. He felt hurt and angry and older than he'd ever felt in his life before. The child belonged back in her nursery.

Claire offered her cheek and then planted a hard kiss on his. Both arms were round his neck in a stranglehold.

'I love you,' she said. 'You're my best brother.'

In memory of my
father and mother

Also in Arrow by Evelyn Anthony

Albatross
The Assassin
The Avenue of the Dead
The Company of Saints
The Defector
The Grave of Truth
The Legend
Malaspiga Exit
The Occupying Power
The Poellenberg Inheritance
The Rendezvous
The Return
Voices on the Wind

No Enemy But Time

EVELYN ANTHONY

ARROW BOOKS

AUTHOR'S NOTE

The house at Cloncarrig and the fox's hide are not a legend, nor did I invent them. They exist, and so did their owner, although his name was not Reynard, and his estate and the follies he built on it are in a different part of Ireland. I have walked the fields and seen the refuge for myself. His friends still hunt the country there, and some swear that they've seen a big dog fox disappear into the folly. Being Ireland, no one hunts it any further, just in case.

Evelyn Anthony
1986

Arrow Books Limited
62–65 Chandos Place, London WC2N 4NW

An imprint of Century Hutchinson Limited

London Melbourne Sydney Auckland
Johannesburg and agencies throughout
the world

First published by Hutchinson 1987

Arrow edition 1987

© Evelyn Anthony 1987

Phototypeset in Linotron Plantin
by Input Typesetting Ltd, London

Printed in Great Britain by
Anchor Brendon Limited, Tiptree, Essex

ISBN 0 09 954020 2

Chapter I

The dawn was breaking as the cars rolled off the ferry at North Wall; there was a sullen, red-streaked sky, with banks of threatening clouds building up on the horizon. After the stale fug in the tiny cabin, she gulped down the clean sea air, the car window wide open. It was a hired car. If they were watching for her, they wouldn't expect her to travel on the night boat from Liverpool, with a rough sea battering at the B & I ship, while the drunks and the seasick threw up in the smelly lounges.

Even so, she had hidden herself in the claustrophobic cabin, afraid she might be recognized. She was difficult to disguise, being tall and strikingly blonde with a face that had appeared too often in newspapers and smart magazines. The charming wife of the youngest member of the Cabinet. Articles about her family life, the handsome Georgian house in Gloucestershire, *Homes and Gardens*, colour supplement, *Vogue* profile material. All the pre-packaged nonsense of a plastic person, she said once, but that only made her husband angry. 'If you hate it all so much, why don't you go back to the bogs?' was his retort. The bogs; that was how he dismissed Ireland. He'd said it once too often, and this time she'd taken him at his word. Slowly the line of cars inched towards the Customs sheds. She drove into the green section. She had nothing to declare. She was waved on by a sharp-eyed young officer, who boasted he could smell a smuggler from fifty yards away. She hadn't realized until she was bumping along the road away from the dock that she'd been shaking like an aspen leaf. There had been no time for a cup of coffee and she'd eaten nothing the night before, going straight to her cabin. She felt weak and her head ached. No cigarettes either: early-open cafés tempted her going through Dublin, but she resisted. The Irish are the most inquisitive race in the world. Every head would turn if a woman walked into one of those male preserves. She couldn't risk that.

The roads were empty in the grey light, and she jumped traffic lights, making smart time. As she turned on to the dual carriageway that ended only a few miles beyond Naas, the rain spat against the windscreen. She fumbled, looking for the windscreen wipers in the unfamiliar car. The little arms flashed back and forth against the glass, fighting the lashing water.

'That's Our Lady weeping for your sins, Miss Claire,' their cook used to say when the heavens opened. So many tears, she thought, and so many sins to be washed away. And so much blood. Centuries of blood-letting; at times the rivers of Ireland ran tainted water that the cattle wouldn't drink. It was so dark she switched on her car lights. 'God,' her husband said, whenever she'd brought him home before her father died, 'what a bloody awful climate . . .' He never noticed the brilliant sunny days, hot as the Mediterranean, when the sky was vivid blue, and the air as sweet as wine.

She saw the signpost, white on green, pointing to the turn off, opposite Kill. How many times she had felt a lift of excitement when she saw that sign and knew that Riverstown was only ten minutes away. Coming back from school in England, being met at the airport, hoping to find Francis the other side of the door into the main building. Running to hug him without being in the least self-conscious. He was her brother, and she loved him best in the world after her own parents. And next came the wonderful, handsome, shabby old house where they had grown up together. Less than a mile now, down the twisty road past Straffan.

The storm had spent itself, and a thin sun was showing through. She stopped the whirring wipers, wound the window down and smelt greedily the scent of grass and overgrown hedgerows that nobody bothered to trim.

There at the end of the road was the turning to their gates. There was a signpost saying 'Clane', and its other arm said 'Naas' in faded lettering. The local children loved to turn them round. Nothing had changed in the last three years. The visitor would still travel miles in the wrong direction.

From the gates ahead, she had left for her wedding in the big Church of Ireland church in Naas. Miss Claire Arbuthnot, shrouded in her English mother's family lace, with pearls shining like drops of new milk round her neck. Claire had heard the Irish maids talking in the kitchen, 'Pearls are tears . . . God love her, she shouldn't be wearin' those on her weddin' day . . .'

Her half-brother had said, 'Why do you have to wear his bloody family jewellery . . .'

'Because it's my wedding present and I'm not a superstitious idiot like you.' And then, because she couldn't bear to quarrel with him the night before she left for a new life, she said, 'I'm wearing your mother's brooch, Fran. It's my something blue.' He'd looked ashamed then, and mumbled about being sorry. On the morning she saw him standing in the body of the church, dark as a gypsy in his morning suit. The little brooch with its sapphire heart was pinned to the silk bow of her dress. She gave him a special smile as she passed by on their father's arm. But the girls' whispering had been right. She still had the pearls, but there had been many tears since she first wore them.

She didn't turn into the gates, although they were open. Her mother always got up early and exercised her dogs before breakfast. Claire drove past, bearing left down a small side road, following the curve of the grey stone wall that surrounded Riverstown.

Billy's cottage was set back off the road, behind a neat little hedge. He had kept lurchers when they were children, and used to take Francis lamping for rabbits. She had been furious that he wouldn't take her too. It wasn't fit for a young girl, he'd explained in his thick brogue, and her half-brother had grinned and mocked her behind his back. The dogs' descendants were still with him, though rheumatism made it difficult for him to go scrambling over the fields at night with the powerful torch to blind the rabbits. They began to bark as she walked the few yards to his front door. There was no bell. She knocked. She saw a lift in the lace curtain and wondered whether Billy had his woman with him. Everyone knew about Billy's woman, but he kept her hidden and it was supposed she must be married. The door opened and he stood there, staring at her, a squat little old man in shirt-sleeves and braces, a cap set on his head. He was never seen without it, except at Mass. He hated showing his bald head. For a moment he stared, and then his face broke up into a huge smile. 'Jaysus, it's yerself! Will ye come in?'

Sitting in his kitchen, with a cup of tea and a begged cigarette, she didn't try to pretend when he said, 'What's wrong wit' ye, Claire?' He'd been there to pick her up when she fell off her first pony; he'd taught her to fish and to know about dogs, and whatever mischief she and Francis got up to, he never told a tale. He was, as her mother had said for twenty years, the laziest codder God ever put breath into, but Claire loved him, and he loved her as if she were his own. She looked him in the eye, and saw him turn and blink. There was tinker blood in him, so her father said. Tinkers always shifted away if you held their gaze.

'I've come to help Frankie,' she said. Fear shuttered his face. Now he wouldn't look near her.

'Sure there's no helping him,' he muttered. He went to the stove and lifted the lid off the teapot to distract himself. 'Pay no thought to him,' he muttered. 'Not God himself could do anything for him.'

'Billy,' she said quietly, 'he's my brother.'

'Only the half of him,' the old man said. He poured more tea into her cup, fumbled with the bottle of milk and dropped the tin-foil top. 'It's the other half that's been the death of him.'

She exclaimed in anguish, and he couldn't keep his

head turned from her. 'Dead! You mean they've found him?'

'No, no, no . . . not yet so, but they're lookin'. He's no time left at all. Have you been up to the house yet?'

'No, and you're not going to tell Mother I'm here.'

'And how would I, seein' she's away?'

Claire said, 'Where's she gone?'

He frowned, sucking at his lower lip. 'Off to stay wit' auld missus Keys down in Cork. You're to bolt and bar the house up, she says to me. He'll not hide himself at Riverstown.' He slid a sly look at Claire when he said that. He had always hated Mrs Arbuthnot. He rubbed his stubby nose. 'I padlocked them gates after herself drove away,' he muttered.

Claire said, 'They were open, that's why I thought she was at home.'

'I'd better go up and take a look,' he mumbled again, but he didn't move.

After a long pause, Claire said, 'Would it be the Gardai who opened them . . . ?' Knowing that the Irish police would have come to Billy for the key.

He was already frightened, and the question irritated him. 'Jaysus, if it's the others in there, waitin' for him . . .'

Claire touched his arm. He was old and she could see the empty teacup was trembling in his hand. 'It's not them,' she said. 'They'd know Frankie wouldn't come home. It could be the Special Branch waiting for me.'

He let out a deep breath. 'You? Oh, Mother o' God, what have ye to do wit' any of this?'

'I told you, I've come to try and find him,' she answered. 'I didn't tell anyone, not my husband, no one. I just got on the ferry. But my husband will guess. He'll guess I've come back and why. He'll tell the authorities in Dublin.'

'I never liked that fella,' Billy snorted. 'You'd no business marryin' a fella like that.'

'I don't like him much either,' Claire admitted. She

9

managed to smile at him. 'You're going to help me, Billy, aren't you?'

He shook his head vigorously. The cap stayed glued on. 'No. Ye'll get divil an' all help from me, gettin' yerself into trouble. Go home to England and yer husband, like him or not, and yer children. What about them?'

She felt very tired suddenly, and angry with him for trying to find a weak spot. 'You don't have to help me,' she said. 'I'll manage on my own.'

He muttered a curse; he knew Gaelic, and spoke it among his own. He had always pretended to his employer that he didn't. 'Ye'll stay where ye are.' He heaved himself up from the kitchen chair and reached for his coat behind the door. 'I'll take the dogs for a walk up by the river and see what's to be seen. If the Gardai's up there, I'll talk to them, so. I'm not to know about the gates . . . There's bread and a bite of ham in the larder. I'll not be long.'

Claire watched him through the window, lifting the lace curtain as he had done. His steps were slow, moving to the kennels where the lurchers lived, fastening them to their leads, shouting at them as they leapt up at him in excitement. He was an old man, and frightened of the death squad of his countrymen, yet allegiance to them was in his blood. A deeper allegiance than his love for the children of the Anglo-Irish landlord he had worked for since he was a homeless lad knocking at the kitchen door to ask for a cup of tea and an odd job. Why should Billy put himself at risk for the sake of his hereditary enemies, whether he'd helped to bring them up or not? And she remembered then the old adage tossed around the dinner table by her parents' friends, when the drink had loosened their tongues, and things were said that stuck in the mind like grit in the eye.

'The trouble is, you just can't trust them. All smiles to your face, and the minute your back's turned, they'll rob you blind. Or walk out and let you down at the last minute.' It was servant talk, of course. But the taint was there, right throughout the race of native Irish. You can't trust them. And you never intermarried. It wasn't just class, as Francis used to say when he raged against the system. It was race, and there would never be peace while that discrimination lasted.

Claire turned away from the window. She sat down in the one comfortable chair; it had come from their housekeeper's room, and had found its way to Billy's kitchen, like the strip of Turkey carpet with the hole in the middle.

The turf stove was alight, and she felt drowsy in the warmth. When they were on holiday from school, she and Francis used to come to Billy's cottage and sit in the kitchen, drinking tea. He taught her brother how to roll a cigarette, and she remembered him doubling up with delighted laughter as the boy coughed and spluttered on his first smoke. 'You'll help me, won't you, Billy?' The stout refusal, and then the shambling figure going up the long path beside the river, up to the house. He wouldn't find her brother Francis there. Nor would the hard-eyed men from Dublin, if her husband had alerted them. Nor, thank God, the merciless executioners of the IRA.

He was being hunted; she was the only person in the world who knew where he would go to hide.

Billy Gorman trudged up the long path to the kitchen garden and the back of the house. On his way he passed the main drive, and he could see that at the end of it the gates were open. He cursed under his breath, shaking his head at his own folly in coming up to the house at all . . .

But he couldn't turn back now. Whoever was inside could have seen him from the windows. He took a cheap cigarette out of his jacket pocket, paused and lit it with a match in his cupped hand. It wouldn't be *them*. It wasn't their way to come in the open. They struck in darkness: the kicked-in door, the burst of gunfire, the hooded killers vanishing like demons into the night. But not always, he remembered. They killed the poor idiot from Sallins in broad daylight . . . He sucked in smoke and coughed. Too late to stop now; better him meeting them than Claire, he thought, and drew courage. For some reason he remembered old Doyle, the gardener, dead now for thirty years, leading him up the same pathway round to the back door and into the kitchen for the mid-morning cup of tea. He'd been a hard man to work for, but he taught Billy everything he knew about that garden and how to take care of it. And when he died, he left the few bits in the cottage to Billy. The back door was ajar. He saw a shadow moving through the kitchen window, and half turned to break into a shambling run.

'Billy! I was just comin' down to look for you.' There, framed in the doorway, was young Joe Burns, looking to Billy like a guardian angel in his blue Garda uniform.

He gasped with relief. 'Jaysus, I thought ye was a burglar . . . I'll tie up the dogs.' The kitchen was cold; the Aga was turned down while Mrs Arbuthnot was away. For a moment or two Billy was too relieved even to ask what he was doing in the house, or how he'd managed to get in when it was all locked up.

The young policeman said in his friendly way, 'It's a careless man ye are, Billy, leaving them gates and the back door open.' He was a pleasant boy, newly recruited into the local force at Clane. He'd been born there and the Burnses had been part of the village for generations.

Billy squinted at him; his heart had stopped hammering with fright. 'I locked up everything meself,' he insisted.

Joe Burns shook his head reproachfully. 'Ye thought ye did,' he said. 'We knew at the station Mrs Arbuthnot was away; she always lets us know, these days. I was passing when I saw the gates not shut properly, so I thought I'd best come in and see if everything was all right at the house . . .'

Billy rubbed his nose and shook his head. 'I'd swear I locked them,' he muttered. The policeman wasn't convinced, but Billy thought, I locked them gates. I locked all the doors. I've been doin' it for thirty years, since old Doyle died. I didn't forget. He looked into the smiling blue eyes of the policeman. There were three cigarette butts in a saucer on the kitchen table. He'd been there for some time.

'Well now,' Burns said, 'ye've saved me the trouble of comin' down to see you. I was on my way when you come up.'

But not in a hurry about it, Billy said to himself. Sitting in a kitchen cold as charity, smoking. Waiting.

'When's Mrs Arbuthnot comin' back?'

Billy said, 'I don't know. She'll ring me up the day before.'

'It must be terrible for her,' Joe went on, 'her son gone missing and all this stuff about him on the radio and television.'

'He's her stepson,' Billy mumbled. 'It's not the same.'

'Ah, you're right,' Joe Burns nodded. 'It's the daughter she had . . . the one that married that English fella. Isn't he in the British Government or something?'

Billy didn't answer; he grunted.

'You've known them all, Billy,' the easy voice went on. 'Is it true what's said about them two?'

'What two?' he asked.

'The brother and sister. It's said they were so close she'd be after coming over when he disappeared. I don't think she'd take a risk like that meself . . .'

'What risk would that be?' Billy gazed at him in innocence. He could scent danger, as his beloved dogs could sight a hare a mile away. And every antenna quivered with alarm. The blue uniform didn't signify safety any longer. Billy didn't know what was wrong, he only knew that something was.

Generations of subservience had taught the humble Irish not to answer any question that might get them into trouble.

Joe Burns lowered his voice, as if they might be overheard. 'She's married to this important man,' he said.

13

'The IRA might do some harm to her. Listen Billy, if ye hear she's come home here, ye'll give me a call at the station. Ask for me, if there's any news of her. I'd like to be the one to pass it on.' He gave a slight grin. 'It'd do my prospects a bit of good.'

'Sure an' I will,' Billy agreed. 'But I wouldn't say it's likely. Jaysus, I can't believe I forgot them gates and the kitchen door . . . Shouldn't we check through the house to be sure nobody's been in?'

Joe Burns said, 'I've already done that, Billy. I'll be off now. Don't worry yerself, I'll not mention a word of it to anyone. And don't forget now; you hear anything, you let me know!'

Billy nodded, promised again, and they went out together. He locked the back door, gathered his dogs and separated from the Garda at the top of the drive.

Burns waved cheerfully to him and walked back to the main entrance. 'I'll see ye,' he called.

Billy didn't hurry till he was out of sight. Joe Burns was lying about finding the gates and the back door open. He was lying when he said he'd checked the house. The door from the kitchen into the main hall was always double-locked, and the key was in Billy's pocket. The whole story had been a lie. Burns had opened the gates and the back door himself and slipped inside. He hadn't been coming down to see Billy. Billy had caught him by surprise.

If there was news of Claire Fraser, Joe Burns wanted to be the first to hear it. As Billy came back down by the river and up the hill towards the cottage, he knew the danger in the kitchen had a name at last. Fear flooded over him. He saw the car with its English number plates parked in full view of the road. He didn't waste time. She'd left the key in it. He could be very agile when he chose. He had an old banger of his own, bought with Philip Arbuthnot's legacy. He backed it out of the shed where it was parked and drove Claire's car in off the road. He heaved the shed doors shut, so it was hidden. He was puffing and out of breath. He'd forgotten to shut up his dogs; they'd waited patiently outside the front door.

He didn't go inside at once. He sat on his own doorstep and tried to think what to do. Frank Arbuthnot had disappeared from his Dublin bank four days ago. The news on TV had been full of it. 'Leading merchant banker vanishes. Fear for his safety.' That was the headline in the *Independent*. Strong hints about his IRA sympathies, as if everyone didn't know he'd been a self-proclaimed Sinn Feinner since he was a youngster. Rumours that he'd been kidnapped or murdered as part of the split that was rending the Provisionals and the old Republican idealists. And Billy had listened to the TV pundits and read the newspapers, and said to himself it was sure to happen in the end. He'd supped with the devil and no spoon was long enough. After what happened to the poor idiot, Donny, at Sallins, just two miles down the road, an Arbuthnot wouldn't be a trouble to their consciences.

And now the child had come back, putting herself in danger for the sake of that brother. He thought of her as the child, though she was married and a mother. He'd dandled her on his knee when she could hardly walk. He sighed a deep, despairing sigh. She must go back to England. He'd drive her to Dublin himself. She couldn't stay in Ireland if he was right about Joe Burns. It wasn't just Frank they were looking for, if they hadn't shot him already and buried him in some bog.

Claire got up when he came into the kitchen. 'You found someone up there,' she said, seeing his face.

He cleared his throat. Better not tell her the truth. Better just argue her into going back where she belonged. 'Only Joe Burns. He's in the Gardai now,' he said. 'I left the bloody old gate open and he came in to check the place.'

Claire sat down again. 'Don't lie to me, Billy. You said yourself you padlocked it. You've never forgotten to lock up in your life. I don't believe it was Joe Burns.'

'It was so!' he insisted. 'Asking questions about

15

yerself. I'm to ring him if you come here, says he. I will, says I. I near had a heart attack thinkin' of you down here under his nose!'

'I've nothing to fear from the Gardai here,' she said. 'I've known them all my life. Joe Burns's father used to work here as cattleman – you know that, Billy.'

'You can't stay here,' he muttered. 'Love of God, Claire, half the police in Ireland are lookin' for Frankie – if they can't find him, how can you . . . an' what if he's murdered?'

Claire said slowly, 'That's the second time you've said it. Why do you think he's dead?'

'Because he mixed himself up in poor Donny's murder.' He spoke very low. 'Ye won't know about that. The poor old divil was standin' on the Sallins railway bridge, watching the trains. He's been doin' it for forty years. Everyone knew Donny was mad for watching trains. No harm in him, he was just a bit of an eejit. There'd been a big robbery in Dublin: hundred thousand taken and the bank manager shot dead.' He lit a cigarette and passed the packet to her. His voice trembled. 'They got off the train, jumping as it went slow under the Sallins bridge. They saw old Donny standin' up there watching them. By Jaysus, they run to the top and stabbed the old fella to death. The Gardai said they thought he'd identify them. So they stabbed him. And anyone could see he was as simple as a child, just by the look of him.'

'I remember Donny,' Claire said quietly. 'We used to give him sweets on a Sunday. He was always standing round hoping there'd be a train. There never was on Sundays. I knew he was dead, Billy. And I know how Frank felt about it.'

'He went to the auld mither and gave her money. He came to see yer mother and talk to her about paying a reward. She'd have none of it, bein' a wise woman.'

Claire didn't have to ask how he knew. Nothing was a secret in Ireland. Her mother's maids would have over-

16

heard and repeated every last word through the village before the day's end.

'There was a lot of talk about it,' Billy went on. 'Some of the local lads were calling Frank names. Decent people kept quiet; it wouldn't help Donny to get into trouble.'

'That's the root of all evil in this country,' she said. 'The decent people staying quiet because they don't want trouble. Letting the killers get away with it. But my brother wouldn't. If he saw something wrong he said so. He'd speak out for a poor helpless old man like Donny, just as he did for Ireland.'

'Aye,' Billy Gorman said. 'And much good it's done him. Now I'll make us a bite to eat. I've put that car of yours in me shed. I'll drive you to the airport and you catch a plane home, like a sensible girl.'

'I am home,' Claire said simply. 'And I'm not going anywhere till I find Frank. Don't worry, Billy, I won't stay more than a few hours and by that time I'll know one way or the other. You won't get into trouble, I promise you.' She got up and came to him; she leant down and kissed him. He went pink to the edge of his cap. 'Let's have the bite to eat, shall we,' she suggested. 'I'm starving with hunger.'

'Billy,' she said after they'd eaten, 'I'll need to borrow your car.'

'Why so?' he asked.

'Because I can't run round in a car with English number plates,' she explained. 'You've told me about Joe Burns. That's the first thing anyone would look at round here.'

'The first thing they'd look at,' Billy countered, 'is a woman drivin' my auld rattlebones of a car! Have ye no sense at all? And where would ye be goin' then?'

'I can't tell you,' Claire said. 'You mustn't know, Billy. It's better not. I'll take the English car and be done with it.'

He slapped his fist on his knee in exasperation. She had him and he knew it. But then, even as a child she'd usually persuade him to let her do this or that against his better judgement. He mumbled and sighed. 'I'll change the number plates from my car to the other one,' he said. 'How long will ye be gone?'

'I don't know,' she said. 'I should be back before it's dark.' She saw the worried misery in his face and added gently, 'Don't worry; I'll be perfectly all right. Will you change the plates, then?'

'I will, so,' he sighed again. 'The sooner ye're gone, the sooner ye'll be back . . . then I'll run ye up to Dublin and get ye on the plane,' he said hopefully. 'Ye'll promise me that.'

'I can't promise anything,' Claire answered. 'But I will be careful.' She followed him to the door; he got some tools out of the shed and squatted down to unscrew the number plates from his old Renault. He became absorbed in the task, grumbling at the stiffness of the holding screws. The task was a blessed diversion; he couldn't stop her going, he could only concentrate on turning the bloody old things till they loosened. If God was good to them she'd find no hide nor hair of Frank Arbuthnot.

Claire said, 'Will it take long? I'd like to go up to the house. Give me the keys, will you, Billy? Just throw them over.'

'Here ye are.' He tossed the bunch to her. She caught them neatly. Frank had taught her how to catch. And how to shoot the rooks nesting high up in the trees with a rifle. Vermin, he called them, when she protested at killing a sitting bird. They slaughtered all the other fledglings and grabbed the space for themselves. Just like the English in Ireland.

'I'll be back in a little while,' Claire said. Billy cursed under his breath as his hand slipped. He didn't look up.

'Mind yerself,' he muttered.

'I will.' She closed the door and waited for a moment, then turned and went into the little bedroom. Neat and clean, evidence that Billy's woman was good about the house. High up on a ledge above a window, she found what she knew Billy Gorman would never give her: the keys to the gun room at Riverstown. She slipped the bunch into her pocket and went out of the door. He was hunched over the car. She turned and set off down the path leading to the river and the house.

The Minister's secretary buzzed him on the intercom. He had arrived late, which was unlike him, and seemed tense and irritable. Very untypical, she thought.

'Mr Brownlow is here, sir.'

'Thanks, Jean; show him in, please. And hold any calls till I buzz, will you.'

Mr Brownlow came in, took off his gloves and met the Minister for Trade and Industry, the Rt. Hon. Neil Fraser, as he moved out from behind his desk. It was a well-known face, he thought, a smooth, production-line politician with all the right connections and ingredients for success. Except that Ministers don't normally look as if they hadn't slept all night.

'Good morning, sir,' he said as they shook hands. 'No news of your wife, I take it?'

Fraser said, 'None, I'm afraid. Nothing your end? Please sit down.'

Brownlow didn't look like a policeman. He looked like a senior civil servant. He said, 'We've traced the taxi, and the garage where she hired a car. And she bought a ticket on the night ferry from Liverpool. So there's no doubt she's gone over.'

Neil Fraser leaned back in his chair. 'I never imagined she'd do such a thing.'

'But you suspected she might have gone to Ireland, didn't you? It was such a pity you didn't contact us immediately you got back and found her gone. We might have got her at the ferry.'

He wasn't going to let the Minister off the hook. In his view Fraser had delayed because he didn't want to face the truth. And that delay meant Mrs Fraser had arrived in the Republic of Ireland, when prompt action could have prevented the whole mess. And a fine mess it might turn out to be. 'She could have gone to friends, or just driven up to London,' Fraser defended himself. 'I could hardly start a major scare until I'd made certain, could I?'

'No, I take your point. But we'd rather have a major scare that turned out to be a false alarm than the real thing and a late start, sir.'

Fraser said wearily, 'Have you been on to Dublin?'

'No, sir. There's some things to be cleared up first. I'd like to ask you some questions. They may be a bit personal. I hope you don't mind.' In case the Minister thought of pulling rank, Brownlow added, 'Your wife's in very great danger; I'm sure you realize that. Getting her out of Ireland is all that matters. We've got to have all the facts.'

'I know that,' Neil Fraser answered. 'I'm going to order some coffee. Would you like some, Superintendent?'

'Thanks very much. And it's Brownlow, sir. We don't use our rank.'

'No, of course you don't. I'm not functioning very well today, I'm afraid.'

Brownlow managed a brief smile. 'That's understandable. Do you mind if I smoke?'

Fraser shook his head. Brownlow was right. He had delayed. Hoping against all hope that Claire hadn't snapped the last link between them and gone to look for that bastard . . . Knowing in his heart, while he telephoned the night porter at their London flat, and went the round of their friends, that she had made her choice. Did this hard-nosed Special Branch officer expect him to discuss that . . . How much of what happened before she left must he disclose?

As if Brownlow could read his mind, he broke in quietly. 'It's her life at stake,' he said. 'If they get their hands on her, they'll kill her. Don't make any mistake about that.'

Neil Fraser leaned forward slowly, and for a moment

covered his face with his hands. Brownlow waited till he had composed himself.

'Ask anything you feel is necessary,' he said, and Brownlow knew he'd get the truth.

'Was there any kind of crisis that brought this to a head? Did you quarrel?'

Neil nodded. 'Yes, we did. We had a serious row two nights ago. I went up to London early that morning and it wasn't made up. That's why I came back on Tuesday night; normally I stay in London during the week – my wife usually spends a couple of days at the flat with me.'

'Lucky you went home,' Brownlow remarked. 'What was the row about?' He had noted the bitter edge to Fraser's voice. A lot of pent-up emotion there, he thought. Not the first row, by any means . . .

'Ireland. And her half-brother.'

'What were your wife's views on the situation over there then? Was she a sympathizer?'

'With the IRA? Good God, no! My wife's family are the sort of people they attack first. No, Claire's not political in the least. She doesn't give a damn about politics – never has.'

Not much of a recommendation for a politician's wife, Brownlow observed. Fraser was being tipped as a future Prime Minister. He prompted, 'Is she worried about her brother?'

Neil Fraser said flatly, 'She's devoted to him. It didn't matter what he did, she wouldn't hear a word against him.'

'And is that why she's gone to Ireland?'

'Yes,' Neil Fraser replied. 'That's what we argued about. I tried to convince her there was nothing she could do. I'm afraid I lost my temper and said if he'd fallen foul of the IRA it bloody well served him right for supporting them.'

'She took this badly?'

'Pretty badly. I shouldn't have put it so strongly, but I never thought she'd actually go . . . I pointed out how dangerous it would be, and – well, how damaging to me in my position if my wife went to Ireland at a time like this.'

'Quite so,' Brownlow agreed. 'Having him for a brother-in-law must have been embarrassing at times.'

'That's exactly what I told her,' the Minister said. 'The press have been decent about it for years; even the Opposition hasn't suggested that his attitudes affected my credibility or my wife's. But going there could . . .' he paused, and then said angrily, 'it could ruin me.'

Brownlow waited for a moment, made an extra note. 'You rang her home in Ireland and there was no reply?'

Fraser nodded. 'That's all I could do, without alerting everyone in the neighbourhood. I tried at regular intervals throughout the night and first thing this morning. There's no one there. Have you been through to Dublin?' he repeated.

'No, and I'm not going to,' Brownlow answered. 'Their people are very good and we have a close cooperation with them. Much closer than the general public knows. But we can't take a chance this time, sir. One careless word could set those bastards on your wife. We can't ask the Irish SB people for help, we'll have to sort it out ourselves.'

'How can you?' Fraser asked. 'What can you possibly do?'

'Send in an expert,' Brownlow said. 'A specialist, used to working over there. Undercover. Find your wife and bring her out.'

'You mean the SAS?'

'I think we'll leave the details out of it, sir.'

The Minister surprised him by getting up. He seemed suddenly positive. 'If that's what you propose, I've got the man,' he said. 'He's a personal friend, and my wife likes him. He knows us both very well. I'll give you the name.' He wrote it down and handed Brownlow the slip of paper. 'I also know,' he went on, 'that he's in England at the moment. I don't want to tell you your job, Brownlow, but if anyone can persuade my wife to come home, and be a good man in case of trouble, it's him. I'd like you to contact him at once.'

Brownlow read the name and the rank, folded the slip and put it in his wallet. If anything went wrong, he could blame it on the Minister's interference. And there was no denying the man's qualifications, if he belonged to *that* branch. He got up. 'I'll get on to it right away. Say nothing to anyone about your wife; tell your staff she's with friends, anything convincing. Act absolutely normally, and with a bit of luck she'll be home before you know it.'

They shook hands again.

'Thank you for coming.' Neil Fraser opened the door to the outer office himself.

Brownlow went down in the lift, found his car in the side street and got in. He told the driver to take him back to his office.

'If that's the kind of bloody fool that runs this country,' he muttered to himself, 'Gawd help us.' Frigging around instead of facing up to where the bloody wife had gone and putting a stop to it at once. His career would be ruined. Much good that'd do her, if what his department suspected was true. Not that he'd tell Fraser. Frank Arbuthnot had been an IRA paymaster for years. Suddenly he goes missing. Very publicly missing. Hadn't it occurred to that burke of a husband that the whole thing could be a put-up job to get his wife over to Ireland?

What a coup for the bastards, if they kidnapped or murdered the wife of a Cabinet Minister. He didn't need Fraser to tell him about the brother and sister. The Special Branch knew everything about Claire Fraser because it was their job to dig around the politicians and their families, especially with an Irish connection like hers. Close as bloody Siamese twins they were. Of course she'd go home, if anything went wrong with him. And wouldn't it be neat for his IRA friends to bait the trap for Fraser's wife with her own brother. Whether he agreed to it or not? From what Brownlow knew about

23

Frank Arbuthnot and his half-sister, he wouldn't be a tethered goat from choice.

He went into the building, up in the lift to the fifth floor, and called a conference among his senior colleagues. An hour later he put in a call to Major Michael Harvey in an army barracks in a secluded part of South Wales.

The path from Billy's cottage wound down towards the river bank. The early rain had left little puddles in the dips along the way. When she and Frank were children, they used to skip the puddles, or sometimes land in the middle, spattering themselves, with shouts of glee. The air was fresh and sweet, the river swept along on its way, swelled by the backwash that made a tiny waterfall further along. Her father had complained to the Water Board every year for the last fifteen of his life that their damned backwashing was washing away his river bank. Nobody took any notice, but official letters were always polite.

The shady ground under the coppice of trees was a blue and white carpet of anemones – what trouble Claire had with that word when she was little, at times it still defeated her. Later the daffodils would muster, blazing like an army of yellow heads the length of the bank and right up to the steps leading to the old house. So many happy memories met her with every step she took. A childhood full of games and innocent adventures, the changing retinue of family dogs, ponies to ride and hunt, with Frank taking the leading rein. Her parents were always up at the front. Only her brother was willing to go home early, towing a child and a fat pony. School was not taken very seriously. She went to the nearest Protestant school, which was over at Kilcock, and learned to read and write with the daughters of their friends.

How often she and Frank had spent the day down by the river, fishing for the cunning trout, or lazing in the damp grass, talking. There were five years between them, but she thought of him as older. Her earliest memory was of him holding her tightly by the hand, when she was just a toddler, in case she strayed too near the rushing river. There were a nurse, and her parents, but they were dim figures compared with Francis. He was tall and strong, and kept her safe. He shared his secrets with her, and from childhood on, Claire would have given her life to please him. Their rooms adjoined, and if she had a nightmare, he was first in to comfort her and laugh the fears away. He told her about the fairies who lived in the holes on the river bank, and how Billy was half leprechaun. They used to giggle and splutter when they saw the old man, thinking of him sitting on a toadstool in the moonlight. She learned about their ancestors from him, and how they came to Ireland and built Riverstown. For a long time, she was afraid to pass the portrait on the stairs of the one he called the Hanging Judge.

She felt so close to him as she retraced the steps of her childhood and young adult life, that for a moment she was overcome by pain. There was a worn and weatherbeaten seat, hewn out of a fallen tree trunk. Claire sat down, as they had done so many times together, and the years fell away as if they had never been apart and she had never married.

'I'm different to you, Clarry.' He was fourteen then, thin and very dark, with the intensity of adolescence.

'How different? You're a boy, that's what's different.' She resented the claim because it raised some barrier between them. She was nine, blonde as a daisy, with big, blue eyes, unaware of her own prettiness. Rather a tomboy, always climbing trees and tearing her clothes and trying to out-ride and outrun everybody else, so she could match up to Francis.

'I know that, you eejit,' he retorted. 'I mean really different. I'm half Irish.'

Claire stared at him. 'What's different then? We're all Irish!'

'No,' her brother insisted. 'You're an Anglo. So's

25

Dad. My mother,' he said, lowering his voice, 'was from the bogs. The Ryans are proper Irish. That makes me half.'

Claire said crossly, still worried, 'Everyone knows that. You're not different to me, Frankie. Mummy's *English* –'

He looked down at that. 'I know,' he said.

Her mother wasn't Frank's mother, because she had died when he was born. There was no conflict. People had step-mothers and fathers. Claudia Arbuthnot was never cross with him or punished him for anything. His father did that. But he was his real father so it was all right. Claire pulled at his sleeve. 'Don't be different to me, Frankie. I don't want you to be different.' Her eyes filled with tears. His were very dark; his hair was black. He was amazingly like Daddy. Suddenly he hugged her, then as abruptly pushed her away and jumped up.

'Don't be such a silly cry-baby. Race you to the old seat!' He was sitting, laughing at her as she hurtled up to him, scarlet-faced and out of breath.

'You bloody pig,' she gasped. 'That's not fair. I can't run as fast as you!'

'That's because you're an Anglo,' he taunted, and was off, daring her to try and catch him. She had a terrible temper, and it always made him double up when she swore at him and clenched her fists. By the time he let her catch him, Claire had forgotten what he'd said, and he had temporarily forgotten why he said it. She only remembered it long afterwards, the night his father turned him out of Riverstown. The day they found the fox.

A few spots of rain fell on Claire. Claire Fraser now, over twenty years later, sitting on the log seat with tears in her eyes. The sun was slipping behind a bank of shower-filled cloud. She got up and quickened her walk up to the house. The key of the back door was in her pocket, the other keys, the stolen bunch, cutting into her hand. Out of so much love, so much misery had come. Out of closeness, such division. Was it true, what he said, that wretched day they said goodbye? 'It's not anybody's fault, Claire. Not Dad's or Claudia's or mine. If you want to know why things have turned out as they are, you've got to go back to the beginning.'

She let herself into the kitchen, where young Joe Burns had asked about her. Questions that frightened Billy into telling lies. Joe's father had worked for her father, and Joe himself had earned a few shillings helping out, when he was a scrawny boy with a runny nose. But Billy didn't trust him. And Billy knew his own people better than any Arbuthnot ever would.

Claire unlocked the door into the main part of the house. It was dark and shuttered in the hall. She flooded it with electric light. There was a whisper of dampness in the air. You couldn't close up an Irish house without the weather getting into the fabric. And there they were, her ancestors, watching her from the walls. Nearly two hundred years unbroken, living at Riverstown. Births and marriages and deaths; the tombstones on Naas church a testimonial, her own father's the most recent. But his first wife, Eileen Arbuthnot, was not buried there. The division had begun with her.

At the foot of the stairs Claire paused and looked up. There was the portrait she had been so frightened by when she was little. A dour, ill-painted picture of a man in a dark coat and tight cravat, with a stern tight mouth and lifeless eyes. The Hanging Judge. He'd hung Irishmen like apples from the gallows tree. Claire turned away. Look back to the beginning. Whoever said that spoke the doom of Ireland.

Chapter 2

The first Arbuthnot came to Ireland in 1798 to try the rebels who had burned the English garrison alive in their barracks at Prosperous. An odd name for a poverty-stricken Irish village in Kildare. Judge Arbuthnot passed sentence of death by hanging, or exile to the penal colonies in the West Indies, on the men of Prosperous. Some had lit the torches and roasted other men alive in the middle of the night. Others had stood by. They suffered equally.

Hugh Arbuthnot took time off from his duties to tour the countryside, and decided that apart from its inhabitants, it was one of the most beautiful places on earth. The fields were green and lush with pasture, the river Liffey flowed through land that was as rich as his Scottish farm was bleak and poor. His people had wrung a meagre living from it. In Ireland, nature had been over-generous. Cattle grew fat, the rivers abounded with fish. The air was mild, and the rain didn't trouble a Scotsman. He applied for a grant of land and this was sold to him for a nominal sum. He neither knew nor cared who had been evicted from it and left destitute.

The site where Hugh Arbuthnot chose to build his house was a rise in the ground, overlooking the river. Fine lime trees formed a natural avenue for the approach; copper beeches and great elms gave shelter from the wind in the east; should the river flood, as he'd observed it did after heavy rain, the house was safe upon its hill. He brought his wife and children over and they settled into the fine house which he called Riverstown.

His son built a stone wall high enough to keep the poachers out, with handsome wrought-iron gates. The stone pineapples on the two piers at his gateway signified that the owner was a justice. He was a shrewd man, not over-kind-hearted, but the misery of the famine brought people dying of hunger to his gates. They were not turned away. The Arbuthnots prospered. They married with a view to inheritance, attended the local Protestant church and contributed handsomely to its building programme. Their sons and daughters went to England for their education, to Trinity College, Dublin, where Catholics were barred, or to English universities.

Younger sons went into the British Army, and one became a distinguished admiral in the Royal Navy.

They tended to choose wives and husbands within their circle in Ireland, and would always describe themselves as Irish. Their excellent record as landlords and non-involvement in local politics saved Riverstown from being burnt down by the IRA in 1922. Neighbours who were not so well thought of stood and watched at gunpoint, while their homes went up in flames.

Philip Arbuthnot was three years old when the Peace was signed that divided Ireland. He was the eldest son, his two brothers having been killed in the Great War. He inherited Riverstown and its eleven hundred acres when he was twenty-seven and married. Neither of his parents had come to the wedding. The rumours said that his bride was already pregnant when he married her. Nobody believed Philip could have done such a thing as marry one of the Ryan girls for love.

Philip was tall with curly black hair and a little moustache that made him look old-fashioned. He was a sportsman and a countryman, uncomplicated in his attitude to people and to life. When he met Eileen Ryan she was sitting on a bank with a dazed look, her bicycle up-ended in a ditch. Her fine red hair glittered like gold in the watery sunlight. Philip stopped, got out and asked her if she was all right.

'I don't know for sure. Where am I?' There was a sweet lilt of brogue in her voice.

Philip knew concussion when he saw it. And at the moment he helped her into his car, he fell in love with her. It wasn't a long courtship. It wasn't a courtship at all, according to Eileen's outraged family, who viewed her meeting with a member of the Protestant gentry with deep suspicion. They didn't want one of them hanging round Eileen, who was too young yet to know what a fool she was making of herself. They didn't see marriage and didn't want to see it. They foresaw only shame and gossip among their own people.

The parish priest was consulted and summoned

Eileen. He came to see her father and advised that she be sent to relatives in Cork and kept there till the danger to her immortal soul was past.

A week later, they eloped to England, and were married in London. The Protestant marriage didn't reconcile his father, who believed that his son had been caught and was marrying because he had some misplaced sense of honour. His mother flatly refused to receive a daughter-in-law who was no better than one of her own maids. The fact that the Ryans were wealthy farmers made no difference. The Ryans were bog Irish. Eventually, they supposed, some means would be found of paying the wretched girl off, when Philip came to his senses.

His father died eighteen months later of undiagnosed cancer of the lung. He didn't disinherit his son, as some of their more extreme friends advised, nor did he tell Philip's mother that he had met his son and daughter-in-law in London. A pretty little wisp of a girl who was certainly not pregnant, she obviously adored Philip. She had a delicacy and charm about her that the old man recognized. He'd seen women in his boyhood with shawls over their heads and bare feet, with the same air of ancient breeding. He wished them happiness, but he didn't ask them to come home.

When he died, his widow moved to a property in Meath and Philip brought his young Irish wife back to Ireland to live at Riverstown. Mrs Gerard, the old housekeeper, had given notice. She was not, she told Mrs Arbuthnot, prepared to work for the likes of *her*.

They drove through the gates and up the avenue of ancient lime trees. It was a bright autumn day in 1938 and as they rounded the bend and came in sight of the river, Philip took her hand and said, 'Look, darling, isn't that wonderful? Just look at the leaf colour all along the bank there . . .' She saw the excitement in his face and smiled to please him. Surely the great blaze of reds and golden yellows was a marvellous sight, but they did nothing to ease the apprehension in her heart. At home they took such things without comment. There was little time to stand admiring the view of this or that season when there was a big farm to run and a house and family to be looked after. 'Oh, God love us, the dirty old east wind is coming up,' her mother would say as the trees turned colour.

'It's lovely, Phil,' she said softly. 'Like a picture painting.'

He squeezed her hand and said, 'A painting, sweetheart. Not picture painting.' He didn't see the faint blush of embarrassment because she turned her head away. All he saw as he glanced at her was his little wife, shy as a fieldmouse, clinging to his hand. Of course she was nervous, he thought, seeing the big white-painted façade of his home come into the open. It was a big place, though the Ryans' farm was substantial enough. She'd nothing to worry about, especially since that old bitch Mrs Gerard had walked off in a huff. Eileen wouldn't have found her easy to cope with. He'd set the staff straight if there was any nonsense . . .

The gardener was waiting for them at the front door. He opened the car door for Philip, who handed his wife out.

'This is Doyle,' he said, introducing her.

'Mrs Arbuthnot.'

Doyle had his cap off and noticed that the new missus half put out her hand to shake his, not knowing what to do.

'Welcome, sir; welcome, mam.'

Philip guided her by the arm into the front entrance and the hall, where a frightening array of girls in uniforms with white aprons and the cook, whom Eileen had known since she was a child, came up one by one and greeted them. She could feel her cheeks burning as girls she'd been to the convent school with in Naas said, 'Welcome, mam' and some had slyness in their smiles.

The cook said, 'Mrs Gerard's gone, sir. Will ye be getting someone else?'

'That's up to my wife,' Philip said firmly. 'But I think

we'd like tea in the library. And early dinner, please, Mary. Mrs Arbuthnot's tired. We had a long journey.'

'Was the crossing rough, sir?' Eileen stood there while he chatted to Mary, who was a distant cousin on the Ryan side. Of course he was at ease; he could joke with his servants and turn away, dismissing them with a happy, 'Good to see you all, and very good to be home.'

How could she do the same, when he wasn't there? He was so happy. When they were alone in the library, a fusty-smelling room full of books behind iron grilles, he hugged her and kissed her.

'It's wonderful to be back,' he said. 'Wonderful you're with me, darling. You're going to love Riverstown. How about a little smile then?'

He sat her down on his knee and kissed her, waking all the wicked senses that she'd been taught to suppress all her life. She was a delightfully fiery little thing, Philip thought, forgetting all about tea, opening her coat and beginning to unbutton her blouse.

It was Eileen who heard the knock and leapt away from him before the door had time to open. The silver tray was set down by Lily, who was senior parlourmaid and in her thirties. She didn't look at Eileen. She addressed herself to Philip.

'What time would you be wanting dinner, sir?'

Philip knew her well. She was his mother's toady, sneaking on the other maids, angling for the hated Mrs Gerard's job.

He said, 'Ask Mrs Arbuthnot.'

Eileen panicked. What time? Philip didn't eat tea like they did at home. He ate dinner and all she could remember was living with him in London; when they rented a flat, he wouldn't let her cook. There was a woman hired to do what she felt was a wife's job. What time? The gleam in Lily's eye was mocking as she repeated the question.

'Cook says, what time would you be wanting yer dinner, mam?'

'Eight o'clock, please.' Eileen remembered their

routine in London. It had taken her months to get used to eating so late and so many times a day.

'Very good, mam.'

The door closed and Philip held out his arms. There was no desire left in her and she shook her head.

'I'll pour the tea,' she said.

'We can go early to bed,' he suggested. 'Or would you rather see round the house first?'

She gave him the cup; a little had spilled in the saucer, because her hand wasn't quite steady.

'I'd rather go to bed with you than see round any house,' she said. 'If we were in London now, that's what we'd do. But not here, Phil. Not with all of them watching and sniggering.'

'Don't be ridiculous,' he exclaimed. 'Nobody's watching! Darling, for heaven's sake, you're the mistress here. You dealt with Lily perfectly well. It's bound to be a bit strange for you at first, but saying you won't make love to your own husband in your own house because of the servants . . .'

'They're servants to you,' she said quietly. 'But I went to school with them. Mary Donovan is a cousin of my father's! How am I going to do it, Phil? How am I going to manage this house and be a wife you can be proud of, when I've been brought up a different way, and everybody in the place knows it?'

He could look quite hard, she thought suddenly. Quite the Arbuthnot, dealing with some nonsense from the Irish.

'If there's any difficulty, Eileen, or advantage taken because you used to know them, we'll sack the lot and get a completely new staff. So put that out of your head once and for all. Now give me a piece of that fruit cake and stop being silly. We'll have a brief conducted tour. By the way, I want you to change the furniture round, get new curtains, that sort of thing. It's your home now. Remember that.'

Her eyes filled with tears. 'I do love you,' she said.

'I'll do my best, I promise you. I'll love Riverstown because it's yours.'

'That's my girl,' he said. 'Try this cake. Mary makes the best fruit cake in Ireland.'

She cut a slice to please him. It tasted heavy and there was too much whiskey in it for her taste. 'Mine's better,' she thought. 'But I can never go into my kitchen and cook for my husband. I can't stand and gossip with Dadda's old cousin and make a fruit cake from Mammy's recipe. I'm Mrs Arbuthnot and my whole life is changed for ever. Thank God I love him, or I'd be out of this house and home before you could say "knife". And I can't talk like that any more either.'

'Phil,' she said softly. 'Let's go on that tour. I want to see our bedroom.'

Only it wasn't theirs. It was a big room with a high, moulded ceiling and a draped bed that stood in the middle of it like a throne. The surfaces were bare; the mahogany gleamed with fresh polish. His mother had left nothing of herself behind. No photographs, no knick-knacks gathered over the years. But it was still her room.

'Mother didn't change things much,' he said. 'The room could do with a turn-out.'

'Blue is a dark colour,' Eileen said at last. 'It could be prettier a pale shade. A new carpet maybe . . .'

Anything to take the presence of the Hon. Blanche Arbuthnot of Dankelly Castle, Co. Louth, out of the room where Eileen was expected to lie in bed with her son.

There was a conference going on in the kitchen. Tea had been made and a big cake like the one served in the library was cut up in thick slices on the table. Lily was holding forth, her pinched face sallow with indignation. The expression 'white-livered' was an apt description of her nature.

'And there she was, sittin' there playing the high an' mighty madam, cocked up in Mrs Arbuthnot's chair.

34

Eight o'clock please, Lily . . .' She mimicked Eileen's voice. 'Mrs Gerard was right to pack her bag and go. If ye'd seen the airs and graces of her!'

She drank her tea and held out the cup for one of the under-maids to fill. She was a tyrant to the girls. Doyle, who tipped his tea into a saucer, looked up over the rim of it.

'I mind her father,' he said. 'Dirty as the auld pigs he tended to, not a penny to bless himself, till his auld skinflint uncle died and he got a hold of the place. He married a bit o' money though. Sure an' they must be pleased seein' the geddle come up in the world like she has.'

He wasn't a malicious man. The searing jealousy of the women didn't affect him. He liked a good gossip and knew something about everybody in the area. He was the same age as old Jack Ryan and well remembered the smell of the pigs he brought with him into the pub of an evening. Jack had been his uncle's heir. He was a rich farmer now, while Doyle was still dirt poor and broke his back in the Arbuthnots' garden with only a lazy boy to help him. If he resented anything it was Jack Ryan's meanness. If he saw Doyle in the pub he'd slide out of buying him a drink.

Mary sat with her elbows on the kitchen table. Her arms were plump and mottled, fat hands cradled the teacup.

'They even brought Father Dowd to her,' she announced. 'Divil a bit of good it did. She ran off breakin' my poor cousin's heart.' She slipped in her relationship to the new mistress with a mixture of satisfaction and gloom. It didn't please Lily or the other maids to hear her claim superiority over them.

'Ye must be shamed out of yer life, Mrs Donovan,' Bernadette piped up from her corner of the table. She was next in line to Lily, five years older than the girl who had come to Riverstown and had the whole world in her pocket, so far as Bernadette could see. All that money, and the fine clothes on her, and a gentleman

35

for a husband. She was damned to hell, of course, she comforted herself. Marrying outside her faith.

'Ah, well.' Mary decided privately that that Bernadette needed putting in her place. 'I've dinner to get for the new master and his lady wife. And to clean up my kitchen before she makes a tour of it. Doyle, ye've got mud on my floor from yer dirty boots!'

'I don't know how I'll bring meself to serve her,' Lily grumbled. 'Sitting in Mrs Arbuthnot's place at the dining table. I'd like to tip the soup in her lap!'

'I'd mind yerself, Lily,' Doyle said at the kitchen door. 'It's himself we've got to please, not her. He'll not put up wit' yer nonsense any more than the Major would.' Philip's father had served in the Irish Guards in the First World War, and was always referred to by his rank. He glanced resentfully at Mary Donovan. 'There's divil a bit of mud on me boots,' he muttered and went out into the back yard.

Upstairs, Eileen resisted as Philip tried to undress her. 'Not in here,' she whispered, avoiding his eager kisses. 'Can't we go somewhere else?' In the end they made love in his father's dressing room, confined on a narrow bed, and Eileen fell asleep. He woke her gently, smiling at her.

'You are a little tiger,' he said. 'You've scratched me to bits. We've got to change, darling, so you'd better get up.'

He saw her bewilderment and said, 'We always change for dinner at home. I know it's a bore, but it's expected. Have your bath, sweetheart, and wear something nice for me. How about the blue we bought together?'

It was a tactful way of explaining that change meant evening dress for her and dinner jacket for him. Poor little sweet, he thought, splashing in the hot water in his father's bathroom. It was all very strange to her, but she'd soon get the hang of it. She didn't mind him telling her things, and learned very quickly. She had modelled her speech on his and asked him to correct her if she said something wrong. Her clothes had been a problem.

That was solved by buying a complete new wardrobe. She was so pretty it didn't matter what she wore. Nothing at all, was better still. They were going to be late, unless he put that thought aside and got ready.

He gave her a glass of champagne in the drawing room before dinner. She looked very beautiful in the long slim blue dress. He'd given her a string of cultured pearls as a wedding present. His mother had taken all the family jewellery with her. There was a little blue brooch pinned to the neck of the dress. It didn't complement anything much, but he hadn't seen it before.

'Where did you get that, darling,' he touched it lightly with a finger, as if it were a toy out of a cracker. She had the brightest smile in the world, and the dress made her grey eyes look blue.

'It's my granny's,' she explained. 'She give it to me on my eighteenth birthday.'

'It's very pretty,' Philip said. 'Grandmother, darling, not granny. It makes you sound like a little girl. And she *gave* it to you.'

'Sure an' I know she did.' Suddenly, cheekily she spun round in front of him, mocking his attempts to turn her into an Anglo-Irish lady. 'Ye'll not make this particular sow's ear into a silk purse, young fella-me-lad!'

Lily, about to knock on the door to announce dinner, heard them laughing and paused, listening. She heard Philip say, 'Quite right, sweetheart. You've married a pompous idiot!' She couldn't make out Eileen's answer but she muttered, 'Eejit, is right,' before she knocked on the door. 'Dinner is served, sir and mam.'

They had been living at Riverstown for two months before the first invitation came. It was addressed to Mrs Philip Arbuthnot and a letter was enclosed with the card. It was written in a sprawling hand that was difficult to read. Eileen, who'd been beaten into writing legibly by the nuns, felt as if the writer didn't care whether her letters were decipherable or not. She knew the name, of course. The family were not rich; much of their land had been sold to pay the debts of successive wastrel sons. The baronetcy was a reward for acts of loyalty or oppression, depending upon which view you took of a small rebellion in the 1720s. They were old gentry, tolerated because they were permanently in decline and had fallen prey to drink and idleness. The family had been relieved of the embarrassment of a huge, unmanageable Georgian house by a convenient fire in the twenties. Sir William Hamilton was said to have started it himself, rather than repair the roof, which let in torrents of water in one wing.

The insurance company, refusing to accept the IRA as culprits, declined to pay. The family found themselves with a gutted ruin and one surviving wing. A local builder obliged by knocking down the remains in exchange for the materials he could salvage, and the place had been known as the Half House by local people ever since. The present Lady Hamilton was English and had some private money. Eileen read the letter slowly.

Dear Mrs Arbuthnot,

We hear that you and your husband are living at Riverstown since the poor Major's death and would be so pleased if you can come and dine with us on December 19th. It is a little close to Christmas, but that seems a good excuse for a party and it's high time we entertained some of our friends. We are so looking forward to meeting you and do hope you can come.

Sincerely,

Claudia Hamilton

P.S. I'll send you an *aide mémoire* if you can.

Eileen passed the letter to Philip. 'What's an *aide mémoire*?'

'It's a reminder; that's what it means, to remind you to come. It's a very nice letter. You'll like her, darling, she's great fun, marvellous horsewoman. He's a good chap, but he's mostly tight. I think we should go.'

'All right,' she said. 'If you want to.'

'If they weren't nice people, I wouldn't dream of it,' he said firmly. 'They'll like you and you'll like them, darling. Sooner or later, you've got to mix with our neighbours and this is a good way to start. Now, I've got to be off. See you at lunch time.'

He kissed her, squeezed her shoulder and was gone. She had been surprised how hard he worked on the place. She, *per contra*, had so little to do. There was a little hand-bell by her place; she rang it for Bernadette to come and clear the breakfast plates away. After that first tour of her new home, Eileen had avoided going into the kitchen as much as possible. Mary's attempts to be familiar with her when Philip wasn't there had been painfully embarrassing.

Sensing his wife's difficulty, Philip suggested she revert to his mother's custom and order the meals through Lily, as if she were the departed housekeeper. Lily's sour resentment was easier to manage than her blood cousin's attempt to presume and profit by their distant relationship.

And Lily's instinct for the winning side soon tempered her attitude to the new mistress. She became ingratiating and saw herself finally taking over the housekeeper's role. There was surprising strength in Eileen Arbuthnot. Shy and lacking confidence she might be, but she was not a woman to challenge outright and gradually the staff accepted her. They grumbled and gossiped among themselves, but Philip knew that his wife was in control.

She left the dining room that November morning and took the dogs for a walk down by the river. The old Labrador and the two Jack Russell terriers loved to go rabbiting along the bank. She hadn't a dog of her own yet. Domestic pets were not a part of Irish life; animals were worked, not cosseted. There was no sentiment towards them and no positive cruelty either. People were poor; even the better-off worked grinding hours on their farms, and if anything was to be fussed over, it was the old people or the children.

It was a mild morning, with a wintry sunshine dappling the ground under the trees. The river washed down on its run through Dublin into the sea, and a solitary man with a low-slung dog at his heels walked along the opposite bank. Eileen loved the river. She didn't fish, of course. Sports were not considered fit for girls. A race or two on prize day at the local school, modesty insisting on decent skirts and proper bloomers underneath them, was as much as the Irish girl was permitted. The others might bring up their daughters to ape men, but not the Children of Mary. She had a young brother, Kevin, who was fond of her in his quiet way. He didn't say much, but he was always kind to her. Her eldest brother thought of nothing but the day when he'd have the farm and be able to marry his sweetheart. He was thirty-five and had a while to wait, everyone reckoned.

The Labrador ambled beside Eileen. The terriers bounded along ahead on their short legs. Philip loved the smelly, aggressive little dogs and was always fussing in case they got stuck down the rabbit holes. Eileen couldn't understand why he felt like that about them. But she took extra care if she was out with them alone.

He wanted her to accept the Hamiltons' invitation. She shivered, pulling the coat closer round herself.

Marrying him was one thing; loving him and defying her family and Father Dowd had taken more courage and determination than she knew was in her. But the injustice of their attitude was the undoing of their arguments. Earning the obedience and respect of the women in the house, who saw her as no better than they were, was yet another obstacle. Many nights she had cried with loneliness when he was fast asleep beside her and risen smiling the next morning to continue the battle. It was all but won and she felt at peace. Even the house, with its big grand rooms and dark paintings of Arbuthnots, seemed less strange once she had altered the bedroom and rearranged the study into a cosy sitting room where she and Philip spent their evenings together.

But meeting the neighbours who knew who she was and that her mother-in-law had moved to another county rather than come face to face with her – that really frightened her. She was native Irish. All her life she had been taught that Philip and his kind were aliens in possession of land which they had stolen from its rightful owners. Oppressors of Ireland and its people, persecutors of the Catholic Church. Alien corn, Father Dowd called them once when he was being entertained at home and he and her father were discussing politics. The alien corn had been rooted out and burnt. Everyone said that the priest had encouraged many of the burnings during the twenties. His own family had been driven by starvation to emigrate to America. The terrible wrongs of the past were stronger than the Christian commandment to forgive. Eileen knew what she had thought of the Arbuthnots and their kind, until she fell in love with Philip. She knew what they in turn thought of her and her people. It had been made very plain over the centuries. And fundamentally nothing had changed. When the old Major, so soon to die, had travelled secretly to see his son and meet her, she recognized his courtesy because he was a gentleman, but there was no welcome and no warmth in him. He came in coldness, as she thought at the time, and left in coldness, to go to his grave.

There was a bench, fashioned out of a fallen tree trunk; the weather was mild enough to sit and watch the river. The old dog sank down by her feet; the terriers scuttled off to rootle through the brushwood. She called after them to no purpose. She remembered that terrible scene with her father, when he forbade her to see Philip again and told her she was going down to Cork till she came to her senses. He didn't listen to her when she tried to explain that they were going to marry. 'Marry in the Protestant Church! No daughter of mine'll set foot in it – I'd see ye dead first!' He didn't want to hear about the compromise they'd come to: an Anglican marriage, the sons to be in their father's religion, the daughters

41

baptized Catholics. All he could see was the shame and disgrace such an alliance would bring on a good Irish family.

She'd gone to her room and cried in misery. And there her mother came to add her warnings. They were gentle, because Bridget Ryan was a quiet woman; Jack Ryan blustered enough for both of them. She sat on the edge of the bed and reminded Eileen what was at stake: the damnation of her soul. Hadn't she understood what Father Dowd said that very afternoon? None of her family or friends would speak to her; she'd be cut off from her own kind. And what about *his* friends? Did she imagine they'd accept her? Wouldn't she always feel a fool, knowing they were laughing at her and her Irish ways. 'Bog trotters,' Bridget Ryan reminded her. 'That's what they call us. Paddy an' his pig. We're all right in our place, but that place is under their feet. Are ye telling me ye'll ever be at home among them?'

The next morning Eileen left the farm. She would never hear from her parents or her brothers and sisters again. She was outcast, as they had threatened.

Now she took Claudia Hamilton's letter out of her pocket and re-read it. Dinner on December 19th. Philip said they should go. 'You'll like her, darling. She's great fun.'

Philip was confident she'd be a success. He was always telling her how pretty she was, how well she ran Riverstown. He was a happy man, in love with his wife and deeply content. Twice he'd driven over to see his mother and come back optimistic that she'd come round to the marriage and visit them one day soon. Everything was wonderful, he said, and she knew it was for him. And if his mother came, she'd have to entertain her, instead of slamming the door in her face for the way she'd behaved. Philip had written a very conciliatory letter to her father, hoping they'd accept him as a son-in-law. Eileen was amazed that he expected a reply.

She got up, suddenly chilled after sitting so long. There was no sign of the terriers. Her spirits sank.

'Buttons, Ruby!'

'They're here, mam, wit' me.' Doyle shambled up the path, the little dogs trotting beside him. 'There's an auld wind come up,' he said. 'Ye'll catch yer death o' cold, sitting there.'

'The sun's gone in,' Eileen said. 'It'll come on to rain soon.'

'It will, so. I'll bring them little divils back to the house for ye, mam. Ye'd best go in before the rain.'

'I will, so,' she said, and for a moment there was a blessed communion between them. Doyle grinned at her and she had to turn away because her eyes filled with tears. She looked poorly, he thought. And sad, sitting there on the bench, not noticing the weather change. It must be lonely living away from your own. She was a nice enough girl and he felt sorry for her. He tethered the little dogs with a piece of twine and he didn't hurry walking back. Doyle never hurried. Time was made for man, not man for time. He'd get to the back door in time for his morning cup of tea and a warm by the kitchen range.

'You look lovely, sweetheart,' Philip said. He had come in from his dressing room and Eileen was waiting, dressed and ready for the dinner party. He wore his clothes so well, she thought, looking at him; not a bother on him, while she had tried on three different dresses before choosing one in desperation. He was born confident, sure of himself. How could he understand what an agony the evening must be for her.

'Lovely,' he repeated. 'Where did you buy that? I don't remember it.'

'I bought it,' she said, 'from that big shop in Piccadilly. It cost a fortune. I'm not even sure I like meself in it.'

'Well, I do,' he said. 'Now, darling, get your wrap on and we'll go. Claudia's English and she doesn't like people to be late.'

He squeezed her hand as they pulled into the drive of

43

Half House. 'You'll be a wild success,' he murmured. 'Everyone will fall in love with you.'

Claudia Hamilton was very tall. She was thin and her bare arms were muscular. She had fair hair that was done in a roll round her head, bright blue eyes and a loud English voice. She greeted Philip with a kiss, which didn't please Eileen – until she realized that it was common practice. They all kissed each other, these strange people. Then she held out her hand to Eileen and gave it a strong clasp that made her wince.

'How lovely to meet you. And what a divine dress. Come along in and let me introduce you.'

She didn't know any of the names; she smiled and shook hands and was passed from one to the other like a parcel. Being inspected, appraised. Philip's Irish wife. Everyone was very friendly. She was given a dry Martini, which she hated and put down almost untouched on a table when nobody was looking. People made conversation with her, avoiding awkward topics like her marriage. London was safe and she answered questions about their stay there and managed to smile and be animated. Claudia was talking to Philip; she wished he was beside her, but after the first ten minutes, he'd been taken away to talk to someone else. She wondered what they were saying to each other. Once she'd seen Claudia watching her and been encouraged by a broad smile. 'You're doing well,' it seemed to say. They went into dinner. She hesitated, glancing anxiously at Philip, who was on the other side of the table.

'You're here, next to James.' Claudia guided her to the seat on the host's left. 'Don't let him drink too much,' she whispered. It was an astonishing thing for a wife to say about her husband to a woman she'd met for the first time.

The food was not very nice; the regiment of cutlery ranged either side of her plate took any appetite away. She managed to get it right by watching the woman opposite to her. She sipped the wine, picked at the first course and let James Hamilton carry the conversation.

44

He did his best. He chatted about the weather, the racing, the poor scent out hunting – did she hunt? Well, of course, she must take it up . . . his wife was mad on it. Break her neck one day if she wasn't careful. Terribly sad about her father-in-law's death. Such a grand fellow. How was poor Blanche these days? Pity she'd gone off to Meath.

'I don't know how she is,' Eileen said suddenly. 'I've never met her.'

Hamilton looked puzzled. His wife had explained the situation to him, but he never listened to what he called women's gossip. He knew Arbuthnot had married a local farmer's daughter, but that was about all.

'Haven't you? Why ever not? She turned into a recluse or something? Not like Blanche.'

'She didn't want Philip to marry me.' Eileen couldn't stop herself. They know, they must do. I'm not going to pretend. I'm not ashamed of anything. 'That's why she went to Meath. So's to be out of the house before I came into it.'

'Really?' He looked at her with interest. What an extraordinary girl. How very embarrassing to say all that in front of everybody. He wondered how many people had heard. Pretty little thing, but Philip must clue her in a bit about how to behave. 'I'm sure she'll come round,' he said.

'She may,' Eileen answered, 'but I won't.'

She drank a little wine and noticed that the girl on Hamilton's right was staring at her. Imperceptibly Hamilton had switched from talking to her to the girl who was still staring at her. The man on her other side was eating. There was a pool of isolation and she was in the middle of it. There were twelve people round that table and they were all known to each other, on kissing and Christian name terms, with the same background and interests in common. The exclusion only lasted a few minutes, but it seemed a lifetime to her.

'Tell me, Mrs Arbuthnot.' The man next to her had stopped eating. 'Do you think there'll be a war?'

'War?' She shook her head. 'War with who?'

'Germany,' he explained. 'You girls are all the same. Never read anything in the papers except the fashion articles. I'm afraid there will be.'

'But we won't be in the war. It's nothing to do with us.'

He paused for a moment and she realized that she had said something wrong. But what?

'Not for some people, I suppose,' he said. 'But I can't see Philip sitting back and doing nothing about it. Anyway,' he gave her a distant smile, 'let's talk about something cheerful. How do you like living at Riverstown?'

She muttered something, anything non-committal would do. He wasn't in the least interested; he went on cutting up his meat and making little packets of food on his fork. What did he mean about Philip? If England went to war, why should Philip go and fight in it? But of course he would. His father had held army rank and won a medal in the last war. Her own uncles, more fools them, had gone off to France to fight and come back gassed.

Her plate was taken away. She refused the sweet. Philip couldn't persuade her to say pudding, when it was ice cream or some sugary mousse. She felt slightly sick. The wretched man was right, of course. She didn't read the English *Times* or the *Irish Times*, which were the only two papers that came into the house. There were no tabloids, none of the women's weeklies with their recipes and home hints that her mother loved reading. War! She wouldn't let Philip go.

She knew that the women left the men to linger in the dining room. She was prepared for the move when it came and followed Claudia Hamilton and the other ladies upstairs. It was a lovely bedroom. There was a big, flouncy bed, covered in silk cushions, pink lighting and fluffy white rugs.

'The bathroom's through there,' Claudia said. She sank down on the bed.

'I'm dying to go, darling.' The girl who had stared so hard at Eileen darted through and closed the door.

Claudia patted the bed beside her. 'Do sit down. And may I call you Eileen? And you must call me Claudia. Lady Hamilton reminds me of my mother-in-law, God forbid!' She laughed and patted Eileen's arm.

Why, Eileen wondered, is it all right for her to say that about her husband's mother, and wrong for me to tell the truth about Mrs Arbuthnot? The other women laughed and an older one, a Lady something, she couldn't remember a single name, said, 'Don't be naughty, Claudia. She's not as bad as all that.'

'She's ghastly,' Claudia insisted. 'She rings up and complains to James that she hasn't any money and she wants this and she wants that. She's not getting a penny from me, I can promise you.' She turned to Eileen. 'My dear, you're lucky. I had to *heave* the old hag out of the house when I got married. Imagine, she expected to live with us!' Eileen didn't know what to answer. A lot of people's old mothers lived with them when they married. No man would turn his mother out of her own house on account of his wife. 'Mind you,' Claudia went on, 'Blanche isn't bad. She's a bit of a battleaxe, but I don't suppose she'll be a bother to you. Maggie, hurry up, what are you doing in there?'

The bathroom door opened and the girl identified as Maggie came out. 'Sorry,' she said. 'Anyone else?'

Eileen got up, glad to escape. She shut and bolted the bathroom door. The bath and basin were pink and there were bottles and jars of bath salts and essences she'd never even heard of. Beautiful towels, as soft as swansdown, with initials embroidered on them. She ran some water and washed her hands. She could hear voices, but not loud enough to distinguish what was said. 'Eavesdroppers never hear good of themselves,' her mother used to say. Eileen didn't try to listen. She flushed the lavatory, although she hadn't used it. She looked pale and tired; there was nothing she could do about it, because she'd left her handbag with her makeup behind on the bed. When she opened the door, they stopped talking, so she must have been the subject.

Claudia got up, opened the door and led the way out. 'Let's go and have our coffee,' she said. 'I know James will keep the men in there for hours.'

They disposed themselves in the drawing room. The girl called Maggie had no alternative but to sit in a chair close to Eileen.

'Do you smoke?'

'No. I never did.' She shook her head. What did Claudia Hamilton mean by 'hours'? How much longer would she have to sit with these women before Philip came in and they could decently go home?

Of course she didn't smoke, she thought, watching them lighting up and puffing away. It wouldn't have been tolerated in her family. Tobacco was for men and a few old tinker women who sucked on a pipe.

'How long have you been married?' She knew that Maggie was being polite, trawling for subjects to pass the time till she could safely move away.

'Nearly a year,' Eileen answered. 'You're engaged, I see – when's the wedding?'

God, Maggie thought to herself, she makes it sound like a wake. I wish the men'd hurry their damned port and come back. 'Next spring,' she said. 'Of course, if this beastly war breaks out we'll have to make it earlier. Maybe it won't, and my father says it'll be over in six months anyway, so none of them will have to go.'

'I don't see why anyone wants to fight for England,' Eileen said. 'Not now we're independent. I won't let my husband go joining up.'

'My brother can't wait,' was the answer. She said it quite casually, as if everybody went to war. 'But men are so silly, aren't they? I don't think you'll keep the Paddies out of it, they love a fight. Ah, here come the chaps. There's my fiancé, do excuse me.'

The Paddies! Eileen had blushed scarlet at the contemptuous word, and the equally contemptuous way it was said. I'm a Paddy, she wanted to stand up and say. And proud of it. To hell with the lot of you.

But she stayed in her chair and Philip came over to her. He noticed that she looked very flushed. He bent and kissed her lightly on the forehead.

'Hello, darling. Sorry we were so long. Are you all right?'

She told the sort of feeble lie she would have despised in someone else. A little social lie, which one of those drawling females would have used. 'I've got a bit of a headache,' she murmured. 'I wouldn't want to stay too long.'

He nodded, taking the empty seat beside her. 'We won't. Just a few minutes more.'

James Hamilton came over. She noticed that he moved unsteadily; his face was very red. 'Whiskey, Philip? Hasn't your wife got a drink? Claudia . . . what the hell are you doing? This poor child hasn't got a drink!'

'I don't want one,' Eileen protested, but he didn't even listen. He was drunk and irritated. He wanted to pick a row. It's not just the Paddies who like a fight, she thought bitterly. My father's never sworn at my mother in a public place in his life.

'Oh, shut up, James,' Claudia called from her seat across the room. 'Not everyone wants to get tight, you know.'

She wasn't even embarrassed. Eileen couldn't believe it. Philip got up. 'I'm afraid we must go. I've a very early start in the morning. I've got to see the men and then go up to Dublin. It's been a lovely evening. Come along, darling, we must say goodnight.'

She thanked Claudia Hamilton. 'It's been lovely,' she echoed. 'A great party. Thank you so much.'

'So sweet of you to come. I'll ring you up, we must have lunch one day soon. 'Night, Philip darling. Let's all get together over Christmas. It'll be such fun.'

He helped put the wrap over her shoulders and she was silent on the short drive home. She felt degraded and diminished without being able to isolate a single snub except that one word, Paddies. But didn't that say it all? Didn't it put the viewpoint of these people towards the Irish? The real Irish.

'It wasn't too bad, was it?' Philip asked her when they got home.

She didn't want to hurt him. She didn't want to disappoint his hopes that she would integrate and enjoy being with his friends. She loved him too much to tell him the truth. 'It was nice,' she said. 'I was a bit shy of them. But they were all very nice to me. Philip, what's this talk about a war?'

'Don't bother your head about it,' he dismissed it lightly. The men had talked of nothing else when they were alone. 'How's the headache, by the way? You're not getting a cold are you, darling? Stay in bed tomorrow if you think one's coming. I'll be out all day, you can stay cuddled up till I get back.'

'I'll see,' she said. She hoped he wouldn't make love that night. She felt too cold and empty-hearted to respond. 'I have a little headache,' she admitted, and that was the third lie she had told him that night.

Over at Half House the party was going strong. Whiskeys and brandies were poured and drunk, cigars pierced and lit, some not too steadily. There was a lot of laughter. James Hamilton had passed from aggressiveness to fuddled good nature, calling everyone his best friend, pressing more drinks upon them. Claudia called for champagne and someone else suggested they put on some records and dance in the hall. And naturally they gave their opinions on the new Mrs Arbuthnot.

'I think she's quite sweet,' Claudia said. 'A bit gauche, but really rather nice.'

'Damned pretty girl,' several of the men agreed.

'I don't think she's nice at all,' Maggie announced.

Claudia spoke up. 'I heard you say something about Paddies. Whatever made you do that?'

'Because she had the bloody cheek to say no one should fight for England if there's a war,' Maggie said.

'We all know she's bog Irish, but she should keep those sort of remarks to herself. I wasn't going to stand for it anyway. We were all very friendly and nice and you made a big effort, Claudia darling, but I don't think it was appreciated one bit. Personally I thought she was hostile and chippy. I love Philip, he's a dear, but I'm not having her in the house.'

'Don't be silly, Maggie, you can't take that attitude.' The woman whose title had baffled Eileen waved her hand at the other girl dismissively. She felt that Maggie Gibbs had gone too far. Of course the girl was gauche and tactless, but that was no reason to be unkind. 'You can't say things like that,' she repeated. 'The Arbuthnots have been here for generations. You can't refuse to have Philip's wife to parties. You don't have to make a bosom friend of her, after all . . .'

'People with her attitude burnt my grandmother's home to the ground in '22,' Maggie declared. 'They brought her out with a gun in her back, a woman of seventy, and set fire to the place while she watched. She went home to England and died. No, I'm not having someone with Republican sympathies near me. And David won't either, will you, darling?'

'We'll see,' her fiancé said soothingly. 'Don't get het up about it now, there's a good girl.' He didn't share his future wife's passionate feelings about the past. It amused him to think how much Maggie and Eileen Arbuthnot had in common, with their rooted prejudices. He loved his home in Ireland and got on with the people. But he was a newcomer. His father had bought a place in Kildare before the Great War. The Gibbses traced their family back to one of Cromwell's captains. 'Come on, Claudia, let's dance,' he said. 'I love this record.'

They circled a few times on the parquet floor in the hall. 'Try and calm Maggie down,' she said. 'Don't let her go round damning that wretched girl and starting a vendetta. I liked her; she's going to find it difficult enough.'

'You like everybody,' her partner said. 'I'll do my

best, but I can't promise. You know these Black Irish, they never forgive or forget.'

'I'll have her to lunch,' Claudia Hamilton said. 'Maybe I can drop a hint or two and put her right, otherwise Maggie will have them both ostracized if she goes round saying that girl's a Republican. The twenties aren't all that long ago, you know. Thanks for the dance, David. You're a divine dancer. I wish James would get on his feet sometimes. Let's go and have a drink, shall we? And by the way, I've bought a marvellous young hunter from old Devlin. He won't be ready till next season, but I'm really going to knock their eyes out with this fellow.'

They went back to the drawing room and settled down into the sofa to talk horses. It was impossible not to like Claudia. Life in Ireland had rubbed some of the English corners down; she had adapted very quickly to the relaxed way of living, and proved herself a great sport who loved a party and hunted like a demon. People were expected to come on time, but that was accepted as Claudia being a bit eccentric. That particular party broke up at five, and two guests were persuaded to go to bed rather than drive all the way back to West Meath.

Another day dawned and the mists from the river swirled and eddied round the banks and crept up to the house the Hanging Judge had built. In the bedroom on the first floor Philip woke as the sun came up. He slept with the curtains drawn back and the top of the window open. Eileen had been horrified, sure it would give them both their death of cold to let the fresh air in at night. He turned and looked at her sleeping beside him. He did love her so much. She was the most girlish girl he'd ever known. Small and soft, with little bones and delicate hands and feet. Most of the well-bred girls he knew were coarse as cows beside her. He loved her courage and her loyalty. Once committed to him, she had withstood her family and, even more difficult, the power of her Church. He regretted the Ryans' intractability because he felt it made Eileen unhappy. They wouldn't have been an embarrassment to have around. They were proud people in their way and would never have intruded.

His mother was rather a stranger to him, so he didn't feel the loss of her so keenly. Nurses had brought him up and by seven he was away at private school in England. She was a busy woman, much occupied with her garden and her charities. She had more time for dogs and horses than for children. She'd call on them one day, he was confident of that. When there were grand-children, she'd reconcile herself completely. She was old and a snob. He didn't blame her; he didn't really care enough to be hurt.

He missed his father, though. They had been friends when he was grown up. They hunted and fished and went racing together, and there was a gap when his father died. He would have warmed to Eileen had he lived long enough to get to know her.

He did want her to settle down and find her place now that they were married. He couldn't instil enough confidence into her, that was the trouble. On the surface he'd helped her to adjust, and a woman less sensitive and intelligent wouldn't have accepted him correcting her speech and table manners. But in his heart he sensed that she was lonely and ill at ease. The servants weren't a problem any more. It wasn't just fear of him that made them change. They respected Eileen. And in spite of themselves they were proud of her. She had dignity, and natural grace. Like tonight, faced with the ordeal of going to a grand dinner party with people who all knew each other and were far removed from her experience, she had acquitted herself proudly and well. If war broke out he'd have to join his father's regiment, but he wasn't going to tell her that. He wasn't going to let anything worry or unsettle her. What she wanted was a baby. He could leave her if there was a child; and he knew, as all his friends agreed that night, that if England went to war with Germany, Ireland might remain neutral, but they could not. He woke her gently, and as the mists sank back into the river in the sunlight, they made love.

53

But it was two long years of disappointment before she conceived.

She felt so sick that it was lunchtime before she could drag herself out of bed and come downstairs. Doctor Baron reassured Philip.

'Sure she's fine,' he insisted, dismissing the silly man's fears. 'She's a fine healthy girl and all she is is a bit queasy of a morning. That'll pass when the baby turns. Nothing to worry about at all.' If she hadn't been Mrs Arbuthnot, he'd have told anyone else to stop spoiling her and give her work to do around the house. That'd keep her mind off herself quick enough. He'd no patience with women putting on airs and moaning about the most natural thing in the world. He'd seen women give birth on their cabin floors and get up and cook their man a meal when he came in . . .

He had little sympathy with Eileen, although he was polite and briskly reassuring. He despised her for betraying her family and her faith. She was a rich lady now; let her take comfort in that. No mother to fuss over her, no aunties and cousins to come visiting and swapping stories about the terrible births they'd had. No old school friends to call and help her pass the time. There were visitors, of course. Lady Hamilton from the Half House and one or two others of her sort. He'd heard their shrill voices when he made a routine call and seen Eileen Ryan sitting up in her big bed looking strained and miserable. He still thought of her as Eileen Ryan, old Jack's daughter. He wondered whether they knew about the baby. They'd have heard it from Mary Donovan. She'd have been up there on her Sunday off, bursting with the news. He saw Mrs Ryan one evening in his surgery. She had a nasty burn on her forearm. Spitting fat, she explained to him. It looked like there might be pus in it. He agreed, and gave her some ointment. He didn't mention her daughter or the daughter's pregnancy. He didn't want to embarrass the poor woman.

Eileen didn't improve much after the three months. She felt weak and seedy and if she went for a walk her ankles puffed up. Mary made her special brews to take the swelling down. Lily brought her breakfast in bed. Doyle picked some choice early plums from the conservatory and sent them up to her.

'Poor soul,' Mary Donovan said, as they stood round drinking the mid-morning cup of tea. 'There's something wrong there, for sure. A breath o' wind'd blow her over!'

'It's a sad state to be in,' Lily agreed. 'Not a move from her mother . . .'

'She wouldn't hear a word from me about it.' Mary was deeply disapproving. 'I went all that way on me day off, and hoped I'd do some good between them. "I've no daughter," she says to me. "Her name isn't mentioned in this house." God forgive us, she was as bitter as gall. I didn't see the auld man. I had me tea with her and the two boys and she didn't press me any further.'

'It's a terrible thing for them,' Bernadette ventured. 'I think my mammy'd be the same.' She was still jealous. She had no man and no prospect of one. She thought of Eileen as 'That one', though these days she didn't dare say so. Lying up there with Mr Arbuthnot and the local gentry fussing round her, as if she was a queen! And the size of the box of chocolates Lady Hamilton brought her last time! She finished her tea and sulked.

'What about the boys?' Doyle asked.

'Not a murmur out o' them,' Mary answered. 'Shamus sitting there like a stuck pig, and Kevin lookin' at his teacup. I tell ye, I was sorry I'd taken the trouble.' She lifted the pot and tipped a little boiling water into it. 'I'll offer a Mass for them all,' she said. 'That's all ye can do when things get so bad.'

Mrs Ryan never came, nor was there an answer to the letter Philip sent her. But when Eileen was in the seventh month, Mrs Blanche Arbuthnot came to Riverstown on her way to stay with friends in Limerick.

Blanche Arbuthnot turned in through the gates of her

old home. The Labrador bounded up in the back seat, excited by familiar smells. She quelled her with a brisk command.

'Sit, Bunny!' She was the Major's gundog and had pined so badly when her master died, Blanche had considered putting her down. But, as if she knew her life depended on it, Bunny had attached herself to her. Now they were equally devoted; she took the bitch everywhere with her.

It all looked so familiar. The green lawns were bright and cut close, the thickets of daffodils had not quite died down along the edges of the drive. Nothing had changed since she came as a bride more than forty years ago. She wouldn't admit that she felt nervous. She switched off the engine, glanced at herself in the driving mirror and got out, letting Bunny jump on to the drive. The front door opened before she had time to walk up to it, and there was Philip, smiling a welcome to her, and behind him was her daughter-in-law.

'Hello, Phil, dear,' she said. 'I've brought Bunny, I hope you don't mind.'

'Of course not,' her son said and then the moment she had been dreading came. 'Mother, this is Eileen.'

She was smaller and slighter than Blanche had imagined. The baby overbalanced her; she moved awkwardly when she came up and held out her hand.

'How do you do, Mrs Arbuthnot,' she said. Her mouth smiled. The light-coloured eyes were full of hatred. Philip couldn't see, of course. He was beside her, smiling in his good-natured way. A faint colour crept up into Blanche's cheeks.

'How do you do. It's so nice to meet you.'

'Do come inside,' the girl said, and stood back to let Blanche go ahead of her.

She had been expecting changes and had steeled herself not to resent them. Philip wouldn't allow anything too drastic, that was one comfort. It was untouched, except that there were very few flowers, sparsely arranged in tight little vases.

'Where are we having tea, darling?' Philip asked, as if he didn't know.

'In the den,' his wife replied.

'The den?' Blanche knew immediately she shouldn't have asked, but the word made no sense to her. Where would you find a 'den' at Riverstown?

'Dad's old study,' her son said. 'Eileen's made it very cosy.'

'We use it a lot,' the girl said, showing her into the room.

Blanche looked round her at the wallpapered walls and the flounced pink curtains and said, 'How very nice. Such a pretty colour scheme.'

She sat down and the Labrador flopped at her feet. This had been her husband's favourite room. There was no trace of him now. She was surprised how much it hurt. Philip looked very well, and kept giving his wife reassuring looks which Blanche wasn't supposed to see. If he was happy that was something, but for how long? How long before the difference in their background began to jar? This dreadful, vulgar room!

Lily brought in a silver tray with tea and sandwiches and one of Mary's marvellous sponge cakes. Blanche smiled up at her.

'How are you, Lily? It's so nice to see you. You're looking very well.'

'Oh, I am, Mrs Arbuthnot, mam.'

She saw the furtive look at the new mistress of the house and thought, 'You know which side your bread is buttered, never mind the fifteen years you worked for me.'

'How do you like your tea?' Eileen asked.

For a moment their eyes met. 'Not too strong. Just milk, no sugar. Thank you.' She took a slice of cake. There was silence. She had never felt so uncomfortable in her life. Her son was married, her daughter-in-law expecting their first baby and she didn't know what to say next.

'How's Mary?' It sounded so forced, but she couldn't leave the silence.

'Mary?' Eileen Arbuthnot echoed.

'Yes, Mary Donovan – you've still got her, haven't you?'

'Oh, yes. She's very well.'

'Can't you tell by the sponge cake?' Philip made a joke out of it. 'Eileen says her whiskey cake is better, but I haven't let her prove it yet.'

'Mary'd never forgive you if it was,' Blanche answered. Or if you went into her kitchen and interfered. But I can't say that. I can't behave naturally because I mustn't give offence. They haven't mentioned the baby. I suppose it's up to me. She cleared her throat.

'Philip told me the splendid news, Eileen. When will the baby arrive?'

'Early August, Doctor Baron says,' the girl answered.

'Baron?' Blanche was aghast. 'Surely he's not looking after you?' She switched to Philip. 'He's an absolute idiot, I wouldn't have him to whelp Bunny. My dear, you must get somebody from Dublin.'

She knew that she had made a fatal mistake. The girl's pale face flushed an unbecoming red.

'He's been our doctor since I was born. He's good enough for me.'

Blanche suddenly felt quite tired. What an effort, and then to see it wasted. There was no point of contact and there never would be. She pulled herself together and said, sounding brisker than she realized, 'Anyway, it's splendid news. One more cup of tea and then I really must be on my way. It's quite a drive.'

Philip said, 'Mother's going to stay with the Dornaways.'

Eileen said, 'Who are the Dornaways?'

'The Earl and Countess of . . .' He was trying to be jolly again. 'Dornaway Castle is quite a place. I'll take you down there one day. They're awfully sweet.'

'They've asked me for ten days,' Blanche said. 'It's such a lovely house, your father and I always enjoyed going there. You must drive Eileen over to meet Bobby and Jill. I'm sure you'd like them,' she added.

The red flush had faded, leaving her terribly pale, with dark rings under the eyes. She said quietly, 'I think they'd be a bit grand for me, Mrs Arbuthnot.'

Blanche put down her cup. 'They're not at all grand. Bobby Dornaway is my nephew. I'm sure they'd be delighted to meet you. It's so nice I can take Bunny. She moped so badly after your father died.' She spoke to Philip. 'I didn't know what to do. The local vet kept saying I should put her down – he's not a patch on old Pat Farrel – he was marvellous with dogs.'

'Pat Farrel is a cousin of my father's,' her daughter-in-law said. 'He's a good man with cattle too.'

'Yes, so he is. Such a nice man. I keep Bunny in the house now,' Blanche hurried on. 'She was so damned miserable in the kennel, poor old girl. So now she's a house dog.' She bent down and patted the silky black head. 'Aren't you, you silly old thing?'

'Will you excuse me a moment.' Eileen got up, glanced at Philip and her mother-in-law. He looked concerned.

'Are you all right, darling? Not feeling sick, are you?'

'No.' She managed a watery smile. 'No, I'm fine. I won't be long.'

'Poor little thing,' he said to Blanche. 'She's had such a rotten time. Been sick practically the whole seven months. By the way, you shouldn't have said that about Baron. He's always looked after the Ryans. Eileen insisted on having him.'

'I'm sorry.' Blanche wasn't used to being rebuked by her son. 'But he's an old butcher. She's not a very robust girl, I'd say. But it's not really my business. I only meant it for the best. Good Lord, Philip, look at the time. I must be getting on my way.'

'I'll go and call Eileen.' He got up and left her sitting alone.

Eileen was not sick. She thought that the spasm of pain would be followed by vomiting, as it often was, but by the time she reached her bedroom it had passed. She crawled on to the bed and hugged herself like a child with no one there to bring comfort. That hateful, arrogant old woman, with her superior airs and her chilly snobbishness, patting her bloody dog and talking about the child she was carrying as 'splendid news'. So cold and unfeeling; Eileen couldn't have imagined anyone behaving in her own son's home as if she were a stranger, making small talk and occasionally bestowing a few words on her daughter-in-law. Dismissing the doctor who had brought Eileen and all her brothers and sisters into the world as someone she wouldn't have to whelp her mangy bitch. Patronizing Pat Farrel, knowing, surely, that he and the Ryans were close relatives on both sides. She didn't mean to cry, but tears came so easily these days, and it was so difficult to stop. She felt angry and degraded, the child she carried equally despised. She couldn't stop crying, and then the pain came back and nagged at her, till she held her hands to her lower belly.

Philip came running down the stairs. Blanche was already in the hall, clutching Bunny's lead.

'Is she all right?' she asked, seeing him come down alone. Her son was white-faced, a sure sign of anger in the Arbuthnots. Lily, coming out of the study with the tea tray, backed in again quickly, out of sight but able to hear.

'She's thoroughly upset,' he snapped at her. 'Crying her eyes out upstairs, poor darling. Why the hell couldn't you have been nicer to her, Mother?'

They stood facing each other in the hall, mother and son who had never been close, locked in the eternal triangle.

'I did my best,' Blanche Arbuthnot answered. 'She wasn't exactly friendly to me. If you care about her and the baby, you'll get a proper doctor to look after her. Don't bother to see me out.'

Philip said, 'She's having pains. If anything happens I'll never forgive you.' He turned and went back upstairs.

From her vantage point inside the doorway, Lily saw Mrs Arbuthnot open the front door and slam it after her. Then she hurried out to the kitchen to tell them all the news.

Blanche got into the car, settled the old dog on the seat beside her and switched on the engine. She was trembling. It was too much, at sixty-three, too much to lose her husband and be left with the son who was the least favourite of her three children, and this dreadful marriage. The house she loved was full of strangeness and hate. Her eyes filled with tears. If only Teddy or Richard had been spared from that terrible war, she wouldn't be cast out like this. They would have laughed Philip out of such a hopeless misalliance . . . even so, he could have married his colleen and it wouldn't have mattered because he was the youngest son . . . I'll never forgive you, she thought. How that whey-faced girl had poisoned him, that he could bring himself to say such a thing to his own mother.

She wiped her eyes and let the clutch in. The exit on to the Naas road was the most dangerous in Kildare. Tears blurred her vision as she swung out, hammering on the horn. She only just missed a donkey cart that was too far over to the left. The driver yelled curses at her, slashing in fright at the helpless donkey. Blanche drove on and three hours later she was safe in Dornaway Castle, where she seemed so shaken that they put her straight to bed.

'I did everything you told me,' Eileen mumbled.

'Yes, darling, of course you did.' He held her hand and soothed her, but she was fretful and kept repeating herself.

'I did my best. She was so horrible . . .' Tears were seeping down her cheeks. He wiped them away, murmuring to her to forget about it, not to worry. He was just so desperately sorry she was upset. Doctor Baron had given her something, she ought to let him put the light out and go to sleep.

'I hate her,' she whispered. 'She hates me and I hate her.'

'Don't say things like that,' Philip begged her. 'Please, sweetheart.'

He had rung for Baron, who came over and examined her briskly. 'She's just having a grumble,' he reassured Philip. 'Nothing to worry about; it can happen around the seven months, but we don't want her going into labour. I've given her a draught. You settle her down now and she'll be right as rain in the mornin'. I'll look in on her round dinner time.'

But Eileen didn't sleep, and by nine o'clock the pain had become stronger. He telephoned the doctor again. A slow-witted girl drove him mad, trying to spell his name, saying himself was out on a call and the missus visiting relatives. No, sure she'd no notion where to find him, but he might ring the house in an hour or so, to see if there were any messages.

When he came upstairs to the bedroom he found Lily standing by the bed, and Eileen clutching her hand and moaning.

'The missus rang for me,' she whispered. 'Sure, God love her, she's goin' to give birth.'

'The doctor's out,' Philip said. 'Nobody knows where he is or when he'll be back! Lily, stay here with her. I'm going to get Lady Hamilton to come over.'

Claudia drove the ten miles separating them at reckless speed. She knew panic when she heard it, and sheer panic was in Philip Arbuthnot's voice. She ran into the hall and up the stairs. She was in a dinner dress, with a coat thrown over it. They had been in the middle of a party when his call came. She saw the housemaid, Lily, standing on one side, and Philip, grey and hollow-eyed with fear, holding on to Eileen. She didn't scream; she moaned and cried with pain, pulling at the bedclothes, jerking her swollen body up and down with the contractions.

Mary Donovan put her head round the door. 'Oh,

thank God your Ladyship's here,' she breathed. 'Shouldn't we go for the midwife?'

Claudia didn't waste a minute. 'Philip, get the car out. Lily, pack some night things for Mrs Arbuthnot, just the minimum. Mary, you come and hold on to her. I'm going to phone the Rotunda and say we're bringing her in now.'

Claudia insisted on driving. 'You look after Eileen,' she said. 'You're in no state to drive anyway. I'll get there, don't worry.'

He sat in the back, cradling his wife in his arms. Every racking pain tore at him; he hadn't wept since he was a child, but his cheeks were wet as he tried to comfort her.

'Darling, don't fight it, try to relax. We're getting you to hospital. You'll be fine.'

'No, no, not hospital. I don't want to go to hospital.' Her fear surprised him. 'Don't take me there,' she whimpered. 'I'll die if I go there. The baby'll die.' And then the pain came, turning her protest into a low cry of anguish.

She had started the second stage of labour when they carried her into the Rotunda and hurried her away into the labour ward. Claudia took charge; Philip stood helplessly while she talked to the ward sister and exerted her considerable authority to get the doctor called immediately. Then she turned to Philip and took his arm.

'Come on, we'll go to the waiting room. They'll bring us a cup of tea.'

It wasn't a long vigil. They sat in the dingy room, with its green painted walls and picture of the Sacred Heart, a tiny red eye of an oil lamp burning in front of it. The smell of disinfectant was acrid.

'She'll be all right,' Claudia insisted. And then, because she had spoken quietly to the ward sister, she thought it best to warn him. 'It may be a bit difficult for the baby. It's very early, you see.'

'I don't care about the baby,' Philip said, and with

those few words he doomed his unborn son. 'I want Eileen safe and well. That's all I care about.'

When the door opened and the sister appeared, he sprang up.

'Mr Arbuthnot? Would you come and see Doctor O'Brien, please.'

'My wife . . .' Claudia heard him say as he went out. 'How's my wife?'

The pain and the exertion had stopped. So had the warm gushing blood that streamed out of her body, taking her life with it. She floated between dreams and fits of consciousness, then she saw Philip leaning over her and she thought someone said, 'You've got a lovely little boy, thanks be to God . . .' but it didn't seem real. Her mother-in-law was real. The anger wouldn't go away. She mumbled in delirium.

'I hate her . . . I hate them all . . . Mammy. Where's Mammy?'

The doctor had left them. There was no more he or anyone could do.

The ward sister said, 'Your wife said she was a Catholic. I've sent for the priest. She's calling for her mother. She wouldn't be here in time. Here's Father Cochran now.' She was surprised and offended when he left the room.

He stood in the corridor outside while the priest prepared his wife for death. He felt nothing. Nature is kind, he thought, sometimes it's kind. As it was cruel to Eileen, who'd bled to death after the birth of her tiny baby. He couldn't cry, he couldn't feel; he didn't know how long he stood outside the door, leaning against the greasy wall. It was a boy, they told him. Very small, but no signs of jaundice and breathing normally, thanks be to God. It was early days, he must understand, but there was hope. He must have closed his eyes because the priest was suddenly in front of him. He was an old man, blinking behind very thick glasses. He carried a shabby bag with his stole and the sacraments in his left hand.

'You can go into her now,' he said. 'It was a beautiful

death she made. She just smiled and went to heaven.'
He said the same to all bereaved. It eased the pain of
loss for the devout. He touched Philip on the arm. 'God's
given you a child,' he said. 'Try to be comforted.'

There was nothing Philip could say. Standing so close
he smelt the fusty clothes and a sour whiff on the old
man's breath. What was beautiful about the death of a
young girl, leaving a motherless child? There was no
comfort her priest could give Philip.

'Thank you, Father Cochran.'

'I'm told the baby's very small,' the priest said.
'T'would be wise if I baptize him now.'

Philip Arbuthnot said, 'My son will be brought up an
Anglican. Excuse me.' He turned his back and went in
to say goodbye to his wife.

Claudia Hamilton made the arrangements. He didn't
want Eileen to lie in the Catholic cemetery in Naas, since
the place reserved for the Arbuthnots was forbidden to
her. She was buried in Dublin. Her family were not
invited to attend.

The baby was strong enough to go back to Riverstown
with a monthly nurse after six weeks and he was duly
baptized a Protestant in the Church of Ireland in Naas.
Claudia was among his godparents. He was called
Francis Alexander William, which were all family names.

Philip was not allowed to be lonely. Friends rallied to
him and Claudia installed a housekeeper and a nanny.
The little boy was strong and he flourished. Philip went
to see him twice a day, encouraged by Claudia, who
hoped the child would make up to him for Eileen. But
he turned more and more to her. James Hamilton had
joined the British Army at the outbreak of war. By the
time he was killed in North Africa, Claudia and Philip
had become lovers.

It was Mary Donovan who suggested that Eileen's
younger brother might slip in to see his nephew before
he left for America. It was a nagging frustration for Mary
to go up to the Ryans and not be able to talk about what

was going on at Riverstown. Surely Bridget Ryan had aged since her daughter's death. There was a quietness about her that Mary had seen before when people were losing their hold on life. Old Jack was drunker at night than usual, and the yob of an elder son glowered by the hearth and waited for *him* to die. One evening Kevin came to the bus stop with her. They stood hunched against the rain and he said in his laconic way, 'How's Eileen's boy?'

Now, two days before he sailed for New York, Mary smuggled him in to see the child. He came in through the back door on Lily's afternoon out. The rest of the maids had been threatened with hell-fire and damnation if they breathed a word. Bernadette had been sacked for cheeking the nurse. Mary had smiled to see her go. The nurse slept in her room for two hours while Francis dozed in his nursery.

Kevin went up the back stairs, Mary chattering like a magpie. He didn't bother to listen. His sister had lived in the big gloomy house for such a little time. She had left no impression. She had come and gone like a shadow.

'He's in here,' Mary said, opening a door.

Kevin had never seen a nursery before. At home the children all slept together and the new baby with its parents till it came off the breast. Everything was white and clinical as if the child were in a hospital. There was no holy picture on the wall, with its little oil lamp, no homely touch he recognized. A cot swathed in draperies and blue ribbon stood isolated in a corner. He approached, and looked in at the boy.

'He's awake, so,' Mary whispered.

He had a thatch of black hair and wide eyes, so dark blue they were changing colour already. There was nothing to remind him of Eileen. Just a black Arbuthnot, like the rest of them. He turned away, and his eyes filled with tears.

'So that's all that's left of her,' he said.

'Don't mind that he takes after *them*,' Mary

66

murmured. 'I've seen babies lose all their hair and come out a different colour.'

'It's what's in him that counts,' Kevin said. 'But he'll never know the Irish half of him. That bastard had him baptized a Protestant.'

'She gave her life for her faith,' Mary said. 'She was too frail in herself. But not in vain, thanks be to God. The nurse who brought him home said the sister baptized him herself the very night he was born. So much good did it do them to take him up to that heathen place in Naas. God's grace is in him, Kevin. It'll come out in good time!'

He leaned down and touched the child with one finger. The skin was soft and smelled sweet. He remembered the sour smell of his tiny sisters that wrinkled the nose.

'Good luck to him,' he said. 'Maybe one day he'll know the truth about himself.' He turned away. He didn't want to sit gossiping in the kitchen with that old slob of a cousin. He wanted to get out of that hated house and everything it represented. Many of his friends were joining the British Army. It seemed a kind of treason. He had relatives in America on his mother's side. He would have shared the farm with his brother in the end, as was the Irish custom, but he didn't want that kind of life. He didn't want to end up a mean and ignorant man like his father, or spend the years bickering with brother Shamus. There was no real future for the Irish in Ireland while the country was divided and people like the Arbuthnots held the land and the power in actuality. In America, it was an advantage to be Irish.

He said goodbye to Mary, cutting the blessings short, and hurried away down the drive to the road. He walked hunched into himself, as if the rain were beating on him, though that afternoon the sun was shining.

It was nearly twenty-six years before he saw his nephew again.

Chapter 3

Claire went through to the gun room. Years ago, it held the family collection of sporting guns, encased in mahogany. It was a male preserve, consecrated to sport, where guns were cleaned after a day's shooting and guests would be shown valuable old museum pieces that had been used by earlier Arbuthnots. It belonged to an age Claire could well remember, when there were big shooting parties at Riverstown, and she followed on foot with her mother and joined the guns for lunch. Frank was a superb shot. That at least he and his father had in common. When they were young there had been no need to lock the gun room. For years, since the trouble began in the North, all firearms, even the most ancient, were kept under lock. Her father gave up shooting quite suddenly, after Frank left home. Occasionally, when she came over from England with Neil, they'd go out and take a few pigeons on a Sunday morning, but his heart wasn't in it.

Neil was devoted to Claudia, but he found Philip frankly daunting. A man who had turned his own son out of the house was not exactly comfortable as a father-in-law. To Neil, hide-bound Englishman that he was, Philip Arbuthnot was best described as Irish, because he couldn't account for him in any other way. Deep down, they hadn't liked each other.

She fitted the key and turned it. The room was shuttered and smelt of oily rags and leather. She switched on the light. The cases were empty. The Purdey guns had been sold after Philip's death, since there was nobody to use them. One gun remained in the rack: Frank's Churchill 12–bore shotgun. And hanging from a hook in its holster, her father's army revolver. She

68

stood hesitating. Where did her father keep the ammunition for it . . . in one of the bottom drawers; she found the clip with the cartridges. She put them in her pocket, unlocked the cabinet and took the revolver down. It didn't fit into her pocket. It was heavy and clumsy, difficult to hide. She took her jacket off and wrapped it up, folding it awkwardly over one arm. Billy wouldn't notice if she put it on the back seat.

She locked up after her. She couldn't think ahead because she dared not. She knew where he was, and she knew that he would need a gun. If the worst came to the worst, she could fire it with both hands.

The car was ready when she got back to the cottage. She forced herself to smile at Billy, clutching the coat with its hidden weapon close to her side.

'Oh, that's great,' she said.

'It was a dirty old job,' he complained. 'Drive it out and I'll put mine inside the shed there. Did ye lock the place up after ye?'

'Yes. It's fine, don't worry.'

She opened the back door and dropped the coat and the gun on the back seat. She reversed the car out and swung it round to give Billy room to put his in its place. The car was his pride and joy. It looked scarred without its bright red number plates. He shut the shed doors, puffing a little, and leaned against them to catch his breath.

'My bloody old lungs,' he grumbled. 'Never been right since the bronchitis last winter. Have ye far to go?'

She shook her head. 'Not too far. I've plenty of petrol. Thanks, Billy. And don't worry about me. I'll be back before dark.'

She let the clutch in and drove towards the road; she waved at him out of the window. He waved back at her and, as the car disappeared from sight, he screwed up his face in anguish and let out a groan of frustration and fear. Not far, she said, and then gave the lie by saying she'd plenty of petrol. Back before dark. Where was Arbuthnot hiding, that half the police in Ireland and the

IRA couldn't find him, and Claire could? They'd always had secrets, those two. Walking together holding hands, not like brother and sister at all. Him watching over her, and her thinking he was God Almighty. She'd grown up into a beautiful fair girl, and every lad in the county had his eye on her, as Billy knew from all the women's gossip. But all Frank had to do was speak against them and that made an end. She could have married a fine young fella, he thought bitterly, with a grand house and a slice of West Meath to go with it, but Frank saw him off. At twenty she'd rather go riding or fishing with him than up to Dublin or down to a dance. So she was packed off to bloody England and came back with an Englishman. He spat in disgust and went into his cottage.

A mile down the road, Claire stopped the car. She got the revolver off the back seat and put it into the glove compartment with the cartridges. She didn't need the signposts on the way. She knew every mile of the back roads to Kells through Kilcock, Trim and Fordstown. How often they'd driven there in Frank's car, towing the double trailer behind them, excited by the prospect of a day's hunting with the Meath. He looked so well in hunting clothes. She was proud to be seen with him, and knew they made a picture when they rode up together.

For a moment her eyes blurred at the memories of happy days, days of innocence. Before Kevin Ryan came back from America and bought the Half House from the last improvident Hamilton, nephew of her mother's first husband who'd been killed at Tobruk. That was when everything changed. Until then Frank had been safe because they had each other, and the things that troubled him were half buried and might well have sunk past danger. But as if Eileen Arbuthnot cried for vengeance from the grave, her brother came back and laid claim to her son.

It was midday, and gloriously bright. Children were out playing in the schoolyards, shouting and enjoying the sunshine; shops were closed up for the dinner hour.

Kells itself was shuttered till the afternoon. She drove past the great Celtic cross, so ancient that its age was only speculation, down the main street, past the gates of the Marquis of Headfort's magnificent estate, now sold to foreigners with money, made the final turn to Cloncarrig.

His voice on that last telephone call came back to her, made only a few days before he disappeared. She knew it so well, and though time and distance had separated them, it made her heart beat double.

'Claire, I wanted you to know . . . they've murdered poor old Donny. Killed him in cold blood. I'm finished with them. I wanted you to know,' he said again. And she had answered, 'Oh, thank God. Thank God! But can you do that – can you break off just like that?'

'I can and I have,' he said.

'Come over here,' she begged him. 'You can't stay in Ireland if you've fallen out with them . . . please, darling Frank, come here to me.'

She heard the mocking laugh, but it was bitter.

'I don't think Neil would be exactly overjoyed to see me. Don't you worry about me. I've friends who'll pull strings. Nobody will dare touch me. And anyway, if I need to hole up till things are fixed, we know where I can go. Remember old Reynard?' And then, dismissing himself, he asked if she were well and happy, and she lied and said she was. 'God bless you then,' was his goodbye, before the line went clear.

Her marriage had ended the night when she told Neil Fraser she was going back to Ireland to look for her brother.

She drove the car slowly, looking for the turning she remembered off the road. It was still there, a gap where a gate should have been, leading on to a rutted farm track. A low drystone wall surrounded the place, but it was crumbling and all along the edge the nettles triumphed. She drove in and bumped along, skirting the worst pot-holes, heading for a clump of beech trees where the car would be hidden from the road. Broad green fields surrounded her, with distant woods

71

bounding the horizon. She stopped, looked round and saw the emptiness of Ireland. Rooks cawed and swooped high in the trees. She took the revolver, the bullets and her coat to wrap them in, and began to walk towards the woods. Beyond the woods lay a valley and in the valley a lake, where the ruins of a fine Georgian house were reflected on a clear day. And beyond that, past a gentle rise, she would find her brother if he were still alive.

The helicopter took off from South Wales an hour after the Special Branch had spoken to Major Michael Harvey. It was an army chopper, but operated under a commercial flying company. Before noon it landed at the heliport and a car was waiting to speed its passenger to London.

He was not at all what Brownlow expected when they came face to face. He was a slight man, a little above average height, but by no means a prime physical specimen. He wore shabby corduroys and a jacket and looked thoroughly nondescript. He could have been anything except an army officer in the most sensitive intelligence branch, renowned for undercover operations in Northern Ireland.

'You haven't wasted any time,' Brownlow said, as they shook hands.

'You said it was urgent. I thought so too.' Harvey sat opposite to him and refused a cigarette. He was a very still sort of man.

'It's a bloody mess,' Brownlow declared. 'If Fraser hadn't mucked about when he got back and found she'd gone, we might have caught her before the boat sailed.'

'I suppose he wanted to be sure,' Major Harvey suggested. 'But it's a pity.'

'You know them socially, I believe.'

'Yes. I've stayed with them several times. Had some days shooting with him. They're a nice couple.'

'How come he knows about you? I thought you people kept top security at all times.'

'I was assigned to look after him for a while,' Harvey

answered. 'We got on very well. He was a high risk at one time. We became friendly.'

'The wife too? How did she take to you, Major? I gather she's pretty pro-Irish.'

Michael Harvey said, 'She didn't want them to shoot her husband; I didn't think she was particularly pro-anything. Besides, she grew up there. So did I, as a matter of fact.'

'Did you?' Brownlow felt he'd been rebuked and it irritated him. An arrogant bugger, he decided. He sat up straight and became official. 'The view is, she's gone over to look for her brother. He's a right bastard.' He dared the Major to defend *him*. 'We've had a lot of conflicting information from over there. The story goes that he's fallen out with his friends in the Provos, and he's either on the run, or they murdered him and dumped the body. The nasty part is that, either way, it could be a ploy to get Mrs Fraser into the Republic, where they can pick her up.'

'That seems the most likely. Would the brother connive at it? The whole disappearance could be a put-up job.'

Brownlow shook his head. 'No way. She's his one soft spot, from what we know about him. I think he's at the bottom of a bog with a hole in his head and they're waiting to scoop her up at the right moment. As I explained to Fraser, we can't say a word to the Irish police because that bloody country's like an echo chamber. One word, and everyone gets to hear of it. The Provos have got contacts everywhere. So it's got to be handled from our end and with the utmost security. And discretion,' he added. 'We want Mrs Fraser brought back home, but no shoot-outs. No repercussions.'

'Is that the official instruction,' Harvey asked him, 'or just a general directive?'

'A general directive,' Brownlow admitted. 'Nobody can tell you how to do your job.'

'Doesn't stop them trying,' was the retort. He looked at his watch. 'There's been no publicity. From what you said on the phone, she's kept a low profile too, which is lucky. Our one chance of sorting this out is to get to her before the Provos know for sure she's in Ireland. So I'll be on my way.' He stood up. 'I'll be in touch. With any luck, I could be back this evening. If I'm not, things have gone wrong. But I'm optimistic. She's not a fool, and she knows what she's dealing with.' He shook hands and went out.

Brownlow pinched his lip between finger and thumb. He knows Claire Fraser a bloody sight better than he let on, he thought. That's why the husband picked him. He's not just a trigger man. Brownlow had been dealing with human vagaries for thirty years. The Major had closed ranks when he criticized Mrs Fraser, and by implication, Ireland. He shook his head. He would never understand them. And by 'them' he meant the English who identified with a country and a people that had never accepted them. He wondered whether Major Harvey, ex-Green Jackets, Wellington and Sandhurst and Ulster undercover expert, would describe himself as Irish. He wouldn't be the least surprised.

The flight to Dublin took just on an hour. Michael Harvey read the newspapers while the stewardesses offered drinks and the passengers examined each other at the start of the flight. He put the papers away and leaned back, gazing out of the window at the bright banks of sunlit cloud as they reached thirty thousand feet. He thought of Claire Fraser, and the first time they had met, at Brandon Manor in the heart of the Cotswolds.

It was three years ago, when her husband was a new Cabinet Minister and there was a scare that he might be a target for the IRA. Informers named him and two other public figures. Michael Harvey was assigned to look after him inside the house. He could mix unobtrusively with their friends and cause no comment. The humbler guardians of politicians patrolled the grounds and watched the roads.

Just after Christmas, when the January weather was at its worst. Fraser was on his way down from London, suitably escorted. Harvey was staying there for the weekend.

'Hallo.' Claire Fraser came to meet him. 'Come in and have a drink.'

'Thanks very much. Sorry to have to inflict myself on you again.'

She had a charming smile. 'Don't be silly. We can sleep at night with you in the house. Gin and tonic?'

'Whiskey and soda, if that's all right. It's whiskey weather today.'

She paused by the table with the bottles and glasses and looked at him. 'That's a very Irish way of putting it,' she said.

'So's the rain,' Michael Harvey countered. 'Reminds me of Rademon on a Sunday. All the pubs shut and nothing to do but go to church. Do you know the North at all, Mrs Fraser?'

'No, we never went up there. My father couldn't stand them. I hope I'm not being tactless.'

He smiled and took the glass she offered him. 'Not in the least. My home was in Galway.'

'Really? We had some cousins down there – the Grahams. Did you know them?'

'My family did. I spent holidays at home, but went to school over here, and then into the Army. The place is sold now anyway.' He sipped the drink.

There was a big log fire, the inevitable Labrador stretched out in front of it, central heating keeping the atmosphere warm; nice expensive furniture and even more expensive country house pictures on the walls. Fraser was a rich man. A hospitable host, full of charm and not jumpy, in spite of the scare. He had done his best to make Harvey feel at home. Harvey was armed at all times, forever primed in case of unexpected noise or movement in the house. Fraser and his wife had shown up extremely well in the circumstances. A lot of people would have been uncomfortable or jittery, having a body-guard at their elbow.

Claire was a very good-looking woman, Harvey considered, watching her pour a drink and sit down opposite to him. Good figure, smart clothes, very blonde. He was completely immune to women when he was on a job. After Belfast, he knew what women could do and smile at the same time. The most he conceded was that Claire Fraser was nice and didn't pester him with silly questions.

'I haven't been home since Easter,' she said. He noticed the word. Home. Keep your eyes open, he'd been told. She has a brother who's highly suspect. 'Neil hates going. And now, of course, we can't.'

'No,' he agreed. 'It wouldn't be very wise.'

'I'm not going to ask you if you do,' Claire said, and smiled.

'No,' he said again. 'I'm glad about that.'

'I talk to my mother on the phone,' she remarked. 'But it's not the same thing. She's promised to come over here in the spring. It's lonely for her since my father died.'

'Wouldn't she move over to England?' He wasn't really interested in the small talk, but the whiskey was soothing and he could relax till Fraser came in.

'Good Lord, no,' Claire said. 'Mother's been in Ireland since her first marriage. She's more Irish than the Irish. She's seventy and she only stopped hunting last season because she's got arthritis in her wrist. Do you know Kildare at all?'

'Not well,' he said, which wasn't true. She seemed anxious to talk that night. Previously, she had said very little and her husband kept the conversation going. But then they hadn't been alone for any time before.

'My mother was married to James Hamilton,' she said. 'They lived at a place called the Half House. He was killed in the war and then she married my father. It was sold ten years ago.' She offered him a cigarette and then withdrew it, 'Oh, I'd forgotten. You don't smoke.'

76

'I never did,' he said. 'Tried it once and couldn't stand it.'

She wanted to say something, he felt, and the cigarette was just a moment's loss of nerve. He waited.

'It was so Irish to call it the Half House.' She sounded casual. 'One of the Hamiltons burnt it to get the insurance and made a mess of it. So they lived in one wing and everybody called it that. It was even on the writing paper, if you can believe it.' She laughed and he joined in. 'Kevin Ryan bought it,' she said. He looked non-committal. 'People couldn't stop talking about it.'

'Isn't he the Senator?' he asked, knowing she wanted the lead.

'Yes, and a big business man. His family were local farmers. He went to America and made a fortune. He's a very powerful man.'

'Have you met him?' There was something uneasy about her. She was asking something from him, this stranger whose job was to shoot the IRA assassins if they came. He didn't know what it was, but now it wasn't small talk and he wasn't just ticking over any more.

'Once,' Claire Fraser answered. 'With my brother. My half-brother. Ryan is his uncle.'

'Oh,' he said.

She got up, fiddled with the drinks, pouring herself another whiskey for something to do. With her back to him, she said, 'Ryan's one of the bosses of Noraid. He turned my brother Frank. He completely turned him. Major Harvey, can you imagine how I feel, with Neil's life being threatened?'

She turned round to face him. His defences went up. There were tears in her eyes.

'You shouldn't feel anything,' he said. 'It's nothing to do with you. And don't worry. Nothing's going to happen to him. I think that's your husband coming in now. Excuse me.' He put his glass down. 'Thanks for the drink.'

Dinner had been strained that evening. Neil Fraser looked tired and on edge, his wife was subdued and made an excuse to leave them early. When they were alone, the Minister offered him a brandy.

'No thanks, I've got to keep my wits about me. Wouldn't do to drink too much.'

'I'm very grateful to you, Major,' Neil said. 'You make my wife feel much happier, knowing you're in the house. She shouldn't worry, but she does.'

'That's only natural,' Harvey said, wondering why he was bringing her into it. 'She's marvellous, considering most women would be throwing a wobbly.'

'How long will it be before they give me the all-clear, do you think?'

Harvey shrugged. 'I wouldn't know. My own feeling is, the greatest danger is in the early days. If they haven't made an attempt by now, I suspect they know the scheme's been blown and they've called it off. But don't quote me. As soon as the situation's normal, you can be rid of me.'

'I've enjoyed having you with us,' Neil Fraser said. 'So has Claire.' He sipped rather too deeply at his brandy. 'The trouble is she feels as if it were her fault. She feels guilty because my life's been threatened. She was quite upset tonight, I don't know if you noticed.'

'No, I didn't. We were talking about Ireland before you arrived. Just chatting.' He was conditioned not to give anything away. Fraser wasn't going to get any lead from him. He wished he'd finish his drink and go to bed. The last thing Michael Harvey wanted was to be drawn into a personal discussion.

'It's her half-brother that's the problem.' Fraser had settled into his chair. He was going to get this off his chest, and nothing was going to stop him. Harvey kept quiet. 'Claire's father married a farmer's daughter. Right out of the blue; ran away and married her in England. There was the most God-awful row with the family. They wouldn't accept her at any price. Then she died having the boy. There was some story about her and Claire's grandmother having a set-to and she had the baby too early – anyway, my father-in-law never spoke to his mother again. Typically Irish, I'm afraid. Seems to me, they live on feuds.'

'It does sound like it,' Harvey admitted. He eased his sleeve up and looked at his watch. Fraser didn't notice or didn't care.

'The old boy married a second time and she's a splendid woman. English-born, actually, and we got on like a house on fire. Claire's much more like her.' He looked gloomily at his empty glass. 'Trouble is, Claire and that brother were inseparable. He was always jealous because she married me. And he's up to his neck in it.'

'Gone over to the other side?' Harvey queried.

'Backwards and forwards to the States, speaks at Noraid rallies. Nothing can be pinned on him, not that the bloody Irish Government gives a damn what people like that do. But it weighs on Claire. Wasn't too easy for me, when I was standing for election. Never mind. They're a hopeless people.'

Harvey moved out of his chair. 'Not all of them,' he said. 'I've known a few who weren't too bad. I think we should shut up shop, if you don't mind. The new night shift is coming on outside and they'll expect the household to be in bed. I hope you don't mind, sir.' The 'sir' was to soften it. He was not surprised to find Neil Fraser was ignorant and prejudiced. He didn't have much time for politicians as a breed.

'Yes, it is late. Goodnight, Major. See you at breakfast.'

He slept in a room opposite the Frasers', with his door ajar. He couldn't help hearing the row. It began with muffled voices that meant nothing. Then they rose in anger.

'He wouldn't help them! Frank wouldn't do anything to hurt you.'

'Like hell he wouldn't – all he's ever wanted is to get you back!'

'You say things like that and you expect me to bloody well sleep with you.'

Harvey got up and closed the door. Then he opened

it again. It was his job to watch over Fraser during the night. He dozed with an eye and an ear open. If they chose to quarrel at the tops of their voices, that was their business.

'You don't want to any more – go on, admit it! It's just another excuse tonight.'

Christ, he muttered to himself. Married bliss. The door to their room opened. She was crying. He felt sorry for the husband. They always cried to put you in the wrong. His ex-wife had cried at him for three years.

'Oh, for God's sake, darling, don't let's go on,' he heard Fraser say. 'Come to bed. I'm sorry. I just wanted you tonight.'

'I'm sorry too,' she said. That was a change, Harvey admitted. 'I'm so sorry, Neil. I'm so uptight about all this I just couldn't.'

The door closed and the voices were a murmur. Harvey settled back on the bed, checked his gun was handy and closed his eyes. He was used to sleeping on the lightest level. It didn't bother him. An odd kind of row, he mused, letting himself drift. Rows about sex were ordinary enough. He and his wife had fallen out over it more than anything else. But what kind of a brother was this Frank Arbuthnot? Clearly, he was very much under both their skins. He dozed.

He was relieved from duty by the end of the week. One more weekend and the security screen could be lifted. Two men had been arrested in Liverpool and their informer in Belfast named them as the assassins. Once this was established, Neil Fraser and the other two targets would be low risks as usual.

'What are you going to do now?' Fraser asked him. 'Or is that a tactless question?'

'I'm due for leave,' Michael Harvey said.

'Oh? Then why not come down and have a day's shooting next Saturday,' Fraser suggested. 'We've got some guns staying with us and it should be a good party. We'd really like to give you a good day. Wouldn't we, darling?' He slipped his arm round his wife's shoulders.

They'd seemed on close terms since the night he over-heard them quarrelling.

'Yes, we certainly would.' She was enthusiastic. 'Do come down, Major Harvey. It's been so dreary for you in the last couple of weeks. We'll have a lot of fun, now that everything's back to normal. And the shooting is marvellous!'

In spite of himself he was tempted. 'I may be a bit rusty,' he said, and they both laughed. 'I mean with a high bird,' he amended.

'Say yes,' Claire encouraged him.

'Do,' Fraser echoed.

'Well, if you're sure you can stand the sight of me . . . I'd love to.'

That was the start of their friendship. It was irregular because his duties took him out of touch for weeks at a time. Whenever he rang up he was welcome to come for a night, or meet them in London and have dinner. He was amused by Claire's attempts to introduce him to attractive women.

'She's awfully nice,' she'd say, preparing the way for yet another girl. 'Very pretty; I'm sure you'll like her.'

And he would cock his head and say, 'I'm sure I shall. But I'm just as happy spending the evening with you and Neil. I'm not in the market.'

He'd told them once that he'd been married. 'Three years and we got divorced. This job doesn't go with a wife, let alone children. So . . .' A shrug – that dismissed so much unhappiness and disappointment. He was glad neither expected any details.

It was an odd friendship; Fraser was a gregarious man, ambitious, keen-witted for the main chance, much sought after. Harvey couldn't see what he had to offer someone like that. Except, of course, a sense of security. He could talk to Michael Harvey and trust him not to make use of what he said. He could sit with his very big brandies when Claire had gone to bed and talk about the Gordian Knot of the Arbuthnot relationships. He couldn't cut it and he was enmeshed in it himself. For such a successful man in his middle years, his reliance on the young army officer was touching. He seemed to Michael Harvey to be very lonely. This was perhaps what they really had in common. It was a marriage in a vacuum, with two sweet children and all the material trappings of affluence and success. But Neil Fraser couldn't reach out and touch his wife. Harvey wondered whether he had ever been able to, even in the beginning. Like a ship on a slow tide, she had moved away from him, without either of them knowing until it was too late and the drift couldn't be stopped.

If Claire had flicked an eyelash at him, Harvey would never have come near them again. But she didn't. She liked him and trusted him as a friend who was valuable to her husband. And sometimes they talked about Ireland and the old days when they were children. They could laugh at the absurdities of life and people that made no sense to those who hadn't lived in Ireland. It was a bond between them, although his links were long broken. His family had sold up and settled in Cheshire. He didn't go over to the Republic or see friends. His background and knowledge had directed him to the branch of military intelligence centred on Northern Ireland. They never mentioned Ulster, except in general terms.

The plane was making its descent on Dublin. The sign to fasten seat-belts lit up in front of him. Dark clouds enveloped the aircraft and it began to bump through them. Somewhere to the rear a child began to wail. He could see the grey ruffled silk of the sea on the left as they banked and came in towards the airport. Inevitably it was raining.

Frank Arbuthnot was missing. Harvey agreed with Brownlow on balance that he was most likely dead and buried. It wasn't his brief to find him. But Claire Fraser was out there and he had undertaken to find her and persuade her to come home. He was quite prepared to use force if that was necessary. He had hesitated when he was asked to go. One mistake could blow his cover and ruin years of careful work in the North. Then he remembered something and knew he was in duty bound to take that risk. A lunch on Sunday in the Gloucestershire garden by the pool. The sun beating down on them and the children splashing and laughing in the shallow end. The most unlikely moment for Claire to talk about a day when she and her brother went walking across the land of a man who believed he'd come back from the dead as a fox.

He went through the green door in the Customs Hall and out into the main lounge. A man with a cardboard saying 'Mr Keogh' in rough pencilled letters came up to him. Michael Harvey followed him out to the hired car. He took the keys from him and drove off. Some distance from the airport he pulled up. The rear seat lifted. The weapons and ammunition were underneath it. A bag with a change of clothes was in the boot. Jeans, a thick jersey, an anorak sold throughout Ireland by Dunne's stores, scuffed jodphur boots. Kildare was racing country. Dressed like that no one would look at him twice.

The first thing, he decided, was to check out Riverstown in case she had been there first.

It was a long walk. The woods were damp and overgrown; she stumbled through brambles and fallen branches. At the head of the valley she was forced to get her breath. It was a marvellous site and, seen from so far away, the house didn't look a ruin. What parties they'd been to when they were young, and Tom Reynard was holding court for his friends and their children.

The Arbuthnots hunted on odd days with the Meath and Tom lived for the sport. He was reputed to be rich, and was famous for his hospitality. He never married, but there were nieces and nephews and always a stream of people staying. Life was joyful at Cloncarrig and Tom, red-haired and ruddy-faced, presided over the dissipation of his fortune without giving it a thought.

'Why the hell should I worry myself about money,'

he would demand, glass full of whiskey in hand, warming his backside by the fire after a day's sport. 'I've made provision for all I'm ever going to need!' And he'd join in his guests' laughter.

'Does he really believe it, Daddy?' Claire asked her father one evening when they were back at Riverstown, after a long wet day and a huge hunting tea.

'Believe what, darling?'

They were sitting in the study at home, toasting by the fire before going in to dinner. Frank was stretched out in an armchair, eyes closed, as if he were half-asleep. Claudia was still upstairs, resting after her bath. She'd led the field with Tom for a five-mile point at the end of the day.

'Believe he'll turn into a fox when he dies,' Claire said.

Philip Arbuthnot smiled. He adored his daughter; he couldn't resist putting a hand on her head and ruffling the bright blonde hair. She reminded him so much of Claudia. 'I think he does,' he answered. 'He's spent enough money on the idea anyway. And if it makes him happy, what's the harm?'

'But when he dies, we'll never be able to hunt in Meath again, in case it's *him*,' Claire pointed out.

Philip laughed at the simple practicality. She was such a natural, uncomplicated child, unlike his son. You never knew for sure what Frank was thinking. He'd loll in his chair as he was doing then, and suddenly come out with some remark that made everyone else uncomfortable. He was going to public school in England after the Christmas holidays were over. It was a late start because of the poor education he'd received at the local Protestant school. He should have gone away to prep school at eight, but Claudia didn't want him to feel rejected just because there was a baby half-sister, so he stayed at home. A tutor and a year's hard studying had just helped him catch up. Even so, without his father's family connection he wouldn't have scraped through the entrance exam. It might be difficult for the boy to go so late, but there was no other way of educating him properly. Philip hoped he would take advantage of the chance and do his best.

'Dad.' He saw his son sit up, lean forward and look at him with the wary expression that irritated him so much. 'Dad, I saw Mr Ross out today.'

'Oh, did you?' The Reverend Hugh Ross was head-master of the local boys' boarding school in Meath. A worthy churchman more addicted to hunting than to academics. Philip hardened in anticipation of what his son was leading up to.

'We had a few minutes waiting around,' Frank said.

Claire saw his hands clench and thought, 'Oh, poor Frank, he's trying to say something that will make Daddy cross.'

'Did you?' his father repeated. 'I didn't even see him to say good day to.'

'He says there's a place at Barraclough, if you'd let me go next term.' He looked down at his hands and then back at his father. It had taken the last half-hour to muster the courage to mention the subject yet again. Listening to Claire chattering about that old lunatic Tom Reynard while he pretended to be dozing and was framing sentences in his mind. It wasn't going to work. He could see by the set of his father's mouth. Anxiety urged him into further risk.

'I'd work very hard, Dad. I'd do just as well, I promise you!'

'I'm sure you'd work,' Philip answered. 'You've done very well to reach your present level. But it needed a full-time crammer to get you there and you're still below average. I've explained it often enough to you, Frank, and I wish you'd accept what I say. An Irish education isn't good enough for someone in your position. None of our family went to school over here. Even Claire will go to England to a decent finishing school, and she's a girl. There's no question of your going to Barraclough, and I shall have a word with Mr Ross!'

'He's only trying to help,' Frank protested. Every-thing about his father said the subject was closed. 'I'm

Irish,' he said, and it sounded aggressive because he didn't want his voice to quiver. 'I don't want to go to England!'

Claire opened her eyes very wide and sat very still. It was the first time in her life she'd heard Frank say something bold to his father. Some kind of crisis had developed in the last few minutes, and she didn't know why she felt afraid.

Philip Arbuthnot's colour faded. 'You're an Arbuthnot,' he said. 'And you're not going to grow up an Irish yob! You go to school in England, and that's the end of it!'

The boy got up. He was tall and thin, his strength outgrown. For months he had lived with the fear of this exile to England, among boys a year younger than himself, separated from his home and his family for a reason he rejected. Fear of his father and fear of the strange environment fused into a passionate anger. At last his father had put into words what Frank had known instinctively lay between them.

'If you say that about the Irish, why did you marry my mother?'

Claire burst into tears. She started to sob out loud. Philip had started out of his chair and half raised his hand to strike his son. Now he turned away.

'Go to your room,' he said. 'Don't you ever dare speak about your mother like that to me. Get out!'

Claudia opened the door. She was flushed and handsome after her rest, wearing something red, with ruffles round the neck. Claire saw her as a red blur through the tears.

'Good Lord, what on earth . . .' she started to say as Claire wept, but Philip interrupted.

'Frank's not having dinner tonight. And I think Claire's had a long day. Go upstairs with Mummy, darling, and you can have a light supper and early bed.'

Frank brushed passed his stepmother and went upstairs. He locked the door of his room. He didn't break down at once. He tried to keep the anger at its peak; he cursed his father, and slammed his fist on the chest by the window so that the photograph of his mother overbalanced and fell on its face. He turned it over. He couldn't flesh her out, however hard he studied the picture. She was just a girl with a sweet smile and a pretty face, her hair drawn back into some kind of fishnet behind. The fashion of fourteen years ago. She could have been any girl in any photograph.

Claudia was real. Claudia, with her made-up face and her bad language in the hunting field, a powerful image which overwhelmed the memory of the frail Irish girl who hadn't survived his birth. She was no mother to him because she'd taken his real mother's place. He didn't like her energy and her enthusiasm; she made too much noise in his life. She had stopped trying to make him like her; that was a relief. The one good thing she'd done was to give him Claire as a sister. If she hadn't started crying, what might not have happened between him and his father?

He slumped down on his bed and gave way to a brief and painful fit of crying. It was over and he was undressed when the knock came on his door. He thought it must be one of the maids with some food sent up by Claudia. It was the sort of thing she'd do, thinking it wrong to punish a boy by making him go hungry.

'I don't want anything, thank you. I'm going to sleep.'

'It's me,' Claire said. 'Let me in, Frankie, please.' She was in her dressing gown and her face was pink and puffed from crying.

'What are you doing,' he whispered. 'You'll get into the hell of a row being out of your bed. Go back, like a good girl.' He couldn't push her out.

She shut the door and climbed on the bed. 'What's the matter with your eyes? You've been howling!'

'No, I haven't!' he denied it fiercely. 'You're the bloody cry-baby, not me.'

'He was going to hit you,' she said, and her mouth turned down at the corners. 'Don't be cross with him.

I'll ask him not to send you to school. But don't say anything more to make him cross!'

The big blue eyes were brimming over again and he sat beside her and put one arm around her. He should have known it was her, creeping out to comfort him.

'I won't,' he promised. 'I'll go to his bloody school, but they won't make an Englishman out of me.'

She leaned her head against his shoulder. 'I don't want to go away either,' she said. 'You heard him say I'd go to England too. What's a finishing school?'

'I don't know,' Frank said. She should go back to her own bed and not risk either of them getting into more trouble, but he liked having the silly little thing cuddled up to him like a rabbit. It was warm and he didn't feel lonely when she was there. She'd cried because she thought he was going to be hit.

'If he hits me,' he said, more to himself than to her, 'Bejaysus, I'll hit him back.'

Claire lifted her head, catching the first word. 'You mustn't say that,' she murmured. 'Doyle says "Bejaysus". Mummy told him off for saying it when I was there. Mummy says "Christ", I've heard her. So does Daddy. What's wrong with what Doyle says?'

'Doyle's the gardener, that's what.' And he's Irish, Frank added to himself. I'm not to say 'Bejaysus'. I'm not to grow up an Irish yob. I'm to be like you. Whether I feel like you or not. I'm to forget that half of me is different.

'What are you saying to yourself?' she asked him. She was feeling sleepy and reassured. She yawned.

'Nothing for you to know,' her brother said. 'Come on, Clarry, go to your bed.'

'All right. Kiss goodnight?' It was their ritual, ever since she'd been able to string words together.

'Kiss goodnight,' he said, wanting her to go. He felt hurt and angry and older than he'd ever felt in his life before. The child belonged back in her nursery.

Claire offered her cheek and then planted a hard kiss on his. Both arms were round his neck in a stranglehold.

'I love you,' she said. 'You're my best brother.'

'Philip, you'll have to talk to him,' Claudia said. 'You can't leave it and have this thing festering about his mother.' She lit a cigarette. They'd finished dinner and were sitting in the study together. For some reason she remembered how awful it was when she first moved in after their marriage. Pink and flowery – in terrible taste. It was a full year before she felt able to suggest redecoration.

'There's nothing festering,' he said irritably. 'He just said the first impertinent thing that came into his head. He's scared stiff of going away to school and all this "Irish" nonsense is just an excuse to get out of it. He's going to Rowden and that's final!'

'I expect he is scared,' she said reasonably. 'Weren't you, at his age?'

'I'd already been away since I was nine,' Philip retorted. 'We kept him at home and mollycoddled him, that's the trouble. Oh, no, darling, I'm not blaming you. You wanted him to settle down and accept you, and then Claire came along – I was furious with him for upsetting her like that – and he was allowed to slack and play the fool at that damned school till he was right behind. That's all there is to it.'

'It's not,' she said, 'and you know it. He feels alienated.'

'Claudia, don't go quoting those bloody child psychology books at me! Alienated, my foot!' He reached forward and rattled the poker in the fire.

'You should talk to him about Eileen,' she insisted. 'I tried once, but he just clammed up completely. I felt he resented it. He's looking for an identity and he hasn't found it with you.'

'I told him about his identity tonight,' he snapped. 'I told him he was an Arbuthnot. If he doesn't like it, he can lump it.' He attacked the fire again, breaking up the turf.

Claudia didn't say anything. She was full of words,

but she was too wise a woman to speak them. He didn't love the boy, that was the real trouble. And the boy knew it. Was it because in some way he blamed Francis for his mother's death – or was the reason less dramatic? What he'd found acceptable in a girl because he loved her aroused antagonism in a son. It was the mixed blood he didn't like, the native Irish in Francis that lived uneasily with all that dour Scots ancestry. But he would never admit such a thing.

She loved Philip and their life was happy in all respects. But he had hardened after Eileen died. He had broken the rules and the punishment had warped him. For years Claudia had tried to reconcile him to his mother. It was hopeless. He said flatly that she had upset Eileen and brought on premature labour. He had never seen or spoken to her since.

At last she said, 'Philip, does Frank know how much you loved Eileen?'

'I don't understand you.'

'Yes you do. Have you *ever* talked to him about her? It might help if he realized how much you did love her.'

He sighed and reached to take her hand. 'You're an amazing woman, you know. How many stepmothers would think of that? No, my darling, I haven't discussed Eileen with Frank, and I don't intend to. He's my son and I love him, just as I love Claire. I shall do my very best for him and, if anything you say is true, getting away to a different atmosphere with other boys will be the answer. Rowden is a fine school and it'll give him plenty of sports and develop a side of him which could never see the light of day in Ireland. He'll learn there's more to being a man than hunting and lolling about the place. Now, give me a whiskey before we go to bed. And stop worrying about the boy. He'll be fine in the morning.'

The morning came, and they breakfasted together. Nothing was said. Frank didn't apologize and Philip behaved as if nothing had happened. At the beginning of January Frank travelled to England with his father to start his first term at Rowden. He got long, ill-spelt letters from Claire every week, telling him what Doyle had done, and how Mary the cook was going into hospital, and the Labrador had taken first prize at the Eadstown Field Day. His father wrote a regular monthly letter and, after Frank had been at Rowden for two years, one of the letters told him that his grandmother Blanche Arbuthnot had died, and left him all her money and her house in Meath.

'Blanche, are you quite sure you want to do this?'

Blanche Arbuthnot finished pouring him a cup of tea. He noticed she needed two hands to lift the silver pot. She had grown very frail. Hugh Lorimer had been her solicitor for years; he was also a family friend. The firm of Lorimer and Leach was long established in Fitzwilliam Square. They were as much part of the Anglo-Protestant establishment as the clients they looked after.

Blanche said, 'My dear man, of course I'm sure. I've thought it over very carefully and you know I don't make up my mind in a hurry.'

He took the teacup from her. 'It's a very final step,' he said. 'Quarrelling with Philip is one thing, but disinheriting him completely . . .'

'Blaming me for his wife's death and refusing to speak to me for seventeen years is hardly "quarrelling",' she retorted. 'It's no good, Hugh. I'm not paying lip service to convention. My money's going to my grandson. And this place. Philip's very well off; John left him Riverstown and everything on trust till my death. He won't suffer any hardship.'

'Tell me, Blanche, does he know you're ill?'

She said casually, 'I think the Dornaways wrote to him, but I haven't heard any more. He's very proud; it's too difficult for him to do anything about it now. And too late, as far as I'm concerned.'

'It's never too late,' Hugh Lorimer insisted. 'Let me write to him.'

'No, Hugh dear. Philip knows I've got cancer. I've

got to put my affairs in order. I want you to draw up the will exactly as I've said, and let me have it as soon as possible.'

'You've never seen the boy?'

'Not officially. I've seen him twice out hunting, when we were following by car. He's the image of Philip. Nice-looking boy, very good seat. I think of him a lot, you know. Cake?'

He shook his head. If the son was proud, the mother was no less so. But she couldn't hide the pain.

'It was so dreadful, his mother dying like that. I know Claudia's been a good stepmother – she's the kindest woman in the world – but I thought he looked a sad sort of a boy. And, since we're talking about it, I want to make amends for the way I treated his mother. I wasn't at all kind, and that's been on my conscience ever since.'

'It's no good blaming yourself,' he countered. 'It was a hopeless misalliance. Most people would have reacted as you did. Her death was a tragedy, but who knows what kind of disaster that marriage would have been if she'd lived? You can't hold yourself responsible for what happened.'

'I don't,' Blanche Arbuthnot said. 'But who can say how it would have turned out? I don't make judgements any more. No, Hugh, I'm talking about something much less dramatic. I've heard rumours round the place that Philip doesn't like his boy. The favourite is my grand-daughter Claire. I want to protect Francis in case they fall out. I know the Arbuthnots.' She smiled, and her face dissolved in wrinkles. She was a bad colour, he thought. Once famous for her complexion, she was almost jaundiced now. 'They're as hard as the Scots and as unforgiving as the Irish. Not that my John wasn't the best in the world. Maybe Francis will think of me kindly one day. I hope so. I've missed knowing my grand-children so much.'

'All right,' Hugh said. 'If you really want it done this way, I'll get it drawn up and sent down for you to sign. You can always change your mind, my dear.'

'Not unless I do it in the next three months,' she told him.

He said, 'I didn't know it was that soon. I'm so sorry.'

'Don't be,' she said. 'I've had a very good life and quite a long one. I don't want to linger on in hospital with tubes and drugs and all that messy business. I shan't suffer much, they tell me, and I'll be here in my own surroundings. It's as good a way as any. Now, my dear Hugh, I'm going to send you on your way. One thing the damned illness does is make me tired for very little. It's been so lovely to see you. Give my love to Jean and maybe you'll come down and bring the will with you? We might as well have lunch, if I'm up to it. Why doesn't Jean come too? Haven't seen her for ages.'

'Why not?' he said. He shook her hand. It was dry and limp. He felt unbearably sad. He left, promising to come down with his wife and make a party of it. It was an empty promise. He hurried the will into proper form and brought it down for signature. Blanche was confined to bed most of the time; he didn't stay long because she was so weary and there was a nurse who bustled him out.

He had telephoned Philip Arbuthnot twice and been fobbed off. He wouldn't come to the phone when he heard who it was. He knew his mother was dying and he either couldn't or wouldn't go to see her. Hugh's last scruples about seeing him cut out of the will were satisfied by writing him a personal letter of appeal. It was answered by Claudia. It was despairing and made him uneasy for a long time afterwards. Philip had no reason to play the hypocrite. He would not be going to the funeral either. Surely, the letter said with a surprising burst of bitterness, Eileen Ryan would rest easy in her grave at last.

Blanche Arbuthnot was buried in the family plot at Naas. Claudia Arbuthnot attended with a crowd of cousins and old friends. The two children were not there. Francis was at school in England in the middle of his studies, and Claire was considered too young. It gave

93

Hugh Lorimer some satisfaction to inform Philip that his son had inherited the estate in Meath and a personal fortune of a quarter of a million pounds.

The TWA jet from New York landed at Dublin airport at just after ten o'clock in the morning. It was a full passenger load; the tourist class was full and Kevin Ryan had just managed to secure a seat in first class. He had slept during the flight and woke refreshed, with a tremor of excitement niggling in his stomach. It was his first visit to Ireland in twenty years. He wondered how much he would find changed. He was very different from the dour young man who'd set off all those years ago. He was thicker set, with a suspicion of belly overhanging the crocodile belt; his sandy hair had been fashionably crew-cut and he wore glasses.

He checked the time of arrival on a big gold bracelet watch, and there were handsome cuff-links with a sham-rock in tiny emeralds in each shirt-sleeve. He was rich and he liked to show it. He dressed expensively, wore hand-made shoes and pure silk shirts. He smelled of aftershave and talcum powder. His wife, Mary Rose, slipped into a mink coat as they prepared to disembark. They had been married fourteen years and there were four strapping children. Kevin peered out of the window at the grey tarmac and the rain, and wondered what the family would say when they saw him and his wife. Photographs had winged their way across, and presents at Christmas and Easter, with Mammy's birthday a speciality. The father was long dead. Kevin had been poor then and unable to get home for the funeral. A visit to the grave was on his schedule. His eyes pricked at the thought. He had long forgotten how he had despised the old man for being mean and ignorant. That was one pilgrimage to make with Mary Rose.

The other he reserved for himself. Not that he hadn't told her the story of his sainted sister Eileen, and how she died giving birth to her child. Hounded to her death by a cruel mother-in-law, neglected by her husband . . .

the same husband who'd carried on with a woman when she was hardly cold in her grave. And then married her. It was a grim tale and the children were brought up on it, along with Mary Rose, who ummed and aahed in horror every time she heard it.

It was part of the folklore among their friends, part of the legend which was growing up around Kevin Ryan, the man who'd married old Heraghty's daughter and made a small furniture-manufacturing business into a multi-million-dollar corporation with branches right across the States. Ryan, the Irish philanthropist and champion of Irish freedom. He had political ambitions, and knew how to make friends at Tammany Hall. And he was generous with his money. He supported orphanages and schools, underprivileged children went on camping holidays at his expense. He was a financial and moral pillar of the Catholic Church, and Mary Rose devoted herself to committees and fund-raising when he decided to run for the Senate. He had been defeated the first time, but that foray into the arena had taught him a lot. A great deal of money and effort had been wasted, but at least some useful lessons had been learned. Next time, he'd won.

He had talked of going home for years; yet excuses came up for delaying till next year and the year after. Kevin didn't know why he put it off because the reasons for doing so were always valid. His eldest son had a mastoid operation; there was a big building programme that needed his personal attention. Mary Rose was pregnant for the fourth time and not feeling too good.

And then the time was suddenly right, and there they were, stepping out on to the blessed soil of his native land. It was right because he was rich and confident enough to introduce Mary Rose to his terrible clod of a brother and his wife, and to Mammy, who was old and senile and sat like a statue in a corner by the kitchen fire. He could show her the house where he was born and the farm, and be proud now, because he was the big success come home, and the family and friends would be in awe of him. Hadn't he actually been elected to the State Senate – old Jack Ryan's youngest lad? It would be a triumph.

He'd hired a smart car for their visit; he joked with Mary Rose about driving on the right side of the road. She shut herself in out of the drizzling rain, and expressed her delight with everything. The roads were quaint, the way they twisted round, and wasn't Dublin just beautiful, with all those darling old buildings . . . He took her on a tour of the city, and she enthused over the faded glories of Georgian architecture and the charm of the bridges spanning the river Liffey. She sighed over the poverty and squalor of the streets they had to pass through on their way out of Dublin. So poor, she said, forgetting the misery of the ghettos in New York; the poor children going barefoot in the dirt.

'Seven hundred years of British rule,' Kevin declared, and she saw the tight line of his mouth. 'You don't undo that in a hurry.'

She was surprised by his hatred sometimes, but then he'd been born there and grown up, while she was second-generation American. He was right, of course. She had been brought up on Ireland's suffering under British rule. But for her husband it was so real. And then there was his sister. What a tragedy that must have been for them all.

Mary Rose was a kind and simple woman, in awe of her husband, as she had been of her father, as she was of her parish priest. She dressed elegantly and had social graces which Kevin didn't have, but her role in life was rooted in the peasant culture of her family's origins. She was the mother and the wife and the queen of the home, as Our Lady had been queen of the little family at Nazareth. She was perfectly content and regarded the liberated woman as a creature to be pitied. She loved her husband and her children, and for Kevin's sake, she would love his family too.

The drive up to the Ryans' farm was muddy and unkempt. The old house loomed up at them with a shelter of laurel bushes and some lean-limbed yew trees. Mary Rose had seen photographs, but they were flattering. On a wet day, it was dark and uninviting, the door and window frames painted green, contrasting with the dirty grey stone façade.

Kevin didn't notice this, or pause to open the door for his wife and take her with him. He sprang out of the car and was banging on the front door. He felt elated, warm-hearted at the sight of the place where he'd been born. His brother opened it, the heavy figure of his wife Bridget in the hallway behind him.

'Hello there, Shamus.'

They grasped hands and pumped up and down, and Mary Rose picked her way through the muddy forecourt and approached, her smile at the ready. The brothers weren't alike, except for the sandy hair. Shamus was thinner and looked quite a lot older. She noticed his collarless shirt was faintly grimy and there was a button missing. His cardigan was not very clean either and had a hole in the elbow. He greeted her very warmly and blushed in the sweetest way when she gave him a sisterly kiss. He surely hadn't used a razor that morning either.

'Come in, come in,' he urged them. 'There's tea in the kitchen and a drink if ye'd rather.'

Kevin detained him for a moment. 'Is Mammy all right?'

'Ah, sure, she's not too bad at all,' his brother said. 'Bridget minds her like a saint, don't ye?'

The plain, large woman in a flowered overall said quietly, 'I do me best. She's no trouble. Wets herself now and again, but that's about all. Come in, she's waitin' for ye. Not that she'll recognize ye, her sight's none too good, but we've been tellin' her for days ye'd be coming.'

It was very warm in the kitchen. Mary Rose took off her mink and handed it to a large redheaded girl, who looked at it and stroked the silky fur before she hung it up on the back door among the muddy anoraks.

'Is it real fur?' she asked. There was a shyness about

her that Mary Rose found appealing. Her own children were much more strident. She called it confident.

'It's mink,' she said. 'Maybe you'll have one like it when you're a big girl.'

'Come and say hello to Mammy.' Kevin caught her arm.

The old woman sat in a corner by the range. She was very upright, like a wizened doll, decked out in a bright flowery overall with carpet slippers on her feet. Her hair was snow-white and brushed back into a neat bun. A very long time ago, she must have been pretty. Kevin bent down and kissed her. She grasped his hand with a thin claw.

'Kevin? Is it ye, Kevin?'

He had tears in his eyes. He held on to her, stroking the poor little bony hand holding fast to his. Twenty years. Half blind and so rapidly aged. He'd forgotten how women aged in Ireland. Hard unremitting work and bearing children made them old before their time.

He swallowed and said, 'Mammy, this is Mary Rose.'

She peered past him. 'Who? Who'd ye say?'

'My wife, Mary Rose.' He repeated it slowly, guiding her hand for Mary Rose to take.

''Tis a pretty name,' Mrs Ryan said gently. 'I can't see ye too well.' She let the stranger touch her for a minute, and then the woman bent and kissed her on the cheek. She smelt like a rose too, the old woman thought. She wished she could see her better. But it was Kevin she wanted. Mary Rose gave place gracefully, and with some relief. There was a uriny smell about the old lady, and she remembered what her sister-in-law had said. She sat down and decided that although it was so early in the morning, she wouldn't mind a drink.

The meeting lasted almost two hours. Kevin and his brother were putting back the whiskeys and talking about things that meant nothing to her. She made conversation with Bridget, who pressed more gin and lime upon her. They began to drift into amiable silence when they had asked each other questions about their children and the schools, and the plans they had for their holiday in Ireland. It certainly was warm and they were really dear people. It was just great the way they took care of the old lady. Back home she'd have been in some nice comfortable clinic. They kept the real values in Ireland, just like Kevin said.

She was glad they weren't going to stay at the farm, though. It would have been too much for poor Bridget, looking after them, when she had so much to do. After a while Bridget asked if she'd like to see over the house, and Kevin's room, which he'd shared with Shamus, of course. Her three daughters were in it now. It was a dark house, Mary Rose thought, climbing the stairs to the first floor. It needed fresh paint and bright drapes, and her high heel caught in the floorboards.

'Kevin's room,' she said, standing in the open doorway. 'It's just wonderful to think of him being a little boy . . .'

Three beds cluttered one wall. It wasn't at all tidy. A large picture of the Sacred Heart gazed down at her, the blue-eyed Saviour with his smooth red hair and silky beard looked faintly sorrowful. A red devotional oil lamp burned on the table below. Mary Rose had listened to a TV debate once when one of the panel had derided the sentimental Aryan view of Jesus Christ. 'He was a black Jew; the Church has turned him into some kind of Barbie doll.' Mary Rose was so shocked she'd switched the set off.

'It's just wonderful to see all this,' she murmured.

They went back downstairs. She said to Bridget, 'Kevin's told me all about his sister. What a sad thing to happen to you all.'

'She got what she deserved,' Bridget Ryan said. 'Deserting her family and her faith. She broke the auld one's heart!'

Mary Rose couldn't believe she'd heard her properly. But there was no mistaking the bitterness of the voice or the gleam in her sister-in-law's eyes. Eileen was a saint to Kevin, but perhaps the folks at home knew more than he did. Deserted her faith. That was very shocking.

'Oh,' she said. 'I didn't know. Kevin didn't say anything about that . . .'

Bridget Ryan shrugged. 'He was the only one had time for her,' she said. 'She was no good, that one. For the love of God, don't mention her name. It's never spoken in this house. We'd best go on down and I'll show ye the sittin' room. I wanted to bring ye both in there, but Shamus says, for Christ's sake they're me own brother and his wife. We're not entertainin' strangers.'

Kevin got up when they came in.

'I've been showin' Mary Rose the house,' Bridget announced proudly.

Her husband laughed. He was a little drunk. 'Sure and she wanted us sittin' in that draughty old morgue of a sittin' room. If she's not polishing the auld bits and pieces, she's naggin' me for new curtains!'

'We're going out tonight, the four of us,' Kevin announced. 'I'm takin' us all out to the Cill Dara and we'll have a fine dinner and a few drinks.'

He too was a little high, his wife noticed. She also noticed that his brogue had thickened and he'd lost his American accent. He had his coat off and was standing in front of the range, with a glass in his hand, rocking on his heels, one hand stuck in his trouser pocket. He looked different. Coarser. She put the thought aside, ashamed of her disloyalty. It was strange to her, that was all. They were nice, friendly people, with all the good-heartedness she'd expected, but they were different from her own family. Different from their friends at home. Her mother hadn't been too pleased with Kevin as a son-in-law. She was a snob; Mary Rose knew her mother wanted a lawyer or a doctor, but there was no one she liked as well as the sharp young Irishman who was working his way up in Heraghty's business. He was a bit too horny to start with, but she had the four children and it wasn't a problem now. From time to time he slept with her and showed he loved her, but business and politics were his priority.

He came towards her and threw his arm round her.

'Isn't she a grand girl?' he demanded. She felt his fingers digging into the side of her breast. Too hard; it hurt. 'Aren't I a lucky fella?' he demanded of them again.

She put her hand up and eased his fingers off. 'Kevin . . .' she whispered.

'We're off to the hotel,' he said. 'A little sleep, eh, me darlin'? Then we'll meet ye all at the Curragh Bar for a few good old jars, and then we'll go on to the hotel. Mind ye dress up, Bridget. Mary Rose has got a trunkful of bloody glad rags . . .'

They left, with Shamus and Bridget waving them goodbye at the door.

'Ye'd best drive,' Kevin told her. 'I don't want the feckin' Gardai pullin' me up for drunken drivin'.' He dozed on the short drive, but unfortunately he was wide awake and very horny when they reached their hotel room. Before he fell asleep he held her in his arms and said, 'Ye don't know what it means to me, coming home again. My heart's here in Ireland, Rose.'

'I know it is,' she answered. She wasn't really thinking about that. She was worrying that they'd made love at the wrong time of the month. Drink never diminished his sexual powers; he was more potent and demanding drunk than sober. She really didn't want a fifth child. He slept for most of the afternoon.

They met in the bar as arranged. The Curragh Bar was a smoky place, its walls plastered with racing pictures and signed photographs of famous jockeys drinking with the landlord. Horse brasses and horse memorabilia everywhere. Mary Rose had no affinity with them or with racing.

Kevin kept on meeting old friends. The drinks were bought and finished and bought again. The talk was loud and nostalgic, incomprehensible to her. She heard Kevin say, 'Jaysus, I'd like to have a place of my own here,' and felt quite shaken. Not a house like that grim old farm, set in the middle of nowhere, with dank trees and mud clinging to you every step you took. It was the drink making him talk like that. She smiled resolutely and decided to get a little high herself. It seemed the only thing to do. Women were drinking in the bar along with their men. It wasn't frowned upon for a woman to start talking loud and making a fool of herself. If you can't beat 'em, join 'em, as her father used to say. Mary Rose switched to vodka and tonic, with plenty of ice and a twist of lemon. Kevin was paying her compliments again, squeezing her waist and showing her off. She did look nice, she admitted, not being a vain woman. Blue suited her and she'd worn her pearl and diamond brooch because he wanted everyone to see it. Her sister-in-law's glad rags were not very glad. She had such a bad figure, that was the trouble. Irish women didn't seem to take any care of themselves. She needed a good diet sheet and daily workouts, Mary Rose decided, and began advising her how to go about it. Bridget listened and nodded and thought to herself 'the silly bitch is jarred' and took no notice.

When they were about to leave for the restaurant, a man standing near the bar came up to Kevin and said, 'If ye're wanting a place here, the Half House is on the market.'

'We might look at it,' Kevin suggested the next day. 'There's no harm.'

He was in high spirits in spite of a hangover after last night. Dinner had been cheerful and alcoholic, Kevin playing host to his family and slipping back into his old environment as if he had never been away. Mary Rose was happy for him and when he suggested looking at the house with its quaint-sounding name, she was enthusiastic. The estate agent came down from Dublin to show them over. He saw what appeared to be rich American clients and insisted on taking them to lunch first. In the middle of his sales talk about the land and the area, it gave Kevin satisfaction to say, 'I was born here, my brother farms up at Bryanstown.'

They drove up the short drive, past a lodge with a roof that looked in need of mending, good grass fields and post-and-rail fencing like broken teeth after years of neglect. The Half House met them round a corner, and Mary Rose exclaimed.

'Oh, isn't it just beautiful!'

The estate agent beamed at her. 'Women bought houses, men bought land', was a proven saying in the business.

Kevin had never been there before. They got out and he stood looking at it for a moment or two before he walked to the door after Mary Rose. It was well named. The wing of a Victorian Gothic pile, with handsome windows and a fine mahogany front door. Three floors of it, and the ubiquitous Irish basement. Splendid trees and a glimpse of garden that had run down badly. The hunting, shooting Hamiltons, so grand in their heyday, were bankrupt and gone. He walked into the hall. He didn't listen to the sales talk, he wandered slowly through the rooms, aware that Mary Rose was showing far too much enthusiasm if he was going to knock the price down. It was a fine big house and the more he saw, the more it pleased him.

On the first floor, his wife slipped her arm through his and said, 'Honey, just look at that view.' The hills were purple in the distance and the magic sky of Ireland smiled in sunny blue above them. Green fields, a coppice of trees, and not a roof in sight.

'Punchestown racecourse is on the right,' the agent announced. 'Only a few minutes' drive away.'

Kevin remembered his father going to the spring meeting, and coming back rolling drunk, with or without winnings in his pocket. Kevin was not a racing man. 'Let's see the roof,' he said.

They were there for most of the morning. They toured the house a second time and Mary Rose began to think about drapes and colour schemes. The whole idea was too romantic and the awful prospect of the Ryan farm-house or its equivalent vanished like a nasty dream. If Kevin wanted a root in the old country, then this, she decided, must be it. And wouldn't the children go wild, when they came over? Wouldn't it be just wonderful to own a gracious old house in the heart of Ireland? They could visit and bring friends over. Kevin was a politician and of course his life was in the States, but hadn't he said only the night before, 'My heart's here in Ireland, Rose.' It would do his election chances good to have the status of a place like this in back of him.

There were outbuildings and stables, all of them run down and needing money spent; or the bulldozer, Kevin decided. The garden could be brought back; a swimming pool could replace the old kitchen garden with its drystone wall.

At the end he said to the agent, 'It needs a fortune spending on it. The roof's bad, there's no central heating, there's damp and the cellars are full of rot. I'm interested, but not at anything like the price.'

'The land's worth it,' he protested.

'Then why isn't it sold?' Kevin demanded. 'Lookit, I'm local and I know the way of things here. I'll need a survey, but I'm not going to pay good money for it unless they bring the price down.' And he named a ruthless sum.

The agent hesitated. The wife wanted it, that was his best hope of a sale. But the man was hard and not likely to be influenced unless he got a bargain. And there hadn't been a serious offer for the property in the last twelve months. He nodded and said, 'I'll have a word with the solicitor looking after Captain Hamilton's affairs. He's in England at the moment. I think we can come to some compromise, Mr Ryan, if you're really interested.'

When they were alone Mary Rose said to him, 'You're not going to lose it, are you?'

Kevin put his arm round her. 'No, Rose, I'm not. But I'll get it at my price, not theirs. I'm not putting money in the pocket of the bloody Hamiltons more than I can help. You want it, don't you?'

'I think it's the most romantic place,' she sighed. 'Just beautiful.'

'Then that's good enough,' he said.

Captain Hamilton, living in a modest flat in Fulham, was only too relieved to get rid of the house and the whole burden of debt. Ryan got the property at half the asking price, and the contracts were signed by proxy when he had returned to America. Two months later the first of the workmen moved in.

Chapter 4

'I'm so excited,' Claire said, 'I can't believe he'll be here any minute.'

Claudia lit a cigarette. 'The plane could be late,' she remarked. 'Don't get too worked up, darling.'

'No, it landed dead on time,' Claire answered. 'I rang the airport. Mummy, don't you realize I haven't seen Frank for two whole years?'

She was bobbing up and down, looking through the window, head on one side listening for the sound of the car. Philip had gone to meet his son. Tactfully, and without Claire realizing the true reason, Claudia had dissuaded her from going to the airport with him.

'Daddy wants to be the first to congratulate him,' she explained. 'It's good for them to have some time alone together.'

Claire was so easy to manipulate, she thought sadly. All anyone needed was to appeal to her kind heart. Finishing school in London and a year in Switzerland had turned the pretty teenage girl into a beautiful and sophisticated young woman of twenty, on the surface. Underneath the excited child held sway, bubbling over because her brother was coming home to Ireland for good. Claudia was disappointed. She had hoped that long separation and new friends would have loosened the bond between them. Maybe he'd changed and Claire wouldn't find him such a hero now that they were both grown up.

'He's done so brilliantly,' Claire said to her. 'Daddy must be thrilled. I remember all those years ago when Frank begged not to go to Rowden and he was way below all the other boys. Daddy must be so proud of him!' She went back to the window. It was a glorious summer's day, with the sun beating down through the huge old beech tree outside on the lawn. Everything was green and lush and in the garden bees droned in the warm air. A car turned round into the gravel sweep.

'They're here.'

Claire hurried out to the hall and through the front door. Her mother followed slowly, stubbing out her cigarette on the way. Certainly Philip should have been proud of his son. He had distinguished himself academically at Rowden and left Oxford with a first in PPE. A year at Harvard Business School had ended with equal success. He'd spent a year with the World Bank in Washington. He was coming home to settle in Ireland for good. She didn't know why it made her so uneasy. Father and son had developed a working relationship which was cordial but without real intimacy. Frank had done everything his father could have wished throughout his academic career. But there was no human warmth in them when they were together. And Claire's absence made the house seem sad and empty. Now both were home at the same time.

Claudia came out on to the forecourt. Frank had matured, she noticed. He was heavier, tanned very dark, rather American in his casual blazer and buttoned-down shirt.

'Hello, my dear. Welcome home.'

Standing there, while Billy Gorman unloaded the bags from the car boot, Frank Arbuthnot saw the familiar scene of so many homecomings. Back for the school holidays. Met at the airport, either by Claudia or his father, with Claire rushing to meet him, until she went off to Switzerland, and he was in America. Letters from home. Dry letters from his father, who hated writing and couldn't think of much to say. Friendly letters from Claudia, keeping him up to date with friends and life at Riverstown. Flowing, gossipy outpourings from his young sister that made his heart ache with homesickness, because they were the real letters. Nothing had changed, except that his father looked older and Claudia seemed more made-up and horsey. But Claire was there, bright as the sunshine in her cotton dress, so blonde and lovely that for a moment his heart gave a ridiculous bump when he first saw her. Suddenly happiness overflowed in him.

'Claire!' He stepped forward and she came straight into his arms. They held and hugged each other and both of them were laughing with the joy of the reunion.

Billy paused, a suitcase in each hand. He grinned at Philip Arbuthnot. ''Tis grand to see them two together, sir,' and Philip nodded. His son looked very well. He had an extra polish acquired after his time at Harvard Business School and the World Bank. He'd talked most impressively about banking during the drive home. He was proud of his son. The wary half-glance that made him think of tinkers was quite gone now. Frank looked him in the face and even put an arm briefly round his shoulders when they met. America had sophisticated him more than Oxford. From now on, everything would go smoothly, he felt sure.

'You're looking very well, Claudia,' Frank said. They exchanged a pleasant kiss. He'd met so many Claudias when he was up at university. Weekend mothers, he described them. Tweedy, lipsticked matrons, with 'sporting type' branded on their foreheads like the mark of Cain. He'd hunted and shot with their sons at week-ends and stayed in their houses; he understood a lot more about his stepmother as a result. It would be easier to accept her now.

He stood and looked round the hall; the same family portraits, the distinctive flowers arranged by Claudia, masses and masses interspersed with leaves and oddities from the garden. The big rug with the dog stains in the corner.

'Where's Belle?' he asked, looking for the descendant of all the Labradors since childhood.

'She's dead,' his father said. 'One of those bastard farmers put down rat poison. A crow dropped the bloody meat into the garden and she ate it.'

'I'm sorry,' Frank said.

'She was in agony,' his father went on. 'Strychnine. I didn't wait for the vet. I shot her myself.'

'It was awful,' Claudia added. 'Don't let's talk about it. Tea will be waiting for you, Frank dear, whenever you're ready.'

'I'll put my stuff in my room,' he said. 'Here, give me those, Billy. They're much too heavy for you to lug upstairs.'

'I'm coming too,' Claire insisted. She had a fleeting impression that her father was annoyed because Frank had taken the cases from Billy.

'Well,' she said, 'are you glad to be home?'

He heaved his luggage on to the bed and sat beside it. The mattress was the same, with the springs sagging slightly in the middle, the hunting prints on the walls, his desk where the dreaded homework used to lie in wait. School groups and university groups framed and displayed.

'God, am I glad,' was all he said, and Claire burst out laughing.

'You've got an American accent,' she pointed out.

'Don't worry, I'll soon lose it. And you've got an English one!'

'I'll soon lose that,' she said. 'Oh, Frank, it's lovely to be back. Nice to have you here too, by the way,' she added teasingly. It was so unbelievably good to be sitting on the bed, talking to each other as if they hadn't been apart at all.

'How was Switzerland?' he asked. 'Did you learn anything apart from how to catch a rich husband?'

'I'll show you what I learned,' she countered. 'I learned to ski better than you can ride, and I've got a certificate of aptitude to prove it.'

'They give you that with the fees,' Frank grinned.

'Feck off,' she said.

He leaned back and laughed out loud. He pulled at the tie till it came off, and opened the shirt at the neck. 'One thing you didn't learn, and that's to be a lady. I've got a present for you. I'll give it to you after tea. I brought some things for Dad and Claudia.'

'Why can't I have it now?' Claire demanded. 'What is it, anyway?'

'It's buried at the bottom of the bloody case, that's why. And all good things are worth waiting for.'

Claire leaned back in imitation of him, stretching her arms above her head. She had beautiful firm breasts.

'I bet you didn't keep the girls in America waiting,' she said. 'We had four of them at Le Rosalie and they were the most demanding, spoilt lot you've ever met in your life. Did you have a lot of girl friends?'

'A few,' he said. 'One very nice one. I was really sorry to say goodbye to her.'

'Oh.' Claire sat up. 'Serious stuff?'

'She thought so, but I didn't,' Frank answered. 'What about you? Find yourself a big blond ski instructor out there?'

'No. The big blond ski instructors were all snapped up by the rich girls. I had to make do with a little waiter.'

Claudia's voice carried up the stairwell.

'Come on, you two. Tea's waiting.'

Frank smiled. 'Nothing changes,' he said.

Claire went ahead of him. She had grown up, he thought. In spite of all the old childish banter, she was a beautiful young woman now. He was very proud of her. He hoped there hadn't really been a waiter.

The old tradition of changing for dinner had been

dropped for a long time at Riverstown. Claudia said it was pompous when the big staff had been reduced to a cook and a gauche girl who was learning how to wait at table. But that night they celebrated Frank's return. Claudia slipped her arm through Philip's. They were drinking champagne in the drawing room before the young people came down. He looked relaxed and happy.

'It's nice to be all together again,' she said. 'Frank is in marvellous form. He's delighted to be back.'

'Yes, he is,' Philip responded. 'He's full of plans for opening a merchant bank in Dublin. I told him he'd have plenty to do running the place at Meath. Also, he's got to decide what to do with the house.'

'He might want to live there,' she suggested.

Immediately he frowned. 'Why should he? He'll inherit Riverstown. I shall advise him to sell it with just enough land to attract some *nouveau riche* from Foxrock and farm the rest. Ah, Frank – help yourself to a glass. We've opened a nice bottle tonight. Cordon Rouge '61. See what you think of it.'

His father and stepmother were standing together, arms linked, when he came through the door. They were very close; he wondered where Claire was. She came in just as he was sipping the vintage champagne. Claudia said it first.

'Darling, that's rather stunning – haven't seen that before.'

It was a vivid sapphire-blue taffetta, flounced impudently at the knee, leaving one smooth tanned shoulder bare. Something blue sparkled in the light as she came towards them.

'Look,' she said to her parents, 'look what Frank's given me.'

He was watching her with a smile on his lips, watching with an expression of tenderness and amusement that only Claudia saw. Philip didn't notice. He saw nothing except the little sapphire brooch that had belonged to Eileen, pinned to his daughter's breast.

Frank said quietly, 'I didn't want to give her some

expensive trash from the States, and I thought maybe Mother's little brooch would do.'

'Isn't it lovely?' she demanded. She put her arm round his waist. For a moment their heads came close; the dark man and the very blonde girl, and Claudia Arbuthnot thought, 'Oh, my God . . .'

'Do let me see.' She swept forward and they separated. She touched the little sapphire pin, and her fingers trembled. '*So* pretty!' she said. 'What a sweet idea.'

Philip spoke for the first time. 'Where did you get that, Frank?'

'Old Mary Donovan gave it to me,' Frank said. There was tension in the room and he couldn't understand why. 'She said it was Mother's. I supposed Mother must have given it to her.'

'She didn't,' he said. 'I put all Eileen's jewellery in the bank. It's never been taken out.'

Claudia said quickly, 'Of course she gave it.' She lowered her voice. 'They were cousins, don't forget.'

Philip turned away. 'She stole it,' he said. 'She must have taken it the night she died.' He spoke to his son. 'You never mentioned it before. How long have you had this? Donovan's been dead for years.' He used her surname, Claire noticed. That was his way of putting any suggestion of relationship in perspective.

'Before I went to Rowden,' Frank answered. 'She said it was Mother's and she'd been keeping it for me. Dad, if this has upset you, I'm very sorry. I didn't know it mattered. I wanted to give Clarry a present, something personal.' He'd slipped into the old childhood nickname.

Philip sighed suddenly. 'Everything your mother had belongs to you, Frank. I was keeping it all to give you one day. Never mind, never mind. You can't ever trust them. It was a nice idea, my boy, giving it to your sister. Very nice. Let's have some more champagne.'

The chasm had opened at their feet and closed again. The dinner was excellent; Philip talked to his son and Frank concentrated upon everything he said. Mother and daughter smiled and chatted, thankful to see them

111

in apparent accord. Claudia was thankful for other reasons. But perhaps she was being over-sensitive. Perhaps she had imagined that moment when they stood together and she'd sensed some awful doom. She filled up her wineglass and told herself sternly not to be so bloody silly.

'We could go over to Meath tomorrow, if you like,' Philip was saying. 'Jim's been a good manager while you were away, so everything's in order.'

'The house is kept open and aired,' Claudia joined in. 'The trouble is we've had a spate of burglaries and the minute anyone knows a house is standing empty, they go in and strip it. Jim and his wife have been living in, and I'm sure that's what's kept the yobs from Dublin away. Do you know, the crime rate has doubled since this wretched business broke out in the North.'

Frank leaned towards her. 'It's an old problem, Claudia, and sooner or later it's got to be faced, and solved.'

'Solved in what way?' Philip asked. 'You'll never get the Unionists to see reason.'

'They'd see it soon enough if Britain withdrew,' Frank countered.

Claire sat quietly, wishing they'd change the subject.

'I'll tell you what'd happen if Britain got out,' Philip said forcefully. 'There'd be bloody civil war and we'd be dragged into it. And that's what the reality is when people talk about a united Ireland.'

Frank said quietly, 'That's not the view in the States.'

'Maybe,' his father said, 'but they don't live here. The Irish-American element is only interested in being anti-British. Most of them have never clapped eyes on Ireland. I hope you put them straight if they talked this rubbish to you! Anyway – I'm free tomorrow afternoon, so why don't we go over to Meath?'

'Why not,' his son agreed. 'I'd like to look it over. I remember I liked the house itself.'

'It's a barracks.' His father shook his head. 'Basement, attics, far too big for this day and age. Your grandmother lived in the old style, so it didn't matter. Riverstown is just the right size for a family house, and even so Claudia works damned hard, don't you, darling?'

'Not really, I enjoy it. So long as I get my hunting and don't have to cook, I'm happy.' She laughed. 'Claire, why don't we go into Dublin tomorrow then, if your father and Frank are going off? I could get my hair done . . . There's a rather nice shop opened up on Grafton Street.'

Claire hesitated. 'I'd rather go and see the house,' she said.

'Another time,' Philip said. 'We'll be busy going over the accounts and driving round the farms. You go off to Dublin with your mother. And don't spend too much money!'

They all laughed then.

Frank said, 'I'll take you over next week.'

'I'll take *you*,' she said triumphantly. 'I've got a car and I passed my test! First time.'

'God help us,' her brother said solemnly. 'They must be paralysed and blind to let you near a car! I'm taking *you*, or we don't go.'

They bantered like children and Philip watched benevolently. His son had changed. The old aggressiveness had gone, leaving a reasonable young man who didn't contradict on principle. Even when he was at Oxford, the discussion on the North would have ended in a sullen row. He felt relieved and happy. Except for the anger burning in him over the brooch. Mary Donovan. What a thing to do . . . what a treacherous creature, after all the years she'd worked for them and the kindness she'd received, right up to the time she died in hospital, the treatment paid for by Philip himself. God, he fumed inwardly, what a people. And there was the memory of Eileen, also wearing blue, with the little cheap tinselly brooch pinned to her dress, standing where Claire had stood that evening in the same room. Going off to Claudia Hamilton's dinner party. It could still hurt him to think of her. Poor little thing, so vulnerable and young, with such a short life left to live.

They left the table and he said, 'Let's have our coffee in the study, shall we?' He didn't want to go back into the drawing room again.

It was such a happy summer. There were tennis parties with friends, a trip to the west, where Claudia had a little fishing lodge, swimming in the sea, cold enough to take your breath – and the joy of riding round the farm. Both farms, because Frank had thrown himself into improving his inheritance at Meath. Claire went over the house with him and agreed with their father. It was too big and needed modernizing; what on earth would a young man do, rattling round in such a place? She didn't want him to move out of Riverstown and she influenced him shamelessly against the idea.

'I won't sell,' he insisted. 'I like it. It's mine, Clarry. She left it to me. I might want to live here one day.'

'All right then,' she countered. 'Let it. That's sensible.'

He hesitated, looking round the rooms on one of their tours of the house. Claudia had undertaken to sort through the clothes and personal possessions of the old lady, and her solicitor, Hugh Lorimer, had gone over the land titles and estate papers with Frank. Part of the farm was tenanted. Frank had dismissed any suggestion that he might try to repossess.

'Nobody gets turned out of their homes by me,' he had said. 'There's been enough of that in Ireland.'

Lorimer had stared at him for a moment and then let the remark pass, feeling he might not be able to handle this young man's affairs with any sympathy.

'I'm not going to let it either,' Frank told Claire. 'I don't want strangers living here, making it theirs. I'll keep on the caretaker for now. I might spend a few weeks a year here – build up some shooting. There's plenty of scope. And hunt a couple of days with the

Meath. Whatever happened to old Reynard's house, by the way?'

Claire shrugged. 'Nothing. The nephews sold off the land and the local butcher bought it. He left the house to fall down; it's no good to him and nobody else wanted it. Dad said they've sold all the lead off the roof and got a big price for it.'

Frank said, 'We'll go over one day and take a look. See if we can see the old devil skulking under a hedge.'

They both laughed. 'Oh, people swear they've seen him,' Claire insisted. 'Even Mummy said she saw a fox vanish in there.'

'Claudia is just as superstitious as the rest,' he said. 'Who's the butcher?'

'Flanagan,' Claire told him. 'He's got a chain of shops in Dublin and he's gone into land. Dad says he's a millionaire. And a bloody vandal,' she added, quoting.

'I don't see that,' he said. 'What does some big Anglo pile mean to him? Why should he care what happens to it?'

'But it's part of history,' Claire protested, not very sure of her ground. 'I mean, it's an old Irish house, like Carton,' naming the grandest ducal house in Ireland, threatened with the same fate.

'It's not part of Flanagan's history,' Frank said quietly. 'If it is, it's a part he'd probably like to see fall down.'

Claire looked at him. 'Don't talk like that in front of Dad, will you? Whatever's got into you since you've been away?'

'I've learned about the other side of the coin,' he said. 'If I was Flanagan, I wouldn't just strip the roof and let the rain in, I'd dynamite the bloody house and everything it stands for.'

'Frank!' She stared at him, horrified.

He shook his head. 'Don't worry; I'm not going to say anything at home. I did it once, that night we came back from hunting over here, remember?'

'Yes,' Claire said. 'I remember. There was an awful row because you didn't want to go to Rowden.'

'That's right,' he nodded. 'I said if Dad felt like he did about the Irish, why did he marry my mother? He never answered, and I've never asked again and never will. But I found a lot of answers in America. Come on, Clarry, we should go, or we'll be late for dinner.'

They drove home in silence. She felt low-spirited and uneasy. Life was such fun and they had so many things to enjoy together. Why had he spoilt it all with those dark words? An idea came to her. It was so frightening that she gasped. Frank turned his attention from the road.

'What's the matter?'

'Frank,' she said. 'Frank, you haven't joined anything, have you?'

'No, if you mean the IRA.'

'Oh.' She gave a great sigh of relief. 'Thank God for that!'

He drove on, concentrating on the road. 'I went to a rally in Boston,' he said. 'I nearly joined something called The Friends of Sinn Fein. But I didn't. I wanted to come home and settle down and see more for myself. It's the cautious Scots in me, I suppose.'

'Oh, don't be so bloody silly.' Claire dismissed it impatiently. 'You're no more Scots than I am. Three hundred years ago Dad's ancestor came from Scotland. We've been in Ireland ever since. Anyway, I'm glad you didn't join anything. Whatever they say in America, Dad's right. They don't live here and they don't know. Changing the subject from boring old politics, are you going to the Butlers' dance?'

'I might,' Frank said. 'If you're going. We've been asked to stay, Claudia says.'

'They'll have that fat lump Olivia lined up for you,' Claire said mischievously. She was in good spirits again, back on safe ground with him.

'She's a very pretty girl,' he retorted. 'You're jealous.'

'Jealous of her big fat bottom? Thunder Thighs, that's her nickname. The dance might be fun.'

He smiled at her. 'Do you really want to go?'

She nodded. 'Do you?'

'We'll see,' he said, teasing in his turn. 'We'll talk about it tonight. Look, there's poor old Donny, waiting to see the Dublin train come by.'

'Let's stop,' Claire suggested. 'I haven't seen him for ages.'

Donny and his obsession with trains was a part of their childhood. When they rode down to Sallins on their bicycles, they'd see him standing on the bridge over the railway line, gazing intently up the track for the train to come. Frank pulled into the side and they got out. He saw them and grinned, winking furiously with one eye in his excitement. No one knew his age for sure, but he was one of eleven children, and simple-minded from birth. Harmless as a baby, as everyone knew, with this passion for the trains that kept him rooted to the bridge in hopes of seeing one. As children they gave him some of their sweets when they bought them from the village shop; later Frank would slip him a bit of money and he'd thank them both with his frantic winking and gaping smile.

'Hallo there, Donny,' Frank said. 'How are you?'

He gabbled happily that he was well, and then said, surprising them both, 'Ye've been gone long away!'

'I've been in America, Donny,' Frank answered.

'Oh, ach,' Donny nodded, and mumbled. 'Ye've been gone long away,' he said to Claire.

'Yes, but we're home now,' she comforted. 'How's your mammy?'

He smiled and nodded, 'Well, well. She'll be comin' soon. She'll box me ear,' and he chuckled at the thought. 'No train yet. So one's coming' . . .' He turned back to gaze over the parapet down the line.

Mammy was a stout and stalwart woman in her sixties, and the sight of her leading her son home for his tea, often by the scruff of his collar, was a local joke.

117

Frank found some change in his pocket. 'Here, Donny, get yourself some cigarettes.'

He was very dirty and the hand that closed over the money was black as a crow's claw. A little spittle ran down his chin, but his eyes were bright with pleasure.

'God bless ye . . . God bless ye . . .' He watched them get into the car and waved to them as they drove past him. Through the rear window Claire saw him turn back to his vigil.

'Fancy him noticing we'd been away,' she said.

'He's not that stupid,' her brother answered. 'Given a little help and special schooling, he mightn't have been as bad as he is. But it's too late now. So long as he has his train now and then, he'll be happy enough.'

'That's the wonderful thing about Ireland,' she said. 'Nobody bothers him. He'd be taken into some mental hospital if this was England.'

'Or America,' Frank pointed out. 'But the Irish aren't frightened or ashamed of handicapped people. To them they're as much children of God as everyone else and they leave them alone.'

'And so they should,' she agreed. 'I bet the mammy goes through his pockets when he gets home and takes that money!'

'I bet she does,' Frank said, and they both laughed.

'A child of God'. Claire thought she'd never heard Frank talk in that way before. Surely he wasn't becoming religious . . . ? She'd have to tease him to find out.

Philip was out, Claudia busy in the house and Claire disappeared upstairs. Frank went into the study and poured himself a drink.

He was abstemious by normal standards; getting drunk didn't appeal to him. He was glad to be alone, to have time to himself to think. The whiskey was enough to soothe without fuddling. He shouldn't have spoken out to Claire. It had worried her and there was no way she would understand. She wouldn't understand how America had affected him. It was a curious liberation, a

118

chance to expand beyond the confines of his class, education and background. A challenge because only achievement counted and he had set out to achieve, from the time he went to an English school with his father's dictate echoing through his mind: 'You're not going to grow up an Irish yob . . .' Nobody could deny what he had done, but they wouldn't understand why he had done it. Not for himself, not for his father, but for the faded image in the photograph. For the whole half of him that was forever denied as if it carried shame. The bog-Irish blood that he was expected to live down. He had decided to live up to it instead. America gave him the example. Men of Irish ancestry were politicians, businessmen, academics, let alone a President who had become a legend throughout the world. He could explore his ancestry with a freedom impossible in his own country. Ireland was an American cult, its history enshrined in the folklore of the descendants of the early immigrants. Frank Arbuthnot learned of the leaking ships with starving refugees from the famine, setting sail for a new life across the Atlantic; of the convicts transported to Australia; of the early heroes of Irish resistance to English rule; of the persecution of the native Church and the evictions of families crippled by rents they couldn't hope to pay. And, inevitably, of the long and bitter political oppression of the minority in the North.

He was too intelligent and too educated to accept such an unbalanced popular view, but for the first time he was in a position to listen and to make his own judgement. The past was a lamentable record, nothing could excuse that. What was needed was a change in attitude, an expiation, if necessary, for the sins of all their forebears. The first goal must be to redress the wrongs of the Irish in the North. That was as far as Frank had been prepared to go when he came home.

He had finished his whiskey. Soon his father would come back from the meeting in Dublin; they'd gather for a drink before dinner and talk about their doings in the day. He wasn't going to relinquish the house in Meath, however hard his family pressed him. It was a restitution to his dead mother; Lorimer had told him as much. He wouldn't be keeping him on as his solicitor. There would be a new attitude and a new regime. A second home where he could feel at liberty and where, for the first time in its history, Irishmen would come on equal terms. 'Don't talk like this to Dad . . .' He smiled, thinking of his sister, so worried that there might be conflict between the people she loved. There was no doubt in Claire, no instinct for self-torture. Generous-hearted, open-natured, she combined all that was best in Claudia and in Philip. She was the one person in the world who made him happy just by walking through the door. For her sake, he would keep the peace at Riverstown, and maybe she would spend time with him in Meath.

At dinner he said, 'If you want to go to the dance at Butlers Castle, I'm game.'

Claudia said, 'Sylvia told me they've got English guests for the weekend. We won't be going, but you should enjoy yourselves.'

Claire said, smiling at Frank, 'It'll be great gas,' and he smiled back at her.

'It always is when we're together. I can't wait to see Thunder Thighs.'

Neither Claudia nor Philip knew what they were both laughing about.

The following week they set off in Frank's car for the trip down to Cork and the dance at Butlers Castle. And that was how Claire met Neil Fraser.

Billy Gorman cut himself a doorstep off the loaf and laid a slice of ham on top. He muttered to himself as he made a pot of tea and searched for mustard to spread on the ham. He wasn't really hungry, but habit made him get the food. Never miss a chance to eat, his old mother used to say. Who knows when the next meal's coming . . . He

120

sat at the kitchen table, poured his tea and ladled the sugar into it. He felt miserable. He was frightened for Claire and frightened for himself. He cursed Frank Arbuthnot. Why had he to be different and bring so much sorrow on his family and danger to them all . . . Bad luck to him, Billy mumbled, wishing him dead for all the trouble he'd caused. How long would she be? Back before dark, she'd said as she left. He took a bite of bread and ham and felt it would choke him. And wouldn't that auld bitch Mrs Arbuthnot choose this very time to go off to her friends in Cork, and leave him to cope on his own? He had never liked her, he grumbled. Old Doyle had told him how she came to Riverstown and took over after the poor little Ryan girl died.

He didn't hear the door open. He felt them in the room behind him, and he put his cup down and very slowly turned. There was young Joe Burns in his Garda uniform and another man with him that Billy didn't know. He pushed back his chair; he was clumsy and the leg stuck in the join of the boards. The table jerked and his tea slopped over.

Joe Burns said, 'Havin' yer dinner, Billy?'

Billy was on his feet, holding on to the chair back.

'I am so,' he said, and his voice sounded thick, with the food still in his mouth. His eyes darted like ferrets from Joe Burns to the stranger. He hadn't heard them knock and his dogs hadn't given a warning.

Joe Burns came closer. 'We knew ye weren't out, Billy,' he said, 'because yer car's in the garage. What have ye done with the number plates?'

Billy gave a moan of fear. Joe Burns spoke gently. The other one had his back to the door.

'We found the other plates,' he said. 'The English ones. She's been here, Billy, and ye never let me know like ye promised.'

Billy started to say, 'I was going to,' and then stopped.

Joe Burns turned to his companion. 'He's a bad heart,' he said.

'Let's see how bad it is,' the man replied.

The gates to Riverstown were locked. Major Harvey stopped the car and got out to make certain. They were padlocked. He lit a cigarette, cupping his hands over the match. He was able to glance from right to left and saw no sign of a car or anyone on foot. Locked from the inside. He knew the Irish custom well. When the family was away the main drive was always barred, the back drive was open. He got back into the car, threw the cigarette out of the window and set off down the twisty road running behind the wall to the rear of the property. Claire Fraser talked a lot about the old gardener, Gorman. She was very fond of him; at times she spoke as if he were some kind of grandfather by adoption. Michael knew how deep such a relationship could run. There'd been no Gorman in his own childhood but a maid at home who'd loved him and spoiled him as if he were her own. It was not unlikely that Claire Fraser, finding that padlocked gate, would have gone to Billy for help. He drove past the rear entrance and the little cottage, a plume of turf smoke curling out of the chimney, and parked in a bend of the road. He got out, and hesitated. He unlocked the boot of the car and slipped the automatic into his anorak, just in case. Then he walked back along the roadside, hands in his pockets, looking as much a part of his surroundings as the trees rooted alongside.

He turned into the little driveway. A garage with both doors shut. Kennels, but no dogs barking at his approach. The cottage front door closed. Gorman could be out. Gone to the pub in Clane for his dinner. Michael Harvey walked up to the kennels. A big sandy lurcher lay dead behind the wire run, the top of its head shot off. A smaller dog lay close by. He stood completely still for a few seconds. There was silence all around him. He recognized it. A very special silence, that was stronger than birds, or the breeze ruffling through the trees overhead. He leapt for the cottage door, his gun exposed in his right hand, and kicked once, sending it slamming open.

He stood in the kitchen. 'Oh, shit!'

The old man had been shot through the head at close range. They had used a silencer on him, as with the dogs, because there were no burn marks. And he'd been badly beaten first. There was blood and a little vomit; the smell of death and pain. Harvey didn't touch him. He backed out, pulling the door shut behind him. The garage. He opened it and saw what had doomed the poor old devil. The car, the English number plates lying on the ground. Claire Fraser had gone to Billy Gorman for help and he'd helped all right. How much had they beaten out of him, Michael Harvey wondered, before they murdered him? He didn't waste any time. If Gorman knew and had given it away, the men who killed him would be on the road to Kells by now. Gorman had been dead for long enough to let the blood on the floor form a thin scum. Harvey broke into a run.

He tried to plan ahead as he drove. His brief was to get Claire Fraser out, but to avoid violence or any overt breach of Irish law – unless there was no other way of rescuing her. He drove fast, bouncing over two little hump-backed bridges on to the dual carriageway to Dublin, cutting through the lazy line of little cars that ambled along with all the time in the world. He jumped several red lights, assured that no police cars were in sight, his horn blasting a warning to anything coming the other way. He knew the route up through Navar and he knew the place; if he found a car hidden anywhere near, he'd abandon caution and go in with the automatic rifle. Just because they'd shot Gorman, it didn't prove he hadn't told them about Claire. The IRA didn't leave witnesses. The one chance was that he didn't know where she was going, and they murdered him in frustration. The only chance, considering the time lapse. But they had the changed number plates to go on and a bush telegraph that worked at extraordinary levels throughout the country. They would know soon enough, if that car was anywhere near a town.

★

The private housing estate at Santry was on the airport road. It was built when land values were rising and the banks eager to lend money. Twenty-five houses, with a square of garden back and front and a garage, architect designed it was claimed, although the fittings were cheap and much of the external woodwork had warped. Joe Burns and his companion were sitting with two men and a girl at a table in the back room of the fifth house on the right of the first quadrangle. A line of washing waved in the back garden; a child's bicycle was parked outside the front door.

The man who had gone to Billy's cottage with Joe Burns was talking. 'He was havin' a fuckin' heart attack,' he said. He had a thick Dublin accent.

The younger of the two men sitting at the table looked at him. He had brown hair and a neatly trimmed beard. He looked like an artist. Joe Burns was more frightened by him than anyone he'd ever come across.

'Then why did you hit him so hard?'

'Ah, we didn't.' It was shrugged off. 'I smacked him a couple of times; Joe gave him a bump or two. Just enough to knock a bit a shit outa him. Isn't that right, Joe?'

'It is,' Joe confirmed. He looked at the three of them uneasily. He'd only seen the girl three times. He didn't like the look of her at all. 'He said he didn't know where she'd gone,' he insisted. 'We did get rough, but not so's to kill the auld bastard. I know my job, Sean. I knew he had a heart. I told ye so, before we went.'

'I'd swear he didn't know,' the other man broke in. 'Lookit, we hurt him bad enough to get it out of him an' he did!'

'So you shot him,' the girl said. It was the first time she had spoken.

'We had to,' Joe explained. 'Sure he was taken bad, but there wasn't time to hang about till he died. We had to make sure. There's no trace of ourselves there. He won't be found till his woman comes back this evenin'.'

'You made a mess of it, you pair of bloody fools!' She

124

spat at them. 'Gorman changed the number plates for her. Of course he knew where she was going. You beat him up and got nothing out of him!'

The young bearded man touched her arm. 'Quiet yourself, Marie. We know the number of the car she's driving. We'll find her. Joe, you get back to the station. Wait at home, Willie. You may be needed later.'

When they had gone the older man spoke up. He had a thick Ulster accent and he was wanted for murders and bombings across the border. His name was Hugh Macbride, but that was an alias.

'She's right,' he announced. 'They fucked it. My lads'd have done a proper job.'

'This is my operation,' the bearded man replied. 'When I need your lads, I'll let you know.'

The two comrades-in-arms didn't like each other. Macbride was a hard man from the North, a seasoned, ruthless fighter who'd spent five years in the Maze prison the only time he'd been caught. He thought his southern counterparts were soft and he despised them. He particularly disliked the young man sitting at the table with him, the respected psychiatrist Doctor Sean Filey. He distrusted all comfortable middle-class revolutionaries. Most of all he resented having a woman like Marie Dempster sitting cheek by jowl with men and giving her opinions. The women of Ulster knew their place. They played their roles with heroism and devotion, but they were never admitted to the higher councils of their men.

He said, 'I'd watch that Garda. He might just decide to save his own skin if things got bad.' He lit a cheap cigarette and inhaled deeply.

Sean Filey dismissed the idea. 'He's a good man; he's true. And he's in too deep now. There's no going back on a murder.'

Macbride only grunted. Plenty of men he knew had grassed to the security forces and the RUC just because they *had* murdered and wanted to get off. But you couldn't convince a man like Filey. He was an intellectual, an educated man. A paper man, Macbride called him. A great one for plans and working out the details. But not efficient enough and strong enough to make them work. Two days ago they'd had Frank Arbuthnot tethered like a goat in this very house, the bait to catch an English Cabinet Minister's wife in a trap sprung by the Provisional IRA. The coup of the decade. Neil Fraser's wife held for ransom. Thinking of the publicity, the prestige the organization would have milked from the situation, made him sick with fury at the way it had been bungled. Demands, negotiations, world-wide attention. And then the contemptuous murder, or even the silence that was more terrifying than a corpse.

Now they had lost the bait, and he had been sent down from the North to pull the operation together before it failed completely. To get Claire Fraser, even if her half-brother had escaped. But he wasn't given the command. Filey was still in charge. The Provisionals in the South were touchy men, sensitive to their brothers in the North. Macbride was only second in command. Filey must not be alienated. Not yet. He stubbed out the cigarette on the floor and ground the end into the linoleum.

'How's about a wee whiskey?' He addressed Marie, as he would have done any woman at home.

'You know where it's kept,' she said. 'Help yourself.'

He gave her a look of menace. It was not the time for confrontation. He had a report to make on her. When they considered it, the members of the Supreme Council would know what to do.

'I'm for a pee first,' he said.

When he had closed the door, Marie Dempster got up. 'He's a pig,' she said.

Filey glanced up at her. 'He's a good man,' he said. 'Not an English gentleman, but a good Irishman. He mayn't have the fancy manners you're used to, but he's fought and suffered for our cause since he was fifteen years old. Next time, Marie, you'll get him a drink if he asks you.'

She turned away from him. She was a dark-haired girl,

with blue eyes and the fine complexion of a consumptive-prone race. One side of her very pretty face was swollen and bruised. 'He suspects me,' she said. 'And you know he does.'

'I cleared you,' Sean Filey countered. 'I was the first one here and he accepted what I told him.'

She shrugged. 'He doesn't believe it. Or if he does, he doesn't care. Back home, he said, they'd shoot me.'

'This isn't the North,' Sean argued. 'You're safe enough, because *I* believe you. You wouldn't let Frank Arbuthnot escape. You want him dead and I know why. The same as you want us to capture his sister. You want them both dead, because your own jealousy is killing you.'

'Leave me alone.' It was a cry of anguish. 'Don't taunt me, God damn you.'

'I'm protecting you,' he answered. 'You chose him instead of me, but it doesn't matter. You've done great things for the cause, Marie. Your mistake was to love outside your own kind. We'll catch him, and we'll catch his sister. Then you'll be at peace. Now, why don't you occupy yourself by making the telephone calls? We'll have Mrs Fraser before the day's out.'

She pushed past Macbride as he came back into the kitchen. He got the whiskey bottle out of the cupboard, offered one to Sean and poured a half tumblerful for himself.

'That's a right bitch,' he remarked. 'Some man should take his belt to her.' He swallowed hugely. He despised Sean Filey because he only drank beer. He always made a point of trying to press whiskey on him. 'Where's she gone?'

'Down to the call box to make the contact calls,' Filey answered. 'If Fraser's wife is within fifty miles of here, we'll know in the next three hours.'

She made eight calls, giving the number of the car they were looking for. She stressed the urgency, repeated the telephone number of the house for all reports and hurried back there herself. She saw Sean Filey in the hall. He had a coat and hat on, and was drawing on gloves.

'I'm going to Fitzwilliam Square,' he told her. 'You can contact me immediately you hear any news.'

She looked round, 'Where's Macbride?' She didn't want to be in the house alone with him.

'Gone,' was the reply. 'He's left a number where you can reach him.' He paused for a moment. 'Do you have enough pain-killers?'

'Plenty,' she said.

'Don't take too many; they can make you sleepy.'

Her mouth twisted into a painful smile. 'Don't worry. I won't miss the telephone.'

She went into the kitchen and made herself tea. Thank God that brute Macbride was gone. Thank God she could sit by herself for a while. Her face was very painful and she had a savage complementary headache.

Frank Arbuthnot had hit her so hard she'd been knocked out. She couldn't get the scene out of her mind. The shuttered upstairs room where he was being kept handcuffed to the bed. The sight of him, watching her every time she brought food and pushed it to him, with hatred and contempt in his eyes. How easy for that cold-hearted devil Seal Filey to dissect her feelings as if she were a specimen pinned to a board, her very heart exposed. What could he possibly know of the agony of loving Frank Arbuthnot? How it could finally turn to such hatred that she had planned to trap him to his death? He spoke of jealousy, with clinical detachment. It's killing you, he said. When they're both dead you'll be at peace. He could analyse, but he could never imagine the suffering and rejection. Or the humiliation of her desire that drove her to Arbuthnot's bed, when she knew he didn't care whether she came or not. Years of living with him in the big house in Meath, with the photographs of his sister Claire mocking her even in the bedroom they shared. Filey would never understand, and he was lucky.

'Marie, help me.' His voice echoed in her throbbing

head. 'Help me, Marie, please.' There was no hatred in his eyes that morning, only agony and pleading. And that was why she'd gone too close, the gun in her hand lowered instead of pointing at him. When he grabbed at her she fired. That was the last thing she remembered before the blow from his free hand sent her reeling and crashing unconscious to the ground. And luckily for her, Sean Filey came by with the gunman, Willie, and found her in the upstairs room. Arbuthnot had escaped and stolen her car from outside. But there was blood on the floor. He had taken the gun with him.

For a time Marie had been in mortal danger. She was questioned, and not just by Sean, but by men from Dublin and from Cork that she had never seen before. She was slightly concussed and vague about the sequence of events. But Sean Filey was her salvation. She had been tried and acquitted without realizing it. Only the Northerner, Macbride, coming hot-heeled from Belfast, asked the questions all over again, and said the same as her inquisitors from the Council in the Republic. Why had a woman been left in charge of Arbuthnot, armed or not? It was a man's job, as the outcome proved.

Filey's answer was truthful; he never lied, she knew that. He wouldn't have lied to save her either. She'd been left alone for two hours that morning because the man who'd guarded the night before had gone home, expecting Willie to arrive. But Willie's car broke down and in the end Filey himself had to drive over to collect him and bring him to the house. Nobody could be blamed, as one with a sense of humour said, unless it was Willie's car. Nobody else smiled.

At every moment they expected a news flash that Arbuthnot had been found or had sought refuge with the police. But the radio was silent and the TV had no news. Hopes began to rise that the bastard was wounded and lying in some lane in Marie's car, with the life seeping out of him, unable to seek help. So the search was set up. Men scoured the roads, the lookout phones were rung, the description of man and car circulated.

But nothing was found. Nothing was reported seen. Arbuthnot had vanished and his sister, Claire Fraser, had left her home in England and was on her way over.

'We'll never get her,' Marie breathed to herself. 'If she's got this far without us finding her, it'll be too late . . . And I'll never have peace in my soul again, because in my heart I'm not sure that it wasn't love for him that made me go too close that morning . . .'

The phone began to shrill and she jumped up, seizing the receiver. She just said hello, and gave the number. The caller spoke a few sentences and then rang off. The car had been seen parked under some trees on the Cloncarrig estate. The time was less than half an hour ago and it was still there. Marie stood up. She was trembling with excitement. She dialled Filey's number; she was put through on a private line. He interrupted his patient very courteously while he took the message.

'He must be hiding in the old Reynard place.' Marie's words tumbled out. 'We'll get them both, Sean. Both of them!'

'I'll make the arrangements,' his voice said in its gentle professional way. 'Don't worry, I'll let the hospital know.'

He turned to his patient and with firmness closed the session.

'A very sick patient of mine,' he explained. 'I hope you'll forgive me. I must go round at once. My secretary will make another appointment for you. She'll give you extra time.' He shook hands with the man, a business executive suffering from depression and alcohol addiction. 'Take care now. And try not to worry. You're going along just fine.'

As soon as the door closed he swept aside the open dossier with his notes and grabbed the telephone. He was on his way back to the housing estate as messages went out to Willie and the two experts who'd been brought specially for the purpose.

The hunt was on.

★

The sun was high in a sky as clear as a looking glass. It beat down on the green fields of Cloncarrig. From where Claire stopped she could see that old Reynard's house was roofless; the windows had fallen out and a green grave-cloth of weeds was creeping up the outside walls. Suddenly tears came into her eyes.

'If I was Flanagan,' Frank had said all those years ago, 'I'd dynamite the bloody place and everything it stands for.' She didn't know what it meant to Flanagan, who owned his chain of butcher's shops in Dublin and had bought up other houses and more land. She knew what it had meant to the Arbuthnots. Friendship and hospitality, the pleasure of good sport and the jolly eccentric with his foxy name and bright red hair, building for his afterlife.

Neil hadn't seen the point at all, when he heard the story. To him, Reynard was an old madman and the friends who swapped hunting stories about the fox that always vanished on the run at Cloncarrig were drunk or stupid. It was all so Irish, he complained irritably. Everyone lived in a fantasy world. No wonder the country was in such a mess. Although she was madly in love with him, Claire hated him when he talked like that and yet he couldn't see how much she minded. Later, when they were always quarrelling, it seemed as if he taunted her deliberately. It was strange that he should come into her mind so vividly as she looked down on the ruined relic of her youth. Two fields away was the first folly built by old Reynard. Neil walked the three miles with her, nudging her with memories she didn't want, a ghost who wouldn't go away. As if he's still fighting Frank for me, she thought, pushing his way into my mind. It was superstitious and silly, but as she climbed through the overgrown hedges, ripping herself free of thorn and bramble, she remembered the dance at Butlers Castle.

Butlers Castle was a hotel now, the family scattered. Tourists slept in the bedrooms where she and Frank had stayed that weekend and the ballroom where they'd danced was now a restaurant. She'd seen travel brochures advertising it and made a vow never to go near the place. Sir Richard Butler was long dead, his daughters married; the only son lived with his mother in a small place in Galway, where he was involved in fishing. Butlers Castle had been sold after his father died. The Butlers were delightful people, but the most inefficient managers of money. A fine estate had gradually slipped into debt and out of their hands.

The castle had been in its last flush of splendour when she went down with Frank for the dance celebrating the famous Olivia's twenty-first birthday. It was cold, of course, and damp in places and there was tepid water for the baths, but nobody minded. The castle was a Victorian monstrosity, built by a Butler who had married money, but it was always full of people. There were four daughters and one son, Charles. If the roof leaked they put buckets to catch the drops and gave a big party for Olivia instead of mending it. Claire had been placed next to one of the English guests at dinner. She knew she looked very pretty; Frank had said the dress suited her, and a number of men came up to talk to her when they were gathered in the hall before dinner. She felt in a happy mood, confident of enjoying herself. As she predicted, Frank was assigned to Olivia. He was a rich young bachelor and the beady eyes of more than Lady Butler followed him that evening.

Claire thought it very funny. She planned to tease him for days afterwards. Her companion was very nice-looking, charming manners, rather stiff, but attractive. She was naturally talkative and vivacious; the Englishman laughed a lot at what she said and never took his eyes off her or spoke a word to the girl on his other side.

'You're staying, aren't you?' she asked.

'Yes, Charles asked me over for a week. We're going fishing.'

'Well, you won't catch anything,' Claire said. 'He

never stops talking. The fish swim a mile at the sight of him. How do you know each other?'

Charles Butler was in his thirties, dabbling in estate management at home and making trips to London on what was said to be a business he'd invested money in. It never seemed to make any, but he had a lot of friends and Neil Fraser was one of them.

'We met with mutual friends. He's great fun; treats everything as a joke.'

'And you don't?' she countered.

'You can't afford to if you're a politician,' he answered.

Claire stared at him. 'Are you an MP?'

'Yes, I've been in the House for five years.'

'Aren't you a bit young?'

He smiled. He had beautiful white teeth, she noticed.

'Yes, I suppose I am. But I always wanted to make a career in politics and I started as soon as I came down from Oxford. I didn't get in overnight, either. I fought two hopeless seats before I was given a by-election with a chance.'

'And you won,' she said admiringly.

'I won,' he agreed. He thought she was one of the most beautiful girls he'd ever seen. And completely unselfconscious. Big, bright blue eyes and a mouth that made him itch to kiss it open.

'Do you always win?' Claire asked.

'If I want something badly enough,' he said.

As soon as the music started, he came up and took her off to dance. The music was old-fashioned, but quite well played by the local dance band. Neil Fraser was a good dancer; he began to hold her closer and closer until she was pressed tightly against him and his cheek was hot against her hair. Claire liked being kissed and enjoyed the limited sexual adventures experienced with young men in Switzerland and in London. None had been serious and she had never been tempted to go to bed with anyone. It was nice to be admired, but she had never been really aroused.

When the music stopped he held her arm and guided her to the bar. She noticed that he fended off any other man who came up to them. He stood over her, rather than beside her, and he touched her continually, as if she belonged to him. Claire found it odd and exciting. She was becoming excited by him and when they danced again, she fitted in with him very quickly of her own accord.

She saw Frank over his shoulder; he had a fair girl in his arms, and they were talking as they danced. Neil Fraser didn't say a word. He moved with her and held her and she felt a throb of satisfaction that was a new experience.

When they stopped he said, 'I want to kiss you. Where can we go?'

'I don't know,' she said.

'We'll find somewhere,' he declared. Holding her by the hand, he eased through the groups of people and out into the empty hall. 'Where's your room?' he asked.

'I'm not going upstairs with you,' Claire said. 'Let's go back.'

'I'm going to kiss you first,' Neil Fraser said, and she didn't resist. It seemed to last for a long time, and the pleasure of it made her dizzy. She felt a fool for a moment, with her eyes shut and her mouth searching for his, when he paused. When he kissed her again he slipped his hand down the neck of her dress and stroked her breast. If he'd suggested going upstairs then, Claire would have gone. But he didn't.

He stopped making love to her and said, 'We'd better go back, I need to cool off. And I think' – he touched her once more – 'you do too.'

'Do I look all right?' she asked.

'You look marvellous,' was the answer. 'It suits you. I'm going to see you again, aren't I?'

'If you want to,' Claire said.

'I want to very much. Do you ever come to London?'

'I'm going over in September. I'm taking a cooking course.'

He smiled at her. 'And flower arranging?'

'Yes, how did you know?'

'I guessed,' he said gently.

They went back into the ballroom. The band was on its second round of the same repertoire, and fewer couples were on the floor.

'Tell me,' Neil asked her, 'who was that very dark chap who kept staring at us when we were dancing? An old boyfriend? He's over there.'

Claire glanced across and laughed. 'Don't be silly. That's my brother, Frank.'

'Oh,' was all Neil Fraser said.

It was odd that Frank never mentioned him the next day. The Butlers were Catholics and went to Mass; their guests came down to a big breakfast and amused themselves until lunchtime. There was no sign of Neil Fraser; Claire was disappointed when she learned he'd gone off to the West early with Charles Butler. She was in a happy mood, as if something especially nice was going to happen, and she wanted to talk to Frank about it. She wanted to ask him what he thought of Neil, but there wasn't an opportunity till they were driving back to Riverstown after lunch.

'I only spoke two words to him,' he said. 'When you were upstairs powdering your nose. He took quite a fancy to you, I thought.'

Claire giggled. 'I took one to him as well,' she admitted. 'He's an MP, can you believe it?'

'Sylvia Butler said he was one of the rising stars in the Tory party,' Frank remarked. 'I think she had her eye on him for Olivia.' He smiled ruefully at the idea. 'I can't see an Irish girl fitting into that set-up, can you?'

'Oh, I don't see why not,' Claire protested.

'People like him live in a strait-jacket compared to us,' he said. 'They have buttoned-down souls.'

She frowned. 'If you only spoke two words to him, you certainly formed an opinion.'

'I know the type,' he said. 'And I don't like it.'

After that the subject dropped. Claire soon forgot both

Neil Fraser and her brother's judgement of him. The weeks went by, and soon she was getting ready to go to London for the three-month course which was supposed to equip her for earning a ladylike living till she got married. All was harmony, as if that summer was a gift from God, and only Claudia felt uneasy watching her daughter and her stepson becoming more inseparable as adults than they had been even as children. But she said nothing, even when Claire refused invitations in favour of some plan she and Frank had made together. She kept her own counsel, because she was a wise woman who believed that things worked out for the best if left alone. And Claire was soon going to London. There was no warning of disaster. Philip was content with his son, Frank was busy with his estate in Meath and enthusiastic about plans for a merchant bank in Dublin.

The weather was fine, the cattle and horses sleek with the rich grass, and Claire was within a week of going. It was Friday and the morning opened with a rainstorm. Claudia looked at the weather and decided she might be lazy for once and have breakfast in bed. Philip kissed her goodbye and went off for the day.

Claire put her head round the door and said, 'Mum, we're going on an expedition. We won't be in to lunch.'

'You and Frank?' Claudia asked, although she knew. 'What sort of expedition?'

Claire came close to her. 'We've a bet on,' she declared. 'I've bet him a fiver we'll get into old Reynard's hide. He says it's all nonsense. We're going over to walk round the follies and see. I've made a side bet of twenty pounds that we find a fox's been in one of them.'

'You're mad,' her mother said. 'It's absolutely pouring with rain.'

Claire looked at her. 'You're not ill are you, Mum? Dad just said you were having a lazy morning.'

'Don't be silly, of course I'm not ill. I'm never ill.' Which was true. 'I just felt it was such a filthy day I'd have breakfast in bed for a change. Tell Sheena you're out for lunch, will you, darling? And tell her to tell

136

Molly to lay for two, not four. You know what an idiot she is – if you don't tell her *everything* . . . and don't catch cold, for God's sake. You've got to travel next week.'

The door closed and Claire had gone. Claudia settled back with the newspaper. There was no post; a new man was delivering, and it was running late till he got used to the district. The old postman was retired at last. He had cycled his district for twenty years, a stick strapped to his saddle to beat off the dogs. He reminded Claudia of a redheaded leprechaun, a grin like a slice of Dutch cheese splitting his face whenever he appeared with the letters. He enjoyed a parcel as much as if it was sent to himself.

She glanced briefly out of the window; the sky was black with malevolent clouds and the rain struck spitefully at the glass. It was a prophetic morning.

The last ditch was crossed and the grey stone folly beckoned them. It was tall and narrow, like a finger pointing upwards. There were no windows, only slits; no doors, but a niche set high up in one wall. Too high for any hound to leap, but within the scope of a running fox. They were both soaking wet, but the rain had stopped and the hot Irish sun was drying out the land. Claire was out of breath. They had run over the last field.

'Therc!' she gasped in triumph. 'Now you owe me a fiver!'

He laughed, his hair plastered down with the rain, shaking himself free of the wet. 'Not till I've got up there and seen for myself!'

The first three follies had been blank towers, with slits that were a painted illusion to deceive the eye at a distance. But this was real, and so was the little entrance to it.

'Five pounds,' Claire shouted at him, as he began a hand-and-toe climb up the outer wall. 'Twenty if there's been a fox in there!' She watched him climb and haul himself up to the edge of the niche.

He called down, 'My God, it's big enough to get inside.'

'I'll come up too,' she said, and began to search for projections in the wall. It was rough built. The other towers had been smooth.

Above her Frank wriggled his way in. Then he leant out and reached down to help her. 'It's a room in here,' he said. 'And I owe you twenty quid.'

Claire stared at him. 'You mean there's been a fox?'

'More than one, by the smell of it. Here, I'll pull you through.'

The stench was so strong that Claire gasped. Then standing in the fusty darkness, they both heard a low, faint growl.

'Jesus,' he exclaimed. 'There's something in here. Stay quiet, Clarry. I'll light my lighter.'

By the little gas flame they found it crouched in a corner, red eyes glowing from the darkness.

'Oh, poor thing,' Claire said, and turned away.

'It's been poisoned,' Frank said. 'Bastards. They're getting twenty-five pounds for the pelts these days. They put poison down the lair and wait for the poor creature to come out to die, then they shoot it. I'd shoot them if I could catch them at it!' He came closer, holding the tiny flame above his head. The fox lay dying; its flanks heaved in spasms and the eyes followed the man with the light who stood above it.

'Oh, Frank,' she whispered. 'I wish we hadn't come.'

'I'm glad we did,' he said. 'You go down and go back to the car. I'll follow in a minute. Go on.'

'What are you going to do?' she asked.

'Stop it suffering,' he said. 'It must have hidden here from the hunt. It got itself here to die. Go on down, please.'

She levered herself over the edge of the niche; Frank held her hand till she found toe-holds, and then she dropped the last few feet. He turned back into the gloom.

He lit the lighter once more and found a stone. The red eyes watched him. 'Poor old Charlie,' he said gently. 'Be a good lad now, and don't try to bite . . .'

He caught Claire up.

'Did you do it?' she said.

'Yes. I think he knew I was helping him. Maybe it was old Reynard. Come on, don't cry. You've won twenty-five pounds, remember?'

'As if I'd take it,' she said. 'Let's go and find a pub and have a drink. I feel sick.'

'It did stink in there,' he said. He put his arm round her. 'Lucky for the fox we came. Think of it like that.'

He took her to the hotel in Kells; the lounges didn't sell food and Frank wanted her to eat something. She had been very upset by the incident with the fox. He was shaken himself, but he didn't want to show it. They sat for a long time in the bar with its garish red walls and laminated fake pine, drinking whiskey. Claire said she wasn't hungry and Frank didn't argue.

'It was almost human,' she said, 'the way it looked up at us. Perhaps we were meant to go today and find him. God, and I've heard people say hunting's cruel!'

'Money makes people cruel,' Frank said. 'Twenty-five pounds is a fortune to some of them. Fox is all the fashion now.'

She leaned over and touched his hand for a moment. 'It must have been horrible for you,' she said.

'Father's always said you should carry a gun when you're out in the country – you never know what you may find that's hurt or trapped. Remember how upset he was about Belle? She'd been missing all day and he found her in a ditch over by Sallins, trying to crawl home. He shot her and carried her back. Mum said he was almost crying.'

Frank remembered the day he'd come home from the States and asked about the dog. She'd been poisoned, his father said, strychnine . . . One of those bastard farmers. He'd felt the same emotion when he found the dying fox, its innards eaten away by a slow poison. Yet twenty-five pounds was more than some families had to live on. It wasn't money that made people cruel, he thought, it was poverty.

His father would never understand or accept that.

Claire said suddenly, 'I don't think we should tell anyone about the hide. If the hunt knows a fox can actually get up there, they'll close it up.'

'I'm surprised they haven't done so before,' Frank said. 'Maybe it's superstition. They don't want to upset old Reynard. We won't say anything, not even at home.'

'It's our secret,' Claire said. 'What a place to hide! No one would ever find you there.'

'No,' he agreed. 'They wouldn't. How about a sandwich?'

'All right,' she said, to please him. The girl in the bar thought what a lovely couple they made.

It was quite late when they got back to Riverstown. Claudia and Phillip were having tea. The rain had started again and seemed set for the night. It was a time to be indoors and snug; they'd lit a fire, although it was early September.

'Hallo,' Philip greeted them. 'Find any foxes? Mummy told me you'd gone off on your wild goose chase.'

'More like a wild fox chase,' Frank answered. 'All we did was tramp for miles and get soaked. So we dried ourselves off at the Headford Hotel and had some lunch.'

Claudia looked up. 'There are some letters in the hall. Some for you, Claire darling, and something from America for you, Frank.'

'I'll get them,' he said.

They were drinking tea and Claire was reading a note from the cookery school without much enthusiasm. Something made her look up. Philip was gazing peacefully at the fire, Claudia was busy with the teapot, and her brother had the letter from America open in his hand.

He said, 'This is from my uncle.'

140

Philip put his cup down. He was frowning. 'Uncle? What uncle? What are you talking about?'

A little red crept into Frank's face. 'My Ryan uncle,' he answered. 'My mother's brother.'

There was a silence broken by his father, who said dismissively, 'Really. She did have brothers, but I can't see why any one of them would write to you.'

Claudia stopped pouring tea. Frank spoke quietly, but the tension was palpitating round them.

'He says he's bought the Half House.'

Claudia looked at her husband and slightly shook her head. There was a hard set to Philip's mouth and a cold expression in his eyes as he held his son's gaze.

'So I heard.'

'Why didn't anyone mention it?' Frank asked.

Claudia put on her cheerful smile and said, 'I don't think we connected it with your mother's family, Frank. Ryan is a very common name.'

'Claudia,' he said quietly, 'if one of the Ryans from Ballymore bought your old home, the whole of Kildare would be talking about it. I must be the only one who didn't know. Why didn't you tell me?' He spoke to his father, turning away from her.

'Now just a moment.' Philip left his chair and stood up. He was taller than Frank. 'You've no right to speak to Claudia like that, do you understand? It cropped up while you were in America, and besides, we weren't exactly pleased. And I don't know why a man who's never seen you in his life should suddenly write to you out of the blue. Unless it's to embarrass us. The best thing you can do is throw the damned thing on the fire!' He sat down as if that closed the subject.

Frank said, 'Apparently he has seen me. He came here when I was a baby. You were in England in the Army. You don't even know what's in the letter; how can you tell me to ignore it? Why don't you read it at least?'

'Philip,' Claudia broke in, 'I told you we should have talked to Frank about this.'

He said coldly, 'Please don't interfere. I've no inten-

141

tion of reading it. If he sneaked into my house behind my back, that's typical. It's a pity he didn't see fit to come and visit your mother after she was married, instead of turning against her like the rest of them.'

'He's explained that,' Frank said. 'He's coming over in November and he's asked me to meet him.'

'No doubt he thinks he'll make capital out of the relationship,' Philip snapped. 'But it won't help him. Nobody decent round here will have Kevin Ryan in the house. Let me tell you something about him . . .'

It's happening all over again, Claire thought in horror, the same scene as when he begged to go to school in Ireland. He was only a boy then, but he's a man now. He won't back down this time.

Her father was saying, 'While you lived in your ivory tower at Harvard, we were getting the backlash of Kevin Ryan and his kind right here in Ireland. Yes, he's Eileen's brother, the one who emigrated to America. He's a gutter politician who's made his career out of raising money for Noraid to pay for the bombings and shootings in the North. He's an IRA front man, backing the murderers who kill innocent people in the name of Irish liberty. You ask why we didn't tell you he'd bought the Half House. Well, I'll tell you why. We were sickened at the thought of people like that living within a hundred miles of us!'

'Philip,' Claudia protested, but it was too late.

Frank looked at his father. He said slowly, 'That's not the reason. You're ashamed because he's a bog Irishman and your ex-brother-in-law. You've always been ashamed of me because I'm half a Ryan. You don't give a damn about what happens in the North – I've heard you say so. Just don't let it creep down here. That's the real attitude. I *have* heard of Senator Ryan, but I didn't know he was my uncle. And I'm going to see him when he comes over in November. I'll judge him for myself.'

They were both standing, facing each other; they were amazingly alike in their anger.

'Frank, I'm warning you,' his father said. 'If you take

up with people like that, you're not welcome in this house!'

'They're my mother's people,' Frank answered. 'As much my family as you are. And you're not going to forbid me to meet anyone. I have my own house, if I'm not wanted here.'

'Then bloody well get out and go to it!' Philip shouted. Twenty-five years of pent-up antagonism exploded in him at that moment. He shouted at his son and showed the hatred that he'd hidden even from himself. The child that was the image of himself, but with the disquieting look and alien ways of a subject race. A despised race, who could never be trusted. A changeling . . .

'Get out,' he repeated, and it was more deadly because it was said in a flat, cold voice.

Claire got up; she was trembling. 'Dad, if you turn Frank out of this house then I'm going with him!'

'Oh, Christ!' Suddenly, shockingly, Claudia exploded. 'What a bloody scene you've made, over nothing! I'm sick to death of the whole bloody lot of you! You'd drive any sane person mad.' And then she rounded on her daughter. 'And as for you, you're going to England next week and that's that. It's time you grew up and stopped holding his hand anyway.' And having said that, she flared at her step-son. 'Your mother died when you were born; you never even saw her. *I've* been the only mother you've ever known! I've brought you up, Frank, and I've never had a thank you from anyone. This is my home too, and it's not going to be disrupted like this. Now I'm going upstairs and you can all go to hell!' As she banged out of the room she burst into tears.

It was as if the roof had caved in. Claudia never lost her temper. She was the level-headed influence, ready to see the funny side or defuse a clash of temperaments. Suddenly she had shocked them. Claire had never seen her mother cry before.

Philip looked at his son. 'I won't have her upset,' he said. 'If you want to hobnob with the likes of Ryan, leave Riverstown.'

'Frank, please,' Claire whispered.

He didn't glance at her. He put the envelope with the letter in it into his pocket. 'I'll go tomorrow morning,' he said.

Chapter 5

Suddenly in that late September, there was an Indian summer. London was hot and stifling when Claire arrived. It was a Thursday, time enough for her to settle into the flat she was sharing, before beginning her course on Monday. She couldn't remember being really unhappy before. After Frank left, the days at Riverstown had seemed the longest and most miserable of her life. There was a pall of gloom over the house; Claire was shocked to see that her father seemed unmoved. Two occasions peaked in her memory. The morning when Frank said goodbye to them both. There was a flat calm after the storm of the night before. He said he was sorry he and his father couldn't agree on certain issues, but he hoped they'd continue to be friends, and held out his hand to Philip. For one dreadful moment Claire thought her father was going to reject it, but he didn't; he said it was a pity, but this solution was the best. He was cold and distant, as if he were speeding a stranger on his way.

There were tears in Frank's eyes when he embraced her. For his sake she stayed composed. For a second or two she clung to him with all her strength, as if to tell him that she loved him and nothing would ever change her. He had said goodbye to Claudia.

'I'm glad you made your peace,' was all his father said.

Then he was gone, and the next day his clothes and personal belongings, representing his whole life for twenty-five years, were collected and taken to Meath.

The second saddest incident in that wretched time was finding Frank at the airport to see her off. Claudia had driven her in, and there he was, waiting outside the departure lounge, looking thinner and drawn about the face.

'Good God.' Her mother didn't look pleased to see him. 'This is a surprise . . .' And then, because she knew how to behave, 'How are you, Frank? Have you settled in? I meant to telephone.'

'I'm fine,' he said, turning away from her. There was no need to pretend any more. She might have brought him up, but he wasn't beholden to her now. 'I wanted to see Clarry off,' he said. 'I thought this might amuse you,' he said to Claire.

It was a paperback of a book long out of print. *Lady into Fox.*

She looked up at him and smiled. 'I'll read it on the flight. Take my mind off crashing. I'll write to you, Frank.'

'Have a good time,' he said. 'I've got to go now. Look after yourself.'

'I will,' she called after him.

He turned and waved and said, 'Goodbye, Claudia,' as if she were a vague acquaintance.

Then Claire's flight was called and she was kissing her mother and hurrying through. At the doors into the departure lounge she turned to look for him once more. Claudia saw her, waved, and then she had disappeared.

'Thank God, she's gone,' she said under her breath. 'It's not a moment too soon.' She drove home and poured herself a very large gin and tonic. She didn't trust herself to mention Frank's appearance to his father. 'Thank God,' she repeated, pouring another stiff drink, 'Thank God, she's out of it. And he's out of the house.'

Being a practical woman, she set about life with her usual vigour the next day. She arranged a large lunch party for the weekend, asking a lot of their old friends. It was as if she had something to celebrate.

On the flight to London Claire opened Frank's

present. He had written on the flyleaf: 'To remind you of old Reynard. Love Frank.'

She took a taxi to the flat in Fulham, which was extravagant, but she had so much luggage for the three months' stay. She felt hot and depressed and already lonely. The girl she shared with was also taking a course, but at a secretarial college and for a year. She was a distant cousin and they'd met briefly one summer. Claire remembered her as a plump girl who talked about young men all the time. But she was kin, and Claudia wouldn't hear of her daughter living in London with strangers. She was at home that first evening; she was very cheerful, full of the fun she was having. They had supper and Claire tried to fit her clothes into one tiny cupboard and a small chest of drawers. It was far worse, she decided, than being at school in Switzerland.

Her flatmate's name was Jenny, and the more she bubbled about the young man who was taking her out at the moment, and the friends and their pub crawls and parties, the lonelier Claire felt. And at the root of that feeling was the chasm that had opened up inside the family. She felt insecure for the first time in her life, and so low in spirits that she filled the jolly Jenifer with dismay. Cousin Claire looked like being a perfect drip, she thought. She was out on Friday, and Claire spent the evening alone, watching the English television, which was full of violent scenes in Northern Ireland. It was so odd to see it, because it made what was happening there seem so close. Riverstown was only sixty-odd miles from the border. For all they were aware of the trouble, it might as well have been six hundred. She couldn't forget home and Frank; London and the flat seemed completely unreal. He'd be so lonely in that big house, rattling around on his own, with the Mahoneys who housekept his only company.

She lit a cigarette, switched on the TV channel to an American comedy and said to herself, 'I'll give this cooking thing a try, but if I can't stand it over here, I'll go back and live with Frank. He'll need somebody to

146

run that house for him. The Mahoneys will run rings round him otherwise.' Unconsciously, she echoed Claudia's opinion of the Irish servant class.

When the telephone rang the next morning, Jenny answered it, and after a moment banged on Claire's bedroom door.

'It's for you,' she shouted. 'Some dishy-sounding man called Neil Fraser.'

And that was how Claire's three months' stay in London ran on to a year. She came home at Christmas and Easter and brought Neil back to meet her parents. Frank was not in Ireland at the same time. They wrote and telephoned, and his news was exciting. He was travelling to America, starting to set up the merchant bank with some US backing. His uncle Kevin Ryan had been over and met him at Meath. He had been a great help and introduced him to a lot of useful people in New York. He spoke of him so enthusiastically that Claire was uneasy. At the end of that year, when she rang Frank to tell him she was engaged to marry Neil Fraser, it was a woman's voice that answered and said he was away, but she would be glad to give him a message. Give, Claire noted, not take. Whoever she was, she wasn't old Biddy Mahoney.

She was staying the night in Neil's flat. They had started the evening in bed, which she enjoyed more and more after losing her early shyness. He was a marvellous lover, she thought, sighing happily. They were going to be blissfully happy. She stretched her hand out and the ruby and diamond engagement ring sparkled in the light. Suddenly her life was exciting and the awful void of Frank leaving Riverstown had been filled by this clever, sophisticated man who made divine love to her and showered her with presents and promises of the wonderful life they would have together.

She had made a lot of friends and met many more through Neil. His father was a widower, and very sweet whenever she went down to stay. Neil had a brilliant political career ahead of him, and she knew people were saying that all he needed was a beautiful young wife and a family to complete the electoral appeal. She was determined to help him and make him proud of her.

He yawned and sat up beside her. They always made love with the lights blazing. Claire had been diffident at first, but he explained, 'Half the pleasure is looking at you, darling . . . Don't be such a little nun,' and then behaved in the most intimate and outrageous way to prove his point.

'Hello, darling,' he said.

She smiled up at him. 'Hello.'

'Did I snore?'

She nodded. 'Like a pig.'

He tweaked her hair. 'You're hell, do you know that?'

Claire played the game. 'Then why are you marrying me?'

He dived at her. 'Because you've got the loveliest boobs in London. Not to mention . . .'

Claire wriggled away from him, laughing. 'No, you don't start that again. You said you wanted to see *Panorama*.'

'I did, didn't I? Well, get up then.'

He was fun, she thought happily. A lot of Irishmen were staid, come to think of it. She was sure their girl friends didn't have a bed life like hers. She dressed and went out to make dinner for them. The cooking school had been a ghastly bore. She said she'd have learnt more from old Molly, the cook at home, but in fact she cooked very well and she'd Claudia's talent for flowers. Neil used to boast that she could make a few dead twigs look like a work of art. She liked cooking for him; only too often he insisted on going out to smart restaurants, and several times to the House of Commons, because he wanted to show her off. He was pleased that his colleagues had reacted so favourably.

His father had expressed disquiet because Claire was so young. 'Only just twenty-one, Neil. It's very young to fill the role, you know. If she's going to be an asset

148

to you, dear boy, she's got to be very tactful and clever.' She was a delightful creature, he added, and pretty as a picture. Neil said firmly, 'London is full of tactful, clever women pushing their husbands. What makes Claire so special is she doesn't give a damn about impressing people or saying the right thing. That's exactly why everyone likes her. Me most of all.' And that was the last time his father mentioned her age. They sat down to dinner and he thought, what a lucky thing I accepted that idiot Charles Butler's invitation to go to Ireland. I might never have met her otherwise. I'm going to be happy with her for the rest of my life, just like I am now, looking at her across the table.

'I rang my brother to tell him we were engaged,' she said.

'Oh? What did he say?' He had a clear memory of the dark Irishman who'd watched them dancing in the ballroom at Butlers Castle. He'd never seen him since, but he hadn't forgotten him.

'He wasn't there,' Claire said. 'It's funny, a woman answered. It wasn't the housekeeper.'

'What's funny about it? Doesn't he have girl friends?'

'Not the sort who stay in the house when he's not there. She said he was in the States. I wonder who she is?'

'How would I know, darling?' he said, and looked at his watch. 'I'm going to turn on the box. I don't want to miss this programme.'

'It's not about the North again, is it – I'll wash up if it is,' Claire said. She didn't really want to watch one of Neil's factual programmes. She didn't know or care about political issues in England and she felt if she heard one more pundit talking about the problem of Ulster, she'd scream. They made much more fuss about it in England than in Kildare. But then, it was their soldiers being killed. She cleared away and left Neil to the television. She wondered again who had answered the telephone in Frank's absence. Maybe her parents would know. It was about time she phoned them again anyway.

She ignored the fact that Claudia had rung her up only the night before.

Philip took the call. He said to Claudia, 'That was Claire; I called you, but you must have been upstairs.'

'I was outside, showing Mack poor old Blue Boy's leg.' Her old hunter had cut into himself out walking, scared, as she put it, by a group of bloody yobs larking around on the road. He'd given himself a nasty gash which had just missed slicing the tendon. She was worried to death about the old boy, and spent more time dressing the wound and looking at him than she did in the house. 'Damn,' she said. 'Sorry I missed her. Everything all right?'

'She's fine,' Philip said. 'Full of beans. Apparently she'd rung Frank and some woman answered. Claire wanted to know who it was.'

Claudia looked up at him. 'What did you say?'

'I said I hadn't the faintest idea,' he said. 'It could have been any one of the hangers-on he surrounds himself with.'

Claudia frowned. 'It's probably that girl Dempster. I gather she's wormed her way in pretty successfully. Not that it matters. It's time he had a steady girl friend.' Personally she didn't care who Frank shacked up with now that he was out of her house and Claire was happily engaged. She and Philip seldom discussed how he lived or his activities. Claudia heard the local gossip but she didn't pass it on. She loved Philip and she didn't want to upset him. Things were shaping up so well, and except for that *bloody* mishap to Blue Boy, she'd never felt more content. Neil Fraser was a good match; plenty of money, a bright future, and most important from her point of view, he was a gent. They all spoke the same language, and God, didn't that make life easier when it came to a marriage. He was crazy about Claire, and she seemed just as much in love with him. Claudia missed nothing that went on in her own house, and she knew perfectly well that they did a bit of corridor creeping when they stayed the weekends before they became engaged. Claire

150

had grown up, and it was thanks to Neil. Claudia was enjoying herself planning a really big wedding, with everyone invited, and Philip said he liked Neil and approved.

Philip poked the turf fire. He always did that when he was worried about something, Claudia knew. She stopped thinking about losing a season's hunting because of the horse's injury, and said, 'You're sure Claire was all right?'

He glanced up at her. 'Yes, of course. I told you, she only rang up to ask about the woman who answered Frank's phone. Isn't this Molly Dempster connected to Eamonn Dempster?'

Claudia had hoped he wouldn't work that out. 'It's Marie, not Molly,' she said. 'I think she's a grand-daughter, but I'm not sure.'

'Then he's really mixing with the scum of the earth,' Philip said. 'The Dempsters have been in the IRA since 1922.'

'*She* may not be,' Claudia countered. 'She's a dentist's daughter, I think. Works in Dublin for some firm of solicitors. Do stop hacking away at the fire, darling, or it'll go out! There's no use brooding about what Frank does. He's going his own way.'

Philip laid down the poker. 'I've heard things,' he said slowly. 'You know what people are like; they can't help talking. Someone in the club asked me the other day if it was true that Frank was setting up an Irish-American merchant bank, and Ryan was going to be on the board.'

'Is he?' Claudia asked. 'Why don't you ask him? After all, you're on speaking terms. He's been here once or twice. Surely he'll tell you?'

'I don't intend to ask,' Philip said coldly. 'We talk about the farms and he asks advice about the property in Meath, but we've no point of contact beyond that. I just have a feeling he's getting into deep water, and I don't want any scandal before Claire's wedding. When that's out of the way, he can do what he likes.'

Claudia sighed. 'He's a fool,' she said. 'If he's getting

mixed up with people like the Dempsters and that dreadful uncle, they'll just use him for all they're worth. He's rich, remember. A rich Anglo with a bad conscience. And an Irish mother to trade on. God, I wish somebody could talk some sense into him!'

'I've made up my mind,' Philip said slowly. 'I'm not going to leave him Riverstown.'

Claudia stared at him. 'Philip! You're not serious?'

'Perfectly serious. He's irresponsible; after the wedding I'm going to change my will.'

'You can't do that,' she said. 'You can't disinherit your own son. He's only young; he may change. He may have his fling with these people and then one day he'll see through them and it'll all be over. You mustn't do anything like that!'

'I love this house,' Philip said. 'It's been in my family for generations. I'm not going to have it filled with the kind of people he brings into my mother's old home. He won't change, Claudia. He's not one of us. Now don't let's discuss it any more. Tell me, what did Mack say about Blue Boy?'

They had been married for over twenty-five years, and Claudia knew when to stop. 'He thinks he's had it for this season,' she answered. 'I could take out Lucky, but he's very strong and a bit green.'

'You're not hunting any four-year-old,' Philip announced. 'If Boy's out of action, go and look for something else. Something reliable and experienced.'

Claudia smiled at him and then gave her horsey laugh. 'If you dare to say a "lady's ride", I'll scream,' she said. 'Does that mean you're going to pay for a new hunter?'

He smiled slightly. 'It'll be cheaper than hospital bills if you take a fall off that lunatic Lucky. Ring round tomorrow, and we might go horse coping together.'

'Thanks, darling,' Claudia said gently. They had a perfect understanding. She thought, 'If Claire ends up like me, she'll be all right.'

Kevin Ryan came back to Ireland just before Frank's

first Christmas at Meath. He had his nephew's letter in his briefcase. He had shown it to Mary Rose, who said what a warm and sensitive person he must be to write like that. Now that the time to meet aproached, it was Kevin who shied away and delayed his trip. He felt uneasy, unsure of what to say and do when he met Eileen's son. Old habits died very hard, and he was afraid his New World confidence would desert him when he was face to face with an Arbuthnot. Finally he came a month late. It was arranged that he would call on his nephew in Meath. They'd spoken on the transatlantic telephone, and the conversation had been stilted. It wasn't helped by a double echo that repeated everything Frank Arbuthnot said twice.

First Kevin visited the Half House. The builders were out and it was being decorated. He was pleased and proud of what he saw. It was a hell of a fine place now. All the old grot of the Hamiltons cleared away, with gleaming bathrooms and plumbing that worked. He'd given Mary Rose a free hand with the money and she ransacked the Dublin antique shops for Waterford chandeliers and handsome furniture. The pictures had cost a small fortune, and he was proud of them. Irish landscapes, big heavily framed scenes of mountain and lake, and a beautiful Lavery portrait of his own wife as an Irish peasant girl. The lovely face haunted Kevin. He took a lot of photographs to show people back home. His children were excited and demanded to come over. His brother and sister-in-law paid him compliments and criticized behind his back. Kevin knew and didn't mind. They'd be jealous and proud at the same time. He understood their feelings. At last he got into his car and set out for Meath to meet his nephew. He felt less nervous because he could talk about his grand new house if it was awkward to find things to say.

Frank opened the front door himself. Behind him the massive Gothic façade was daunting enough. He saw a short, grey-haired American, with a scarf wound round his neck and a curious forward stoop as if he were sheltering from a cold wind.

It was Kevin who spoke, prompted by years of political glad-handing at strange doors. 'Frank, isn't it? I'm your Uncle Kevin,' and held out both hands.

They were settled in front of a big turf fire, the smell sweet in the large old-fashioned room. One on either side in two armchairs with a decent whiskey in their hands.

Frank couldn't stop looking at him. He was like the photograph, and yet not really. The same thin face and narrow features, sandy grey hair and pale eyes. His mother had been delicately pretty. Her brother was wiry, expansive in gesture and with a ready laugh. From the moment he grasped both Frank's hands, he had felt a sympathy between them. Leaving his old home had been inevitable, but Frank had never felt so lonely in his life. The businesslike visits to his father made it worse. He felt so painfully rejected that he put off going to see Philip. He wasn't missed in the house. Claudia was friendly, but she never pretended to miss him. He felt keenly that his father was relieved when he said it was time to go. They both stood up with the speed of anticipation; Frank had seen them do it before when hurrying an unwanted visitor on their way. He had looked forward to this meeting, because he dared not do anything else. He dared not let it fail, because of the price he'd paid. And it wasn't going to fail. Sitting opposite his uncle, Frank felt a warmth and a kinship with an older man for the first time in his life.

'I remember sneaking in to see you,' Kevin said. 'In through the back door, with our old cousin, Mary Donovan, taking me by the hand. Did you ever know her, Frank?'

'When I was little, yes. She always gave me biscuits when I went into the kitchen.'

'She was a grand woman,' Kevin announced, forgetting how he had despised her as a slovenly old gossip.

'Yes, she was,' Frank nodded, remembering how

154

she'd slipped him his mother's brooch, with the whisper not to tell on her, it was as much as her job was worth.

'You were a lonely little lad,' his uncle went on. 'Lying all by yourself in the room, with your poor mother gone, and your father away fighting for the English. I said then, one day I'll come back and see Eileen's boy. And so I wrote the letter to you. You know, you've a look of her.'

There *was* something, Kevin decided, a fleeting expression that was Eileen in spite of the black Arbuthnot colouring. All his apprehension had gone. He felt confident and in command of the situation. He'd forgotten that his nephew was young enough to be his son. He felt warm towards him, and some instinct detected that Frank needed acceptance as much as he did.

He wondered exactly how much of the circumstances of his mother's marriage and her death the young man knew. He decided to enlighten him a little at a time. He began gently that night, feeling his way. He stayed to dinner at his nephew's insistence. The whiskey flowed; he didn't like wine and wouldn't pretend he did. He took in the comfort and the shabbiness of a typical upper-class Anglo big house, with its mass of silver on the table and fine glass, with holes in the curtains from years of wear and patches of damp by the cornice. He saw the housekeeper or cook or whatever she was waiting on them both, and felt that in spite of it all, Frank Arbuthnot was lonely and looking for something more. If he'd been his son, he couldn't have been more welcoming. It made Kevin feel good, and it wasn't just the drink warming his heart. He recognized the identity that had so alienated Philip. For all his English accent and his gentleman's manners, he was an Irishman. The Ryan blood was strong in him, and the tinker ancestry they shared made signals across the generations.

It was long past midnight when Kevin said goodbye. They'd made a firm date for Frank to go to New York and stay with him and meet his young cousins.

'And Mary Rose,' his uncle said. 'She'll take to you, Frankie, just like you were her own. And she's a grand woman. Quite the little lady she is too.' His brogue was thicker, and he wrung his nephew's hand and finally embraced him before he climbed into his car. For all the emotionalism, even the theatricality of his farewell, there was a genuine feeling of affection.

Watching him drive away, Frank saw beyond the swagger of the Irishman made good. In his way, Kevin was a considerable man, a man of shrewd intelligence and strong ambitions.

Families of enormous wealth and power in the modern world had sprung from stock like his. He made the old-established overlords like Philip Arbuthnot seem tired and bloodless.

Frank didn't go to bed. He went back to the dying fire and built it up, and poured a nightcap whiskey. He didn't feel tired. He felt elated, excited. There was drink in him, he admitted that. It might exaggerate what he was feeling, but it wasn't responsible for it. He had gambled on meeting his uncle, with his future and his family ties at stake, and he decided that night that he had won. He had met the other side of himself and it filled the void at last. He had reached out across the class and racial divide of Irish life and touched hands with his mother's people. He knew now that he was closer to them than to the father and stepmother sitting so smugly at Riverstown. He learned so much about himself and his mother's brief unhappy life in the guarded revelations of his uncle. There was more, much more, but that would come in time. And he would make his sister understand. She was the only one who mattered. He was a little drunk, a little unsteady putting the guard to the fire and walking up the stairs to bed. And he was sad too, because there was no one in his whole big house to talk to about what had happened.

There are no secrets in Ireland. Philip's friends in the Kildare Street Club were not the only ones to hear that there was a rift between them and Frank had moved to Meath. The cause was known too. It lost Frank sympathy among his friends, and aroused interest among others he didn't know. It began with an invitation to lunch from a well-known writer who'd recently bought a house a few miles away. The writer was an American of Irish descent who had made a fortune out of heavily erotic cult books. Being a newcomer, he was anxious to make friends and innocent of all intent when one of the literati from Dublin suggested he approach Frank Arbuthnot.

It was a Sunday and Frank's trip to New York was only ten days away. The writer lived in a big Georgian house in a handsome park; he had a pretty American wife, who considered him a genius and treated him accordingly, and a collection of stray dogs, picked up from the street corners and the country roads where they'd been abandoned. The writer was regarded locally as an amiable eccentric who wrote dirty books, and no one took him seriously. No one expected him to stay long in Ireland when the novelty wore off. People had seen his kind before.

It was a lavish party; drinks flowed and the atmosphere was talkative and stimulating. Frank, who knew only two people in the dozen invited, was soon enjoying himself. He felt as if he, rather than the writer, was the centre of attention. A charming professor of history at University College Dublin treated him to amusing anecdotes and introduced him to a young psychiatrist who'd come back to Ireland after three years at the Institute for Psychiatric Studies in Boston. He had a beard and a serious manner which Frank found attractive. His name was Sean Filey. He seemed to be making gentle fun of the writer, who was becoming more expansive about the role of sexuality in art. At lunch Frank was seated next to a girl he hadn't met. She was very pretty and vivacious, and she paid him a lot of attention.

'I was late getting here,' she explained. 'My car wasn't behaving itself this morning.' She added that she lived in Dublin. Her name was Marie Dempster. 'Do you live near?'

Frank explained, and gave the name of the house. She opened her blue eyes very wide.

'Old Lady Blanche Arbuthnot lived there, didn't she?'

'Mrs Arbuthnot,' he corrected. 'She was my grand-mother.'

'Was she really?'

He smiled at her. She looked so surprised. 'Yes, really. Do you know the house?'

She glanced down; she seemed shy suddenly. 'Well, no. I know of it, because my father had a little farm not far away. We wouldn't exactly be on the visiting list.'

He thought, good God, she's blushing. 'Then why don't you come over and see it?'

The girl glanced up at him. She had a beautiful smile, with very white teeth. 'Only if you'll be there,' she said. 'I'm not a great one for old buildings.'

'It's not that old, or that important,' he said. 'But I'd be delighted if you'd come some time. Come and have lunch next weekend. After that, I'm going to the States for a while.'

She looked disappointed. 'I can't next weekend, I'm going to a concert and I've got friends coming round. Do you like music?'

'Not a lot,' he admitted. 'We're not a musical family. But I will be in Dublin next Thursday. If you're free, we could have dinner.'

'I'd love that,' Marie Dempster said.

She didn't drive back to her flat in Dublin. She drove to the house on the estate on the airport road, and waited for Sean Filey. The first move had been made.

Kevin was at Kennedy Airport to meet him. It was bitterly cold, with snow playing whirlwind hide-and-seek round the rooftops as they drove out on the northern Route 73 to Boston.

'It's great to see you,' his uncle said. 'Just great. I've told Mary Rose and the children all about you. We've a

big party arranged for you to meet some of our friends.'
He wagged his head at Frank and added, 'People who'll
be useful to you, me boy. Good Irish-Americans with
the money. We'll have a hullava a good time while you're
here!'

Frank had never had a welcome like that from his
father. The new sensation of warmth and belonging came
over him, stronger than the first time they met. The
Ryans lived in a big modern house in a smart suburb of
Boston. The windows were all glowing with lights and
the snow fell in a fragile curtain as they drew up to the
door. The houses were in a high-security estate, with
closed circuit TV and armed guards on the gates. It was
an ugly reminder of the violence that clouded American
life. The rich and the privileged were targets, but at least
they knew how to protect themselves.

When the front door opened, a pretty, brightly dressed
woman came to meet him, and said, 'Frank? I'm Mary
Rose. Welcome to our home,' and reaching up she kissed
him. 'I've heard so much about you,' she went on,
beaming at him. 'Kevin's just never stopped telling us
all about his wonderful visit with you. Now come on in.
The drinks are waiting!' And she trilled with laughter,
as if his arrival was the best thing that had happened for
years.

There were four children. Good-looking children in
various stages of adolescence and one little red-haired
girl who smiled and smiled at him and went on staring
till her father took her on his knee.

'This is Eileen,' he said. 'Named for your mother.
Same red hair, same bright eyes.'

'Aw, Daddy,' the little maiden said, squirming with
embarrassment.

Frank smiled at her and thought, 'This is a real family.
This is how I'd want to be with my children.'

When Mary Rose was in the kitchen and the children
had gone back to the television set, Kevin poured a
whiskey and raised his glass. 'It's a great day for me,'
he said quietly. 'Having Eileen's son in my house.'

'It's great to be here,' Frank responded.

They talked politics till dinner was ready. Broad politics, without probing too deeply. By the time Mary Rose came to the door to call them, Kevin had established that he and Frank had more than family ties in common. He might have a WASP name, but his sympathies were with his mother's people. All he needed was guidance in the right direction.

The party in his honour was lavish. There was a buffet laid out for fifty guests, drink flowed in the best Irish tradition. Outside help had been brought in who knew their job, and Mary Rose, gleaming in a black sequin dress and expensive diamond jewellery, greeted their guests. There were politicians, several priests, one with the purple of a Monsignor in his shirt front, well-dressed women who proclaimed their husbands' success with minks and more diamonds. Kevin moved among them, slapping backs and kissing cheeks, parading Frank from one group to the next.

'My nephew from Ireland. My dear sister's son.'

There were lively and attractive girls who eyed him speculatively and brawny young men who talked about sport and business, vying with each other. Older men, with hard achievement behind them, took a quieter view of this nephew of Kev Ryan's, brought out like a rabbit from a hat. He was nice enough, but there was nothing of the Irishman about him. Then they recalled the old tragic story of Kevin's sister and her marriage, and the English accent and manners made sense. He had spent time in America, and the Harvard Business School impressed them.

After the supper Kevin gathered a few of the older men together in a room he called his den, and asked Frank to join them. They talked American politics and business, and the two men Kevin most wanted to impress drew his nephew into a discussion on banking and the world economic trends. Over his nephew's head, Kevin received a nod of approval, and allowed himself a proud smile. Frank was doing him credit in the closed community of the Boston Irish. These were the leading citizens, these two. Multi-millionaires, second generation, with intermarriage binding them. Not Kennedys, but coming upward after them. He'd been right to bring Frank over, right to introduce him. His own political ambitions would be strengthened; a fine home in the Old Country, as they called it, and a member of the establishment among his family. Kevin looked at his nephew and let his pride show. He shook hands with his guests with Frank by his side like a son. Watching it, Mary Rose felt just a little jealous, because he should have paid more attention to their own Patrick, who was turned seventeen and needed promoting. But it was an unkind thought, and she suppressed it. He was such a charming young man, with beautiful manners. Different, but so charming. It was touching to see Kevin and him together. He did make Kevin seem just a little rough sometimes, and that was another disloyal thought she had to put aside. She was so firm with herself that she went out of her way to spoil her new nephew and press him to come again real soon and stay much longer.

One night when his visit was coming to an end, she sat up in bed and said to her husband, 'Honey, when are you going to tell him the truth?'

Kevin wanted to go to sleep and not talk, so he grunted. 'What truth? It's late, Rose, I wanna get some sleep.'

'When are you going to tell him he's a Catholic?' she asked. 'Kevin, listen to me. It's your duty. You've got to tell him.'

Painfully, Kevin heaved himself upright. He was tired, and his liver had taken a lot of punishment, but Mary Rose had touched a nerve. He was a deeply religious man. Being a devout Catholic was as much a part of him as being Irish.

'I'll tell him,' he said. 'I'll tell him before he goes home. But I've got to pick the moment, Rose. It'll be a shock to him.'

At that moment his wife was as near to reproaching

him as she had ever been. 'God's grace can never be a shock,' she said. 'It'll open his mind and heart to the truth. What would your sister Eileen say if she could hear you?'

'Jesus, Rosie,' he muttered, lying down and turning on his side. 'I'll tell Frank. I promise.'

Before, he had been ready to drop into a deep sleep. Now, long after Mary Rose was adrift beside him, Kevin pondered on his sister, and what indeed she would have thought. And in the darkness he faced a different truth from the truth of Mary Rose. His sister had married outside her Church. She'd abandoned her faith for the love of Philip Arbuthnot, and there was no mention of her asking that her child should be baptized. She'd died with the deathbed repentance he'd always found uncomfortable. He didn't know then what she would have thought about her son being baptized a Catholic in secret, and maybe it didn't matter. What really mattered was the effect it might have upon his nephew. If anything would draw him closer to his Irish ancestry, then this revelation might be the thing.

There was a telephone message from Marie Dempster among the many calls waiting for Frank when he arrived home. For a moment he couldn't place the name. But it was only a few seconds' lapse. Of course: the pretty girl he'd taken out to dinner before he went to the States. Marie Dempster. Mrs Mahoney had written everything down in her painstaking hand. Miss Dempster wanted Mr Frank to telephone as soon as he got back. There were two messages from Claire, asking him to ring a London number. He tried that first. The girl she was living with answered. Sorry, she was away for the weekend. Yes, she'd say her brother called. He felt so disappointed not to speak to her, he didn't bother to ring anyone else till the next morning.

Marie Dempster sounded pleased to hear from him. She had a nice voice, and she didn't waste time on the telephone.

'I thought you'd be back by now,' she said. 'I did enjoy our dinner and I'd love to hear about your trip. Why don't you come here and I'll make dinner for you? Are you busy this weekend?'

Frank hesitated. He wasn't busy. He had come back from America with so many impressions and a strange feeling of fundamental change in himself. And no one to talk to, because Claire was away. If she'd been at home, he'd have taken a plane to London.

'No. I've no plans made,' he said. 'I'd like to come.'

She gave him the address and said Sunday at seven, if that wasn't too early. 'I'm looking forward to it,' she said, and then hung up.

It was a flat in a house off Baggot Street. There were five flights of stairs to climb. The address was a good one, but there was no money left over for luxuries. She'd created a pleasant room out of very little. When he said how nice it was, she was dismissive.

'I made the curtains and covered the chairs myself,' she said. 'And I like plants. I spend money on flowers and plants. It reminds me of the country. I've some wine, will that do?'

Frank said, 'That'll be great,' and wished he'd thought of bringing her something. He wasn't used to girls living on their own, with no money to spare. There were so many things he didn't know about how other people lived. A life of comfortable privilege, cushioned against reality. That was the sum of his experience, he thought, half listening to her making small talk while she prepared supper in a walk-in kitchen too small to hold two people. He didn't notice the food; the wine was cheap and unpleasant, but she had taken so much trouble he praised everything. And he talked about America.

She asked him a few questions, the sort of questions he expected, and then said suddenly, 'I'd love to go one day. I'd like to live there and get a really decent job. There's no future for me in the firm I'm in.' It was a well-known firm of Dublin solicitors, not too far from where she lived.

He said, 'Why not? They're very good people.'

She leaned towards him. Her blue eyes were shining with anger. 'Because my name is Dempster and I'm a Catholic,' she said. 'I've been there four years, Frank, and the job of private secretary to the senior partner is coming vacant. I should get that job. I'm a very good secretary . . . the best they've got there. But they've brought in a girl from outside. She's from the right background. Church of Ireland and good Cromwellian name!' She turned away and rummaged in her bag for a handkerchief. She blew her nose and cleared her throat. 'I shouldn't have said that to you,' she apologized. 'I had a bit too much wine. But I've been boiling over it for days.'

'I'm not surprised,' Frank said. 'I've never heard of anything like it. It's what you'd expect in the North, but here . . .'

She looked at him. 'In the North I wouldn't have got a job with them in the first place,' she pointed out. 'They're honest about their discrimination. No Catholic need apply. That used to be in all the "Situations Vacant" in the papers. That's what the trouble is with us in the Republic. Just because we're not being kicked around by Britain any more, we think there's nothing left to do. No injustice right under our noses!' She seemed so agitated, twisting her handkerchief in her fingers, a bright flush on each cheek. She got up and went through into the cupboard that called itself a kitchen. 'I suppose I've said all the wrong things to you,' she said from inside it. 'Now I'll never see you again.'

He felt so sorry for her, and so indignant. He got up and met her as she turned to come back into the room. She looked miserable and anxious. As she said to Sean Filey afterwards, it was the best bit of acting she'd ever done in her life.

Frank put both hands on her shoulders. All his life he had comforted Claire. It was as natural to him as breathing to be gentle with a girl.

'Don't be silly,' he said. 'Of course you're angry. Give the bastard notice. I'll help you get another job.'

She smiled and blinked away tears. 'You're not a solicitor,' she murmured.

'No,' Frank said quietly, 'but I'm about to open a merchant bank right here in Dublin. There'll be a job for you in a month or two's time, if you manage till then.'

'You really mean it?' She had beautiful blue eyes, with the heavy dark lashes and eyebrows that were peculiar to the Irish. She glanced downward and looked shy. Then unexpectedly she put her arms round his neck and kissed him. 'You do mean it, don't you?' she said. 'You're a very special sort of a man, Frank.' She kissed him again and opened her mouth to him. She was too experienced and subtle to go to bed with him the first time. She guided him to a pitch of sexual desire, and then buttoned her dress and drew back saying how sorry she was, and she shouldn't have got carried away.

As she'd expected, he didn't insist. The perfect gentleman, she thought contemptuously, angered by the fact that she was hot for him herself and wouldn't have minded being bundled into bed. But she had her part to play.

'It's not that I'm a virgin,' she explained. 'I just don't sleep with a man till I'm sure.'

'Sure of what?' Frank asked her. He leaned over and did up the last of the little buttons that covered her breasts. He brushed his hand over them, and she caught her breath sharply.

'Sure if I could love him,' Marie answered, and then, 'Stop touching me, Frank. It isn't fair.'

'I don't want to be fair,' he said and kissed her neck. Then he moved away and stood up. She watched him from the sofa. He kicked one of her shoes by mistake. 'When will you come down to Meath? You said you'd like to see the house.'

He was getting his coat on. He bent and brought out her shoes from under the sofa. He smiled at her. She hated him for smiling at her like that. Filey had told her to go slowly. 'Be careful. He's not one of your gawbeens. He's clever and he's sophisticated. Get your hook in deep.' Filey was wrong. He might be clever, but he wasn't sophisticated or he wouldn't be fooled by the little girl act. He'd have seen through her. No sophisticated man would be going home because she'd given him that guff.

'When do you want me to come?'

'Wednesday's a good night,' Frank said. 'I'll ring you tomorrow night. Goodnight, Marie. Thanks for this evening.'

She didn't move. She didn't want another goodnight kiss, or she might forget Filey's instructions. He was a fool and he was going to swallow the hook with herself and her sob story as the bait. She despised him, but she had never wanted a man so much in her life. She went to bed and lay awake, unable to cool her own fever. Wednesday was three whole days away.

Frank felt he'd made rather a fool of himself that night, offering her a job, nearly ending up in bed with her. He thought he'd better cancel their date for Wednesday. Next morning he actually dialled the number but there was no reply. He didn't want to take advantage. English and American girls knew how to look after themselves. He had an old-fashioned view of the naïvety of Irish women. He admitted he found her very sexually attractive. She had suddenly appealed to his sympathy and stirred all sorts of muddled emotions in him. And they *were* muddled. Coming back from America he found it a blessing and a curse to be at home. The fine old house at Meath succoured and reproached him at the same time. His grandmother had left it to him, with her fortune. He owed his independence to her. And yet he couldn't bear to see her photographs about the place, because of the picture Kevin Ryan had imprinted on his mind. The image of a cold, contemptuous old patrician, scorning her pregnant daughter-in-law and bringing on premature labour.

The Mahoneys fussed over him, and their subservience reproached him too. They should have been on friendlier terms, less servants and master than fellow Irish. But he knew nothing would have disconcerted them more than an attempt on his part to be familiar. The warmth of a kind and affectionate family was lacking in the emptiness of his handsome house. And above all he missed Claire.

He had always missed her, he realized, from the time they were separated in boarding schools, through his days at Oxford and the years spent in America. But they came home to Riverstown and the old happy fusion took effect. Now that link was broken. They would see each other, but it would never be the same. And then, on Monday night, she telephoned. He forgot all about cancelling Marie Dempster.

Claire had been trying to get through for an hour, while the maddening recorded voice repeated that all lines from England were engaged. Neil was taking her to the theatre and she didn't want to be hurried. The bustling Jenifer had breezed in and out and just remembered to tell her that her brother had called while she was away. Finally the lines were clear and the eccentric telephone exchange in Meath connected her.

'Frank, it's me! How are you?' She glimpsed her reflection in the glass above the telephone. It smiled happily back at her. It was so good to hear his voice again. They hadn't been in touch for weeks.

'I'm fine,' he said. 'It's great to get you at last. I phoned, but you were away.'

'I was staying with a friend. Rather a special friend. Listen, he'll be here in a minute and I'll have to go. I wish I could come over, but I'm broke at the moment. You've no idea how expensive London is. I've got so much to tell you. Listen to me, babbling on. How are you? How was America?'

'Interesting,' he said. 'Clarry, I'd love to see you. I've

got a lot to tell you too. I'll stand you the air fare, but I don't want to make trouble for you with the parents. I don't think they'd like me paying for you to come here.'

'Is it still that bad?' she asked him. 'I hoped maybe things had settled down. Frank, there's nothing wrong, is there?'

There was no use trying to deceive her. 'Not wrong, no. I'm fine; but I've got a lot of things on my mind. Why don't I come and see you?'

'Don't be silly.' Her response was instant. 'There's no bed for you here; you can't swing a cat in the place it's so small. Don't worry about the money. I can manage it. I'll slip over, nobody need know. Can you meet me on Friday? I'll let you know the flight.'

'You're sure? It would be great to see you.'

'I'll be there,' Claire said. A few minutes after she rang off, Neil Fraser was ringing the front-door bell in the street below.

Neil intended asking her to marry him that night. But he didn't. After the theatre when they were having dinner in the smartest private club in London, she asked him to lend her the air fare to Ireland.

'Whatever for? Darling, you can have anything you like, but why not ring up your mother if you want to go back?'

'Because I'm not going to Riverstown,' she explained. 'I'm going to stay with my brother Frank. I told you, they've had a falling-out and it's difficult.'

Neil shrugged. He had heard about a family row but hardly bothered to listen. Certainly he didn't take it seriously. All families quarrelled, but it was soon made up. Claire had not attempted to explain the circumstances. She knew instinctively he wouldn't understand.

'Surely it's not still going on,' he said. 'This was months ago, when you first came over to London.'

'It is, and I can't see an end to it. No, maybe I can. Maybe something will happen that will bring Frank and Dad together.' Like a marriage, she thought suddenly.

'He sounded rather miserable on the phone. I spoke to him tonight. I said I'd come over and see him. I hate asking you, Neil, but I haven't a penny in the bank till my next allowance. I'll pay you back the minute I get the money.'

He said, 'Of course you can have as much as you want. When are you going?'

'This Friday,' Claire said. She saw him frown.

'We're going to stay with the Miltons,' he said. 'It's been arranged for ages. We can't let them down.'

She said quietly, 'I can't let my brother down. I said I was coming. He needs me, Neil. I can go to the Miltons another time.'

He was very angry. James and Pru Milton were not just friends who could be inconvenienced. Milton was one of the Prime Minister's PAs. It was very important for him to go, and to bring Claire with him, if they were going to get engaged. He had planned to ask her that evening and take her down to Gloucestershire as his fiancée. It was impossible to cancel the arrangements. Their joint destiny shifted its course for those few seconds while he hesitated.

'Please, Neil,' she said. 'I'm really worried about Frank. I must go over.'

He loved her too much to see her look unhappy. Their lives swung back on course.

'All right,' he said. 'I'll go to the Miltons. You go to Ireland and put your mind at rest.' He leaned across the table and held her hand.

Claire gripped his fingers tightly. 'Thank you, Neil. I won't forget this. You're a darling man, as they say at home.'

The Miltons were very understanding when he explained that Claire had to go to Ireland unexpectedly. He lied about her father's health, and was annoyed when Claire found the excuse funny.

'Why not my grandmother's funeral?' she asked, laughing at him.

'Well, I could hardly tell them that you'd gone to hold your brother's hand!'

The retort was sharper than he meant. But he drove her to Heathrow and then set off for Gloucestershire. He was sure she would marry him; he couldn't imagine a future without her, and when they were married, all this over-dependence upon her family would stop.

Frank was waiting for her at the airport. The flight had been bumpy, and she looked pale. He hugged her for a moment.

'Good trip over? Not so good?'

'Bloody thing bounced up and down like a rubber ball,' Claire said. 'There was an old nun in the next row saying her rosary at the top of her voice. I nearly died of fright! Oh, Frankie, darling, it's so lovely to see you!'

'Come on,' he said. 'Let's get home,' and arm in arm they walked out to the car.

She leaned back in the big armchair and stretched her arms above her head. The fire roared in the grate, a brandy as sweet as benediction waited in its swollen-bellied glass beside her. Everything was warm and Irish and familiar, and there was Frank sitting opposite. England and Neil seemed a million miles away.

'I'd forgotten what a lovely house this is,' she said. 'Grandmother had great taste. What have you done with all her photographs?'

He said quietly, 'I've put them away.'

Claire opened her eyes wide. 'Why? Oh, not because of that old story about your mother? I don't believe it, Frank. I don't believe she did anything to hurt your mother. I think Dad went hysterical and had to blame somebody. You ought to put them back. After all, she left everything to you.'

'Conscience money,' he answered. 'I didn't believe the story either. But I heard it in America. It's true, Claire. My mother went into premature labour because of the way she treated her.'

'Oh, God,' she sighed. 'What good does it do to rake

up old wrongs? It's all so long ago, Frank. Put the photographs back; forget it.'

'My uncle told me something else,' he said. 'It's funny, Claire, but I can't get it out of my mind. The night I was born, I was baptized a Catholic.'

She stared at him. 'You couldn't have been! Dad was there!'

'Apparently the nurse did it,' he explained. 'I was very small and it's common practice among Catholics if the baby's in any danger. It doesn't need a priest to be valid.'

'You don't believe in it, surely to God? It's just a lot of superstition . . . babies going to hell if they're not baptized!'

'No,' he answered, 'I don't believe in that part of it. But it's a strange feeling, that's all. To be brought up one thing all your life and then find out you're something else.'

She picked up the brandy glass. She didn't like the way he was talking at all. 'Brother dear' – she tried to sound light-hearted – 'if you take any notice of what some silly old biddy did all those years ago, you need your head examined! How can you be any different?'

He raised his head and looked at her, and then into the fire. 'It makes me more Irish,' he said.

The fire blazed up suddenly, as something in the turf ignited.

'We're all Irish,' she insisted. 'Living in England has taught me that. Even Mummy would feel a foreigner if she went back now. I certainly do.'

'I always did,' he countered. 'And I spent most of my young years there. School and university. I'm more at home in the States.'

'Because you were mixing with all the other Paddies,' she smiled. 'Getting jarred and singing "The Mountains of Mourne". You've always harped on this "different" thing. I remember you saying it to me when we were children. Darling Frank, it doesn't even make you happy. Be proud of being Irish, but don't let it get under your skin like this. Calling yourself a Catholic – just because this uncle you've just met tells you some old wive's tale. How do you know it's true?'

'Because the nurse who baptized me told Mary Donovan. And she told my uncle.'

'If I say this is a lot of old biddies' gossip, you'll call me a snob, I suppose?'

'It seems to me,' Frank said gently, 'that it's worrying *you.*'

Claire nodded and finished her brandy. 'Yes, it is. Because it's having an effect on you, and you're my brother and I love you. What's got into you, Frank? Is it America – was Dad right when he told you to leave old Ryan alone? All this business about our grandmother . . . putting the photographs away . . . you've known the story since you were a child, so why is it suddenly an issue? This nonsense about being baptized a Catholic, when you've been christened and brought up Church of Ireland all your life. What's the matter? Can't you tell me what's really at the back of it?'

She got up and came to him, balancing on the arm of his chair. She slipped her arm round him. She felt so motherly, she could have stroked the dark bent head.

'He never loved me,' she heard him say. 'He couldn't look me in the eye. There was always something about me he hated. I tried to forget it, Clarry. I tried to please him, but nothing worked. He was all right with me on the surface, but the first opportunity he turned me out.' He twisted round to look at her. 'I go to my own home once a month or so, and we talk about the farm and the cattle prices, like two strangers. And he can't wait for me to go.'

'Oh, Frank,' she murmured, and held him close. 'Oh, how awful for you. I didn't know it was as bad as that. I kept hoping it would mend with time. Maybe it will. I believe it will.'

'How could he have loved my mother and feel as he does about me?'

She had no explanation. It was not the moment to

172

pretend. 'I don't know,' she admitted. 'Perhaps you're too alike. Perhaps if you looked like her, he would have loved you. I don't know,' she said again.

'He regrets it,' he said. 'He regrets marrying her, falling out with his own family. And so long as I'm around he can't forget it. He can't pretend it didn't happen. Can't you see it, Claire? It's like a haunting. She dies, but I survive. Then years and years later her brother comes back and buys Claudia's old home. Just a few miles down the Naas road. It must have crucified him.'

'If you go on like this, you'll end up in St Pat's,' Claire said.

'I've got to get my life straight,' Frank said. 'I've got to find out who I really am and what I want to do. I'm not crazy, Claire, but I feel as if I'm in a vacuum. I'm planning to open a bank in Dublin; there's a lot to do to improve the estate. I'll have Riverstown one day. But it doesn't seem to have any meaning for me.'

'It's leaving home,' she said. 'That's what makes you feel like this. Thinking Dad doesn't love you.'

He looked up at her. 'Do you think he does? Honestly?'

'I think he's uncomfortable with you,' she said after a pause. 'He finds it difficult to show his feelings. And he's very obstinate and proud. Frank darling, I've got an idea. Why don't I talk to him about it? Not at the moment, but when I come home next. He may be feeling just as unhappy as you are. Why don't I do that?'

'Haven't you already done it?' he asked her, and she couldn't deny it. She tried to forget that chilling relief in her father when his son had finally gone.

'Yes, of course I did. But you'd just had the row. Time heals everything.'

'Not with the Arbuthnots,' he said.

They were silent then, each watching the spurt and flicker of the firelight. Once she ran her hand over his hair. She had never known him in need like this. He had always been the strong one, giving her security.

173

Now it was her turn to mother him. And he's never really had a mother, she thought sadly. My mother was kind and dutiful, but I don't think she ever put her arms round him and did what I am doing now.

'Why don't I get us both some more of that brandy?' she suggested.

'It makes a good nightcap,' he said. 'I've taken to having one in the evenings.'

Claire brought him a glass and slipped down on to the floor by the fire, leaning against his chair. 'So long as it's not two or three,' she said.

'It isn't,' he answered her. 'Not that at times I haven't been tempted.' He looked down at her, with the bright hair gleaming in the rosy light, and her sweet face puckered in anxiety about him. He thought, Wouldn't it be wonderful if she could stay? Wouldn't the whole house come alive? Instead he said, 'I've talked enough about myself. Now I want to hear what you've been doing.' Something nagged at the back of his memory. Something she'd said in that brief telephone call. A special friend, was it?

For a moment Claire hesitated and then made up her mind. 'You remember that man I met at Butlers Castle, the English MP?'

He frowned. 'Yes, I remember him.'

'I've been seeing a lot of him in London,' Claire said. 'He seems very keen.'

'I'm sure he does,' Frank said. 'He was pretty keen that night, I remember. Are you keen too?'

She paused. 'I don't know. I was so miserable when I first went over. I nearly came home. Then he turned up, and started taking me out and introducing me to lots of people. He's very nice,' she added. She thought suddenly, I won't say I've slept with him. Frank'd have a fit. I wonder if it shows?

'You're not even twenty-two yet,' he said. 'For God's sake don't rush into anything. I didn't like him, I told you so.'

She sighed. 'I know you did.'

174

'He's so bloody English,' Frank went on. 'Have a good time if you like, but don't get too involved. That kind of man is not for you.'

Claire didn't argue. She wasn't going to lie to him, but she didn't want to upset him either. He was prejudiced against Neil, without knowing anything about him. If she did decide to marry him, Frank would come round. And as he hadn't even asked her yet, what was the point of making an issue?

'Your home is Ireland,' he said. 'You won't be happy anywhere else.

Marie Dempster was nervous. She had smoked one cigarette after another while she waited for Sean Filey. He was late, which was unusual. He was a punctual man, rather rigid in his habits. He came into the bungalow and called out.

'Marie?'

'I'm in here,' she replied. He came through the doorway into the sitting room, and grimaced.

'Ach, look at the smoke in here. Why can't you give up that dirty habit? If you could see what it does to the lungs!'

Marie said angrily, 'They're my lungs and I'll smoke if I want to.'

He didn't argue. He took off his overcoat and gloves, unwound the scarf from his neck and laid everything neatly on the back of a chair. She looked tense and irritable. He wondered what had gone wrong with her date with Arbuthnot. The first evening had been a success. She was jubilant when she reported to him. Perhaps a little over-confident, he thought at the time. He'd warned her not to rush. Arbuthnot needed careful managing.

'Any coffee?' he asked. She got up, obviously unwilling.

'I'll make some,' she said irritably.

He followed her into the kitchen. He preferred it to

175

the drab and stuffy sitting room. Kitchens were cosy places. His own family always gathered there.

He said, 'Let's have a cup in here.' He gave her time to relax before he asked the question. 'What happened on Wednesday night?'

'Nothing,' she said flatly. 'I went down to his house; we talked about this and that, we had dinner and he said goodbye.'

Filey looked up sharply. 'Why the change?'

Marie shook her head. 'I don't know,' she said. 'He was very nice, the perfect gentleman, as you'd expect, but his mind wasn't on me, Sean. I tried to get him up to the flat this weekend, but he said, no, his sister was coming over from England and he was spending the weekend with her.'

Filey knew she had expected to stay the night and consolidate the advantage gained after Frank came back from America. He sensed that she was furious and bewildered by the rebuff.

'I couldn't get through to him at all,' she said. 'It was like a shutter coming down. I didn't know whether to push myself or take the hint and pretend the other night had never happened.' She moved her empty mug away. 'I should've slept with him then,' she said. 'Compromised him properly.'

'I don't think so,' Filey answered. 'I told you, this will take time. He had family matters on his mind; did he say why his sister was coming to see him?'

'No,' she said. 'It didn't sound like trouble either. He sounded happy enough.'

Filey saw the lowered look and wondered how she could be jealous when she hardly knew the man.

'I'll ring him up and try again,' she said. 'The sister will have gone home by now. He showed me a photograph of her.'

Sean said with a little cruelty, 'Is she pretty?'

The answer surprised him. 'She's a beauty. Very blonde. Not like him at all. You'd never dream they were related.' She opened her bag, lit a cigarette. 'Sean, I've been thinking.'

'About what?'

'About this idea of recruiting him,' she said. 'It sounded great when we discussed it. But I sat in that house the other night and I thought to myself, Is it really going to work? He's from a different world; he's one of *them*. Oh, he plays with the idea of being Irish, but to me it's just a lot of bloody fantasy. It's a big romantic gesture and he's loving it . . . that's what's Irish about him if you like, but how real is it? Could we ever trust him, supposing he does join?'

Sean Filey looked at her. 'He has a role to play for us,' he said quietly. 'Beyond that he knows nothing. We'll trust him as far as it suits us and no further. We need that bank of his, Marie. We need him because he *is* one of them. So far as his motives go – if he likes to play-act, good luck to him. Just so long as he does what we want. You're discouraged. Don't be. The grand house put you off, didn't it?' he asked gently.

'A bit,' she admitted. 'And he was different, too. He was part of it. I saw the old bitch of a housekeeper looking at me when she brought the dinner and I knew she was wondering what some little piece from Dublin was doing sitting there.'

Sean reached over and laid his hand on hers. It was friendly, but he sometimes regretted they no longer slept together.

'You won't contact him,' he said. 'I'll do that. I'm having some friends in for an evening. There's a poet I can get to come and read his verse. He'll accept, Marie, and you'll be there. Then it's up to you.'

Neil Fraser met Claire at the airport. She'd told him the time of her flight back, but didn't really expect to see him. The House was sitting for an important debate. Monday was a bad day, he said, but he'd come if he could. He was in the arrivals hall by the gate. He hurried up, took the little overnight bag and kissed her.

177

'Hello, darling. The car's outside, come on, we've got to rush.'

It was sweet of him to come all the way to meet her; he had just got time before he'd have to go into the lobby and vote.

'How was the weekend?' she asked him. She felt so pleased to see him, she hugged his arm and the car nearly swerved.

'It was fine,' he said. 'The Miltons were disappointed not to meet you. I said we'd go down for lunch in a fortnight. They were very nice, and I think he'll be a useful friend. How was your brother?'

'Rather miserable,' Claire said. 'He's in such a mess, Neil, you wouldn't believe it!'

He glanced quickly at her. 'Mess? What do you mean?' Not a scandal, surely – not at this stage when he wanted to present Claire to the people who mattered.

'Oh, he's got himself so mixed up,' she went on, not realizing why he was anxious. 'It's all my bloody father's fault. Frank feels he doesn't fit in and he's always had this bee in his bonnet about his mother being bog Irish and it making a difference. I can't talk him out of it. If Dad had been a normal father, he wouldn't have given it a thought!'

Neil hid his relief. No scandal, that was all that mattered. He didn't understand what she was talking about apart from that.

'My mother's done her best, but I don't think she ever gave Frank much affection. She's not a demonstrative type, except when it comes to a sick horse. No, that's not true, she's marvellous really. I'm just upset about Frank, and there's nothing I can do while I'm over here. Never mind; it's lovely to see you, and I'm so glad you came to meet me. How long will you be at the House?'

'A couple of hours. I can get you into the Strangers' Gallery if you'd like to listen to the debate and wait for me.'

'No, thanks. I'd rather go to the flat and wait for you there.'

He took his hand off the wheel for a moment and laid it in her lap. 'I've missed you,' he said. 'And I've missed this.'

'So have I,' Claire answered. When they were in bed Neil made love so excitingly she could forget everything else. And she hoped it would help her forget Frank, at least until the morning. She guided his hand back to the wheel. 'Watch the road,' she said, and they both laughed.

He dropped her at his flat in Fulham and drove off back to Westminster. He couldn't help thinking that her brother's identity crisis was hardly worth cancelling such an important date with the Miltons. But she was a determined girl; very strong-willed. He liked that in her, though it was a nuisance at times.

Sean Filey lived with his parents; there were five in the family and Sean was the youngest of the three boys. But he was the only one who had followed his father into medicine. Brian Filey had been a doctor for forty-seven years. He found his clever son too high-powered, and secretly he thought a lot of modern psychiatry was rubbish. But he was very proud of Sean all the same, and his wife doted on him. They hoped he'd settle for a nice girl and get married soon. He was the only one of the family still single. The house was a comfortable old-fashioned villa, built at the turn of the century. The Fileys had lived there all their lives and Sean had the upper floor to himself.

He arranged his party three weeks ahead, with alternative dates in case Frank Arbuthnot couldn't make one or other. There was a young poet gaining a wide reputation for his verse; and a group of people he hoped would enjoy something different.

He was friendly and relaxed when he spoke to Frank, reminding him of their meeting at the novelist's house. He slipped in a sly joke at the writer's expense, which made Frank laugh. Frank accepted. He wasn't interested in poetry, and he had an awful feeling some of it might be in Gaelic, but he liked Sean Filey. If he was going to be an Irishman, then he would break out of the old Anglo circle, with its talk of hunting and land prices, and mix with the Irish: the writers and artists and intellectuals who had never been welcomed to Riverstown, or to his grandmother Blanche's house.

When he arrived he felt ill at ease, in spite of Sean's efforts. He was introduced to everyone, but they all knew each other and after a few words they drifted away. The poet was a bearded, shabby man, with a sing-song Cork accent. Frank didn't think he was particularly young, but then there was so much hair on his head and his face it was difficult to tell. He shook hands limply with Frank and his eyes slid away, looking for someone else.

Twenty minutes after he'd arrived, Marie walked in. She was out of breath and very flushed, which made her look even prettier.

He heard her say to Sean, 'I'm so sorry, Sean, my old car let me down again. I had to take a taxi. I was so afraid you'd have started.'

She looked across at Frank and smiled, but she didn't come over immediately. He was suddenly glad to see her. He should have telephoned after they'd had dinner at home, but then Claire came, and he'd forgotten. He made his way over to her. She had a glass of wine in her hand. Sean had provided red wine and beer and there were big plates of ham sandwiches and fruit cake. His mother had offered a proper cold spread, but Sean said No, most people would have eaten before they came.

'Hello, Marie,' Frank greeted her.

'Hello, Frank. I didn't know you were coming. How are you?'

'Fine, thanks.'

'I should have thanked you for the lovely evening,' she said. 'I loved your house.'

They sat together, side by side on hard little chairs, and the poet advanced into the centre and began to read aloud from a book of his works. Everyone was very quiet; there were twenty people in that room, and they sat as still as if they were at a funeral. He read beautifully. The language flowed, full of imagery and original ideas. Frank had expected to be bored. He became entranced, and when the first reading ended, he joined in a loud burst of clapping.

From his seat at the back, Sean Filey watched him speculatively. He knew the poems well. They had affected him too the first time he heard them. It was good that Arbuthnot had come under the same spell. Their name was Ireland. They spoke of beauty and sadness, of longing and reflection, of love that blended into a love deeper than the love of men and women. The hairy young man from the suburbs of Cork City was the spiritual heir of the great Irish ballad makers, the poets and bards who brought the people their country's history through verse and song. When the monasteries perished and the ancient manuscripts were burned by the barbarians from over the sea, the songs and the stories were kept in the people's hearts and passed on from one generation to the next. He gave this simple explanation at the end of his reading, and he made it very moving. There was more applause. Sandwiches and cake were handed around. The poet was surrounded and holding a little court.

'You liked it, didn't you?' Marie said to him.

'Yes. He's remarkable. I'm ashamed I've never heard of him before.'

'Sean discovered him,' she explained. 'Apart from shrinking people's heads, he's a great one for helping Irish artists. There's two critics here tonight, one from the *Independent* and another from the *Cork Examiner*. There'll be a report in tomorrow's papers. That'll help. It's funny, I never liked poetry at school. But I like this. It sings, doesn't it?' She smiled up at him.

Frank said, 'But they're sad songs.'

'Ireland's been a sad country,' she responded. 'Who else has got a national heroine called Deirdre of the Sorrows?' She looked at her watch. 'I'll have to go,' she said. 'Could you give me a lift home, Frank! It's not too much out of your way. My car's on strike again.'

'You'll have to get a new one,' he said. 'Of course I'll drive you home.'

Outside the door on Baggot Street she turned and said, 'Come up for a minute. I'll make us some coffee.'

He couldn't have refused if he'd wanted to, and he didn't. Inside her flat, she closed the front door, stripped off her coat and put her arms round his neck. She kissed him, and touched his lips with her tongue.

'I nearly didn't go tonight,' she said. 'Now I'm glad I did.'

Frank didn't go home to Meath till the following morning.

She called Sean Filey in her lunch hour.

'He stayed,' she said briefly. 'And I'm seeing him tonight. I think we're on.'

'Good girl,' was his response. 'Now get yourself the sack. We don't want him forgetting about that job in his bank he promised you.'

He rang off and Marie went back to her table in the snack bar where she had lunch. Cold-blooded bastard, she thought. 'Good girl.' He'd have played pimp to his own sister if it served his purpose. No wonder he made love like a bird. A peck and a fluttering and a quick glance at the watch . . . Not like last night. She'd taken the initiative and then found it taken away from her. She was determined to keep it in perspective. She said that to herself several times. He made music with her. Nobody else had even strummed the first note. But that was just a bonus. There was no call for her to think how his hair grew back from his forehead and how she liked stroking it in place when they were lying together. Or the shape of him under the light, with good shoulders and a fine chest with a black fuzz of hair drawing the eye down to his navel. She had let her coffee get cold thinking about him. Get the sack, Filey had told her. Remember the job he promised you. I'll do better than that, Marie said to herself. I'll work in his bank and I'll end up moving into his house. That way I'll really have him in my hand. And if he makes me happy doing it, why not . . . ?

'If only Frank was here,' Claire said. 'Then everything would be perfect; it's such a shame he couldn't get back for the party.'

Claudia lit a cigarette. Preparations for the big engagement party and for a spring wedding were taking their toll of her nerves. Now she looked sharply at her daughter and frowned.

Claudia said, 'You cabled him the news. He could have come back in time for this. Anyway, don't let Neil hear you going on about it. I should think he's sick to death of hearing about Frank.'

Claire turned away. Her mother's attitude was openly hostile to her step-son now, as if she were free to express a long-concealed dislike. Neil came down the stairs just in time, before she said something angry.

'You look super, darling. Doesn't she, Claudia?'

'I think we chose the right dress,' was the reply accompanied by a smile.

She likes Neil all right, Claire thought.

Claudia said, 'I think people are arriving. Now, you two, you do the honours, nobody's come to see me. And of course your father's disappeared as usual, just before the party starts. I'll go and find him. He hates shaking hands.'

Neil slipped his arm round her waist. 'Why are you looking so pissed off – had a row with Claudia?'

'No,' she said. 'She gets on my nerves sometimes, that's all. Here's old Fred King; they've got a marvellous stud at Kilcock. He's sweet, you'll love him.'

Shaking hands with the old man, gnarled as a leafless tree and eighty if he was a day, Neil doubted it. They were swamped by people; Claire repeated names and he shook hands and accepted the congratulations with what he hoped was a good grace. They were all very nice, very warm, but he didn't miss the beady looks that raked him up and down. Claudia appeared and guided them into the main reception rooms, where people were getting drinks and the noise was above safety level. This was Establishment Ireland, he thought, glancing at the men with their old school and regimental ties, the women who would have been at home in any English country house. The same sort of people as the other guests at Butlers Castle, where he had met Claire, except they were the parents' generation. He stood beside her, a drink in his hand and chatted to a succession of people who came up. He found himself locked in by a woman in her forties, weasel-sharp eyes probing him, a long thirties-style cigarette holder in one hand. He couldn't remember her name.

'Ah,' she said. 'So you'll be taking Claire to live in England?'

'Yes, we've bought a house in Gloucestershire, near Tetbury.'

'I know Tetbury,' she said. 'Used to stay there with people called Hunt. He died and she ran off with a man young enough to be her son. Talking of sons, I do feel so sorry for Philip. First that wretched Frank goes to the bad, and then you come along and steal his daughter away.' She stared at Neil with open malice. 'It won't do you much good having a brother-in-law who's an IRA sympathizer, will it?'

'Excuse me,' Neil said. 'I must find Claire.' He turned his back on her and pushed his way through the crowd. He came up and caught her elbow. 'Darling, who's that frightful old cow in the green dress over there – the one with the holder?'

Claire looked across. 'Min Harding,' she said. 'She's ghastly. I don't know why she was invited. What's she been saying to you?'

Neil hesitated. An IRA sympathizer . . . it couldn't be true. Claire never mentioned anything like that. He decided not to spoil the evening. Of course it wasn't true.

'Oh, nothing. I just thought she was an old cow.'

184

'She is,' Claire agreed. 'And the most barefaced liar. She'll say anything about anybody.'

He was instantly relieved. 'It's a great party,' he said.

'Yes, it is. I'm glad you're enjoying it. It is a bit of an ordeal meeting everyone, but they've been dying to meet you and the wedding's too long to wait. I just wish Frank was here too.'

She'd said it several times. He was surprised to feel hurt.

'Well, you'll have to make do with me,' he said.

Claire smiled up at him, and he was happy again. 'I think I can manage that,' she said.

Three thousand miles across the Atlantic Ocean, Kevin Ryan was giving his nephew lunch at the Columba Club. It was a handsome Victorian building, old-fashioned inside and out. In its way it was a mirror image of the gentlemen's clubs that Irish immigrants had never been allowed to join. There was a lot of solid mahogany panelling and heavy furniture, a big gloomy restaurant with excellent food. Membership meant acceptance into the Irish-American hierarchy, both in business and in politics. Kevin had lobbied hard to be elected. Now he was one of its most distinguished members. He leant towards Frank across the table.

'We'll have the bank's opening the same week as we warm the Half House,' he suggested. 'It'll be a double for us, Frankie. Everyone'll come!' He watched his nephew closely, in spite of the broad smile on his mouth, the pale eyes a touch narrower than normal.

Frank wasn't himself. Mary Rose said so, and she had an instinct for such things. Women had instincts, because God in his wisdom had been miserly with brains. But they weren't to be discounted for all that. Frank looked drawn and puffy under the eyes as if he hadn't slept. He seemed aloof, even with the little redhaired cousin who was his favourite among the Ryan children, which worried Kevin. He didn't want him slipping away from him at the last minute. Up until a few days ago, they'd been a big happy family, with Frank settled in as one of themselves. He'd sunk into himself after that cable came.

Kevin said, 'Frankie, you're not listening to a word I've said. What's troubling you? Won't you tell me?'

For a moment Frank didn't answer. The cable had come and he'd read it, unable to believe that it was Claire telling him she was going to marry Fraser. It was long and full of enthusiasm and endearments, but the basic truth made him sick to his stomach. He was losing her to that pompous bastard. He thought of seeing him paw her on the dance floor at Butlers Castle, of him owning her and taking her away to live in England. Without knowing it, he had crumpled and mutilated the cable in his hands.

He had gone down to dinner with Mary Rose and Kevin and the children and said nothing, because his loss was like a wound. He couldn't discuss it because they'd spout good wishes and bonhomie, and he didn't trust himself to hide his feelings. His jealousy and shock couldn't be shared with anyone. And in the hours without sleep that followed, night after night of them, while he tried to think what he could do, he did despair. He loved Claire. He could have lost her to someone who would have made her happy, and conquered himself in the process, because he loved her with a pure unselfishness. But not to this. Not to a man who typified everything most hateful to the Irish, a man who wouldn't understand her and love her for the woman she really was. She'd warned him that time when she came to Meath, and he'd been too blinded by self-pity and his own dilemma to do more than mildly discourage her. He blamed himself bitterly. Her parents were delighted, the cable said. They were giving a party and she insisted he come home. He didn't even take in the date. Go to a big reception for all their old friends and neighbours, and see Claire with Fraser beside her. No, Frank admitted, he couldn't face that. Let them have their party. Let them celebrate what he knew would be a disaster of a marriage.

'Frank,' his uncle said. 'Tell me, lad. What's wrong?'

He focused on Kevin and saw the kindly look and the way he had of cocking his head when he was anxious. Why not tell him? Why not confide?

'My sister Claire is getting married,' he said at last.

'The poor boy,' Mary Rose said. 'No wonder he's upset. But why would his sister marry a man like that?'

From Frank to Kevin, and from Kevin to his wife, Neil Fraser had emerged as a vicious right-wing Tory politician dedicated to keeping the minority in Ulster under the Protestant Unionist heel. No one, least of all Claire, would have recognized a single characteristic of the real man. Kevin cleared his throat, and just in time he swallowed, rather than spat. Even now the old habits tended to slip out. But it was hatred, not phlegm, that made him want to spit.

'Because she's no bloody different,' he said. 'She's one of them, and poor Frank doesn't see it. It's no bad thing, Rose. It'll open his eyes to who his real family are, that's for sure.'

'We all love him,' she said, knowing that it was the right thing to say. And to feel, of course.

'I'm going out tonight,' Kevin announced.

She was surprised. He hadn't mentioned any change in plan. Normally he kept to his routine. His office by eight a.m. and home to the family by seven. A whiskey or two, sometimes more if he was tired, then dinner and TV and bed. Except for Fridays when Mary Rose took them all off for Rosary and Benediction.

'Are you taking Frank somewhere?'

He shook his head. 'No. I've a business meeting. You take care of him tonight. Don't wait up for me, Rose. I may be late home.'

When Frank came in that evening, Mary Rose was especially thoughtful. She pressed a second drink on him, kept little Eileen up beyond her bedtime because he loved to play with the child and conveyed that she was only too ready to listen if he had a private sorrow to confide.

'Kevin's going to be late,' she said after dinner was cleared away. He was such a nice boy, she thought. He always helped with the dishes, though you could see he'd never had to do anything domestic for himself. 'Would you like to sit with me for a while and be cosy?' she enquired.

Frank said, 'What a nice idea. Is there anything on television worth watching?' Kevin had told her, of course. She was so friendly and kind-hearted he couldn't hurt her feelings by shutting her out.

Mary Rose trilled her gay laugh. 'My,' she said, 'I just love the way you say "television". It's so cute!'

They settled down into the deep flowery sofa, with the massive colour set watching them with its blind eye. Normally Mary Rose took a chair nearby. 'That's your Mommy's chair,' Kevin would say to his children, and no one else used it. This time she came and curled up beside Frank.

'Frankie dear,' she said. 'Kevin told me about your family trouble. I just wanted you to know, I feel for you. I really do.'

For a moment he was afraid she was going to pat his hand. Family trouble was a quaint way to describe Claire's engagement.

'Thanks, Mary Rose. I'm sorry if I've seemed a bit out of sorts. It was such a shock to me, that's all.'

'And you'd no idea?' she murmured. Kevin had been sparing with the details.

'Oh, I knew he was taking her out,' Frank said. 'I was at the dance with her when she met him. But I didn't believe it would come to this. I thought she was just having fun in London and he'd drop out when she came home to Ireland. It's my fault, that's what's getting me. I could have stopped it, if I'd thought about her instead of myself!'

Mary Rose didn't know what to say next. The Tory

politician and his bride sounded rather well-matched as Kevin described them.

'Is she like you? She's a half-sister, as I recall.'

'Not to look at,' Frank answered. 'She's blonde, not a bit like Dad or me. We've always done everything together since we were children. I've never been as close to anyone as I am to her. I'd mind losing her whoever it was. But he won't make her happy. That's the only thing that matters.' He looked at Mary Rose. 'She's a lovely girl,' he said simply. 'She deserves someone special. And it isn't Neil Fraser or anyone like him.'

'Oh, dear,' was all she could think of to say. Kevin was right when he said Frank couldn't see his sister as she really was. Even after she'd chosen such an awful man to marry. He was surely a devoted brother. She couldn't imagine one of her boys talking about a sister like that.

'Would you like me to have a Mass said for her?' she enquired. 'I could fix it with Father Joe before you leave.'

For a moment he was so irritated that he actually got up rather than sit beside her. 'She's not dead,' he said. 'She's just marrying the wrong man. Sorry, Mary Rose. I know how much the Church means to you. I don't see it the same way, that's all. Have a Mass said if you like; it's very sweet of you.'

He turned away, ashamed that he'd been curt. But the insistent, gentle pressure on him to join the Ryans on a Sunday had been the only jarring note during his stay. He would not go to Mass with them. Not even when little Eileen asked him. He suspected Mary Rose of prompting the child.

She looked up at him from the sofa. 'If you had the Faith, you don't know how much it would help you in your life,' she said.

'Maybe,' Frank answered. He felt he was nearer getting to know the real woman at that moment than ever before.

'There've been times when I doubted,' she went on.

'Times when I didn't have the strength to do my duty by Kevin and the children. I remember when my daddy died. I broke up for a while. But God helped me come through. I have real faith now, Frank, and I'm happy. I just wish you could have that happiness too.'

'You're a very good woman, Mary Rose. My uncle is a lucky man.'

There was a pause between them then. She got up with a little sigh and took her place in her own chair.

'I'll pray for your sister,' she said. 'You won't mind that, will you?'

She had a sweet smile, he thought. At times he wondered whether there was anything behind it, like the nice things she was always saying about everyone. A sharp or critical comment never passed her lips. He had wondered how Kevin could live with such undiluted Christian charity – if it was that, and not a stupid woman taking refuge in a saintly pose. Now Frank was certain. It was not a pose. Mary Rose was living her religion.

'You go ahead and pray,' he said gently. 'If there's anyone listening, it's probably to you.'

Kevin Ryan's business meeting went on till after midnight. It took place in a large private house twenty miles outside the city centre. There were half-a-dozen men present, shut up in a downstairs room. Whiskey and cigars were on the table. The two prominent citizens of Irish descent who had met Frank Arbuthnot on his first trip over, were among the six at the meeting. A man in his mid-forties presided. He was not American, and he had entered the United States on a false visa.

They had discussed items on the agenda and the last but one concerned the new Boston Irish merchant bank that was scheduled to open in Dublin in the next month. It was Kevin Ryan's responsibility and he had made a long and detailed report. They were supplying the money, which would give them an eighty per cent holding. Frank Arbuthnot would finance the remaining twenty per cent. The non-American who presided over the meeting had been born in Downpatrick, but spent the last five years living in the Republic under an alias.

'This changes the picture,' he announced. 'If Arbuthnot's brother-in-law is a Tory MP, I don't see how we can risk him saying something to his sister that could be passed on.'

He looked round the table. One of the funding politicians nodded.

'It makes a difference,' he agreed.

Kevin gathered himself for the fight. He had been expecting the top Provisional leader to make exactly that point.

He said, 'You're wrong, Joe. You're both wrong. My nephew is sick to his stomach at this marriage. I spent the day with him. I know what he thinks of it. I know how he feels. I tell you, he was over-close to the half-sister. Now she's betrayed him, as he sees it. He'll come nearer to us. Already he says I'm like a father to him. And he's like a son to me. I tell you, this is a blessing. This cuts the last link with that family of his.'

He looked from one to the other. They all knew him and trusted him. He had proved a shrewd and cunning comrade in arms over the years.

'If I didn't trust him,' he said, 'I'd be the first to say forget it, set up with someone else.'

'There isn't anyone else,' the Provo leader pointed out. 'Arbuthnot's the cover man we need for this. Anyone from our side would be suspected. Dublin's not blind to what goes on. They've a tight eye open for money being laundered for us.' He lit a cigarette and coughed. He had weak lungs, legacy of a miserably impoverished childhood and medical neglect. Three years' imprisonment under the Internment Act of '71 hadn't helped. 'So we need him, but how much does he have to know? We'll have a plant there, right beside him as soon as the bank opens, isn't that right?'

'Eammon Dempster's granddaughter,' Kevin announced. 'We all know what the Dempsters did for Irish freedom. She's going to work for my nephew. They're close, as you might say.' He gave a sly grin. 'I wouldn't be surprised if he didn't marry her one day. But answering the question how much does he have to know, I'd say there's no way we can get the amount we've in mind through the bank without him finding out. Would you agree with that, Pat?'

'I would,' the older man said. 'We've got to trust him. We've got to recruit him and make him one of us. Otherwise it won't work on any scale at all. And I'm not putting a million dollars into this unless it's making a proper contribution to the Cause.'

Kevin said, 'Leave this to me. I'm closer to Frank than anyone. Get this sister's weddin' out of the way first. He'll join us and he'll work with us. I'll guarantee it.'

'He's got to commit himself before July,' the man from Ulster said.

Kevin nodded. 'He will,' he said. 'By the time the bank opens, he'll have taken the oath.'

Chapter 6

'Oh, Frank, I'm so glad to see you. Why didn't you come to our party?'

'I was up to my eyes in bank business,' he said. He had never lied to Claire before. But things were changing already, even before she committed herself to another man. Truth is the first casualty when people drift apart. He'd read that somewhere, and never imagined it could apply to them. It seemed so odd to meet in Dublin instead of at Riverstown where they belonged. But it was his suggestion and she didn't argue. They sat in the lounge of the Hibernian Hotel. He'd booked a table for lunch. It was mid-week, and the hotel was full. He thought she looked thinner. 'I sent you a cable, after all,' he protested. 'Was it a good party?'

She sipped her drink. Gin and tonic. She called it a G and T, which was something she'd picked up in England. He hadn't heard it before and it grated on him.

'Yes, it was great. Everybody came. But I missed you. It wasn't really bank business, was it? You're not pleased, are you?'

Suddenly there was no need for lies. 'You don't have to pretend, Frank. I know you.'

'That's why I didn't come,' he said. 'I couldn't believe it. I couldn't pretend to be happy about it. Are you sure it's what you want? You haven't been rushed into it, have you? You can always break an engagement.'

'No,' she answered. 'I've been living with him for six months. I didn't want to tell you, but I do know what I'm doing. I want to marry Neil; nobody's making me do it.'

He said slowly, 'But do you love him? There's more to it than bed.'

She laid her hand on his for a moment. Neil's ring glittered. 'I do love him,' she said. 'We're very happy together. Apart from bed, and that's marvellous. The only thing that will spoil it for me is if you and Neil don't get on.'

He said, 'Then that settles it. If you love him, you'll hear no more from me about it. And so long as he makes you happy, we'll get on fine.'

'Now I really am happy,' she said. And he knew then that whatever he felt, he must conceal it.

'Let's have lunch,' he suggested. 'Then you can get all the details off your chest. I can see you're bursting to tell me all about it.'

It was a long lunch; he bought champagne, and a lot of the businessmen nearby envied him such a stunning girlfriend. He was told all about the wedding dress and the bridesmaids and the flowers. In spite of the emptiness in his heart, she made him join in and laugh with her, as if it were the happiest prospect for him too.

'You're going to be principal usher,' she announced. 'Neil's got some friend he was at school with as best man, and there won't be too many people from England. Can you believe it, he said some of them are scared to come over?'

He didn't take it up, and Claire went on. 'Four hundred guests; Dad's going to be broke at the end of it. And Mummy's in her element. You'd think it was her wedding instead of mine!'

'I can imagine,' he said. He could imagine only too well. Claudia would be delighted with Neil Fraser as a husband for her daughter. She would get the maximum out of organizing every last detail to perfection. He wondered what his father thought of Neil. But of course he would never ask him.

'I think this might actually mend things between you and Dad,' she said, surprising him.

'Why should it?' Frank asked.

'Because he's happy and he seems much mellower these days. I thought he'd be bad-tempered and fed up with all the fuss, but he's entered into everything. Frank darling, make a big effort with him and see what happens. You may be surprised.'

He said gently, not to disappoint her, 'I'll try.'

'And by the way,' Claire said, as they were driving back. 'What's this I hear about a live-in girl friend at Meath? I think she's answered the phone to me once or twice. It certainly wasn't old Biddy Mahoney.'

'She's a nice girl,' Frank explained. 'We get on well; she's going to work in the new bank in July.'

'She's a Paddy, isn't she? And don't bite my head off for saying it!'

'She's Irish,' Frank said firmly. 'And a Catholic, and her grandfather fought alongside Michael Collins. You can't be more "Paddy" than that!'

'Is it serious? If you're thinking of making it up with Dad – he'd have a fit.'

'I'm not thinking of making it up with him, *you* are. And it wouldn't be any of his business if it was serious.

194

So happens, it's not. It's a good arrangement and it suits us both, but that's as far as it goes.'

'For her too?' Claire questioned.

He sped away from a set of traffic lights. 'I've never said I loved her. There are no strings for either of us.'

After a moment Claire said, 'Will I meet her?'

'I don't see any point,' Frank answered. 'But I'll tell you what I would like. I'd like you to meet my uncle Kevin Ryan. Just quietly, next time he's over. Will you do that for me? Dad and Claudia needn't know.'

'Frank,' Claire answered, 'if you want me to meet him, of course I will. I don't want to upset them before the wedding, but I'm not a child to be told who I can and can't see. Just give me a ring when he's here.'

He turned to her briefly, and then back to the road. He was a fast driver, and often took risks unnecessarily. It was her only criticism of him. 'He's been very good to me,' he said. 'He's a bit of a rough type, but you'll like him. And he's heard such a lot about you.'

Marie Dempster looked at her watch. Lunch with his sister had meant the whole afternoon. It was past five o'clock and Frank hadn't come back.

She had missed him during the long trip to the States. He had told her to invite friends down, treat the house as her own. He didn't want her to be bored or lonely. He never said that he'd be lonely without her. There were times when she thought of him in the bosom of the Ryan family and forgot that she and they were allies. She hated them for having him to themselves, while she waited in Ireland, hoping for an occasional phone call.

Sean Filey kept in close touch with her. Once or twice she was tempted to sleep with him, as if doing so would punish Frank for leaving her. But she knew Filey would reject her. That was over. All that mattered was the place she had made for herself in Frank Arbuthnot's life. So far as Sean was concerned, she was succeeding past success. And so he would think, she said savagely to herself, with ice water in him instead of blood. He might know every last twitch of sexual behaviour and motivation and be able to analyse its meaning like a toad's reflex, but he knew nothing about love, and love was becoming Marie's problem. Not just the passion that erupted like volcanic fire, but the cruel torment of the spirit that was unrequited love. She grudged the time they spent apart during the day. He had business in Dublin, business about his farms. At least she could busy herself as if she were his wife, running his house, chasing those lazy old servants who'd been used to twisting a man round their fingers.

But when he travelled she was miserable. And when he left her after the wonderful night they'd spent together, and stayed out most of the day with his sister, she was consumed with jealousy. She went upstairs, had a bath, changed into a pretty dress and made her face up carefully. Now she had the use of his money, she bought expensive clothes and scent and went to the best hairdresser and beautician in Dublin. She had been a pretty girl, in a provincial way. Now she was glamorous, even beautiful. He was happy with her, she knew that. He found her highly attractive and satisfying as a lover. She knew that too. But she did not hold his heart. After months of living with him, Marie knew her rival couldn't be fought on ordinary terms. She could have challenged another woman and won. But in no way could she compete with a sister. There was a photograph in his bedroom, showing them together on a beach in the West. Sitting with an arm round each other. She must have been about fifteen. They were laughing. It was a typical holiday snap, enlarged and framed instead of being stuck in an album where it belonged. The studio portrait was a different matter. That had a proud position in the drawing room on the piano. It had a fine silver frame, which Biddy Mahoney forgot to polish. Marie didn't mind it being tarnished. She ate the old woman alive if the brasses and the silver in the dining room weren't squeaking clean. She hated that smooth smiling image, framed in very blonde hair. And yet she longed to see her in the flesh, to torture herself by watching them together and having her suspicions confirmed. Now she was getting married. And going to live in England permanently. Marie pinned her faith on distance. When she wasn't on his doorstep maybe he'd forget about her . . . But he hadn't forgotten so far, and they'd been apart since he was thrown out of home.

She came downstairs, packaged for him, she thought, like the whore she was in reality. She'd have given her soul to run to meet him and know it didn't matter a damn how she looked. Six o'clock. She swore out loud. He'd come in looking innocent and friendly, unaware of her resentment, which she mustn't ever show him. She wasn't just a jealous mistress who could afford a tantrum. She was part of a conspiracy. Sometimes it consoled her to know that he was being duped, and she was part of that deception. But then when he took her in his arms, nothing else mattered and she would as soon have told him the truth about Filey and his precious uncle Kevin. If only she believed they could go on living together afterwards. But Marie knew that would be the end for her too. By entangling Frank, she kept him. There was no other way.

She opened the drawing room door. The room was blazing with the late evening sun. She caught a breath in rage. How often had she told that old bitch to let the blinds down, before the furniture got faded. She turned and stormed into the kitchen quarters. As she expected, they were at the kitchen table, drinking one of their endless cups of tea. The old man was in his shirt-sleeves, dirty from the garden. Marie'd set him to growing vegetables and he dug and hoed in silent protest at the backache and the rheumatism. Marie addressed Biddy, ignoring him.

'Why haven't you let the blinds down? Don't you see the sun's pouring in?' She stood with her hand on the door handle and the other was clenched into a fist at her side.

'I was on me way to do it,' Biddy protested. She pushed herself away from the table and the tea.

'It was rainin' only a little while ago,' her husband came to her defence. He'd worked for the Arbuthnots and their kind all his life. He'd never heard one of them speak to Biddy like that. Dempster was shouting at her, like a bloody fishwife.

'Don't tell lies to me! Get on and do it this minute. Next time you forget, I'll speak to Mr Arbuthnot about you!'

There was a pause. She saw their faces upturned to her, and the contempt they didn't dare express except by shirking and disobeying as much as they could behind Frank's back.

'I'll be drawing the blinds then,' Biddy Mahoney said. She skirted round Marie, moving with maddening slowness, and an even more maddening dignity.

Marie glared. 'You'd better talk to her,' she snapped. 'Or I'll have the both of you out!' Then she pulled the kitchen door shut with such force that the teacups rattled.

Mahoney sat still. They were well-paid, and they got on with Mr Frank. It had been an ideal job for them both till he brought this little Dublin whore into the house. He wasn't going to stand by and have Biddy shouted at by the likes of that one. He finished his tea.

Marie heard Frank come in. He opened the drawing-room door and saw her sitting there with a drink in her hand, and all he noticed was the smile.

'Hallo,' she said. 'It must have been a good lunch.'

He came and sat beside her. 'Not bad,' he said. 'I sorted things out, that's the main thing.'

He looked calm and relaxed. Her hope of a quarrel died. He was angry about the marriage, she knew that much. Filey accepted the reason. Naturally he would hate any member of the English establishment as a brother-in-law. But Marie wondered if there was any man in Ireland he'd consider worthy of that sister . . .

'So you'll be going to the wedding then?' she asked.

He glanced at her in surprise, and for an instant saw something in her eyes he didn't like.

'Of course,' he said. 'Now tell me what you did today.' The subject of Claire was closed.

'I had trouble with Biddy again,' she said.

Claudia was at her desk, ticking off replies to the wedding invitations. Nearly everyone was coming. The small contingent from England had to be housed with neighbours. Neil's father would stay at Riverstown. The caterers from Brown Thomas in Dublin hadn't sent the menus in spite of two telephone calls. She heard a tap on the door and said absently, 'Yes?'

Biddy Mahoney stood there, wearing her Sunday hat and best coat.

'Good God,' Claudia said. 'Biddy? What are you doing here? Come in.'

'I'm sorry to disturb ye, Mam. Jim drove me over; he's in the hall.'

Claudia left her desk. 'Sit down, Biddy. What's the matter?'

'We've been thrown out of the house,' Biddy said.

Claudia could see that the old woman was near to tears. Thrown out. They'd looked after that house for nearly ten years, ever since Blanche Arbuthnot died. She went bright red with anger. 'You've been sacked?' she said. 'I can't believe it. Why?'

'There's a woman livin' there now.' Biddy looked embarrassed.

'I know there is,' Claudia said grimly.

'She complained of us, Mam. She come in the other day, screamin' at me like a banshee over forgettin' somethin' and the next thing is Mr Frank sends for me and Jim and says we've got to treat her with proper respect or he won't keep us. So my Jim says she shouts at me and nags at him over the old vegetable garden till we can't sleep at night for worryin'. He's a quiet sort of a man, and he put it fairly.'

'I'm sure he did,' Claudia agreed.

Biddy said, 'But 'twas no use. She'd put in her poison against us. Mr Frank says he thinks it best we look for somewhere else.'

'God Almighty,' Claudia exploded. 'He must be off his head. Surely he didn't just tell you to go like that?'

'No, he gave us a month's notice and a present. He was generous enough. She was smilin' like a cat with the cream in her all the next day. We did our work and never a word passed. Then he's away for the night and she comes and tells us to pack up and get out be the next mornin'. So we're gone. This very day. Jim wouldn't stay another minute after the way she talked to us. He's got his pride.'

'Have you anywhere to go?' Claudia asked.

'My sister'll have us till we find another place,' Biddy answered. 'I wanted ye to know the truth, before some lie gets told to ye. Divil a reference we'll get either, if I know her. She'll be after tellin' Mr Frank we just walked out and left her flat when he was gone.'

'Don't worry about that,' Claudia said. 'I'll give you a reference. You won't need anything more than that. Have you any money, Biddy?'

Biddy said, 'We have. Mr Frank wrote us a cheque when he sacked us. We're all right for quite a time. I'm sorry about it, Mam. It's her comin' to live there that's the cause. There was never a cross word till she came. She's changed him. He's not the man he was.' She got up, and held out her hand.

Claudia shook it. 'He certainly has changed,' she said, 'if he'd be influenced by a creature like that.'

At the door Biddy turned back. 'There's an old sayin', Mam. If ye lie down with dirt, ye get up with fleas!'

Claudia couldn't have expressed it better.

The Half House was finished. The last curtain had been hung, the pictures were in place, and Mary Rose received her accolade from Kevin. With his arm round her waist he squeezed excitedly.

'Jesus, it's the grandest house in Kildare! We can give

those bastards a run for their money now.' He looked round him and laughed. 'Who'd a thought old Jack Ryan's son would live in a place like this, eh? I mind when I went to America, the auld man says to me, "Kevin," he says, "you'll come to no good leavin' your home. I'll have to give your share of the farm to Shamus now . . . " He didn't want to do it, Rose. I was more his favourite than me brother. But if he can see me now, I wonder what he'd say?'

'He'd be so proud of you,' Mary Rose said. She thought, it means more to Kev to own this house than to sit in the United States Senate. Irish roots ran deep indeed in native soil. 'It's all your doing,' she went on.

'And yours, darlin'.' He seldom used that word outside their infrequent lovemaking. Then it was more of a stimulus than an endearment. 'You made it look like it does. In spite of me,' he added slyly, and she smiled up at him.

He had questioned the light colour schemes and the foreign-looking furniture with all the gilded brass. He liked a warm red and big handsome mahogany pieces himself. But Rose had taste; so had the queer young decorator she'd brought in from Dublin. Kevin refused to call homosexuals gays on principle.

'We're going to give a party,' he announced. 'We're going to show the lot of them round here!'

She said, 'You won't be inviting those snobs of Protestants, surely. Not to our home?'

His brogue deepened. 'Sure, an' they wouldn't come. Do ye think I'd pour drink down the throats of Arbuthnot at Riverstown and his sort? Like fuckin' hell I would!'

'Kevin,' she protested. 'Not that word!'

'There isn't a better one for them,' he defended himself. 'They'll hear about it, but they won't be getting any invitation. Except for Frank. That'll get up their noses enough . . . and we'll have people from Dublin. I've a whole list, with the bank tied in with it all. It'll be a great party, Rose. And I want you lookin' like the Queen of Ireland on the night!'

Mary Rose chided herself. 'Oh Kev, I forgot to tell you, I was so excited this morning. Frank called. He wants to bring his sister over to meet you. I didn't know what to say.'

He frowned and said quickly, 'Why would he do that? Why would I want to be meeting her?' And then he paused and corrected himself. 'You didn't say anything, Rose, did ye? I don't want to upset him.'

'Of course I didn't,' she answered. 'He loves his sister; I told you that. I didn't say anything except you'd call him back.'

Kevin let go of her. He hunched his head forward still further, a sign of anxiety that Mary Rose knew very well. He was remembering his boast to the men of power in Boston. 'It's a blessing in disguise. This marriage cuts the last link with the Arbuthnots.' It seemed that he was wrong about that. He made up his mind.

'Let him bring her,' he said. 'We don't have to be over-friendly, just pleasant. It'll do no harm to show him we've no prejudice against her. You make the call, Rose. Tell him I'm tied up, and suggest they come tomorrow for a drink. That keeps it short.'

Then he excused himself and put in a call to Sean Filey at his consulting rooms. There were two members of the Dail he particularly wanted to come to the party, and Filey knew them well. The more support he gathered for the new banking venture, the easier it would be to attract genuine investment on a large scale. And that meant the sums being channelled through from America would be easier to conceal. There was a large shipment of arms and ammunition waiting for payment in the Middle East. That would be the first clandestine transaction, and he intended that Frank Arbuthnot should be responsible for making the payment. Once he had acted as paymaster for a Provo arms deal, he could never go back on his commitment to the Cause.

*

Claire had never felt more uncomfortable in her life. She had been tempted to tell Claudia, rather than sneak off and meet Frank, pretending they were going to choose a wedding present up in Dublin. Then she decided not to risk a row with her mother. For a row there would certainly be. Claudia was touchy and suffering from what Philip described as wedding fever. He was tolerant of her moods, and advised Claire to be the same. When she protested that she was the bride and ought to be the one with the nerves, he only laughed and said she was too Irish to be bothered by the odd arrangement going wrong. All her mother's English blood was coming out, that was the trouble.

The morning of the day she was going to meet Kevin Ryan behind his back, Philip gave her Blanche's Georgian necklace to wear on her wedding day. His mother had taken the family jewellery with her rather than surrender it to Eileen Ryan, but she was too honourable not to will it back to her son. Claire didn't know how to look him in the face when he handed her the big leather case and kissed her.

'That's my wedding present, darling,' he said.

'Oh, Dad! Oh, it's gorgeous. Are you quite sure?'

'Absolutely,' Philip answered. All the Arbuthnot brides for the last hundred years had worn that necklace on their wedding day. His daughter Claire would be the last. He didn't say so. Feeling deceitful and wretched, Claire went off to meet her brother, and drive in to the Half House by the back entrance.

He noticed immediately there was something wrong. She told him about the necklace.

'It's my own fault,' Claire said. 'It was cowardly of me to tell them lies. I should have said straight out where I was going.'

Frank disagreed. 'No, you shouldn't,' he said. He pulled the car in to the side of the road. 'Look, we don't have to go. I know I asked you because I'm fond of my uncle and I wanted you to meet him, and maybe you would like him too. But I shouldn't have mixed you up in this. I'm sorry, Clarry. Come on, we'll forget it.'

'No, we won't,' she said. 'The whole thing is so bloody stupid if you think about it. Why shouldn't you be friends with your own mother's brother? Why shouldn't I spend half an hour with him, and not feel like a criminal?'

'Because that's the way Ireland is,' he responded. 'Them and us. That's what I'm fighting against. But you don't have to; you'll be living in England soon and none of this will touch you any more.'

'Now you're making me feel guilty,' Claire said. 'Of course I'll care what happens at home! Don't you think I mind about you having to leave Riverstown and being only just on speaking terms with Dad and Claudia? Oh, do drive on, for God's sake . . . we're going to be late.'

Ryan was a small man and she hadn't expected that. Small and sharp-featured, with a curious head carriage like a tortoise poking out of its shell. His wife was very American, very polite and quite cold towards her. They both shook hands, said all the right things, while conveying their hostility. Claire had been brought up with good manners. She knew how to cope with a situation which was essentially unpromising and carry it off. She praised the house and decorations, which she privately thought rather vulgar and pretentious, and avoided all mention of the fact that her mother had lived there during her first marriage. Nobody said anything about the Hamiltons, but the significance of the change of ownership was implicit in the Senator's every word and gesture.

The Ryans were proprietary with Frank, which irritated her, and he was obviously very intimate with both of them. Subtly she was isolated. There was a triumphant undercurrent directed at her, as if Kevin Ryan had won a battle that she didn't know was being fought. In the end she got up to go, because the sense of being hated made her angry. And worried. Worried for Frank, who was so sure these people were his friends because of the blood tie.

'Thank you for showing me the house,' she said to Mary Rose. 'It's lovely. I'm sure you'll be very happy here.'

Ryan had a cool, dry hand that rested very briefly in hers as he said goodbye. He embraced his nephew.

'We'll see you soon, Frank. Mind yourself now.'

They drove off and she saw them standing side by side, and the Senator's wife waved, like someone in a Hollywood movie, as they rounded the corner and went through the back drive.

'They were a bit shy with you,' Frank said. 'They're normally very warm-hearted.'

Claire looked out of the window. 'I'm sure they are. I don't like either of them, Frank. And I don't trust him.'

'You've been prejudiced, that's why,' he said. 'Anyway, thanks for coming. For what it's worth, they both liked you. He told me so when we were leaving.'

Claire said, 'Then I'm wrong. I hope I am. Where are we going? This isn't the way home.'

'We're going to choose a wedding present,' he answered. 'That's what you told everyone at home and that's what we're going to do.'

'The only present I want from you is to make it up with Dad,' she said.

'I've told you, I'll try. But I wouldn't bank on him responding. I thought you might like some Waterford glass.'

'That sounds nice,' Claire said. Her eyes filled with tears. He was cold to her for the first time in their lives because she had said what she thought about that unpleasant man and his frosty wife. She felt hurt and confused. She didn't want to go to Dublin with him and choose Waterford glass or anything else. She wanted to go home to the safe haven of Riverstown. More than anything, she wanted to be with Neil.

'Well,' Mary Rose asked, when they went back inside. 'What did you make of her?'

He sneered. 'If I told you, you'd go on at me for using dirty language,' he said. 'She's typical of her class and her kind. She needs a boot up the ass. Come on, for Christ's sake let's have a decent drink and forget we had to have her here.' He poured himself a whiskey that made Mary Rose wince.

'I didn't take to her at all,' she said. 'So different from Frank. He's so warm and loving. You wouldn't think they were related. I'll have a vodka on the rocks, dear. And not too big.'

'He's different,' Kevin agreed, 'because he's my sister Eileen's son. He's a good lad. Don't worry about him.'

She sighed gently. 'If only he'd take to the Church,' she said. 'I pray every night that he will.'

Kevin sent down a quarter of the whiskey in one gulp. She was a good, almost a saintly woman, his wife. Too good to be told too much about the harsh realities of freeing Ireland. Let her pray on for his nephew.

'He'll come round in time,' he comforted. 'You said it yourself. God's grace is in him.'

There was a family dinner the night before the wedding. Neil's father had arrived and made a good impression. Philip liked him. Claudia had begun to relax, like a general in sight of victory. The caterers had been tamed, the flower arrangers had worked miracles in the church and the big marquee outside on the main lawn was a bower of flowers and foliage. Everything was poised for the next day, and there was an air of excitement throughout the household. Even Philip was infected and brought out a private bottle of vintage champagne for Colonel Fraser before the rest of the family arrived. There were twenty-three in all to dinner. Aunts and cousins and old uncles who'd dug themselves out of the bogs, as Claudia said, to celebrate Claire's marriage. God knew how some of them got there at all, they were so old. Philip actually thought two had died till he got letters from them. There were young relations giggling and laughing over their drinks, all dressed in evening clothes, Claudia looking very handsome in dark blue. And Claire in green, with the Arbuthnot necklace glittering in the light. Frank arrived early. His father introduced him.

'This is my son Frank, Colonel Fraser. I'll get you a glass. This is rather special.'

The Colonel smiled at him. 'I hear you're a banker,' he said amiably. He had light eyes and bushy eyebrows that were gingery grey. There were traces of Neil in him, the same staccato way of speaking that made everything sound like a command. His wife was dead; one less of them for Claire to cope with, was Frank's reaction.

He said, 'Yes, I'm opening a new merchant bank next month in Dublin. It's American-backed actually.'

'Oh? Well, that must be a good thing. Difficult times for you over here at the moment. Your father was just saying the trouble's started creeping down to the South. Robberies and things like that. I hope you'll have good security in your bank.'

Frank said quietly, 'I don't think we'll be in any danger. This is very good champagne.'

Then Claudia came in and she walked up to him in her purposeful way and kissed him briskly. 'Hallo, Frank. You've got a drink, I see. One for me, Philip darling. Claire's on her way down now. We must finish this bottle before the hordes arrive. You can't waste a '64 vintage on mere relatives." She laughed her hearty laugh, joined by Colonel Fraser.

Frank came up to his sister. For a moment he looked at her. The visit to Kevin Ryan and the silent, miserable trip to Dublin afterwards was forgotten at that moment, as if it had never happened.

'You look great,' he said. He wanted to put his arms round her and hold her as if they were children again, but he couldn't with everyone watching.

'Frank, darling,' she said. 'It's so wonderful to be all

together tonight. Look what Dad's given me.' She touched the circle of diamonds at her throat.

He said, 'I thought you'd wear them tomorrow.'

She led him towards her parents. 'Neil's given me the most marvellous pearl necklace. He's asked me to wear that instead. Dad doesn't mind, do you?' She linked her arm through Philip's and smiled up at him.

'Of course not,' he said. 'They're magnificent. Three perfectly matched rows. You're a very spoilt girl.'

Colonel Fraser beamed. The more he saw of his daughter-in-law and her parents, the more he liked them. The brother was a dour fellow. Neil hadn't talked about him much. Apparently he didn't come to Riverstown that often. Lovely bride she'd be, he thought. Do Neil a power of good to have a wife like that. Essential if he was going to get ahead in the party.

There was a knock on the door. Molly, eyes shining and pink-cheeked with excitement, came in to say, 'The cars are comin' up the drive, Mam,' and they exited into the hall to greet them. Claire was unashamedly happy. Everyone kissed her and exclaimed over her dress and Philip's wedding present, and after dinner she rushed upstairs and down again with Neil's pearls to show them all.

Frank was surrounded too, beset by relations he hadn't seen since he was very young. Some of the young cousins started flirting with him. He'd forgotten the warmth of being in a family circle. He was disappointed to find himself seated far away from Claire, but he dismissed as imagination the feeling that Claudia was keeping them apart. If only the bridegroom was different. If only this wedding meant she'd live in Ireland. Couldn't she look at that pompous old man and see that the son would end up like him? No, she couldn't. He forced himself once more to accept the inevitable and hide his feelings. She was so happy, he had no right to quibble. But why did she have to wear his bloody pearls instead of her own family heirloom? His anger fastened on that intrusion. When he was examining them, he was able to whisper to her.

'Clarry, don't you know the superstition? Pearls are tears. You should wear Dad's present on your wedding day.'

'You've been listening to Sheena and Molly,' she teased him. 'Tears, my eye. Don't be silly, Frank. Besides, I'm wearing that sapphire pin you gave me. It's my "something blue".'

'Are you? That's very sweet of you.'

She thought, Oh God, I know he's so unhappy deep down. 'It's like taking a bit of you down the aisle with me,' she said quietly. 'I love Neil, but it won't make any difference to us. You'll always be my best friend.'

Philip watched them from his place on the sofa, murmuring a word here and there to his cousin Alice, who'd come all the way from Cork. How could Claire be so fond of him? He didn't understand it. He would never understand how his son could inspire that degree of loyalty and affection. Now he could look at him and admit that he had never found him lovable; never felt him a congenial companion, either as a child or a man. He had concealed his dislike and his contempt for his son ever since Claire's engagement was announced. But after tomorrow there would be no need to pretend. He had been to see his solicitors and the changes had been made. If he died that very night, Riverstown was safe from Frank Arbuthnot. Safe from the kind of man who had thrown the Mahoneys out on the word of a slut who didn't know how to treat them. Safe from the sponging intellectuals who frequented his house in Meath, flattering the rich fool that they accepted him as one of themselves. Safe from the native enemy who wanted to destroy everything the Arbuthnots represented.

He sipped a nightcap whiskey and decided that his daughter ought to go to bed if she weren't to be tired for her wedding. Frank was staying with them that night. It was the last time he would sleep under the roof of Riverstown.

Neil and his best man stayed at Lawlor's Hotel the night before the wedding. Breaking with tradition, he had seen Claire in the afternoon of the family dinner party and given her his present. He had felt shy and uncertain of himself for the first time. He was in an alien environment, however friendly and well disposed. They were a very close-knit group of people, many interrelated, all with similar backgrounds. And there were so many of them. Cousins and half-uncles and great-aunts.

The Frasers were thin on the ground, their own friends few in number. He'd already arranged a large reception at the House of Commons after their honeymoon. That would take care of his political and social obligations. He couldn't wait to get the ceremony and the reception over with, and take Claire away. The pearl necklace was not a family heirloom. His grandfather was a middle-class businessman who'd made a fortune. He wouldn't have dreamed of spending thousands of hard-earned pounds on jewellery for his wife. Neil had seen the old diamond necklace and felt inferior because he had nothing comparable to give her. He had heard people in Ireland talking derisively of 'new money' and felt it was probably said about him.

They didn't care about being rich. They were the least material-minded human beings he had ever met. Money bought a good horse or paid for a day's betting on the Curragh. It helped maintain the big houses nobody could afford to heat and look after properly, but the houses weren't status symbols and if they had to be sold off, nobody thought the less of you. It was all so different from the attitude in England. Victorian values would have been greeted with hoots of laughter in that easygoing company. Men of ambition were suspect. If he'd been required to live in Ireland, Neil would have withered with boredom and frustration. He found the relentless drinking very difficult. And he hated the changeable climate, where sun blasted briefly through the heavy clouds before the next downpour of rain.

But he said nothing to Claire. He didn't want to say or

do anything that might disturb the wonderful harmony between them. Neil had expected pre-wedding storms and rows. Everyone had them, he was told. But Claire was sunny and sweet, joyously excited about their marriage. He loved her so much that it was like a physical ache when they were apart. He had made an effort to get on easy terms with her brother, but that proved impossible. One family lunch at Riverstown was not enough to break through to him. It was an uncomfortable experience. Neil wasn't over-sensitive to atmosphere, but the chill between father and son and the painful anxiety of Claire made him squirm. And filled him with impatience. He thought it a poisonous situation and the sooner Claire was out of it the better.

He woke up that morning to see the sky bright blue outside the hotel window and his marriage only a few hours away. By eight o'clock they would be on the plane for Paris. And then on to Cannes the next morning. He had asked her to wear his pearls on the day. He didn't understand why it was so important to him. He would have denied that it was laying claim to her against her family. If she would break the tradition and defy the idiotic Irish superstition about pearls and sorrow, he would feel she'd taken a further step to independence. By which he meant dependence upon him. But he would have hotly denied that too.

'Of course I'll wear them, darling.' Her response had been instant. 'I'm wearing the little blue brooch Frank gave me. I'll have something from the two people I love best in the world.'

He had needed all the warmth of her kiss to reassure him, even so.

Marie Dempster was at the back of the crowd that gathered outside the church in Naas. She had slept so badly the night before, the dark glasses were a boon as well as a disguise. There was no need for Frank to stay at Riverstown. Risking a quarrel, she had reminded him of the way he'd been turned out, of his rejection and humiliation because he refused to submit and deny his mother's family. He didn't see through her; he thought she was reproaching him for being weak and compromising. But the attack bounced back at her.

'I don't have your bitter heart,' he said, and she recoiled. 'This is my sister's wedding. Nothing is going to spoil her day. She hopes my father and I will make it up. I don't believe we will. But we'll all be together at home for that one night. If you see it as a betrayal, I see it as just good manners. Now, let's drop the subject.'

She was frightened that she'd gone too far. She didn't mention it again. So she set out in the car to drive to Naas and see the famous wedding. See the sister come out in her white finery and stand there smiling, while Marie skulked in the crowd to get a glimpse of her. It was self-torture, but she couldn't help it. There had been a brief shower and some threatening clouds which lifted, driven by a light wind. The crowd round the church door was growing denser as passers-by joined in. The Irish love weddings and funerals, Marie thought. Any excuse to gawp, be it a bride or a corpse. There was a burst of organ music and the knots of people, mostly women and girls, craned forward. The sun actually shone as Claire stepped out of the doorway on her new husband's arm.

There was an official photographer snapping at them, calling for the bridesmaids to come forward. Claire and Neil stood smiling and posing for a few minutes. She didn't see the woman in the headscarf and sunglasses. There was no portent of the future. Then they got into the big car with its festoon of white ribbons, and drove off to waves from the crowd. Marie turned and vanished before the guests came pouring out. She couldn't risk Frank seeing her.

The reception went on long after the bride and groom had driven off to Dublin airport. Everyone kept saying what a grand party it had been and what a beautiful girl she was. Claudia had a lot of champagne. She was tired, triumphant and happy. Claire was married and from now

on all would be well. She saw her step-son and her smile
died away. His power was broken now. Thank God.
Thank God she wouldn't have to pretend any more. He
moved towards her. She looked round for Philip, but
couldn't see him. A number of guests were staying on
in the hope of being asked to have dinner. She hoped
he wouldn't be one of them. Frank came up.

'That was a wonderful wedding, Claudia,' he said. 'I
don't know how you organized it all so well.'

'It came together at the end,' she said. She drank more
champagne. 'The service was lovely, I thought. And she
looked a dream. He's such a sweetie; they'll be very
happy.'

He said quietly, 'I hope so. I can't see my father. I
want to say goodbye.' Claudia raised her eyebrows.
Frank could see that she was a little drunk.

'Oh, must you rush off? Well, it's been a long day.
There's Philip, over there talking to Colonel Fraser.
Goodbye, Frank.'

They didn't kiss or shake hands. 'Goodbye, Claudia.'

Colonel Fraser said, 'Are you leaving? Oh, what a
pity. Well, it's been a wonderful day. Wonderful
wedding.' He shook hands with Frank and said it again.
'Simply splendid, the whole thing.'

Philip hesitated. He didn't want his son to stay. And
yet it mustn't become embarrassing for Neil's father.

He said, 'Are you sure you can't stay? We've provided
some kind of buffet for the hangers-on.'

'No, I'm sorry,' Frank said. 'I've arranged something.
I'll see you soon, Dad. Goodbye, Colonel.'

'Nice lad,' Fraser said. 'Strong family likeness
between you. I suppose he'll be the next to take the step,
eh?'

Philip ignored the remark. He saw his son edge
through the group of guests, pausing to speak and then
move on, till he left the marquee. Philip realized at that
moment that he had lost his daughter and was suddenly
sad.

'I'm going to get a decent drink,' he announced. He

went off to find the two things that always eased him if he were troubled. Whiskey and Claudia.

The flight from Dublin to Paris was smooth. Neil held Claire's hand. He felt the wedding ring on her finger. She was his wife now. Their life together had really begun. He pressed his knee hard against hers and whispered that he couldn't wait to get to the hotel. He wanted her so much. Everything about her excited him; it was as if they'd never slept together and it would be a new discovery. Claire let him touch her when nobody could see. The warm tide of sex lapped round her. It had been a wonderful day. A day of happy memories that she would savour long afterwards. And she loved Neil as well as wanting him to make love to her. They were going to be ideally happy.

Poor Frank, she thought. He's going to miss me. But maybe he'll find someone. Someone really special who'll make up to him for everything. I'll ask him to come over and stay for a few days as soon as we get back.

Frank didn't go back to Meath. He started the car and drove to the exit on to the Sallins Road. He stopped in the gateway and then turned right. Claire was gone.

He noticed the little sapphire pin, transferred from her wedding dress to her bright red suit, as she came and kissed him goodbye. She wore a flowery hat that pricked his cheek. He would never forget that moment, because it finally changed his life. More fundamentally than his leaving Riverstown. Her love had always been his anchor. It hadn't lessened, but there was another kind of love which Neil could give her. There would be children, a new life, a home made out of Ireland, so that the sea separated them. For all her promises that nothing would change their old relationship, Frank knew that from now on it could never be the same. He drove steadily down the road through Sallins, slowing as he came to the railway bridge. There was the familiar figure of Donny, engrossed in his wait for the train that didn't come. He didn't stop the car; Donny didn't notice him or wave.

He went on, driving with resolution now. His father's last remark was a slip of the tongue, he realized that. Philip would never be cruel in a petty way. 'We've provided some kind of buffet for the hangers-on.' It was a Freudian slip, if you believed in that sort of thing. His friend Sean Filey would explain it in his grave way, as if that took the sting out of it. Frank didn't want Filey, or Marie, who'd be waiting, trying to hide her jealousy, when he got home. He indicated and swung left through the entrance to the Half House. It looked warm and friendly, with the lights blazing in the ground-floor windows.

Kevin Ryan opened the front door to him. 'Frankie,' he exclaimed. 'This is a turn-up for the book – come in, come in!'

Frank said simply, 'Can I take a drink off you, Uncle?'

Kevin saw the morning suit and knew he'd come direct from the wedding party at Riverstown.

'You can take supper and a bed for the night if you want,' he said.

The door closed firmly behind them both. It was late when he suggested that Frank might like to give Marie Dempster a call and get her to come over . . . wasn't it time she met Mary Rose anyway . . . ? Frank didn't object. He'd forgotten she was at Meath; he'd almost forgotten the wedding and his father letting him go off alone while the ragtag of spongers were made welcome. He was drunk, and he had Kevin to thank for it. Not drunk so that he slurred his words or missed his footing. Anaesthetized was the right description. Feeling no pain, as the English said, and then brayed their empty laughter afterwards. He hated them. He hated the man who had taken Claire away from him. He hated his stepmother because she had encouraged the whole thing. He hated his father because he hadn't ever been as kind to him as his poor dead mother's brother Kevin. But he wasn't hurt any more.

Mary Rose whispered to her husband, 'Do you think she ought to come over? I mean, okay they live together, but he's never introduced her socially.'

Kevin grinned. He knew what she meant, and he thought the mixture of snobbery and prudishness quite funny. But then he'd a few drinks in him too.

'She's his girl,' he said. 'It's her place to be with him tonight. She'll ease him.' He eyed Mary Rose and thought, And you'll ease me, whether you like it or not. We'll warm the bed tonight, and the house next week. He said, 'We're all part of the same family, Rose. He's our kin, and she's a grand girl. I'll make the call. She'll come.'

He met Marie in the hall. Jesus, he thought, peering at her, Frank's the lucky one.

'Your man's drunk,' he said. 'And not surprising. He comes here like a stray dog after the grand Arbuthnot weddin'. Go in and look after him. Sure, you can stay the night with us.'

'No thanks, Senator Ryan.' She answered formally, and without warmth. 'I've come to take him home. He'll be better there with me.'

Ryan eyed her, and this time without admiration. A cool, uppity piece. She could do with a boot up *her* arse.

'Suit yerself,' he said. 'He's through in the sittin' room. Mrs Ryan's there with him.'

She wouldn't take a drink. She shook hands with the little American woman and wondered how someone so dainty in herself could fall for a yob like Kevin Ryan. Then she got Frank on his feet and, with her arm supporting him, he walked outside and got into her car. His own, she explained, would be collected later, if they didn't mind. He fell asleep as she drove. She glanced at him briefly. Sleeping, he looked vulnerable. Drunkards disgusted her, but there was nothing maudlin or undignified about him. Just sad, so that she ached to make him love her and be happy. She thought, maybe it'll happen now. Now that she's gone. Maybe he'll see me with new eyes.

Claudia woke the next morning with a hangover. Philip was already up. She called out to him.

'Darling, are you in the bath?'

The door opened and he came out. 'No. Don't you want to go back to sleep? You must be exhausted after yesterday.'

She smiled. 'I am a bit tired. And I've got a fairly bloody hangover. But wasn't it a great success?'

Philip sat on the bed beside her. 'Yes, it certainly was a good wedding. All due to you. Clever old thing.' He leaned forward and kissed her. 'I miss her, don't you?' he said. 'I keep expecting her to come in and say good morning.'

Claudia gripped his hand. 'So do I. When I woke up I thought, I must ask Claire how she enjoyed it. Silly, but she's very dear.'

Philip said, 'She'll be all right with Neil, that's the main thing. He's a good man. Bit stuffy and English, but she'll change all that. I must say, she looked a picture.'

Claudia looked at her watch. 'Where's Sheena got to with the tea? She's always late, that girl. But they were good, weren't they? Worked like blacks to get everything ready. Those bloody Dublin caterers got my back up . . .'

Philip smiled. Claudia had declared war on the caterers from the start and the household staff had joined in the fun, running with complaints about the professionals from the city. Everyone had enjoyed watching the missus doing battle, and adding a little fuel to the fire.

She sighed and leaned back on the pillows. 'We've got to drive Jack Fraser to the airport,' she said. 'As soon as I've had my tea I'll get up. He's rather nice, when you get to know him a bit. He's very fond of Claire.'

'So he should be,' Philip retorted. 'He was even nice about Frank.'

Claudia said, 'What are you going to do about that?'

'About my will? I've done it.'

She sat upright, her eyes wide. 'Oh, my God,' she

said. 'You mean you've changed your will already? Why didn't you tell me?'

'You had other things on your mind,' he answered. 'It's all done: signed, witnessed and lodged with Hunter. I've left Riverstown to you. Unentailed.'

Claudia heard the knock on the door and said, 'Come in, 'morning Sheena,' as the tea-tray was set on the night table. Then she looked up at Philip. She chewed her lip, and then stopped because it hurt.

'I don't think you should do this,' she said. 'He is your only son. Can't you tie it up in a trust, put conditions round his inheriting?'

'No,' Philip said flatly. 'The conditions I'd place on his taking over Riverstown wouldn't stand up in any Irish court. That was Hunter's view. I've left the house and everything to you, darling. My hope is that you'll leave it to Claire's son, if she has one. But there are no strings. There's no way Frank can fight you because you're my wife and entitled to my property.'

'Oh, Christ,' Claudia sighed again. 'What happens when he finds out? What on earth is he going to say to me?'

'Oh, I'm going to let him know myself,' Philip said. He took up the teapot and poured two cups. 'Nobody's going to blame you. I've made the decision and if he wants to kick up a row, he can do it with me. Here you are, drink this.'

She took the cup and sipped. 'What's Claire going to say?'

'I'm safeguarding you,' he said. 'That's what I'll tell her. We can't worry about that. She's got a life of her own now. She was far too wrapped up in Frank anyway.'

Claudia said, 'She was rather. Darling, go and have your bath.'

When he had gone she poured some more tea and lit a cigarette. He hated her smoking in bed. It all sounded so calm and reasonable, but she knew it wasn't. It was a blow aimed at her step-son's heart. She wondered how clear her own conscience was in respect of Philip's decision. She didn't like Frank. Perhaps if she hadn't had Claire, she might have accepted him more as her own. And she had seen the brother and sister draw closer together when they should have been moving away. That had worried her, even frightened her. Philip had noticed too. It was the first time he had made any comment, but he had noticed.

Was that why he hated his son? Because only hatred could account for what Philip had done. First turning him out of the house. They'd quarrelled. She remembered the scene only too well, and her own furious reaction to the stupidity of both. But all families rowed, and then made up. Even if they weren't very fond, it was the tribal instinct to keep the family intact. Philip had thrust his son out. The excuse sounded thin, even to her. Perhaps he had always resented his existence and subconsciously wanted to be rid of him. Not because he felt he had too much influence over Claire; Claudia dismissed that. But for other, deeper reasons. Her head ached and she stubbed out the cigarette.

She didn't want to take Frank's inheritance. She didn't need Riverstown, and if Philip died first, she took it for granted that she would move out and his son would move in. She remembered her own Hamilton mother-in-law digging herself into the Half House till Claudia paid for a little house out of her own pocket to get rid of her.

She didn't like her step-son, but she didn't want to hurt him. She thought, Philip has left me an option. If I don't say anything, it might still be all right. If Frank sees sense, and there's plenty of time, then I can simply give it to him later on . . . She contented herself with that. Besides, she knew her husband. Once he had made up his mind, nothing she or anyone else could say would change it. She got up and started hunting for the aspirin.

The Boston Irish Bank opened with a lunch party and an evening reception on 15 July. The lunch was limited to investors from the United States and the Irish institutions. The Chairmen of the Bank of Ireland and of the Allied Irish Bank were present, with members of the Dail from both political parties. Marie made all the arrangements and hired staff and caterers. She had been appointed Frank's personal secretary and assistant. She didn't attend the lunch, which was for men only, but she stood close beside him at the large cocktail party that evening.

Sean Filey was among the guests. He stood in the main hall of the handsome Georgian building in Merrion Square, with one of the principals from Boston. He noticed the flower arrangements, the efficient waiters, the smooth way in which Marie moved among their guests, greeting those she knew and asking others if they had everything they wanted. She had changed, he thought, changed as fast as only a woman can when she adopts a different lifestyle. There was little of the small-town secretary visible in the beautifully dressed woman playing hostess to the top men in Irish business and politics that night. She looked happy and self-assured. An actress revelling in a star part. Only Filey knew that the audience was just one man. She had become obsessed with Frank Arbuthnot. Everything she did was to gain his approval and draw him closer. She acted with Filey too, pretending that Frank was under her influence.

'I'll talk to him,' she'd say, when they had their meetings in the house on the airport road. 'He'll do it if I ask him.'

Filey wasn't deceived. He saw the insecurity behind the façade. Most of all, he saw the absence of emotional love in Frank Arbuthnot. Generous, yes. She had a red Mercedes, real jewellery, even the ultimate bourgeois status symbol: a mink coat. He was kind and considerate; Sean had seen them together often enough to notice how well he treated Marie. He gave her the kind of respect that a man gives to a woman he doesn't love, just because he doesn't love her. And in her heart, he reckoned, Marie knew. He was interrupted in his analysis by the American beside him.

'Well, we're off to a helluva good start. Kevin promised and Kevin delivered. He always does.' He looked at Sean Filey and grinned.

'I'd say it was Frank's father who delivered,' Filey remarked. 'Come on over and meet our best young poet. He's there, talking to the crew from RTE.'

'No,' the American said. 'I don't want any goddamn TV coverage. What do you mean, Frank's father? I don't get you!'

'He cut Frank off, left the family house and everything to his English wife. I think that's what really brought him over to our side. But don't let's spoil the Senator's claim to glory.'

He smiled, and Ryan's Boston friend thought, what a snide son of a bitch, and moved away.

It was a great success. There was wide coverage in the newspapers and on television. The new merchant bank was well supported in Ireland and its American affiliates were men of wealth and social prominence. Kevin Ryan was on the board, but he kept a very low profile, refused interviews and disappointed those who hoped he might enter political controversy on the side of the Catholic minority in the North. He brushed all suggestions aside. He was in Ireland as a private citizen. He and his family had a home in Kildare, close enough to his brother's place, and he was very happy to talk about that. The big house-warming party he gave was closed to the media, and gradually interest in him died down because not long afterwards he returned to the States.

By the end of September, Frank Arbuthnot joined his uncle in Boston. Marie stayed in Ireland. She was busy finalizing the transfer of the money from the Middle East via Italy and finally Lucerne, before Frank arranged its channel through to clients in the bank. The shipment of arms would set out from Holland as soon as the payment was completed. There was new staff at Meath. They came through Sean, who recommended them to Frank. A good couple, he said, very reliable and honest. One of their younger boys had got into trouble for doing drill up in the mountains. It was only kids playing at being patriots, but the boy got six months and the father lost his job. It would be a kindness to give them a home. Frank agreed immediately. Sean wasn't surprised. He knew how to make Frank Arbuthnot feel guilty. He would never have credited him with a kind heart. The Brogans' son had been sentenced for possessing explosives, and was a dangerous man with two violent robberies to his credit. The Brogans knew where their duty lay. And this time, Marie had no servant trouble. She talked like that sometimes, until Sean rebuked her.

'You're becoming a little lady from Foxrock,' he said, and the contempt pulled her back on course.

The money for the arms deal went through and the shipment came into Ulster via a fishing boat. There was a notable rise in attacks on British troops during the next six months.

Frank Arbuthnot was committed now beyond any hope of opting out. His life assumed a regular pattern. He made three trips a year to the States on bank business. Once he took Marie with him and they flew down to Florida for a holiday. He and she worked a five-day week in Merrion Square.

There were regular secret meetings in the house on the airport road. He didn't know that Marie's visits to her family or to see old friends were a cover for her attendance at those meetings. Once she suggested that he might be included. Jim Quinlan, the senior Provisional officer, looked at her and said flatly. 'No. He's with us because his own kind turned him out. He's still one of them. I've never trusted a bloody Anglo and I never will.'

Filey didn't disagree. Afterwards he said to her, 'That was stupid, Marie. Jim didn't like you saying that. He's told me to have a word with you.'

'They've had more money in the last year through Frank than they've had since the trouble started,' she protested. 'He works heart and soul for the Cause.'

'So do we all,' was Filey's answer. 'When's his next trip to England, by the way?'

She flushed. 'What's that got to do with it?'

He said, 'You don't mind then? You don't mind being left alone while he goes to see her?'

Marie turned away from him. 'Why should I mind if he spends a few days with his sister? She's the only family he's got left.'

'I'm glad you've stopped being jealous,' Filey remarked. 'All the same, Jim's right. We trust him as far as we need to, and no further. Your first duty is to the Cause. That's why you're with him. Remember that.'

She went from the meeting first, to get home before Frank.

Jim Quinlan spoke to Sean Filey on one side.

'Did you put her straight?'

'I did. She meant no harm; she's a sensible girl.' He lit the senior officer's cigarette for him.

'Keep a watch on her,' he said, drawing in smoke. 'Sensible girl or not, she's living with the bastard. We don't want her getting too involved with him. Just in case we change our mind about him.'

'Don't worry about Marie,' Filey assured him. 'I'll vouch for her.'

Jim glanced at him. 'Give her a miss for the next couple of meetings,' he said. 'Let her cool her heels for a bit. I'll be off now, or I'll be late for duty.' He worked as a guard on the railway.

Marie drove home to Meath. The Brogans had everything ready when she got in. The fire was lit in the big drawing room, the curtains drawn. There was ice in the bucket and the drinks set out. They were efficient and hard-working, because they took their orders from her and not from Frank Arbuthnot who paid them. She poured herself a vodka and tonic, kicked off her shoes and sank down on the sofa. She was the mistress of the house and the mistress of the man who owned it. She could do what she liked, spend what she wanted, change this and that, and he never demurred. But the photograph of Claire Fraser stood inviolate in its silver frame on the piano. Once she had put it away. He hadn't been in the room five minutes before he noticed.

'Don't you dare touch that,' he exploded at her. She hadn't made that mistake again. But hatred of the smiling image grew until she couldn't sit where she could see it. That bastard Sean, she thought, tasting the sharpness of the vodka. Putting the knife in and turning it. 'You don't mind being left while he goes to see her.'

Mind! Those visits nearly drove her mad, and worst of all was the need to hide her feelings. She hadn't stopped being jealous, as he so cruelly suggested. She was more jealous and insecure than ever. Frank was isolated from his family, his sister lived in England, he had been totally rejected by his own father. He should have turned to her and responded to her love for him. But he didn't. He gave her presents and had settled money on her – Filey didn't know about *that*, she thought spitefully – they worked together and slept together, but he had never said he loved her. And now that bitch was having her first baby and he was booked in to fly over as soon as it was born.

She heard the front door open, and jumped up quickly, hunting for her shoes. She emptied the glass of vodka and put it back on the tray. When he called she came out to the hall to meet him. She smiled and kissed him. He put his arms round her. His affection had begun to cause her pain rather than hope.

'Hello,' he said. 'How was your mother?'

'Not too bad,' she lied. 'It cheered her up to see me. We had a good old chat, and she loves that. Were you busy?'

He nodded. She linked her arm through his and drew him into the room where the fire beckoned.

'Busy enough,' Frank said.

'Did you miss me?' She made it sound coquettish.

He smiled. 'How could I? I had Mrs Warren sitting on my knee all afternoon.'

Marie trilled her laughter. Mrs Warren was the ugliest

and stoutest of all the secretaries. So funny, but not the answer she craved: 'Of course I missed you, darling.'

'I'll get you a drink,' she said.

Frank relaxed in an armchair. All the chairs were giant-sized in the house. Marie nearly disappeared if she curled up in one.

'I don't really want one,' he said.

She turned and looked at him. She had one weapon to fight with, and she was using it more and more. She went over and turned the key in the door.

'If you don't want a drink,' she said, moving towards him and lowering herself on to his knee. 'How about this . . .' and she guided his hand to her breast.

'Darling,' Neil Fraser said. 'What a clever girl you are.'

He held Claire's hand. She opened her eyes and smiled at him. He thought she looked more beautiful than ever. But very tired and pale, with a luminous softness that touched him deeply. As deeply as the sight of his baby son.

'He's sweet, isn't he?' she said. 'It didn't take too long, either.'

He said, 'I'm sorry I didn't stay to the end. I couldn't take the last part. Seeing you in pain.' He brought her hand up to his lips.

'Don't be silly, darling,' she said gently. 'It wasn't as bad as all that.'

She had refused an anaesthetic, insisting upon experiencing her baby's birth. That and Neil's flight from the delivery room hadn't endeared them to the gynaecologist.

'Are you glad it's a boy?' she asked him. 'I knew you wanted one, though you never said so.'

'I'm just glad it's a healthy baby,' Neil admitted. 'I kept thinking while I was waiting downstairs, I don't care about anything so long as Claire's all right. I'm so proud of you, and I love you so much.'

She saw there were tears in his eyes. She was surprised. She had imagined him being proud and pleased, behaving like a typical first-time father with a boy as a bonus. But not like this. He was more emotional than she had ever seen him. He did love her. More than when they married nearly two years ago. Even when she was sick and clumsy and short-tempered carrying the baby, he had surprised her by his patience and care. I'm very lucky, she thought. I should be glowing with happiness. But I'm not. I wasn't sorry when they took the baby away. It was such an awful anticlimax . . . I'm just very tired and it was all a bit of a shock. I'll glow tomorrow, I expect.

He said eagerly, 'You are happy about him, aren't you, darling? It wasn't too bloody for you, was it?'

'No,' she said. 'Of course it wasn't. Have you rung everyone?'

He nodded. 'I phoned as soon as I heard. Father's delighted, and I got through to Philip and Claudia. They're thrilled. They're flying over tomorrow.'

Claire said after a moment, 'Did you let Frank know?'

'There wasn't time. I came straight in to see you as soon as I'd spoken to Claudia. I'll do it later.'

'Don't worry.' She squeezed his hand. 'I'll speak to him. Why don't you go home, darling? You've been hanging round here all night.'

'I'm all right,' he insisted. 'But you're tired, aren't you?'

'I am a bit,' Claire admitted. He bent over and kissed her.

'Thank you,' he murmured. 'He'll be a great little chap. Now you sleep and I'll be round at lunch-time.'

She turned to watch him to the door; he paused before closing it and waved almost shyly at her. Then she was alone. The whole wrenching experience had left her numb and shocked. But she wouldn't say so to Neil. He'd been so anxious about her, almost guilty because she was suffering pain. And he was so pleased. That was very touching. The baby was sweet. Poor little thing, she thought, it can't have been much fun for him. Her parents would be thrilled with their first grandchild.

They'd be ringing everyone. All the relatives in the four corners of Ireland, toasting the new baby. Corks popping and congratulations. No one had let her brother know. She stretched out her hand and touched the bell. The nurse came in very quickly.

'Hello, Mrs Fraser. I'm Nurse Adams. I've just come on duty. How are you feeling?' She thought Mrs Fraser looked grey-faced and exhausted. She must have had a rough time. Still, these people with their natural childbirth . . . 'Bit tired, I expect,' she said, not waiting for an answer.

Claire said, 'I'd like the telephone plugged in, please.'

Ten minutes later she was speaking to Frank in Ireland.

'You're an uncle,' she said. 'Little boy. Yes, he's fine . . . I'm okay. Well, it wasn't much fun. Don't ever have a baby if you can help it. No, of course I'm all right . . . I'm not crying . . . Frank, when are you coming over? I wish you were here now.' The tears were rolling down her face, soaking the pillow. 'Neil's absolutely thrilled. Everyone's thrilled except me. I feel as flat as a bloody pancake. I don't know what's the matter with me – no, Mum and Dad will be over tomorrow. I don't care. I want you to come, please. You're the godfather, remember. How's Ireland? Give it my love.'

She listened to him talking for a few moments. All her life he had been near to comfort her. She didn't understand why, but she had never needed him as much as she did now, and he was miles away across the Irish Sea. And the telephone line crackled, making it difficult to hear.

The nurse opened the door. 'Mrs Fraser, I think you should go to sleep now.'

Claire didn't have the energy to argue. It had taken enough effort to get the telephone in the first place.

'I'll ring off now,' she said. 'Let me know when you're coming. Yes, I will. Goodbye, Frank love.'

Obediently she let the nurse arrange the pillows and

settled down to sleep. She closed her eyes. Her husband was delighted. Her parents were thrilled. She had a new baby son. The tears went on trickling. She felt lonely and homesick, and nothing seemed to matter at all.

Marie had been listening to the telephone call. She came forward with lying words of congratulations, but Frank didn't seem to hear them.

'There's something wrong,' he said.

Hope flared in her. 'Oh, no! Your sister's all right, isn't she? Is it the baby?' She didn't hope for that.

He said impatiently, 'The baby's fine. But she doesn't sound right. I swear she was crying when she rang off.' He was frowning.

Marie said, 'Oh, I shouldn't worry about that. Lots of women cry after they've had a baby. It's quite normal.' She shrugged a little as if it needn't be considered.

Frank looked at her. 'Not Claire,' he said. 'I know my sister. I'd better go to London today.'

'If she's depressed,' Marie said after a moment, 'surely her husband's the one to deal with it.'

He didn't answer. She wasn't sure if he was silent because he was angry or because she had touched a sore spot. 'I must go to London today.' In the name of Christ, Marie cried out inwardly, hasn't she got a husband and a mother and a father if she needs looking after? Why does it have to be *you* who goes running?

He said suddenly, 'You're right. Of course, you're right. But she won't tell him. She'll put a brave face on it. We had a cousin who got post-natal depression. She was ill for three years. I'll speak to him.'

At the end of ten days Frank flew to London. Claudia and Philip had only just gone back and Claire was about to go home. She was feeling a lot better. The sense of sinking misery had stopped, thanks to the prompt treatment which resulted from Frank's warning to Neil. She didn't know why Neil spent so much time with her, or why the baby was put beside her for long periods with the nurse sitting, chatting, in the room. She saw her parents and didn't notice they were worried, or realize that she passed days crying for no reason. The room was so full of flowers they had to put the vases on the floor and into the corridor at night. Neil had given her a ruby brooch which must have cost a fortune.

She felt better but she kept asking when her brother was coming, and she didn't see the look of anguish on her husband's face every time the question was accompanied by more tears. And then he did come. The door of her room opened and instead of Neil, or the doctor or her nurse, there was Frank with a big bunch of flowers wrapped in cellophane.

The pills and the therapy were working, but when she saw him the last cloud lifted and she laughed with real joy. She rang for the baby and felt quite moved for the first time when she held him. Frank said what a fine little fellow he was. She talked and talked about the birth, as if now she could speak the truth and not pretend she hadn't hated it and been afraid. He listened and stayed beside her, his finger caught in the sleeping baby's tiny fist.

At last Claire sank back and said, 'I've nearly burst keeping all that in!' And he knew she was not in danger any more.

Outside the room he met Neil. They shook hands. Neil Fraser looked years older, he thought, than the last time they had had dinner in a London hotel. And now there was something in his eyes which he didn't even try to hide.

'How is she?' he asked.

Frank said, 'She'll be fine now. But I wouldn't rush into another baby.'

Neil said slowly, 'So I've been told. I'm sure it's done her a lot of good to see you. She's coming home tomorrow. Why don't you come and stay for a few days? I know she'd like that.'

Frank said, 'That's very kind of you, Neil. If you think it'll help, I'd be delighted. But I don't want to be in your way.'

'Not at all. Do come. Make it in time for dinner.' He

turned, reaching for the door handle. 'See you then,' he said and went inside.

He saw the brightness in her face and his heart was light for the first time since the baby was born. She was better and she held out her arms to him with her old warmth. But relief was mixed with a new pain. He had been shown the brave face. She had turned to her brother for help. For all they were married and had a child, Claire still didn't really belong to him.

The child was christened in the old Norman church in Gloucestershire. Claire looked well and happy, holding the baby in her arms for the photographers outside. There were four godparents: her brother Frank, a Hamilton cousin, a distant relative of Neil's and the star of the quartet, an influential member of the Tory 1922 Committee. Claudia and Philip stayed for the weekend, with Neil's father. A brisk young nanny looked after the little boy. He'd been christened Peter Francis Hugh.

His uncle Frank was in America, but he sent a cable and gave a handsome Irish silver mug. He was right not to come; Claire accepted that. Neil was secretly relieved. There would be no embarrassment, no atmosphere to spoil the day. Frank and his father were not on speaking terms. Personally he thought it incredible for Philip to cut his only son out of his will because they disagreed about politics. Ireland was such a mixture of muddle and prejudice that none of it made sense.

Claire was in blooming health after a holiday in Portugal. She was more beautiful, he thought proudly, watching her against the background of a sunny English garden. Tanned and thin again, with a mature self-confidence. His colleagues in the House said she was the perfect wife for a rising politician. Now that his personal life was settled into a routine – wife, baby, country house and London flat near the division bell – Neil began to concentrate intensely upon his career. Claire was full of enthusiasm; their sex life was as satisfying as ever. There was nothing to stand in the way of his career. It was the best way of forgetting that in spite of all the benefits, a gap had opened up between them since the baby's birth. Seeing her animated and laughing with their friends, Neil sometimes wondered if he were not imagining a subtle change in their relationship.

The girl had grown into a woman. She had lost the curious innocence which had attracted him when they first met. It was said that Irish society kept its young women unsophisticated by contrast with their English sisters. Neil used to laugh at Claire for being childish. He longed for that vanished simplicity now. A stranger lurked behind the ready smile, and held aloof from their heated lovemaking. He was aware of it even on this special day, when the sun shone and his child cheeped like a contented nestling in Claire's arms. But he was a man who despised self-pity and suspected flights of imagination. His emotions had been in low gear until he married; now he was determined to get them under control again. Work was the cure for weakness and self-doubt.

From the day of the christening, Neil set himself a new priority. He was going to rise in the newly elected Tory Party. His son was eighteen months old when Neil Fraser was made a Junior Minister in the Prime Minister's first Cabinet reshuffle.

Three months later there was a report in *The Times*, with a photograph, of his brother-in-law addressing an audience in New York on behalf of Noraid, with some of the most notorious IRA supporters in the city perched in a row on the platform behind him.

He knew Claire had seen it. He waited for her to comment, but she never said a word. She lunched with him at the House and sat through a debate in the afternoon as he was making a speech. She was there, but not with him, as if she could avoid the issue of what her brother's public statement must mean to Neil's career.

After the debate his Minister had spoken to him privately. He would be expected to make a firm disavowal of his brother-in-law in the House that

231

evening. Questions were already being raised in the press. Neil responded cautiously. He gave his opinion of his brother-in-law as a crackpot eccentric who shouldn't be taken seriously. The Minister said he was sure that was the case, but a stronger condemnation would have to be made. The Opposition would raise issues of security, and the powerful pro-Unionist faction in his own party, apart from the Members from Ulster themselves, would hound him unless he could convince them that he and his wife had severed all ties with an avowed enemy of Britain. The words, 'and your wife', were spoken with emphasis. Neil said, Yes, of course, Claire shared his view and would certainly support whatever he said.

On his way home to dinner, before returning to the Commons, he wondered how he was going to open the subject. He didn't need to, because the telephone was ringing as he opened the flat door. It was Philip telephoning from Ireland.

'We saw the paper today,' he said. 'Claudia and I were horrified. We wanted you to know how damned sorry we are – it must be so awkward for you, Neil.'

'It has been,' he admitted. 'There's been a lot of comment.'

'He's gone mad,' Philip said angrily. 'If anyone asks me, I shall say so. I've been fuming about it all day, thinking what an embarrassment this must be for you.'

'I shall have to make a statement tonight,' Neil told him. 'I hope you understand. I can't mince words about Frank and what he's done. The real problem is, I don't know how Claire will take it.'

'You're not suggesting she'll support him? For God's sake, put her on the line and I'll talk some sense into her – it's disgraceful!'

He turned and saw Claire standing behind him in the doorway. He covered the mouthpiece for a moment.

'It's your father,' he said. 'He wants to talk to you.'

She shook her head. 'If it's about Frank, I don't want

to speak to him,' she said quietly. 'That's why he's rung, isn't it?'

'Yes,' Neil answered.

She turned away. 'Say I'm out,' she said, and closed the door.

It was the first serious quarrel they had ever had. It began with Neil being reasonable. Calm and objective. He asked why she had ignored something she knew must have a serious effect upon his political standing. He didn't wait long for an answer because he saw by her face that he wasn't going to get one. He described the interview with the Minister and the ordeal he was facing in a few hours' time. He began to shout, because the shut look and the silence goaded him into losing his temper.

'Even your father came out on my side,' he said furiously. 'You wouldn't even speak to him.'

'He would, wouldn't he?' she countered suddenly. 'He hates Frank. He'd side with anyone against him. Of course he'd ring up. What was he doing? Ranting and raving? No, I wasn't going to listen to him. I won't ever let him talk to me about my brother and I told him so when I heard about Riverstown.'

He took a step towards her. 'Claire, don't you understand? This isn't some family feud we're talking about – this is my political career! It's been laid on the line for me. My wife's brother is an open supporter of the Provisional IRA. Do I have to remind you that two months ago five British soldiers were killed and injured in an ambush in the North? I've got to condemn him in public in the House.'

He paused and tried to calm himself. He wished to God he hadn't lost control and shouted at her.

'You've got to endorse it,' he said. 'I've got to say that *we* reject everything he says and stands for. Otherwise my position will be made impossible.'

He turned away, and went to pour himself a drink. His hand was shaking. He tried to make peace.

'Do you want something?'

'No, thanks,' Claire said. 'So you're going to make the statement. If you want to include me in it, I can't stop you. I hope it'll be enough.'

He sat down; he set his glass untouched upon a table. 'Don't you care about me at all? Don't you care that what he's done has put me in the most bloody impossible position? No.' He shook his head slowly at her. 'No, you don't. He comes first with you, doesn't he?'

He waited, afraid that she might destroy everything between them by telling him the truth. But she didn't. She came and sat beside him.

'Of course I care about you and what this means to you,' she said. 'I didn't know what to say when I saw the paper this morning. Can't you understand that? I thought, oh, God, Frank's made it all public now, and what's Neil going to say. I couldn't condemn him, Neil, because I understand the way he feels. I don't agree with any of it, but I know why he thinks it's right. He's lost so much because he took this stand. I knew you'd be furious and I hoped it wouldn't be noticed, or matter all that much. I was running away, I suppose. But I can't turn on him, darling. You say whatever you like in the House, and if involving me helps, then of course you must do it. But I can't lie about it and pretend what I don't feel.'

He said slowly, 'Supposing you're asked right out – what are you going to say?'

'That I've nothing to add to my husband's statement.'

He picked up his drink. 'It might be a good idea if you keep out of the way for the next few days,' he said after a moment. 'Go down to Gloucestershire. Don't talk to the press.' He felt a surge of disappointment and hurt, and it betrayed him into folly. 'It would help if you came to the House this evening. It would strengthen what I've got to say.'

He knew when she got up that he had made the plea in vain.

'I can't,' she said. 'I can't sit there and hear my brother abused and denounced. Not even for your career. I'll go home tonight. You'll do better without me here till this blows over.'

Claire was on her way to the country when Neil made a statement that caught the headlines the next morning. It was one of the most scathing denunciations of the IRA and its methods heard in the House of Commons since the Prime Minister's speech after the death of Airey Neave.

Neil Fraser emerged with his reputation enhanced. When he went to his home in the country that weekend, it was the first time since they were married that he and Claire didn't sleep together after nearly a week spent apart.

Chapter 7

Frank knew what had happened as soon as he saw her. She had arrived first in the Gloucestershire pub, and when she got up to meet him, her condition was obvious.

Then they sat down, side by side in the privacy of the gloomy little parlour, and a waitress came and asked if they wanted a drink before they went in to lunch. They hadn't met for nearly three months. Frank didn't mention Neil. He'd driven up to the country to see her. They varied their meeting places; sometimes it was London, but he was uneasy about her being recognized. He didn't want to cause trouble for her with her husband. And trouble there had been, some months after the famous speech, the first time she told Neil that she was seeing Frank. After that, they made their arrangements in secret.

'Claire,' he said. 'You're pregnant!'

'Trust you to notice.' She smiled at him. 'Quite right, I'm nearly five months.'

He said, 'Why? Why have you let it happen? You

235

were told not to have any more! For Christ's sake, what sort of a husband is he!'

'He made just as much fuss as you're making,' she rebuked him. 'He even talked about an abortion, but I scotched that one pretty quickly. I want the baby, Frank. I know what I'm doing. It won't be the same as last time.'

He shook his head. 'How do you know?'

'Because I'm not going to fool around and try the natural motherhood bit. It'll be really easy, and anyway Peter can't grow up an only child. He wants a brother or a sister. Remember the fun we used to have when we were little?'

He said gently, 'Of course I remember. But we grew up wild. It's not the same for children over here.'

'No, it isn't. I've got a good nanny, but as soon as this one's born I'm going to get rid of her. She's too heavy on Peter and half the time I'm in London. Frank, you'll have to find me a nice local girl and send her over. Will you do that?'

He didn't remind her that an Irish nurse in a Minister's household might give the security people a heart attack. He didn't want to emphasize the division that existed. He just felt anxious and angry that she had been allowed to put her health at risk. A proper husband wouldn't have taken any chances. He'd have made *sure* she couldn't conceive.

'Are you feeling all right? Not too sick?'

'Not sick at all,' Claire answered. 'It's quite different this time. Maybe it's a girl. Don't look like that, Frank, there's a darling. I've checked with the doctor and the gynae and I'm going to be fine. All I had was a minor fit of the baby blues, and the minute you came over, I cheered up. Tell me, how's everything at home?'

By home, she meant Ireland. Riverstown wasn't mentioned by either of them now. It only spoiled their few hours together.

'Much the same as usual,' Frank told her. 'Nothing really changes. It's very expensive, inflation's gone mad.

We're all banking on finding oil to bale us out. Can you imagine Ireland turning into an Arab sheikdom?'

She laughed. 'Billy driving a Rolls-Royce and having his girl friend come out into the open – God, wouldn't it be crazy? How is he? Do you ever see him?'

'Once or twice, when I've been in Naas,' Frank said. 'He looks just the same as ever. Still got his dogs. Still goes on about his bronchitis, and smokes like a chimney. He said you hadn't been on a visit for a long time.'

'I know,' she said. 'Neil can't really go now. And it's difficult for me, because he gets so het-up. I've told him it's perfectly ridiculous to talk about me being in danger, but he won't listen. Give me a cigarette, will you? Thanks.'

He lit it for her. 'How are things?'

Claire looked at him. 'Between Neil and me? Up and down. That's why I thought another baby would be a good idea. I haven't made him very happy, I'm afraid.'

Frank said, 'You mean he hasn't made you happy. Why don't you pull out before it's too late?'

'Leave him? Don't be bloody silly, Frank. I'd never walk out on Neil. Apart from Peter and whatever's under the table at this minute, what would I do?'

'Come home where you belong,' he said slowly. 'Start again. I'd look after you. You'd find someone else, someone who was one of us. I mean it. Life's too short to be unhappy. He'll get over it.'

She stubbed out the cigarette. 'I shouldn't have said that.' She pushed back the chair. 'Don't talk to me about leaving him, Frank. I can't and I won't. He loves me, and it would break his heart.'

'You mean it would hurt his career,' he retorted.

'Not any more.' Claire dismissed that. 'Half the politicians in the country are divorced or second-time married. It's not like Ireland. Nobody cares about that kind of thing. Come on, let's go and have lunch and talk about something cheerful. I want to hear all the news, who you've seen and what everyone's doing.'

Towards the end of the lunch, she said, 'Frank, I've

got to ask you – are you sure you're right supporting the Provos now? They've done some terrible things lately. Do you really believe it's the right way?'

He hesitated. No one but Claire would have asked him such a question now. And no one else would get the answer he gave.

'I don't think it's right to go as far as they've gone, no. I've had some pretty basic doubts after the Mountbatten murder. And I've said so.'

She said slowly, 'That was so dreadful – unspeakable. But Frank, can you say things like that? Isn't it dangerous? If anyone thinks you're changing sides?'

'There's no question of that,' Frank insisted. 'I believe in a United Ireland. I want to see the British Army out of Ulster. There's a war going on up there, whatever people over here try to make out, and the soldiers are fair game.' He leaned towards her. 'It's killing civilians that shakes me. I'll tell you something.'

'What?' she asked.

'I went to see a Catholic priest.'

Claire gasped. 'I don't believe it? Whatever for?'

'I was baptized a Catholic,' he said. 'You know that. So I went to talk to old Father Donaghue.'

Claire knew the parish priest in Sallins. A kindly man who had been the spiritual mentor of every servant at Riverstown since she could remember.

'Frank, what on earth did you say to him? He must have thought you'd gone mad!'

The instinctive reaction made him smile. An Arbuth-not sitting in the priest's parlour at Sallins.

'He was a bit surprised,' he admitted. 'We had a cup of tea together. I told him about being baptized.'

'He must have been thrilled,' Claire said. She didn't understand why the idea irritated her so much.

'Thrilled he wasn't,' her brother answered. 'You know, we've always looked down on the Irish priests. I was just the same. Bogmen, our father used to call them. But old Donaghue would have surprised you. He just sat there and let me talk.'

'Talk about what?' Claire asked.

'About my feelings for Ireland, and the conflict of not knowing where I really belonged. I asked him if he thought I should study the Catholic faith and see if that would help me.'

'I'll bet he jumped at that,' she said.

'No, he didn't. He said by all means, if I was genuinely interested, he'd be glad to give instruction. But not while I supported violence against my fellow men. These were his words, Claire: "There's no place for men of blood in Christ's Church".' He said after a moment's silence, 'I never went back. But I got the message. It wasn't at all what I'd expected.'

'It's not what I'd expected either,' she said. 'Frank, you mustn't get mixed up with all that superstitious nonsense. How could someone like Father Donaghue cope with the problems of someone like you?'

He said gently, 'I thought he coped with them rather well.'

'Oh, I wish I didn't live here,' she exclaimed. 'If I was near, you wouldn't even think of doing such a thing. I can just imagine the gossip!'

'There won't be any gossip,' he said. 'No priest breaks the seal of Confession. You needn't look like that. How many people you know have been to a psychiatrist?'

'There's no comparison. One's medical, the other is just mumbo jumbo!' She saw the expression on his face. 'I'm sorry, I didn't mean to say that. It's just that I can't take you and all that Roman business seriously.'

'Of course you meant it, that's the way you were brought up. So was I. Being a Protestant was part of being in the Establishment. I remember our father actually saying it about someone he knew who'd changed over. "No gentleman in Ireland is a Catholic." I thought, Why not? Just because it's the native religion – the peasant's Church. It's the same old system, them and us. You should try to see things without prejudice and not go on repeating the old bigotry.'

Claire fumbled in her bag. Her eyes had filled with

tears. 'Darling Frank,' she said. 'I'm so sorry. I'm a tactless idiot. I'll never talk like that again.'

He smiled and she was instantly forgiven. 'Oh, yes, you will,' he countered.

'Well, I'll try not to,' she amended. Then she thought of something. 'Is your girl friend a good Catholic?' It must be her influence. Silly not to have realized it.

Frank said, 'She's an atheist. She wouldn't go near a priest. So you can't blame her. We'd better get the bill, that waitress is giving us dagger looks.'

Outside the pub he helped her into her car. He bent down to the window.

'Look after yourself. And for God's sake, don't worry about me. I know what I want and I know what I'm doing. Write to me, won't you?'

'Yes, I will.' She looked up at him. It always hurt to say goodbye. It hurt long after she had got home.

He watched the car move off and waved. He didn't notice the two men sitting in a Ford Escort in the car park. He didn't know that they had pulled in soon after he drove up to meet his sister. One of them noted the time on his pad. They began to follow Frank as he drove back to London. Every meeting he made was monitored, but the only ones of significance concerned the Minister's wife. Sooner or later he would have to be told.

When the baby girl was born, Neil was away on a fact-finding tour of the Middle East. Claire went into labour two weeks early. Claudia flew over as soon as she heard. Philip was not feeling well. He had just got over a very bad cold, and he was tired. He wasn't as young as all that, she pointed out. There were no complications; Claire had an easy delivery under close supervision. Neil sent flowers and a cable, but he couldn't break off his tour. It was a calm and happy occurrence and she liked feeding the little girl. She had been unable to feed the first child.

It was comforting having Claudia there. She moved into the Gloucestershire house and took charge of every-

240

thing. When Claire came home after five days, she found a new nanny installed and her mother presiding over the household as if she'd managed it all her life.

'I sacked that girl,' she explained. 'I caught her walloping Peter for some silly little thing, and I told her to pack her bags and get to hell out before you came back. This girl's very nice; poor little chap, he mustn't have his nose put out by the new baby. You must make an extra fuss of him.'

Claire said, 'You fuss enough for both of us. You are marvellous, doing everything. It's so lovely to be home. I hate hospitals. That awful smell.'

Claudia enjoyed herself till Neil came back. Then she was off, she declared, and nothing would persuade her to stay.

'The last thing a man wants when he gets back is to find his mother-in-law stuck in front of him. You're a perfect family now, darling. Take my advice and call a halt. Two's quite enough and you've got a pigeon pair . . . she's a dear little thing, isn't she? Lucy suits her down to the ground. I think she's going to be the image of Neil!'

There had been a letter from Ireland and a big basket of flowers delivered to the house. They came from Frank, but Claudia didn't comment. There was nothing to be said about him now. He had put himself beyond the pale. Any idea of going against Philip's wishes and giving him Riverstown was out of the question. She considered her step-son's behaviour utterly despicable. She actually called him a traitor to herself. Thank God Claire was happy, nice new baby and such a fine husband. He really was going right up the ladder. One day, as she said to Philip, he might be in line for Prime Minister.

When she got back she found Philip in bed. He'd had a dizzy fit while he was walking in the garden. Billy had helped him back to the house and the doctor advised him to rest. It was nothing to worry about, he insisted. Knowing how he hated being ill, Claudia didn't fuss.

She accepted his explanation and spoke to the doctor behind his back. The dizzy fit had been a slight heart attack.

She didn't want to worry Claire, and instinctively she turned to her son-in-law for support. He was kind and reassuring. He wouldn't tell Claire unless her father got worse. He was so anxious not to upset her equilibrium so soon after the birth. Anything *he* could do . . . Claudia promised to call on him. Philip did as he was told and rested until he was passed fit to get up for a little every day. He looked tired, but not ill. Claudia's worry eased.

Six months later he died in his sleep.

'You'll never believe it, but he's going to that funeral!'

Sean Filey knew Marie had a furious temper, but this was different. She was slit-eyed with rage. It made her look ugly.

'It's his father,' he remarked. 'Of course he'll go. Why do you care?' He knew very well why she cared. He knew that time had fed her jealousy until she was possessed by it and blind to reason.

'His father,' she mocked. 'A father who cut him out of his will, treated him like dirt all his life – he ought to be celebrating the auld bastard's dead!' In moments of high emotion, her brogue crept back.

'Perhaps he is,' Sean suggested. 'Going to the funeral doesn't mean he's sorry. I still don't see what it's got to do with you.'

She stared at him, and then said something that surprised him.

'Because if he was heart and soul with us, he'd spit on the grave before he went! I'll tell you why it's to do with me, and it's to do with you too – I don't trust him.'

Filey said slowly, 'What the hell are you saying?'

She slumped into a chair. 'You've heard him say we shouldn't hit civilian targets. I've heard him say more than that. He's got doubts, Sean.' She raised her head and looked him boldly in the eye.

242

Filey said quietly, 'Has he now – since when? Why haven't you reported this before?'

She was not to be cowed; she had gone further than she meant to because she was goaded by anger. But it was the truth, and she thought bitterly, Why should I protect him . . . after yesterday, why should I go on codding my own people just to save his skin?

'I wanted to be sure,' Marie answered. 'I noticed things had changed after we got Mountbatten. He was moody, not himself at all. I opened a bottle to celebrate. He wouldn't join me.'

Filey said nothing to that. Marie sat still. It served him right. She should have warned Filey months ago that he was weakening. Yesterday had been the watershed, she thought. Yesterday when I told him what a worm he was to pander to that family. He showed me his true colours then. He's going to hold that bitch of a sister's hand, that's what it is.

'He's still passing the funds through,' Filey said at last. 'So he's still useful. But for how long, that's the question? I'll have to report this to the Council. You'll be asked to repeat it all.' He looked at her and said, 'It is the truth, isn't it? You're not condemning him for reasons of your own, are you?'

She got up. 'If you think that, then go on trusting him till he turns us all in. I'm going now. You do what you like, but you can't say I haven't warned you.'

When she had gone he stayed on in the house. He made himself a cup of tea. She was insanely jealous. Jealousy could warp a personality until they couldn't see truth from lies. Or vengeance from loyalty. But he couldn't deny that Arbuthnot had reacted badly to civilian casualties in the North. Sean had despised him. He saw it as weakness, not humanity. There was no place for scruples in a desperate struggle. Nothing but single-minded, ruthless action could achieve their goal. There would be innocent victims as in any other war. But if Marie was right, and the shift in Frank Arbuthnot's attitude was fundamental, then something might

243

have to be done about him. On balance it was safer to give her the benefit of the doubt and call a meeting with Jim Quinlan.

Marie drove on to see her mother. She was good to her family, generous with the money Frank gave her. She hadn't been to visit her mother for some time. That was the reason she gave to herself for not going straight back to Meath. She couldn't forget the dislike in his eyes the night before, or the angry dismissal as he slammed out of the room and went to sleep elsewhere.

'Keep your tongue off my sister! If you ever say a word against her again, you can get out and stay out!' he had said.

Marie's mother was pleased to see her, but suspicious when she lingered past her usual time.

'What's happened to that fine fella of yours?' she demanded.

'He's all right,' Marie answered sullenly.

Mrs Dempster knew her daughter. 'Ye've not been fightin' wit' him, have ye? Divil another man ye'll find as generous as that one . . . Jaysus, look at the clothes on ye, and that grand car.'

Marie wished she'd shut up. She was fond of her mother, but the old woman's speech and ignorance grated on her. So did the house where she'd been born. It was alien to her now. The cheap furniture, the garish carpet in all the colours of the rainbow, bought with her last cheque. The plastic flowers on the table, and the sugar-sweet picture of Our Lady, blue eyes raised to heaven. Marie hated that most of all. It symbolized the Ireland she wanted to see changed for ever. Irish women were pious, submissive, enslaved by men and the Church. Her mother was typical. She left the politics and the fighting to her menfolk; she talked of her own heroic father who'd fought in the Easter rising in 1916, but Marie knew it didn't mean more than a chance to boast among their neighbours. She had no sympathy or understanding of her daughter's revolutionary ideals. Except to laugh at them and point out how she'd taken to the rich life like a duck to water. Marie couldn't argue with that. But nothing altered her desire to sweep away the Ireland of her mother's generation. She wanted to see it a proud, united country, rid of its oppressors down to the last babe in arms.

She found a bottle of gin under the kitchen cupboard. The auld one liked a nip now and then during the day. She poured herself a drink. She had to go back. She had to face him and try to mend their quarrel. The truth was, she said aloud to herself, she couldn't imagine life without him. Her mother would say it was the grand house and the servants to wait on her she'd miss. But it wasn't so. It was Frank she wanted. To see him sitting in the chair opposite at the end of the day, like an old married couple. She'd dreamed of that for a long time. But no longer. He'd never marry her. She'd had to swallow that and it was a bitter draught. But she could accept it so long as they were together, sharing their lives by day and living at Meath. Marriage was a middle-class convention. She could do without it. But not without him. Most of all she wanted him in her bed at night. That was a hunger that grew with the years. It tortured her and enslaved her because her need for him was stronger as his need for her grew less and less. She finished the last of the gin and grimaced.

Her mother came back. 'I've wet the tea,' she said. 'Ye'd best be gettin' back home then. It's not good for a man comin' back to an empty house.'

He was not there when Marie opened the front door. She always knew if he were near. She called and Mrs Brogan hurried out into the hallway. She had a healthy respect for Marie Dempster, even though she didn't have a ring on her.

'Where's Mr Arbuthnot?'

'He's away over to Kildare,' she was told. 'He phoned to say he'd be in for dinner.'

Marie nodded abruptly and turned away. The Brogans must have heard them shouting the night before. She went upstairs to their bedroom. Kildare. She said it aloud. *She'd* arrived for the funeral, that was it. That sister had come over and he'd gone to meet her. She sat down in front of the dressing table. She could have swept all the lotions and bottles on to the floor and smashed the lot. She looked drawn and sallow, with deep rings under her eyes after a sleepless night.

He'd made her suffer so much. He'd tortured her for years with his love for someone else. Looking in the mirror as if she were face to face with her own soul, a terrible thought came to her and she didn't dismiss it. She loved him, but she'd gone to Sean to try and do him harm. If she'd succeeded, if they believed her, anything might happen. It might be a relief. An agony, but a relief at the same time. But it wouldn't be enough if only Frank paid for her misery. It should be both of them . . .

Mrs Brogan met him when he came in. 'Miss Dempster's upstairs. She asked if you'd go up.'

He'd spent the day making arrangements for his father's funeral. Claudia was far more shocked by Philip's death than she admitted. She'd accepted his offer and left the details to him. Neil couldn't come to the funeral because it wasn't safe for him to be in Ireland even for a few hours. Frank sensed how much she wished it was her son-in-law taking the responsibility. Claire was only flying in and out the same day. In spite of himself Frank was conscious of grief. He had loved the father who never loved him, and he was surprised to find he was capable of mourning him. He had forgotten about Marie. The night before, he'd shut himself up in a spare room. When he came down next morning she had gone. It had been a sickening scene. She had suddenly flared up at him, spewing her poisonous jealousy about his family, lashing out at Claire, whom she had never even met. Now she was back. He supposed he had better go upstairs and see what could be salvaged in the relationship. On his part, not very much, he suspected.

When he came into the room, she ran into his arms, begging him to forgive her. There was nothing else he

could do. But he refused to let her tempt him into bed.
And sitting opposite him in the handsome dining room,
Marie knew that she had lost her only hold on him.

It didn't rain at Philip's funeral. There were no Holly-
wood-style mourners under a mushroom growth of black
umbrellas. The sun shone, the service was dignified,
with a moving choice of readings and Philip's favourite
hymn, 'Abide with me'. The church was full, and after
the burial in Naas cemetery, the congregation came back
to Riverstown for a buffet lunch. Everyone clustered
round Claudia, saying what a grand man he was and
how they were all going to miss him. There was more
emphasis on funny stories and anecdotes than sadness.
The concept of the wake had carried into Anglo-Irish
custom. The widow needed cheering up, the dead man
would rather his friends had a decent drink and a laugh
in his memory than went about with long faces. People
were polite to Frank, but not warm. He had betrayed
his father's class and lifelong convictions. It was good of
Claudia to have him in the house at all. And of course
everyone knew that he wasn't going to inherit the
Arbuthnot family home. Two hundred-odd years, and it
was bypassing the male heir and going to the wife. Most
of Philip's friends thought it too drastic. There were
black sheep in every family. But it was a mistake to
break the line like that. One of Philip's cronies from the
Kildare Street Club had too much to drink and started
making remarks about the IRA. He was hurried off
home and Frank knew nothing about the incident.

The lunch went on until late afternoon. Claudia was
going to friends in Cork that evening. Since Claire had
to fly back to London, she couldn't possibly be left alone
in the house. As the last of the guests were leaving,
Claudia came up to Frank. She looked very haggard and
old, in spite of the make-up. She hadn't cried during
the funeral. She wasn't the kind of woman to make a
public display. She had done her crying in private.

'Thank you for arranging everything,' she said. 'It was

247

very well done. Old Greenway gave a very good address. Your father would have been pleased. So many people came . . . that was nice.'

He said, 'I'm sorry he's dead. I'm sorry so much went wrong between him and me, but I want you to know I'm here if you need anything.'

Claudia wished he'd go. He was driving Claire to the airport. She had seemed stunned and silent all through the day. Claudia didn't want to talk to him about his father. The house was full of Philip, as if his spirit had stayed behind. Later it would be gone. Later she could come back and resume her life. He was sorry, he said. He looked unhappy, she admitted. She had noticed their friends giving him the cold shoulder in a subtle way. What a pity, she thought, but bad blood will out. He had only himself to blame for being the outsider on that day. He was so like Philip as a young man standing in front of her. So alike and yet quite different. Mongrel blood, she thought, and was immediately ashamed.

'Frank,' she said. 'You know there's nothing in the will. But if there's anything you want out of the house, please let me know. Some of the pictures . . .' She let the sentence die.

'Thank you,' he said. 'It's kind of you to offer. But I don't want anything.'

'Think about it,' Claudia insisted. 'You may change your mind. Now, if Claire's going to catch her plane, she really ought to go.'

In the car Claire took off her black hat. The sun made a bright halo of the blonde hair.

'I feel numb,' she said. 'I don't know what's the matter with me. I can't believe I'll never see him again.'

'You mustn't upset yourself,' Frank said. 'He wouldn't want that. He doted on you.'

She turned towards him. 'I loved him, Frank, but it was never quite the same after what he did to you. If Claudia wills me Riverstown, I'm going to give it to you.'

'I wouldn't want it,' he said gently. 'But I knew you'd

say that. I've got my own place and I'm happy there. Besides, Claudia will live to be a hundred, so don't start thinking like that.'

'What are your plans?' she asked him.

'Nothing special, I'm very busy. I've a trip planned to the States in the autumn.'

Claire looked at him. 'You're not going to speak at another rally, are you?'

He didn't answer. 'You couldn't get away, I suppose? I'd love to take you round the East Coast.'

'I don't think Neil would like it,' she said. 'What a stupid bloody world we live in! There we are, me not able to come back to my own country, except I've got to fly in and out like a criminal, and you can't come and stay with me because of my husband's political career. We meet in hole-and-corner pubs for a few hours and talk on the telephone when he's out of the house! I'm fed up with it, Frank. I'm fed up with his friends and the phoney life we lead. I'm the perfect Minister's wife, with the two regulation children and a regulation Cotswold manor house with a swimming pool and a herbaceous border. Sometimes I feel I'd give my soul for a bit of Irish mess and madness!'

He slowed down as they turned into the airport. 'Leave it then,' he said. 'Bring the children over here. You shouldn't have married him in the first place.'

'I can't,' she said. 'Don't keep saying it.'

She didn't open the car door. He saw that for the first time her eyes were full of unshed tears.

'With Dad gone and everything different, I feel so lost. And nothing makes up for it. Not Neil, not even the children. Don't get out, say goodbye to me here. I don't want that waving goodbye in the departure lounge.'

He put an arm round her. 'Wipe your eyes,' he said. 'Goodbye, Clarry. You made up to Dad for everything. Remember that and don't grieve. I'll ring you in a couple of days. When's a good time?'

'Any time,' Claire said. 'I'm finished pretending.' She

got out of the car and hurried through the doors into the airport building without looking back.

Three men met at the house at Santry. Sean Filey, his superior, Jim Quinlan, and Hugh Macbride, who'd come down from the North. Filey had called the meeting to discuss Frank Arbuthnot.

Macbride was impatient. His was the pressing problem and he hadn't come across the border to listen to their troubles.

'For God's sake,' he interrupted, 'if the bastard turns lily-livered, you don't have to sit and talk about it. Get rid of him!'

Filey said coldly, 'Your money supply will soon dry up if we do.'

Macbride brought his fist down on the table. 'That's why I'm here! We're running short of funds. America's dried up since Mountbatten.'

'That's temporary,' Quinlan protested. 'Give it a few months for public opinion to settle. Noraid will get the cash flowing through to us again.'

'We haven't got a few months,' Macbride snapped. It was easy for them to talk about time. They had time in the Republic. The Brits weren't breathing up *their* arses. 'We've lost two major arms stores in the last nine months. Fifty Armalites, ten thousand rounds of ammo, boxes of grenades and explosives. And no money coming through. We've had to halt operations.' He lit a cigarette, then threw the match on the floor. 'We've been offered a big shipment,' he went on. 'It's a new supplier and he wants the money up front first.'

'He'll have to wait,' Filey said. 'It won't be long.'

'He won't wait,' Macbride said flatly. 'He's got other customers. We need a hundred thousand pounds and we need it by the end of June. Otherwise we lose the shipment, and we'll lose more than guns. We can't afford to stay quiet. It's hard enough keeping our people together. If we lie low, they'll start to drift away. I've come down to ask you to get the money for us.'

'How? A hundred thousand — how in the name of Jesus are we going to get that?' Quinlan demanded.

Macbride glared at him. 'The way we've had to get it before now,' he said. 'Rob one of your fat Dublin banks.'

There was a long silence. Then Sean Filey said, 'Why do you have to come down here for that? You've got banks in Ulster.'

'We've got fuckin' fortresses,' Macbride countered. 'It'd take an army to get near one of them. We've milked that cow dry, I can tell you.'

There was another silence. Then Quinlan said, 'If we do it, we'll need Arbuthnot to bank the money and launder it through.'

Macbride stubbed his cigarette out. He coughed, cleared his throat and swallowed. Sean was certain that at home he'd have spat on the floor.

'It's a fine time to have doubts about him,' he remarked.

'Doubts or not, he's the only one,' Quinlan retorted. 'We're not risking our lads to have them picked up at the border with the money on them. It goes through the usual channels and your man can be paid in Monte Carlo.'

'You'll get it then?' Hugh Macbride demanded.

'You'll have the money,' Quinlan promised. 'The how and the where you can leave to us.'

The meeting broke up, and Sean offered Jim Quinlan a lift in his car back to the centre of Dublin.

Quinlan said, 'How much of what Marie said do you believe, Sean? I remember when she wanted him admitted to the Council. Can we trust him with this?'

Sean weighed his answer. Neither had felt free to go into the matter in too much detail, with Macbride listening. His answer to everything was a bullet.

'I think she's part right, but only part. He hasn't pretended to like some of the things we've had to do. He's soft, because his kind could afford to be. Except when *they* felt threatened. But he's been straight with me and said so. I think we can rely on him for one more major contribution. After that . . .' He shrugged.

He dropped Jim Quinlan off at Heuston station and went on to his practice in Fitzwilliam Square.

Neil's official car met Claire at London Airport. The Minister was delayed in London and would be coming up later by train. She had expected him to meet her. But, of course, he was busy and, after all, he'd sent his car. She thought, It's funny, he's doing everything wrong, without knowing it. And whenever he tries, it's in the wrong way and for the wrong reason. She felt tired and drained. If he were late she could skip dinner and go to bed. But when she came into the house the drawing-room door opened and there was Michael Harvey. And her son, Peter, in his pyjamas, holding on to his hand.

'I hope you don't mind,' he said. 'Neil asked me to spend a couple of days with you. I got leave unexpectedly. And Peter wanted to wait up till you got home.'

Claire came and kissed her son, who wanted to be picked up and hugged. He was very heavy, or else she was very tired.

'I'm so glad you're here,' she said. 'Of course Neil couldn't tell me. You know where I've been?'

'I know,' he said quietly. 'I'm so sorry. Here, old chap, don't strangle your mummy. Come on, don't let me down now. You promised to go to bed if I persuaded Iris you could stay up.'

She watched the little boy scamper happily up the stairs. 'He's mad about you, Michael,' she said. 'Let's have a drink and then I'll go and change out of this awful black. Will Neil be home for dinner?'

'Yes, he rang about half an hour ago, wanting to know if you'd arrived.'

'The traffic was bad,' she explained. She liked Michael Harvey, but now she couldn't escape and go to bed. Not to sleep, but to cry if she wanted to, to be alone and try to collect herself before life knocked on the door the next morning and expected to be lived.

He gave her a stiffer drink than usual, she noticed. He sat down and said, 'Neil was very upset he couldn't go with you.'

'He shouldn't be,' she answered. 'He can't go to Ireland even for a funeral, in case someone throws a bomb at him. Any more than I could stay a night with my mother. She had to go to friends. I'm so bored with it all, I can't tell you. Do let's talk about something else.'

Harvey thought, She won't forgive this. I know the Irish. She'll hold this against him for ever. Because if it was the other way round, she'd have chanced it and gone with him. Poor sod, he's on a hiding to nothing here. Women don't give a damn. All they see is the personal issue. Like my wife did. By all means, let's talk about something else.

When Neil came in, they were watching a television comedy and, so far as he could see, Claire seemed quite relaxed. Thank God for Michael Harvey. He was a good buffer when tension rose between them. And he was someone Neil could talk to. In his own way he seemed to sympathize with Neil and understand. Most men would have taken one look at Claire and sided with her.

After dinner she excused herself and went to bed. The two men stayed up talking. Not about the problem in their midst, but about the wider issues in their respective worlds. When Neil went upstairs his wife was asleep, and he was careful not to wake her, although what he most wanted was to take her in his arms and ask her all about her father's funeral, to comfort her as deeply as he knew she was hurt. But the moment had eluded him, as it so often did these days, and she would have slipped a little further away from him as a result. When they woke together the next morning, she smiled brightly at him, brushed all enquiries off by saying she was fine, and locked herself into the bathroom to keep him at bay.

The following evening, in Michael Harvey's hearing, she telephoned her brother in Ireland. He went out of the room, closing the door. His two days' unexpected leave was neither leave nor unexpected. Someone had to tell the Minister that his wife was meeting Frank Arbuthnot in secret when he came to England. As a friend Neil Fraser trusted, Michael Harvey was the choice. He saw at that moment that Claire had made it easy for him. He went out to the garden, where Neil was sitting in the warm dusk, smoking a cigar.

After they'd spoken he said, 'How much do you tell her about what's going on?'

Neil said slowly, 'Confidential stuff, do you mean? Nothing. And she never asks. She's not interested. She'd never pass it on.'

'Not intentionally,' Harvey countered.

Neil looked at him. 'You don't understand,' he said. 'It's not that kind of relationship.'

'Just the same, I'd be a bit careful. It's amazing what someone can let drop without realizing it. *He* might pass it on, or he might not. You can't take the chance.'

Neil smoked on in silence. Michael Harvey felt very sorry for him. He had never suspected that Claire was deceiving him. It was certainly a shock.

'You say she didn't make any bones about ringing him up?' he asked after a time.

'None at all. I think she wanted me to hear. Probably wants you to know too. That's a very good sign, believe me.'

'If you say so.' Neil finished his cigar. 'I'm not sure. I think she's sending me a signal.'

Harvey looked up sharply. 'What do you mean? What kind of signal?'

'That from now on, she's going her own way. I should have gone to that funeral. I should have told the Security people to stuff it and gone with her. They tried to stop her going, but there was no way. I made a terrible bloody mistake, Mike.'

Harvey agreed with him, but he didn't say so. 'And what would have happened if you'd been targeted and they'd made their hit? I'll bet you that there was a contingency plan in case you turned up at Riverstown. Even if it was some poor half-baked kid who'd been told he was doing it for Ireland. Someone, somewhere, was waiting to take a pot at you if you'd shown your face. If Claire's blaming you, then it's time someone pointed out the facts of life. I thought she'd have got the message after that last scare, when they picked up the jokers in Liverpool. Would you like me to remind her about that? After all, that's how I'm here now.'

'Thanks, but no. We didn't go through that time without rows, I'm afraid. She sees everything in terms of criticism of her brother.'

Harvey remembered the night he overheard them quarrelling. He was on duty as a bodyguard then, and the human element was none of his business. It was impossible to be objective now. He knew and liked them both, but his sympathies were leaning more and more towards the husband. Thank God he wasn't married any more.

'Why did you lie to me?'

Claire didn't flinch. 'I had to; the last time I told you we'd met, you went through the roof.'

'After that speech in New York,' he reminded her.

'After your speech in the House,' she countered. 'Talking about the Irish as if they are murderers and terrorists. It did you a lot of good with your party, but how do you think I felt about it?'

He turned away from her. 'I don't know,' he said. 'I don't know how you feel any more, or how you think. But don't lie to me next time he sneaks over to see you. Tell me. It'll save a lot of embarrassment.'

'All right, then you can tell your spies they don't have to watch me any more. God, to think of it!'

'They're not my spies,' Neil Fraser said. 'They're watching your brother because he's an enemy of this country, and a number of people have been killed by the people he supports. I was threatened myself, if you

255

remember. See him if you have to, but don't put me in the position of not knowing next time.'

He closed the door of their room and went out. He hadn't told her that Michael Harvey was his informant.

It took two months to plan the robbery on the Kildare Street branch of the Bank of Ireland. Quinlan chose that particular branch because the armoured truck bringing in the week's takings from a number of large stores and businesses came on a Friday morning. It was impossible to hijack the truck or stage an armed raid during the transfer of the money because there was a heavy escort of police which surrounded the truck and the bank during unloading. Security was far too tight. So it was decided to send a group of three men into the bank in the early afternoon. There would be sufficient cash in the tellers' safe for weekend withdrawals. Three men could grab the money and get out quickly.

Quinlan set a regular watch on the bank for a month, using a rota of the men who would carry out the robbery, so they were familiar with the interior, the exits on to the street, and the identity of the under-manager and the chief cashier. He planned everything down to the last detail. He chose men with a criminal past, one of whom had organized a successful wages snatch in Limerick two years before, when the local IRA were hard-pressed for funds.

Sean Filey was informed, but not involved in the planning. He was not a man of action; his role was to watch Arbuthnot via Marie and the Brogans, and to keep him in line till the money was in their hands and could be paid into the Boston Irish Bank. The first thing he did was to speak to Kevin Ryan in the States and ask him to cancel Frank's trip over. It would be a big help to a project on hand if Kevin came to Ireland instead. His nephew was in need of moral support. Kevin listened and said he'd think about it. Moral support had only one meaning. Frank was wavering. Kevin wasn't surprised. Even Mary Rose had been shocked by the violence in the North and the murder of the Queen of England's cousin. Kevin had trimmed his sails to the wind of public opinion and cancelled a speaking tour. It might be good for Frank if he went over to Ireland, and good for him too. His own batteries needed recharging. He called Sean Filey back and said he'd come and stay for a few weeks at the Half House. And he'd set his nephew straight at the same time.

It was a beautiful spring. The land burgeoned into its dazzling greenery, the hedgerows spilling over with clouds of white May. It was the time of year that Frank loved best. The daffodils would be ablaze at Riverstown now, and the river in full flood, washing away the bank and messing up the trout fishing. He thought of his home, and whatever he said to Claire, his grandmother's house was no substitute for the place where he had grown up.

And Marie's presence was becoming a burden. He didn't look forward to coming back with her in the evenings and pretending that their relationship hadn't changed. She grated on him, because she was tense and insincere; most of all he recognized that she was miserably unhappy, and that he was the cause. It couldn't go on, but he didn't know how to end it. They made love because she could still arouse him, but the aftermath was emptiness, with a tinge of self-disgust. She would have to face the fact that after their years together, nothing had grown and most of what they used to have had died. For him, he realized, but not for her. That was his dilemma.

It was mid-May and they were driving back from Dublin together. She said suddenly, in the bright voice which was an affectation, 'There's a fantastic new restaurant opened on the Curragh. One of the girls was telling me about it at lunch today. Why don't we go out tonight and have dinner?' She didn't wait for him to answer. 'It'd do us both good to get out and have an evening. We're stuck at home too much. And I've a pretty new frock I want to wear for you.'

She was trying so hard he hadn't the heart to refuse. Perhaps it might give him the opportunity to talk to her.

'Why not? I'll ring up and book a table.'

Marie put her hand on his knee and stroked it. 'You're so good to me,' she said. 'You spoil me, Frank. When we come home, I'll do a bit of spoiling for you.'

She came down the stairs and stood, so he could admire the dress. It was certainly pretty. By any standard she was a woman who made heads turn. She'd have no difficulty finding another man. They'd be falling over themselves if she were free, and thanks to him and her job, she had met a lot of influential people.

'You look very nice,' he said kindly. 'That colour green suits you. It's not too bright.'

'Green for Ireland,' she said, and clung to his arm as they walked to the car.

They were driving along the main Naas road through Sallins when he slowed down as they approached the bridge.

'What are you stopping for?'

'There's old Donny. I'll just say hello and give him a few bob.'

'Who's Donny?' she asked.

'He's a simple old fellow, loves to stand and watch the train come through from Dublin. He's been on that bridge as long as I can remember. When Claire and I were children we used to give him some of our sweets on a Sunday.'

He pulled in to the side. Marie frowned. There was a dirty figure in a torn jersey leaning over the parapet.

Frank called out, 'Donny!' and he turned. He had the watery eyes and slack mouth of an idiot. He grinned and waved. Frank opened the door.

'Come and say hello,' he said. 'It'd make his day.'

She got out reluctantly. She had beautiful new shoes and the gutter was dirty. Frank seemed quite at home with the half-wit. He called her over and said, 'Donny, this is Miss Dempster, a friend of mine.'

He stared at her and grinned, and a trickle of saliva ran down his chin.

Marie said briefly, 'Hello, Donny. Frank, darling, we'll be late.'

'Where's Claire?' she heard him ask. 'When's she comin' back?'

'Soon,' Frank assured him. 'How's the mammy keeping?'

'She's keepin' herself well. Would ye have a cig on ye?' He waited, head cocked on one side, and extended a very dirty palm.

'I haven't,' Frank said. 'But here's a pound. Buy yourself a packet. Take care now.'

'God bless ye,' Donny said. 'There'll be a train in a minute.'

Frank got back into the car. Marie was already in her seat. 'Poor devil,' he said. 'He lives for the sight of a train. I don't think he knows whether he's seen one or not. It's the waiting he likes.'

Marie grimaced. 'He's so filthy. Why do you bother giving him money? He'll only go to the pub.'

He said, 'Donny's never been in a pub in his life. All he has is the trains and a few cigarettes. He's harmless, everyone round here knows him.'

'People like that make me sick,' she said. 'I bet he's not as simple as he makes out. I can't bear idiots, they're so creepy.'

Frank saw her in the driving mirror: the hard mouth drawn down, the look of disgust on her face. For all her political convictions, there wasn't room in her heart for one helpless child of nature. He thought suddenly, That's why I could never love her. She has no compassion.

He knew what would happen when they got home. She stopped by the stairs and reached up to kiss him, her tongue probing against his lips.

259

He drew back. 'Marie,' he said quietly, 'it's no good. You know it's no good.'

She stepped away from him. 'Why do you say that, Frank? It's always great with us. Let me show you tonight. Let me try.'

He shook his head. 'No. Why don't we go in and sit down? It's time we talked this out.'

He gave her a drink; she was very pale and silent. 'We've had some wonderful times together,' he said. 'But it hasn't been right for a long time. We've both tried; I know you have perhaps more than me. It hasn't worked, Marie.'

'You're not in love with me,' she said flatly. 'That's the reason.'

'I've never said I was,' he reminded her. 'You understood that from the start.'

'Oh, sure I know what you *said*.' Her tone was bitter. 'But I hoped I could make you change your mind. The trouble is, you're in love with your own sister.'

Frank didn't move. She waited, having dealt the dagger blow, but nothing happened.

After a moment he said, 'I want you out of this house tomorrow. If you need more money than I've already settled on you, you can have it. I also want you out of the bank. From tomorrow.' He turned and walked out, closing the door quietly after him.

Marie stood alone in the room, marooned in the silence. There had been no row, no exchange of insults and reproaches. She could have coped with that, perhaps salvaged something at the end of it. He might have hit her, and she would have welcomed it. Instead there was that cold dismissal. He'd given her notice to quit as if she were a servant. Not just the house, but the job. Everything was cut from under her. Sean Filey would want to know why. She felt such a surge of hatred that her stomach heaved. For a moment she thought she was going to be sick then and there.

She had aimed at his heart, and only succeeded in mortally wounding herself. Upstairs Frank undressed and went into a spare room to sleep. He didn't know which disgusted him most – Marie, or himself for having taken up with such a woman. By tomorrow she would be gone. And something fundamental would change in his life when she was out of it. His aversion to her was part of that change.

She didn't go to her mother. She packed some clothes, and told the Brogans she was going to visit relatives in Galway. They noticed the size of the suitcase and judged it would be a long stay. She couldn't take everything. The accumulation of ten years needed a trunk. He'd been very generous, she thought savagely, looking at the cupboards filled with clothes, the dozens of pairs of shoes, the mink coat and the fashionable silver fox jacket, hats in boxes, drawers full of underclothes. She'd send for them later.

But now she needed to get out of the house and have time to think, and plan what explanation to give to Filey and his superiors as to why she had lost her position at the Boston Irish Bank. They'd care much less about her personal relationship coming to an end. The job was another matter. How could she explain that she had been sacked? They wouldn't like it, if they thought she'd brought that on herself. She'd have to find another reason, something that would take the blame off her and lay it square on Arbuthnot. She thought of him as Arbuthnot now. No more as Frank. Hating him was a relief; she only wished she'd realized before how much less painful it would be than to love him. Now she could ease her own pain by injuring him, and it gave her a fierce satisfaction. He'd pay. He'd pay for the rejection and that final insulting dismissal, showing her how little she meant to him. Not worth a good row, even, when any other man would have laid into her with his fists for what she'd said.

But first she had to get away and work out how to protect herself. The thought came back to her as she drove off in the smart BMW sports model he'd bought her a year ago. There must be a way to punish that sister

261

as well. Some means of wreaking a vengeance upon her, just when it seemed Claire had triumphed over her.

She set off on the road to Dublin and booked herself in to a quiet suburban hotel. She stayed there for a whole day before she put a call through to Sean Filey. By that time she had worked out her story to the last detail.

Kevin had arrived at the Half House with Mary Rose and their eldest son, Patrick. He was glad to be home; the splendid house always gladdened his heart. He'd retire there, no question. He hadn't said so to Mary Rose, but it was easier now that his brother had died. She'd found the family a bit of a trouble. There'd been jealousy and backbiting, as you might expect, but Mary Rose took it to heart. His lump of a sister-in-law was to blame, and now that Shamus was gone, Kevin didn't bother himself about her. The sons were farming and the unmarried daughter was at home looking after them all. He wanted his son to get acquainted with the place, and get to know people. He had pleased Kevin by saying how impressed his friends at college would be when he showed them photographs. He was not a clever young man, but he was steady. With his father's money and his grandfather's business behind him, he'd do all right. His mother thought he was the best son in the world. She'd made murmurs at one time about the priesthood, but Kevin had quickly ruled that out. A daughter a nun was one thing, but his eldest boy had a business to take on. Not to mention the Half House one day.

One of the first calls to come for him was from Sean Filey. It was brief.

'We've got more trouble with your nephew,' he said. 'Have you seen him yet?'

'I've only been here two days,' Kevin snapped. He didn't like Filey. He didn't feel comfortable with intellectuals. He suspected that all psychiatrists analysed everyone they met, as a matter of course. He didn't like beards, either, because he felt they were grown to hide something. He'd read that somewhere and he was sure it was true. 'What the hell do you mean by trouble?'

'He's thrown Marie out of the house and the bank. He's in a dangerous frame of mind. And right now we need him badly. You're the one to steady him. Just for a while longer.'

Kevin hesitated. It sounded bad. Bad for his nephew too. He was fond of Frank.

'I'll call him now,' he said. 'Leave him to me.' He repeated his boast. 'I'm like a father to him.'

'It's just wonderful to see you, Frank.' Mary Rose gazed up at him. He thought she had aged since his last visit. Her hair was greyer and there were little networks of lines. He was glad to see them. They were his family. He could always trust them.

Kevin had sounded warmer than usual when they spoke. 'We've missed you, Frankie. Come on over.'

Kevin didn't rush his fences. They had a long lunch, and he eased Frank into a confidential mood with wine and gentle banter among the four of them. Then he signalled to Mary Rose and his son that he wanted to be alone with his nephew. Man's talk, as Mary Rose called it. She slipped away, taking Patrick with her.

'Things have been bad in the North, I hear,' Kevin began. His sharp eyes saw a change of expression.

'They've been bad down here too,' Frank said. Suddenly he spoke his mind. 'Why did they do it? Why did they blow up that boat and kill those poor devils?'

Kevin held his tongue. Frank went on, frowning, obviously troubled.

'Don't they know that's no way to win public support? And to be honest, I find this business of shooting down RUC men in front of their wives and children bloody terrible too.' He looked at his uncle. 'The direction is changing,' he said. 'What was a war in the North for freedom and justice is becoming more and more of a terrorist campaign.'

Kevin said reasonably, 'I know how you feel, Frank.

263

But let's look at the record. The struggle in the North has been going on for years. People in Britain and America are taking it for granted. It doesn't make the headlines any more. Some poor bastard of a Catholic gets dragged out of his bed and murdered by the Orangemen and it gets a couple of inches down the inside page. It's not nice killing men in front of their families, but it's been happening to our people for years. Now they're giving the sons of bitches a dose of their own medicine. As for the killing of that fella Mountbatten and the others – well . . . !' He spread his hands as if to say, it was something that had to be done. Albeit regrettable. 'We don't want his kind in Ireland. And it served its purpose. It showed them we can strike anyone, any time, no matter who they are.' He leaned across and put his hand on Frank's arm. 'It's a dirty business, because they've made it so. Right from the start, when they set about a peaceful crowd demonstrating for their basic human rights, and laid into them with clubs, up a street where they'd barricaded them in. Remember that? Remember Bloody Sunday, Frank? Troops firing on unarmed men and women. Thirteen dead. We have to fight, and fight on their terms, if we're ever going to have a chance of winning.'

'After all the killing and the sacrifices,' Frank said slowly, 'it doesn't seem to me we're that much further forward.'

'I think we are,' his uncle said. 'And we can't give in, just because of all the blood spilt and the suffering of our people. We've got to win, don't you see that?'

'Yes,' he answered. 'I do see it. And I want it as much as anyone. It's the methods I don't like. I've helped our Cause and I'll go on helping. There's a big payment coming in soon. I'm going to deal with it. Nothing alters my commitment. But I'll speak my mind when I see something creeping into us that's rotten.'

'Speaking your mind to me is one thing, Frank,' his uncle said. 'But I'd be careful not to shoot your mouth off anywhere else. Things are hard for us at the moment and it won't do you any good to go round criticizing.'

Frank said, 'Is that some kind of warning? If it is, I won't take it.'

'Ah, don't be a bloody fool.' Kevin changed his tone. 'I'm just giving you advice, that's all. How's Marie? I meant to say bring her, but I thought we'd have some time to ourselves.'

'We've split up,' Frank said. 'And she's left the bank.'

'That's a pity. I thought she was a fine girl. We all thought you might make an honest woman of her one day. Isn't her leaving the bank a bit awkward for you?'

'No. It would have been more awkward having her there. I can handle the next lot without any help from anyone.'

'Was it a fight you had?' Kevin asked him, testing out Sean Filey's hinted explanation. 'It must have been a helluva fight to break the two of you up after all this time.'

Frank didn't want to discuss it. He didn't want to think about Marie.

'I settled money on her,' he said. 'She's all right, don't worry.'

Kevin felt a tinge of resentment. He recognized that way of closing the subject. For a moment Philip Arbuthnot spoke through his son.

'What's the next big payment, Frankie?' Kevin asked, cocking his head on one side as if he too had lost interest in Marie Dempster.

'Sean says it's a hundred grand,' he answered. 'It's due in at the end of next week.'

Ryan asked the question Frank had asked Sean Filey. 'That's a lot of money. Where's it coming from?' He got the answer Frank had been given.

'I think it's better not to know,' his nephew said. 'I don't ask for details; the less one person knows, the safer it is for the others. But I'm getting the cash, and I'll put it into a new account at the bank where it can be transferred, as soon as I know where to send it.'

'Won't you have trouble with Exchange Control?' Ryan queried.

'It'll be the first time,' Frank said. 'Most of our business is for overseas clients. There's never been any problem. There won't be this time.'

Ryan got up. The private talk was over. He thought he had defused the situation. He hoped so; he was fond of his nephew. He wished he could have made the warning stronger, but he didn't dare. In his present mood, Frank might have courted real disaster by refusing to handle this shipment of money. The idea filled Kevin Ryan with alarm. He patted his nephew on the shoulder.

'If my sister Eileen can look down on you,' he said, 'she'll be a proud woman. Come and walk out with me for a while; there's a grand bit of sunshine and I've done a few things round the place I'd like to show you.'

When Frank left he sank into a chair and switched on the television. Mary Rose thought he looked glum and irritable. As soon as Frank's car set off down the drive his bonhomie had dropped like a mask. She knew he hated watching the particular quiz programme which was babbling in the background. She thought, Maybe he'll talk about it.

'I thought Frank looked tired,' she remarked. 'Is he working too hard? Why don't we invite him over to Florida for Christmas?'

'We could do,' Kevin grunted. He looked up. 'Marie's left him. Yeah, sure, we'll invite him over. Good idea.' He settled low in the chair, glaring at the screen. 'Listen to that fuckin' idiot of a woman! Jesus, a two-year-old'd know the answer.'

Mary Rose ignored the language. She said gently, 'I'm glad she's gone. She wasn't the right girl for Frank. I just couldn't take to her, honey. I did try, but I just couldn't . . .'

'He won't do much better,' Kevin said.

The money would be in by the end of the week. It might be a good idea to invite his nephew over to the

States much sooner than Christmas. As soon as possible, till he'd calmed down. There were plenty of nice girls back home. He needed his mind taken off politics. And the frightening overtone of distrust stemming from Sean Filey and the others needed time to sink below the surface. Kevin knew that it had always been there, the sleeping crocodile sunk in the mud. Now it was stirring. And Frank himself was threshing round in the water.

He said to Mary Rose, 'I can't watch this shit. There's one thing I miss about back home, and that's cable TV.' He got up to get himself a whiskey. It might stop him worrying.

On the morning of the robbery, Sean Filey was at St Patrick's nursing home, treating three private patients. Jim Quinlan was on duty at Heuston station. He had arranged the roster so he would be there for the Dublin to Cork train. Marie Dempster was at the house at Sanky. She was driving out to Sallins at the time arranged. She'd rented a flat near Howth Bay. It was quiet and had fine views over the sea. That morning she sat by the radio, smoking and drinking cups of strong coffee. She wasn't made-up in her usual careful way, or smartly dressed. Jeans, a shirt, a scarf tied over her hair. The sleek BMW was left behind at Howth. There was a hired Ford Escort parked outside.

Frank was in his office, talking to a client who wanted the bank's support in a share flotation for a ceramics company in Wicklow. It sounded a promising issue, and likely to attract strong support in the market. He heard the wailing sirens in the background and paid no attention.

In the foyer of the Kildare Street branch of the Bank of Ireland the manager lay shot dead. A girl was crying hysterically, police were cordoning off the area and gathering the bank staff into the back rooms. The acrid cordite smell of gunfire lingered in the air. A stolen Renault 5 was lost in the traffic headed towards Heuston station. There were three men, apart from the driver,

267

the hoods pulled off their heads, the shotgun on the floor between their feet. The suitcase with the money crammed into it was stowed in the boot. They heard the sirens wailing, and one glanced through the rear window. None of them spoke. The manager had played the hero, lunging for an alarm button instead of doing what he was told. He'd been shot dead before he had time to reach it.

The Renault pulled into the station forecourt. One man checked his watch. They got out, nobody hurrying. One heaved the suitcase out of the back. A porter lounged nearby.

"Bye now, thanks for the lift,' one called out for his benefit, as the driver set off. They walked through to the ticket office. One bought three tickets to Cork, while the other two waited, guarding the suitcase. They looked relaxed and very ordinary. One bought a newspaper and opened it at the sports page. A number of people were catching the train. The three walked through the barrier, each with a ticket and apparently quite unconnected. They boarded the train as soon as it came in and made their way to the rear.

Quinlan met them. 'Follow me,' he said. He unlocked the guard's van. The man with the suitcase looked round.

'We had trouble. Feckin' manager. Declan shot him.'

Quinlan didn't react. 'I'll lock you in; five minutes before Sallins I'll open it. You know what to do then. Good luck.'

He went out. The man called Declan fumbled in his pocket for a cigarette. His hand was shaking badly.

'None o' that!' he was told sharply. No butts or spent matches must be left behind. Like a fool he had taken off his glove. He drew it back on and settled down on a box to pass the time. Shooting the manager had shaken his nerves. It wasn't the first time he'd killed a man, and once they'd dropped the money and were clear, he wouldn't give it a thought. There were mailbags in the van. The older man, a long-term criminal who'd been on the Provos' payroll for some years, pondered them for a moment and then decided not to push their luck. They had the money safe, and they'd be well paid. Besides, they were convinced supporters of the Republican cause. They checked their watches again. The suitcase was taken up. They stood, swaying slightly with the movement of the train, and at the exact time, Quinlan opened the door and glanced in briefly.

'Be ready,' he said. Then he was gone. They came out into the corridor. The countryside hummed past them. Sallins was up ahead. Quinlan timed it perfectly. The first carriage had passed under the bridge when he pulled the emergency cord. As the brakes went on and the train began screaming and juddering under their impact, he raced up towards the driver's cabin. It had almost stopped by the time he reached it.

'Bloody yobs,' he shouted. 'I saw 'em pull the cord . . .'

Donny heard it coming. He couldn't believe it at first, and he craned forward over the edge of the bridge, cupping a hand to his ear. His mouth stretched into a huge, delighted grin. He jumped up and down, gripping the parapet with both hands, and gave little cries of excitement.

'The train,' he babbled, 'The train's comin' . . .'

It was one o'clock and the rest of Sallins was eating dinner or sitting over a drink in Cargill's lounge. The shops were shut. It was the hour of the Irish siesta, without the sun. Donny saw the big, beautiful miracle of the train as it approached, and to his astonishment and joy it started to slow down. The Dublin-Cork train didn't stop at that tiny station, it sped through, giving him a brief glimpse of its glory. Now it was actually stopping. Nearly stopping, coming to a slow, slow crawl, so that he could see its shiny roof and lovely carriages sliding away under the bridge. It was the most exciting moment of his life, and he wet himself a little without knowing it. For a brief moment he thought it stopped, but by then there was only the tail end of it on his side. Then it started to move again, gathering speed. He turned to watch it, giggling with happiness, and as it vanished down the track he turned again and saw the three men coming up the steps from the platform.

They'd dropped down from the rear as the train slowed to a near halt. People's heads were poking out of carriage windows way up front, staring ahead looking for whatever had caused the driver to put on his brakes. No one saw them leave the guard's van. Quinlan would come back and relock the door. The incident would be put down to teenagers fooling with the emergency cord, and there'd be no connection with the Dublin bank robbers.

Except that there was a witness up there on the bridge who'd seen them leave the train.

'Declan!'

It was a command. Declan thrust one hand into his coat and bounded up the few steps leading to the bridge. Donny stared at him. He was still grinning and mumbling to himself. He didn't see the knife. In a frenzy of rage and fear, the man called Declan stabbed him over and over again, holding him by the front of his ragged jersey as he plunged the weapon into his heart and lungs. Donny didn't even cry out. He died with the memory of the lovely train imprinted on his mind. The first vicious stabbing pierced his heart before he had time to be afraid.

He crumpled into a heap, blood spreading like a rain puddle all round him. The three men were gone, leaving him there. Across from the bridge, down a side road, they saw the Escort parked and the woman sitting in the driver's seat. She opened the passenger door, expecting them to put the suitcase in and go.

'Drive us to the next town,' she was told, and before she could protest they'd piled into the car, slamming the doors.

'We were feckin' seen,' was the snapped explanation. 'Get on, will ye, for Christ's sake!'

She started the car, began to drive too fast, and was ordered savagely to slow down.

'Drive normal. Into Naas. We'll get the bus.'

Marie turned to the man beside her. She had begun to tremble. A witness. Oh, God, it had gone wrong.

'Who saw you?'

'Some auld fella on the bridge. He won't be tellin' anyone. This'll do, here.'

They got out when she pulled in to the kerb. She tried not to see the others. She kept looking ahead of her. The suitcase was on the back seat. One hundred thousand pounds in notes. She'd heard the news flash on the car radio. The manager had been murdered. Now there was another man dead. She couldn't think properly till she got back to the house, and that case was hidden and the car shut away in the garage. Only then, with whiskey sluiced into a cup of coffee and the shakes subsiding, did Marie realize that the witness on the bridge must have been the Sallins idiot, Donny.

The neighbours were sitting round with Donny's mother. Someone had brought a few bottles of Guinness. His married sisters were there and the two brothers. They were dazed and aimless, making tea, clearing cups off the kitchen table, staring anxiously at the mother who was the mainstay of them all. The father had died years ago of drink and misery, leaving her to bring up five weanlings, as she said. And one of them missing a sixpence . . . Donny, poor harmless creature that he was, stabbed to death in the middle of the day on Sallins bridge.

For a long time his mother sat with her apron pulled over her face like a shroud, weeping as Irish mothers had done for their sons since time began. Now she had calmed herself and taken a glass of Guinness. The Gardai had been and gone. One of them had left two pounds on the mantelpiece. She'd known them all her life. Donny's body had been taken away. There were words she hardly understood like 'autopsy' and 'inquest'. But it was murder, she understood that. When one of her

271

daughters bent and whispered to her that Mr Arbuthnot of Riverstown was outside asking if he might come in, Donny's mother just sat and stared. She broke into a storm of tears as soon as he came into the room. The neighbours huddled in the background. Mr Arbuthnot himself coming to a place like this! Donny's eldest sister wiped her hands on her skirt and asked if he'd have a cup of tea. He looked terribly upset, she told everyone afterwards.

Frank knew Ireland. He said thank you, if there was tea ready, he'd be glad to have a cup. He said gently, 'Mrs Brennan, I heard about Donny on the news. It's a dreadful thing for you.'

He looked into the lined and weary face; the hands wringing in her lap were worn with rough work and twisted with arthritis. Every day as long as Donny stood on the bridge, she'd come out and led him home, scolding him all the way. But she'd cared for him and borne the burden for all those years.

Frank leaned down and said, 'Whoever did it will be caught, don't worry. They'll pay for it. Donny never hurt anyone in his life.'

'He was a good lad,' she said, and let her tears flow, mopping them with the crumpled apron. 'He never harmed so much as a fly on the wall. Who'd do it, Mr Arbuthnot, sir? Who'd kill a poor child o' God like him?'

Frank didn't answer.

News on the car radio was linking a bank robbery with an incident on the Dublin-Cork train when someone pulled the emergency cord at Sallins, where the poor simpleton had been found stabbed to death. Frank knew, even as he looked into Donny's mother's face, that he would get a call to say the money for the arms shipment was ready for collection.

'Don't worry about anything,' he said. He spoke to Donny's brother. He worked in the local slaughter-house, and kept not only his own family of four children, but helped his mother as well.

'I'll be in touch,' Frank said. 'Your mother'll need

money for the funeral. I'll see to that. She's not to go borrowing. You tell her that.'

'I will,' Donny's brother mumbled. 'I will so. She's some put by for herself, but that's all.' He stared after Frank as he said goodbye and left the house.

Sallins would talk about that visit for years to come.

Frank drove back to Meath. Mrs Brogan came out to meet him. He saw the husband in the shadow of the kitchen door.

'Isn't it terrible news, sir?' she said. 'That poor man murdered in Dublin?'

'Yes,' he said. 'Terrible.'

He went into the study and shut the door. He sat down and switched on the television for the latest news. Mrs Brogan went back to her husband.

'Did ye see the face on him?' she demanded. 'White to the gills. Maybe it's robbin' the bank he doesn't like – too close to home.'

Brogan said, 'It looks like our lads, Mary.'

'I'd say so,' she said. 'Good luck to 'em. I'll say a little prayer they won't be caught.'

'You don't understand.' Marie's voice rose. 'He stopped the car to give that dirty old creature money. He'll go mad over this!'

Sean said, 'Lower your voice. You don't need to shout. He won't like it – so, what does he do? He's agreed to take the money and pay it through to the supplier in Monaco. He's in up to his neck. Calm down, woman, for Christ's sake. You're losing your nerve.' He turned away from her.

Marie moved after him. 'He'll shop us,' she said. 'He'll give the lot of us away. That'll buy him immunity.'

'From Dublin maybe,' he answered, 'but not from us. He knows what happens to informers. He'll shout the odds, but he daren't do more.'

She said bitterly, 'He's not afraid of us. He's never seen that side. He's never in his life had to keep his mouth shut for fear of anyone. Arbuthnot's no poor yob from Cork who can be scared witless by the threat of a kneecapping. I know him,' she went on. 'I know him better than you or anyone else. I told you why we broke up and I lost the job. I stood up for what we were doing, and he raved at me. Murderers, cowards . . . that's what he called our people in the North. But you don't want to know, Sean. You'd rather risk everything than listen to me!'

He swung round on her. He never lost his temper, but he did then.

'I know what you told me,' he shouted. 'I know I backed you with Quinlan and the others. But I didn't believe you, Marie, and I still don't. You're jealous because he doesn't love you, and now that he's sick of you, you'd see him dead if you could! But I won't kill him to please you. Not till I know he's a real danger. Now I'm shouting,' he said in exasperation.

'Prove it,' she taunted him. 'Ask him to accept the money. See what he says!'

'I'm going to,' he answered. 'I'm going to Meath tomorrow. Now shut up. I've had enough.'

He went out, banging the door. She heard the car start up and screech as it turned out on to the road. She knew Sean. He was afraid, but he wouldn't admit it. The plan to rob the bank had misfired. Two men were dead, one because he was brave and foolish, the other because he was in the wrong place at the wrong time.

The public was roused. The IRA was being accused in the media; the circumstantial evidence was growing, linking the murder of the idiot at Sallins to escaping robbers who feared he could identify them. Nothing could be proved, unless one of the killers was caught. Or Quinlan came under suspicion. She wasn't worried about that. He was too experienced to slip up, and there'd never been a blot on his record with the railway in thirty years. The money was hidden in the house. There'd been no arrests, no new developments after two days. The local pubs and lounges were taking collections for Donny's widowed mother. They were safe, except for Frank Arbuthnot.

He went into Dublin to his office as usual. The staff thought he seemed withdrawn and tight-lipped, as if he had something complicated on his mind. He did business as usual, accepted an invitation to lunch at the Hibernian with two brokers. He told his secretary to cancel the appointment with Doctor Filey at his home that evening. He had to stay in town on business. He read the news-paper reports and listened to the news bulletins. They weren't going to be caught. There were no clues. The guard on the train said he'd seen a youth pull the cord and then run down the corridor. He couldn't catch him. The car stolen on the morning of the robbery had been recovered in a side street off the Quays. Forensic tests detected traces of a recently fired shotgun on the rear floor. A porter at the station remembered seeing a similar car draw up and some men getting out, but he couldn't remember the number and couldn't give a description of anyone. They weren't going to be caught.

Kevin Ryan telephoned. Frank didn't take the call. He didn't want to talk to his uncle. He knew the moment of decision was upon him.

There were violent, ruthless men within the frame-work of the Provisional IRA. And they were part of a horrible scenario of vengeance and terror in the North. Now that terror had struck two streets distant, and knifed a helpless old man because he happened to be in the way. He wouldn't touch the money, until the men responsible for killing Donny had been punished by their own people, and he'd been given proof of it. If they refused – he had made up his mind what to do.

He left Dublin and drove to Riverstown. Claudia was in the study. They hadn't seen each other since his father's funeral. She had aged. But nothing else had changed. She flushed angrily when he was shown in.

'What the hell are you doing here?'
'I came to see you about Donny.'

She said, 'Donny? What about him? Why do you burst in here without even ringing up?'

Frank said, 'Because I knew you wouldn't see me. Claudia, I want to do something for the family.'

He saw the bitterness in her face. 'Why don't your friends in the IRA provide for them?' she countered. 'After all, they killed the poor devil.'

'It's not proved,' he said, and it sounded feeble.

She shrugged. 'Balls,' she snapped at him. 'Everyone in Sallins knows it was them. That's why nobody's come forward. The porter at the railway wouldn't even give a rough description after he realized it wasn't just a robbery. You make me sick, Frank, talking about helping the family. You and your speeches in New York and your public support for the bloody murderers – what do you want to do, salve your conscience with money?'

'I want to offer a reward for information,' he said. 'And set up a proper fund for Mrs Brennan. I want you to join me, Claudia, and get your friends to contribute. If we offer enough, someone will inform on whoever did this. They always have.'

'So it's said,' she said contemptuously. 'Offer them enough and they'll betray their nearest and dearest. Why don't you get your charming uncle to do something about it? Ask him to put his hand in his pocket for this? I bet you'll get a short bloody answer! I wish you'd go,' she added and turned away from him.

'Then you won't help?'

'No.' The answer was final. 'I'm sorry about Donny. But I'm not going to get a bomb thrown through my window just to make you feel better.' She turned round to him. 'If your chickens are coming home to roost, then it's about time. You're one of them. You do something about it.'

'I'm going to, Claudia,' he said. 'The bank manager had a wife and three young children. It's not just Donny.'

He went out, and left the house. She stood by the window and watched him get into his car and drive away.

Suddenly she remembered the flash of premonition that had come over her so many years ago, when he and Claire stood side by side, smiling at each other. The same sense of tragedy swept over her again. It was so strong that she tried to open the window and call him back. But the catch was on too tight, and the next moment the car had disappeared.

By the next morning the story was being whispered throughout Sallins. Not only had Frank Arbuthnot gone to see Donny's mother and paid for the funeral, but he was up at the house telling the missus he was going to pay big money for information about who'd done the killing. The missus wouldn't have any part of it. Wise woman, they agreed. It didn't do to meddle with things like that. All you'd get was trouble.

The report came direct to Sean Filey via Joe Burns, who'd heard it in the Gardai station. He didn't dare contact Jim Quinlan. Quinlan thought he was being watched. Filey had to deal with this alone. He couldn't trust Kevin Ryan either, if he felt his nephew might be at risk. He'd intervened once and it hadn't gone deep enough to survive the shock of the idiot's death. He suffered two days of suspense after Frank cancelled their meeting. The excuse could have been genuine. He had tried to believe it was, if only to allay his own fears. He decided to be calm and rely upon rationality instead of instinct. He decided not to rush Arbuthnot, not to betray any suspicion. Then he got the call from young Burns, and he knew then he had to act. He phoned Mrs Brogan.

'Is Mr Arbuthnot expected home tonight?'

'He is,' she answered. 'He's in to dinner. He rang me from his office this afternoon.'

'Good,' Sean Filey said. 'I'm on my way over.'

Chapter 8

'What you're asking is impossible.'

'I'm not asking,' Frank Arbuthnot said. 'I'm demanding it. I want the men who murdered Donny Brennan punished. And I want proof of it, Sean. Nothing else will do.'

They were standing, and Filey was conscious of the difference in their heights. He felt overshadowed for the first time in their long relationship. He had never lost the initiative before. Now it had been wrested from him by the man he had manipulated and despised. He felt a conscious hatred of him, and recognized that it had been there from the beginning.

'You really mean to tell me that the life of one old half-wit is more to you than our victory in the North?'

'There is no victory in the North,' Frank retorted. 'There's just another load of guns at stake, more killing, more violence. And never mind who gets hurt. All you can see in this is one old, useless idiot that nobody's going to miss, isn't that right?'

'No,' Sean countered. He knew he was arguing for the future of the whole careful enterprise he'd built up through this one man.

'No, that's over-simplifying. Every man's life is important. But sacrifices have to be made. You know that. You've accepted it. This is just a childhood memory that's been violated. This ties in with sweets on a Sunday when you were a boy. It's sentimental self-indulgence, Frank. Be reasonable, for God's sake. They had to do it. He could have identified them!'

Frank said quietly, 'Donny couldn't identify his own mother. They didn't have to kill him, Sean. There's no excuse. They shot down the poor devil in the bank too.

I know, he went for the alarm. But isn't there any limit when it comes to killing in cold blood? Is it always right, because somehow it's part of the fight for Irish freedom?'

Sean Filey paused for a moment. The argument was lost and he knew it. He threw down his challenge.

'Yes,' he said. 'Whatever we have to do, we'll do.'

'Then you can count me out,' he heard Frank say. 'If that's the price, it's too much for me to pay. No principle in the world is worth more than the poorest simpleton in Ireland. That's what it comes down to. You can find someone else to deal with that money. I wouldn't touch it.'

Filey said quietly, 'You're breaking your oath, you realize that?'

'Yes. But you needn't be afraid I'll go to the police. There are other ways of helping them catch those swine. But I won't betray you or anyone I've worked with. You can be sure of that.'

'Your word of honour?' Filey asked coldly. Like the promise you made when you joined. Words of fealty sanctified in the blood of our fathers and grandfathers . . . Hatred chilled him. It made him shiver. Arbuthnot was going to offer a reward for information. But that wouldn't constitute betrayal.

Frank said, 'I don't think you take that very seriously. But in my case you can. No one will ever learn anything about the organization from me. I didn't make this decision without thinking very hard. But I'm not prepared to go along with what you represent any more. Would you like a drink before you go?'

'I don't drink with traitors,' Filey said.

'Only with murderers!' was the retort as he opened the door and went out.

It was very quiet in the room. There was a fine mantel clock of his grandmother's and the gentle ticking sounded like gunshots in the silence. There was a knock on the door.

Frank called out, 'Come in.'

'Shall I serve the dinner now the gentleman's gone?' Mrs Brogan enquired.

'Thank you, Mary. Ten minutes, if it won't spoil.'

'Oh, sure, it's a casserole. It won't spoil at all.' And smiling, she withdrew.

He lit a cigarette. He'd open some wine when he went to the dining room. Alone, after years of living with Marie. It was a blessed peacefulness by contrast. The empty bed was sweeter than an embrace when he sank into it.

He went to the phone and dialled England. Her voice answered.

'Claire? It's me. I've got something to tell you. I think you'll be glad . . .' And while she asked him worried questions he thought of a joke to ease her mind.

'I can always hole up in our secret place. Remember old Reynard?' And then he said goodbye, God bless you, and hung up. They wouldn't dare touch him. They might talk about it among themselves, but they wouldn't dare. He threw the stub of cigarette into the empty grate and went into the dining room to eat alone.

Filey didn't interrupt her. He let her talk, the plan shaping, filling out with details. She couldn't sit still. She was walking round the kitchen, pausing to emphasize the point. She was flushed and bright-eyed. Her excitement was almost sexual, he thought, watching her. Yet everything she said made sense. Killing Arbuthnot was the obvious remedy. But wasn't it a kind of defeat, an admission of failure? What she proposed would turn it into a massive triumph. A propaganda coup that could bring a ransom with it.

'If you kidnap him,' Marie said, 'she'll come here trying to find him.'

Filey said, 'You really think she'd take that risk?'

'I know it,' Marie declared. 'I've listened to them on the phone to each other. I've read the letters she writes him. She wouldn't give that husband what'd drop off

280

her finger. It's darling Frank she cares about. She'll come. All we need is the publicity.'

Filey imagined that jealous spying, carried on over the years.

'Did you ever say anything to him?' he asked her.

She stopped moving and turned to face him. 'Yes,' she admitted. 'That's why he threw me out. That's the truth of it, Sean.'

'I thought it might be,' he said. 'Not that it matters now. He's turned against us. I can't involve Quinlan in this. But I'll talk to Macbride.'

'Why?' she demanded. 'Why does he have to stick his nose in? We've got enough people – we can keep him here till we get her. Jesus, I can't wait to see his face!' She sat down and lit a cigarette. Her hands were shaking.

A little mad, Filey thought. She's become a little mad with her jealousy. It's made her capable of anything.

'I have to bring Macbride in,' he explained. 'Our lads can't take the money to the North, it's too risky for them. He'll have to make his own arrangements. A boat would be the best way. And he has contacts with the Dublin Council. He can keep Quinlan informed. I'll get on to him. Meantime, we've got to work out the timing and place to take him.'

'I know his routine backwards,' she said. 'I can do that. We'll need someone to make the upstairs room secure.'

By the next morning the window in the upstairs room was whitewashed. A bed had been moved into it. A strong padlock had been fitted to the door.

Macbride had asked one question only: 'How much time have we got?'

'Not much,' Filey answered. 'As soon as we're ready, it'll be done.'

'Don't hang about. He could make up his mind to spill his guts out to the Gardai any day.' And then he added, 'Good luck. That sister'd be a big fish to catch.'

There was a car park to the rear of the bank. It was overlooked by blank walls. It was marked 'Private', with little bays reserved for senior employees. Every day at nine-thirty, Frank Arbuthnot drove in. As Marie Dempster said, you could set your watch by him.

It was all timed to the last minute. Brogan had phoned through when he left for Dublin; the black Peugeot 505 was cruising round the area until nine-twenty, when it turned into the cul-de-sac and slid into a vacant parking bay. There were always two kept for bank visitors. A strange car wouldn't cause comment. Filey wanted to carry out the kidnapping after the bank closed, but Marie insisted that Arbuthnot didn't come back every after-noon, or leave at the same time in the evening. The morning was the safest. The risk was a member of the senior staff arriving late. Marie could vouch for Frank's punctuality, but she couldn't be certain that Dublin traffic and human nature might not wreck their plan. If the car park was full, they had five minutes or less to seize their quarry and drive off. They'd discussed alternatives and abandoned them.

Meath was out of the question. The Brogans mustn't be involved in a police investigation. They were loyal to the core, but not sophisticated enough to cope with an interrogation. Dublin was the place to make the snatch, and it must be done without evidence of a struggle. An ambush on the road was ruled out for the same reason. Arbuthnot must arrive at the bank, leave his car and then vanish.

It was a very wet morning. Frank drove into the centre of the city, glanced at his watch and cursed the traffic. Dublin was grey in the rain, the river Liffey ruffled by a sharp little breeze that whipped it spitefully. The pavements shone like polished slate. A billboard mocked Frank as he drove: 'Come to sunny Cork with Loughlin Holidays'. A smiling family group waved at him, the sky blue in the background. Further on, a news stand, protected by a flimsy plastic sheet, had the scrawl on the *Independent* board, 'Robbery. No clues'.

'I won't betray you or anyone I've worked with.' That was his promise to Sean Filey. And that contemptuous question, 'Your word of honour?' He had expected the anger, been prepared for bitterness and reproach. But not for the hatred. It wasn't a hatred new-born out of the situation. It must have always been there under the surface of what Frank thought was friendship. The lights changed and he moved on. Work was the antidote. It stopped the agonizing self-examination that drove away sleep and peace of mind. So much had been thrown away, so many things destroyed in his pursuit of an ideal. If an ideal it really was, he thought, in growing doubt. Or just a search for himself that led him nowhere in the end.

Thank God for the bank. Thank God for work and more work, so that he couldn't think too far ahead. Ryan wanted him to go to the States. Now that was closed to him. His uncle and his friends were united in the common cause that he'd abandoned. There'd be no welcome for him there once it was known. He turned into the cul-de-sac. It was nine-forty. Not bad, considering the weather and the traffic. The spaces were all full. He didn't even notice the black Peugeot. He reached behind him for his brief-case, got out, locked the car door. At the same moment Willie left the Peugeot. He came up to Frank. They met within a few feet of the black car. No chances were to be taken. Those were Filey's instructions. 'Don't pull a gun on him, he's the kind to have a go at you. Send Pat round and get him from behind.'

'Mornin',' said Willie in his nasal Dublin twang, with a broad smile. 'It's Mr Arbuthnot, is it?'

'Yes.' Frank paused.

Pat straightened up from where he'd been crouching, brought the cosh up and then down with all his force on to the back of the man's head. Willie caught him as he went down. The boot of the Peugeot sprang open and the two of them had him heaved up and bundled inside in a few seconds. Willie slammed the boot down.

'Now ye bastard,' he said. 'Ye'll take a little ride.'

*

They'd taken him upstairs. Willie'd stopped on a quiet road outside Dublin and he and Pat had tied the unconscious man's hands and taped over his eyes. They didn't dare gag him in case he choked. She'd watched from behind the curtain when the car drove up. She'd seen him briefly, manhandled in through the front door, and heard the shuffle and scuffle of resistance as they forced him up the narrow stairs. Willie'd stuffed a greasy rag into his mouth to stop him shouting till he was safe inside. She stood very still, her heart hammering with a savage excitement.

He'd turned her out after all those years. He'd taken everything she had to give, most of all her brand of fierce proprietary love, and tossed it away like rubbish. Now he was going to pay for that. His betrayal of their political beliefs meant nothing to her any more. All she could think of was him imprisoned above her head, at her mercy now, as she had so often been at his. She wondered if he'd beg. No, Marie thought, not for himself. But wait. Wait till we bring her face to face with him. He'll beg then, and I'll be there watching.

Willie cut his hands loose, seized one wrist and locked it into a handcuff, which was then snapped round the bedpost. He pulled the rag out of his mouth and ripped away the tape blinding his eyes. He looked down at him, with Pat standing in the rear. He was holding a gun and pointing it at their prisoner.

'Now ye listen to me, you fucker,' Willie snarled. 'Ye open yer trap to make a sound and I'll be up here and knock the teeth down yer throat. Not that there's anyone to hear ye! But no noise out of ye – no fuckin' trouble or, be Christ, I'll make ye wish ye'd never been born!'

Then he went out. Pat followed. He lingered in the doorway for a moment and levelled the gun slowly and deliberately at Frank. He didn't say a word. He just looked, and the look said everything. It was more terrifying than Willie's threats. Then Frank was alone.

There was a blinding pain in his head where he'd been coshed. He tried to sit upright and the room spun round.

He leaned over and retched. His right hand was pinioned to the bedpost, which was heavy and solid. He sank back and closed his eyes. He couldn't remember anything before he came to in the black, cramped space, and found himself blindfolded and tied up. Concussion, he thought, that's the headache. That's why I'm sick and can't remember. Stay quiet. You can't do anything like this. Stay very quiet. They haven't killed you. Remember that. They want something from you first. Slowly he stilled the fear that threatened to turn into panic. You're weak and shaken. Your only hope is time, and soon enough you'll find out why you've been brought here. Then you can begin to fight them.

'Pat give him a fair old crack on the head,' Willie said.

Sean Filey glanced at the impassive young man sitting by the fireplace, cleaning his nails with a matchstick. He met a blank and hostile stare.

'He could be concussed,' Sean said.

'He could so,' Willie agreed. 'I heard him bein' sick after we left him. That'll keep him quiet for a few days anyway.'

Filey got up. 'Marie's coming in and out. You've got the rota for guarding him. She'll see to the food and one of you go up and hold a gun on him. I'll be round tomorrow. Watch yourselves meantime.'

Pat stayed the first night. He went up towards mid-afternoon, opened the door briefly and watched the man lying on his back on the bed. He was breathing and seemed asleep. Frank watched the dim figure through a slit of eyelid. The room was mercifully shaded by a little whitewashed window. Light hurt his eyes, and the pain in his head was a continuous throbbing ache. The nausea had stopped. The door closed again and he could hear the man's footsteps going down the stairs. He lay still, willing himself to sleep.

A full bladder woke him. Someone had been up and left a lamp burning in a corner, too far away for him to reach. There was a chamber pot, a roll of lavatory paper and a jug of water with a tin mug placed beside the bed.

It should have been a difficult and humiliating task to relieve himself. Willie hadn't reckoned on him being left-handed when he fastened him to the bed. He lay back, listening. His head ached, but he felt no dizziness when he moved or sat up. His arm was very stiff, suspended above his head. He lay and he listened. There was no carpeting, just bare boards, nothing in the room but the bed and the lamp on the floor. He could hear a murmur of voices from below. He sat up again and looked down. The floor was thin. Modern planking, unlike the thick wood used in old houses. The ceilings were not soundproof. He was above them, but all he could hear was the murmur. He couldn't isolate any words. If he could make a hole, there was a chance . . . His pockets had been emptied. There was nothing he could use. He felt a great surge of rage sweep over him, followed by a helplessness that could have brought him to tears.

He passed the night in fits of sleeping, and starts of waking panic when he dreamed the door was opening and the man with murder in his eyes was standing there. But when it did open, it was late morning, and it was Marie Dempster with a tray in her hand who stood and smiled at him, with the gunman at her back.

'How are you feeling, Frank?' she asked. 'I've brought you a bite of breakfast.'

The alarm had been raised by mid-afternoon. The girl who'd replaced Marie as Frank's secretary phoned through to Meath when he didn't come in, because he had clients waiting. He had left for Dublin at his usual time, she was told. When she noticed his car in the parking bay, the senior investment consultant advised her to contact the police and the hospitals, in case he'd walked off somewhere and been run over. A detective came round with a constable, took details, examined the car and went back to report.

From the computer print-out on Francis Hugh Arbuthnot, the Chief Superintendent decided to call in the Special Branch. The item was on the early TV news and in the evening edition of the Dublin papers. 'Banker vanishes', the headlines cried in thick black type. 'Mr Frank Arbuthnot, prominent merchant banker, disappeared after leaving his car in the park outside the Boston Irish Bank this morning. Mr Arbuthnot left his Meath mansion at eight-thirty this morning and has not been seen since. There is growing speculation that he may have been kidnapped. The Arbuthnots are a wealthy Kildare family . . .' Sean Filey switched the set off.

The black Peugeot had been stolen in Wicklow at dawn that morning. It was left a mile away from the owner's house. Sean had told Willie to drop empty coke cans, sweet papers and a crumpled packet of cheap cigarettes inside. All the windows were left open and the door had been given a dent with a hammer. The infuriated owner was told by the local police it was teenagers joy-riding, and he was lucky the damage was so slight. Nothing was missing from the boot and nobody bothered any further. Arbuthnot had been swallowed up as if he'd stepped into a bog. And a bog was where he would end, as soon as they had got Claire Fraser in their hands. If Marie was wrong, and the sister didn't come, then he'd be executed as a warning to others.

The publicity was just what they wanted. It made the six and nine o'clock news on BBC and the ten o'clock on ITV. Filey watched them both. The slant was different, but even better for their purpose. 'The brother-in-law of Trade and Industry Secretary Neil Fraser is feared kidnapped from his merchant bank in the Irish Republic. Mr Frank Arbuthnot, member of a prominent Anglo-Irish family and Chairman of the Boston Irish Bank of Dublin, disappeared after leaving his home in Meath.'

Billy Gorman saw the item on RTE. He sat hunched in his chair, staring at the set, muttering 'Jayney', over and over, because he was frightened out of his life by what he was hearing. Sallins had been buzzing with talk of the reward Arbuthnot was going to offer. A number of people said he should mind his own business. Others said worse.

Up at Riverstown, Claudia saw the same programme. She watched it right through and sat on with the sound turned down for a long time afterwards. 'Your chickens are coming home to roost,' she'd said. It looked like a terrible prophecy now. Soon the phone started ringing. She answered it. She said the same thing to the next three callers.

'Yes, it is frightful. But if it is the IRA, he brought it on himself. I just hope it doesn't mean trouble for the rest of the family.'

And then came the call she'd been dreading. The call from Claire in Gloucestershire.

Claire had taken the children to a birthday party. There were twenty little boys and girls. Lucy was the extrovert; she toddled forward to join in, while Peter hung back holding on to his mother. He was a shy child, and Claire had to coax him to play the party games. After a time he was enjoying himself. The noise was shrill and deafening. The little girl who was seven that day cut her cake and blew out the candles to screams of encouragement. There were balloons and a present for each guest. Claire knew the family slightly, but she was aware that her children had been asked because the Frasers were a social prize.

They drove home, the children playing with their too expensive gifts in the back. Claire remembered the simple presents of her own childhood, when a packet of coloured pencils was a treat. She switched on the radio as the news was finishing and listened to the weather forecast. Warm, south-easterly winds, maximum temperature twenty degrees centigrade.

It should be a nice weekend. And for once the house wasn't going to be full of people. Neil arranged house parties weeks in advance, and he had a long and varied list of guests. Most of them were connected with his political career. Claire had been bored by what she called his lobbying weekends for years. But she went through the motions. She arranged lunch and dinner parties, played tennis and walked with them on the Sunday afternoon, Neil's Labradors trotting obediently at their heels. This weekend she could swim in the pool and lie around reading without being interrupted. When they first moved to the house, she and Neil used to have crazy tennis matches, slamming the balls at each other and shrieking with laughter. That had stopped long ago.

She took the children upstairs to the nursery. The girl Claudia had engaged after Lucy's birth was still with them. They ran happily towards her.

'I'll come and say goodnight after they've had their baths,' Claire said. She went back downstairs, poured herself a glass of wine and tucked herself up on the sofa. She switched on the BBC six o'clock news.

Neil had been driving flat out to get home after the call came through. Because of the family connection, he was told about his brother-in-law's disappearance before it became public. As soon as he came into the drawing room and saw Claire, he knew that she'd already heard. He saw her white and stricken face and hurried towards her.

'Oh darling, I know. I know. Don't cry.' He put his arms round her.

She drew into herself as if he were a stranger.

'I'll die if anything's happened to him,' she said. 'It's the IRA. I warned him, I begged him. Oh, my God, my God . . .'

'Claire,' he protested. 'For God's sake, don't go to pieces like this! He'll probably turn up – he could have gone off somewhere without telling anyone. Don't work yourself up till we know a little more!'

She wrenched away from him. 'Oh, it's easy for you to say that. They'll kill him. I know they will!'

He couldn't calm her. He couldn't reason. Nothing he said seemed to penetrate at all. In the end he said, 'You stay here. I'll get through to London and see what I can find out. They may have more news.'

For the first time she seemed to listen.

'Will you? Will you do that? Oh, get through now, for God's sake.'

When he came back she was quieter, as if she had worn herself out. Her face was blotched and the tears were still running unchecked. He gave her his own handkerchief and slipped his arm round her. This time she didn't pull away.

'I've spoken to people who'd know the full details,' he said. 'It does look as if he's been kidnapped. It could be for ransom.' He didn't mention the other suggestion. 'It may be murder,' he'd been told. 'He's been putting the Provos' backs up lately. If they don't find his body by tomorrow, then it could be a ransom job. Let's hope so, for Mrs Fraser's sake.'

She listened, wiped her eyes and then said, 'I want to ring my mother. I want to talk to somebody who understands. I told him to get out.'

Neil said nothing. Yet another secret kept from him. It wasn't the moment to ask about it.

'I'll get the number for you,' he said. 'Would you like a brandy; calm the nerves?'

'No, thanks,' Claire shook her head. 'It was just the shock. I'd been worrying for days, ever since he phoned. I'm all right now. Sorry I made such a scene. I haven't got the stiff upper lip, I'm afraid.'

He so wanted to be gentle and comforting. He wanted to forget how much he hated that half-brother and wouldn't have really minded if he'd got what he deserved. Perhaps Claire knows, he thought suddenly. Perhaps that's why she put up the shutters again. Someone who understands. That hurt him, and for a moment he was selfish enough to be angry. Claudia wouldn't be sorry. She felt the same about Frank as he did. He went to the telephone and dialled.

'Don't cry,' Claudia said. 'It doesn't help to upset yourself. We've just got to hope it's all a mistake. He may turn up. You've got to keep calm and think of Neil and the children, darling. The Gardai came round a little while ago, and they've promised to let me know if anything comes through. It was that nice boy, Joe Burns. You remember, the father worked for us for years and he used to help out at times. Don't worry, he's probably all right.'

'He isn't, Mother,' Claire said. 'And you know it.'

There was a pause, then Claudia said, 'He did come here after that poor old fellow Donny was murdered. He was talking rather dangerously, I must admit. He wanted to offer a reward for information. I said it was the IRA and he knew perfectly well it was too. I wouldn't have anything to do with it, but you know Frank. He hasn't listened to any of us for years.'

Claire said, 'He rang me and told me he was finished with them. Mother, I'm coming over.'

She heard Neil say, 'No!' very loudly in the background.

'Don't be ridiculous,' Claudia spoke sharply. 'That's absurd. Rushing over and leaving your husband and children. It certainly wouldn't be safe, and you're not staying here. I've decided, I'm not staying either till this is cleared up. I shall go down to Maura Keys in Limerick for a few days. Put Neil on, please, darling. I want to talk to him.'

Claire said distinctly, 'No, I won't. You'll only gang up together. Poor Frank. My poor brother. Nobody gives a damn about him except me.' Then she rang off.

Neil came towards her. 'Claire, for God's sake, darling.'

'I know what you're going to say,' she said. 'But please don't. Not tonight. I couldn't stand it if we argued. Mother was bad enough. I can't stop thinking about it. They're merciless, Neil; they won't just kill him. If they think he's betrayed them in any way, they'll hurt him.'

'Has he betrayed them? Why didn't you tell me?'

'We don't talk about him,' she pointed out. 'We only row if we do. He phoned me some days ago. He said he was finished with the IRA. I wanted him to get out and come here. I would have asked you if he'd said yes. But he wouldn't. They can't touch me, that's what he said. Oh, Neil, I'm so frightened of waking up in the morning and hearing something dreadful.'

'You won't,' he assured her. 'Our people said tonight that no news will be good news. They're usually right.'

There were sleeping pills in the cupboard. He insisted that she took one. He lay awake beside her. He heard her catch a breath in her sleep, as if she were crying in a dream.

If he's dead, I've probably lost her, he thought. She'll never get over it. If he isn't and there's a long nightmare ahead, God knows what will happen . . .

In the morning she woke before him and switched on the radio for the early news. Frank's disappearance was not among the headlines. Claire lay back against the pillows. After a night's rest it was easier to think rationally. Her response last night had been hysterical with shock. No news would be good news, Neil had said. The day was not over; there was plenty of time for the nightmare to become a news item. 'Banker found dead'. She shuddered and shut the thought out. What had he said when they spoke last . . . how long ago? It was only days, but it seemed like a lifetime. *They won't touch me.* Yes, but something else . . . *I can always hole up for a few days. Remember Reynard?* She turned and grabbed Neil by the shoulder.

'Wake up! Oh, wake up, darling. For God's sake.'

He started up, alarmed, and saw by the look of her that it wasn't bad news.

'He may be all right,' she said. 'He may have gone into hiding! If he was threatened, that's what he did! Oh, Neil, it's a chance. If he's not found and there's no ransom or communiqué from those brutes, it's a very good chance! He even said something like that. I was in such a state last night I forgot all about it.'

'Well, maybe that's the explanation. If he thought they were going after him, it makes sense. But where would he be?'

She looked down at her hands. It was their secret. She

292

wouldn't mention it to Neil. He'd dismiss the idea as a piece of Irish lunacy and she couldn't afford that. If he took that last hope away, she'd never forgive him.

'He didn't say,' she said. 'But he'd know somewhere.'

Marie laid the tray down on the bed. It was the morning of the second day. He hadn't spoken a word or responded to her taunting. The silence maddened her. She wanted him to rise to her, to curse and abuse her. Anything but that contemptuous look, as if she were the dirt under his feet.

Willie alternated with the dour Pat. One stayed the night, the other relieved him the next morning. Marie spent time in her Howth flat, and slipped out to cook for the man on guard and torment their prisoner.

'The police came to see me yesterday,' she mocked him. 'I told him we'd not seen each other for weeks. I said I was so sorry, but I'd no *idea* where you might be.'

Willie was sick of standing there with the gun while she nagged and jeered. It was a waste of his bloody time, and she wasn't getting anywhere with the sullen bastard.

'Come on out of it,' he muttered.

Frank spoke to him. 'I want to go to the lavatory.'

'Use the piss pot!'

'It's full.'

Willie jerked his head at Marie. 'That's yer bad luck. Come on,' he repeated.

Frank didn't expect he'd be taken to a lavatory, but it was worth trying. He couldn't shift the frame of the bed. The handcuffs were a sophisticated type that couldn't be picked open, even if he'd had anything thin and sharp to do it with. But he'd made a small hole between the floorboards with the fork he was allowed to eat with. He didn't try to keep it; that would have been noticed immediately. He eased himself over the edge of the bed, crouched down and dug away at the wood. It was difficult; the fork was a miserable tin thing which could easily bend. The hole was tiny, not deep enough to let him hear them talking clearly in the room below.

He listened to the sound of their steps going downstairs, and then began to work gently, scratching out a few splinters at a time.

There was a routine. Marie brought the tray twice a day. They gave him ten minutes, and then Willie or the sinister Pat came in and collected it. The smell of the chamber pot was sickening. It was emptied at night, and left under the bed all day.

He ate the food quickly. It was a slab of stale ham, with a hunk of bread and a rancid-tasting margarine.

'I'm afraid it's not *haute cuisine*,' that fiendish woman had simpered at him, mispronouncing the French words. 'But it'll just have to do!'

He was hungry. He was better and the headache was only a slight discomfort now. But he mustn't seem too strong. He lay down and pretended to be sleeping when they came. By the evening, if he got the fork again, he might be able to distinguish what was being said.

But the evening came, and Marie wasn't there. Pat brought him a saucepan of tinned soup and a spoon. It had a blunt end which wouldn't go between the boards.

Friday and Saturday passed. Claire stayed by the television set, watching every news bulletin. Neil assured her they'd be told before anything was released to the media, but she insisted on listening to the hourly radio news bulletins as well. Neil played with the children. He tried bringing them to Claire, but she was unable to draw comfort from them. At the end of that long, agonizing Sunday, she said to him, 'I think he's gone to ground. Oh, Neil, how can I find out?'

'You can't,' he said. 'You'll just have to be patient and keep your spirits up.'

He only hoped her optimism was justified. Private enquiries through their liaison with Dublin didn't support her theory. Quite the opposite. If a ransom demand was not made within the next forty-eight hours, then Arbuthnot had been summarily executed by his old associates in the IRA. They might decide to leave his fate a mystery and consign the body to one of the deep primeval bogs. A major Sunday newspaper carried the story as their second lead. Frank Arbuthnot was written about in terms that made Claire throw the paper down in helpless rage.

'What a pack of lies! All that stuff about millionaires and giving money to the Provos – God, I've never read such filthy lies in my life.'

'I'm not exactly pleased with it myself,' her husband pointed out.

Claire dismissed that. 'It can't hurt you, Neil. Stop thinking of your bloody career for five minutes, can't you? Everyone knows what you think about Ireland, you've said it often enough. They've made my brother out as some kind of thug.' Then she said, 'Oh please, not Lucy and Peter. Go back to Iris, darlings, Mummy's got a headache. No, Lucy, I said no. Go back to the nursery. Where the hell is Iris?'

And then his patience snapped for the first time. 'There's no need to take it out on the children. They don't know what's happened. You've made Lucy cry.'

'Just because she can't get her own way. And don't talk to me like that in front of them.'

Neil ushered the bewildered brother and sister out, calling for their nanny. Then he came back into the room. Claire was smoking. She had chain-smoked and eaten almost nothing since Thursday night.

'Claire,' he said. 'You've got to pull yourself together. I know you're upset, but I won't have the children treated like that. Most mothers would find them a comfort.'

She turned to him slowly. She looked pale and ill, but by now he was too angry to feel sorry for her. Nothing counted with her but that half-brother. Nothing! He was near breaking point himself.

'You may as well know I've decided to go to Ireland.'

Instinctively he'd known that was coming too. He said, 'You can't do that. It would be insane to go there at this time. I absolutely forbid it.'

'Because it would look bad in the press? Bad for you, I mean?'

He held himself in. 'Yes, it would look very bad. But that's not my reason. I don't want you going to Ireland because you could be in real danger. You can't do that because of Peter and Lucy, even if you don't care about me.'

She said quietly, 'I can't stay here. I can't stay at home not knowing what's become of my brother. If you loved me, Neil, you wouldn't expect me to.'

'I love you,' he said. 'But I expect you to put your family first. You're not to think of going to Ireland. Your own mother said the same.'

'She's not Frank's mother,' Claire answered. 'I'm the only person in the world who loves him. I'm the only one he's got. Don't make this an issue, Neil. Please don't.'

'It is an issue. And it's you who's making it. I've lived with him coming between us for ten years. I've had enough of it. If you walk out on us now, it's for good.'

She didn't answer. She walked past him out of the room. He left for London on Monday morning without seeing her again. She drove Peter to school on Monday. She hugged and kissed him.

'I'm sorry I was cross yesterday, darlings. I just had a nasty headache and I felt grumpy.'

Peter looked up at her. He had a shy, uncertain mannerism that sometimes made her think of Frank when he was very young.

'Will you play with us when I come home, Mummy? You're not going to London to stay with Daddy, are you?'

For a moment she hesitated, but only for a moment. Neil's accusation had hurt, because it was partly true. She saw her son's anxious face and changed her plans. One more day. She owed the little ones that.

'I'm not going to London,' she said. 'We'll have a special game and you can have supper with me tonight, Peter.'

One more day to be endured to prove to herself that she loved her children. One more day of torturing suspense that ended like the others. No new developments, the bulletins said. No ransom demand, no fresh clues.

On Tuesday morning she hired the car in Broadway and set out to catch the night boat to Dublin.

Kevin Ryan flew home to the States a month early. He packed up and left the Half House with Mary Rose and his son Patrick, and nobody asked him why. The headlines about his nephew's disappearance glared at them from every newspaper. Mary Rose was pink around the eyes. They didn't speak on the drive to the airport, and when Patrick started asking questions, Kevin took his head off. Mary Rose glanced sideways at her husband when they were strapped into their seats. They'd been twenty-five years married and she was still trying to come to terms with the man who'd said of his own flesh and blood, 'He's turned traitor, the dirty bastard. He deserves all he gets, and that's an end of it! No more, God damn it! Rose, shut your mouth, I tell you!'

For a moment she'd seen his balled fist lifted to strike her and recoiled.

Next morning he said briefly, 'We're going home. We'll come back when this trouble's over.'

He was her husband and there were things it was better for a woman not to know. She had to accept it. She'd spent a long time praying for Frank Arbuthnot, wherever he might be. She dared not contemplate what might have happened to him. As the plane taxied and took off she had an unthinkable thought: 'I never want to see Ireland again.' Then she slipped her hand into her pocket and began to say the rosary.

Kevin Ryan looked out of the little window as the grey shreds of cloud sped past and suddenly changed to a dazzling sun-filled blue as they reached thirty-five thousand feet. He felt bitter, as if there were bile in his mouth he couldn't spit out. Bitter and old. And the explanations lay ahead of him. There was no greater shame than betrayal by a member of the family. He had to fan his anger. It kept the sorrow in him at bay.

Frank got the fork back on Sunday. It was thrust into a plateful of tinned stew. He couldn't wait for the brutish Willie to go out. Then he was over the side of the bed and down on his knees, picking away at the gap between the boards. This time desperation made him careless. He bent the edges, but he'd made a sizeable hole. There wasn't time to do more. He swallowed half the tepid mess on the plate and set to straightening the tines of the little tin fork. Marie hadn't shown herself. He was thankful for that mercy at least. The plate was taken away, no word was spoken to him, and he was alone. He'd be alone until the evening now. He got down to the floor again and tried scratching with his fingers. A few slivers of wood came away. One spiked him under the nail. He pulled it out and went on. The hours passed. His fingers were raw, but the gap had widened.

They'd taken his watch so he had no idea of time. He heard a noise and scrambled back on to the bed. His pinioned arm was numb from the pressure of the metal bar round his wrist. He heard the door open and pretended to have been asleep, blinking and rubbing his free hand across his eyes. She was standing there. A shadowy figure was behind her as always; the distant light in the passage glinted on the levelled gun.

'I've brought your supper,' Marie announced. 'I hope you haven't missed me.'

She moved towards him, holding the tray in front of her. Frank had a wild impulse to kick out as she came within reach and send it flying backwards into her face. But that would have pleased her. That would have proved she'd reached him at last. He looked past her to the doorway. It was the gunman – Pat, this time – standing guard.

'Willie says you didn't eat your lunch.' She stopped,

admonishing him. He refused to look at her. He didn't see the angry colour flood her face.

'You answer me when I speak to you, you bastard! You'll get no food tonight!'

He couldn't let that happen. 'Don't take it away,' he said. 'I'm hungry.'

She paused and a slight smile touched her lips. 'Are you now? Ready to speak to me at last, are you?'

He had to play for time. He had to get the fork once more. 'Why are you doing this?'

She said in a shrill voice, 'Because you're a dirty betrayer. Turned against us on account of that snivelling loony at Sallins. That's all Ireland meant to you – a filthy old snot-nose, and you're ready to shop our lads on account of him! Here – take your dinner. I hope it chokes you!'

She banged the tray down on the foot of the bed. Then she had gone and the door was shut and locked. He worked feverishly at the hole in the floor. It was wide enough to see the thin line of white plaster underneath. He did the same as he'd done in the morning. He shovelled in the food. Baked beans this time.

Pat came to take the plate away. He stood in the doorway. He didn't come close like Willie. This was a real professional.

'Put that tray on the ground. Now push it over. Use your foot.' He was well beyond reach when he picked it up.

Frank said, 'What about the pot? It needs emptying.'

The eyes stared at him, glowing with hate. 'I'll empty it over you,' was the reply. Then he was gone.

Frank sat quietly for a few moments. He was going to be killed. He knew that the man who would pull the trigger had just left him. He could sense his impatience. But why delay? Why keep him alive and take any risk? He could have been shot dead after they'd seized him, and thrown out on to the road, a warning to anyone else who might think of changing their mind.

He could hear voices below him, and music. It was

muffled but louder than he'd ever noticed before. He got down and, straining to the limit, managed to get his head down and his left ear close to the hole he had made.

In the room below, Marie was sitting in front of the television. It was a religious programme, and she turned the sound low. All those moon faces mooing hymns like a lot of bloody cattle. Pat came down. She looked up at him. He put the plate into the sink.

'How long are we goin' to keep him up there?' he demanded. He'd asked the same question before.

Marie said irritably, 'Till she comes. I've told you. Sean's told you. Stop asking the same thing every minute, for Christ's sake. You'll get your chance.'

'What happens if she don't come?'

Marie wouldn't consider that. She was living for the call to say that Claire Fraser had been spotted at the airport. She'd fly, of course, wasting no time. They had friends looking out for her. Some on the day ferry too, but only as a precaution.

'She'll come looking for him,' she snapped. 'She won't stay snug in England when he might be in trouble! They've a close kind of a relationship, those two. I ought to know.'

She lit a cigarette, puffing it angrily. The dour young man got on her nerves. He was itching to kill Frank. For some reason beyond her understanding, that grated on her. She preferred the Dublin gangster, Willie, with his rough threats and foul mouth. She turned up the sound and the credits began rolling over the screen to the background of a final hymn. Upstairs, listening to the verses coming clearly through to him, Frank knew now why he was being kept alive.

He wrenched and wrenched in helpless fury at the handcuffs. He tried to heave the bed near to the painted-out window, and then realized that they'd hear him down below. He sweated till he was wet through. Claire. That was what they were waiting for. They were waiting to seize Claire, and using him to bait the trap for her. He could see the reasoning behind it all. She was the prize.

To kidnap and murder a British Cabinet Minister's wife would be a propaganda coup like the murder of Mountbatten. It proclaimed the power of the IRA and its ability to choose a target, however well protected, and destroy it. His uncle Kevin had said as much. 'We can strike at anyone, any time, no matter who they are.' It was Marie, of course, who'd put them up to it. 'They've a close kind of a relationship, those two . . .' Her dreadful twisted jealousy had seen Claire's love and loyalty as something they could exploit. Claire would come back to Ireland, drawn by God knew what trick. She'd come, and they'd die together, watched by that demonic woman.

He lay awake, judging the time by the television programmes. He got down and listened, and heard the news. No clues to the whereabouts of missing banker Frank Arbuthnot. Claire would come. Claire would be followed and seized. The door to his prison would open and they'd bring her in for him to see, before they killed him.

The night passed. He lay in mental agony until he heard sounds from below. They were awake and moving around. He got out of bed again and crouched on the floor to listen.

'I'll be off then,' Pat said. He'd made himself breakfast. That lazy bitch never did a hand's turn if she could help it. He'd eaten the same old rubbish as the one upstairs.

'Willie's not here,' Marie pointed out.

'He's late so, but I can't wait. I've me job to get to. Here, give him the key of the cuffs and the gun. And don't go near *him* till Willie gets here!'

Frank stayed very still. He heard a door closing. Marie was alone in the house. She had the gun and the key to his handcuffs. He got up slowly. A few minutes for the one with the killer eyes to be on his way. A chance in millions that he could get Marie to come upstairs before the replacement got there. He had to try. He had to take that chance, however hopeless, and pray to the God above for time and carelessness on her part. He made up his mind. He let his body fall heavily to the floor and then he began to scream as if he was in pain.

The sudden noise made Marie jump to her feet. The cries were terrible. She heard her own name, 'Marie! Marie!' ending in a moan of agony. She hesitated. She swore furiously, looking quickly out of the window. No car turning in, no Willie. It came again, more piteous than before, 'Marie . . .' She picked up the gun, slipped the safety catch off and ran upstairs.

He was lying on the floor, grotesquely twisted, the pinioned arm at a horrible angle. He groaned and cried out as she opened the door and came a few steps into the room. She held the gun pointed at him.

'My arm's broken,' he moaned and then lolled back as if he were fainting. 'Help me . . .'

'Oh, Jesus Christ!' Marie exclaimed. She came towards him, and as she grew near, subconsciously she lowered the gun.

It was too late for her to move back. His left fist lashed out with every vestige of strength. At the same moment she pulled the trigger. The blow caught her on the side of the face and threw her backwards, crashing against the wall. She was knocked out instantly. The gun clattered on to the ground. The effort had nearly pulled his right arm out of its socket.

She had the key of the handcuffs. He heaved and pulled at the heavy bed, inching to within reach of where she lay. She had a cardigan on. The pockets were empty. She'd have put the key in her bag. He could have broken down and wept with disappointment. At any moment the thug Willie would arrive, and then his only hope was gone. Even if he held him up with Marie's gun, he was comparatively helpless secured to the bed. He manoeuvred the bed backwards, reaching for the gun. He had to take the only chance left. He brought the muzzle up to the lock mechanism on the handcuff round the bedpost, his wrist as far away as possible, and pulled the trigger.

The bullet shot the locking device to pieces. At the same moment he felt a sharp blow, as it ricocheted off the wall into his side. He didn't notice the pain in his calf, where Marie's shot had grazed the skin, making it bleed. He only knew that he was free and he might have only a few seconds to get out of the house. He was unaware of pain, just a slight burning in his leg and a tiny trickle of blood that spattered the floor as he moved. He was down the stairs and by the front door. Nobody was in sight. There was a car parked outside. The BMW sports he'd given Marie as a Christmas present. The keys. He had to have the keys. They'd be in her bag. She never left them in the car. He found the bag on the kitchen table and the keys were in it. So were the keys to the handcuffs. He had her gun and a fast car. Once he got behind the wheel he could make the nearest Gardai station, as soon as he knew where he was. He didn't feel weakness or shock.

He pulled the front door shut and ran to the car. He was perfectly steady. He opened it, slid into the front seat and winced momentarily as a spasm twisted him. Then the key turned and the superb engine was alive. He backed the car, turned it and put his foot down. He was out of the little drive and on the road. He still didn't know where he was.

The phone in the house began to ring. It rang and rang. When Willie got no answer, he rang Sean Filey, and told him his car had broken down and he couldn't get through to Marie to tell her.

'I'm coming to get you. Be on the doorstep.'

It was no use Sean going to the house alone. He was unarmed and unequipped to deal with trouble, and he knew something had gone wrong. It was a ten-minute detour to fetch Willie, but he had to make it.

Frank slowed at a crossroads. There was the Smurfit building. He knew where he was. He hesitated and saw the red car coming towards him with Willie at the wheel. To be caught now, at this last moment . . . A very sharp pain ran through him and a feeling of dizziness. He didn't hesitate. He didn't think. He had to escape, to outrun that car and get to safety somewhere. If they caught him, he couldn't warn Claire. He swung the wheel and sent the car hurtling towards Kells. The car he'd seen turned after him.

Marie regained consciousness. She moaned and touched her face. Slowly, with much pain, she managed to get to her feet. He was gone. The shattered handcuff was lying on the floor. Her gun was gone. But there were bloodstains. She must have hit him. She tried to walk but sank down again, her legs giving way. There was a big bump on her head where she'd struck the wall. Her face felt as if it had been kicked in. She tasted salt blood in her mouth. And then she heard Sean's voice from below, calling her. She heard him coming up the stairs, and Willie's voice just outside. He'd got away. He'd tricked her and escaped. But she'd wounded him. There was a bullet in him somewhere. That would save her life.

He left the main road as soon as he could and went across country. He drove down the twisting pot-holed roads at desperate speed. There were villages and pubs. He slowed, hoping for the green Gardai sign, but he couldn't see one. The red car with Willie in it was in sight. He didn't need strength to drive; the steering was light as a feather and the response to anything he asked immediate. He picked up speed again, leaving the pursuer a little dot. The roads were against him. The car cornered beautifully, but he couldn't make the best use of her dramatic speed. He was in pain when he breathed now, and fighting the dizziness which came and went. Marie's bullet must have hit him. He forgot about the little wound in his calf. It had stopped bleeding. He had to slip that car. He had to outrun Willie or he'd be recaptured . . .

He came back on to the main road near Kells and he had to slow with the stream of traffic. The car came into view from behind. Straight over there was another sign: Cloncarrig. Reynard's old house. The hide, the secret place where nobody could find him. If he could get there . . . He cut across the road, causing two furious drivers to hoot and shout after him for risking a major accident. He sent the car flying down the country road, and saw the wall of the house loom up on the right. His body was numb and his head felt light. There was a track off the road. One field away was the folly with the secret room. He'd approached the house from the opposite side of the country. He pulled in off the road and stopped the car. He thought he was thinking fast and clearly. He had to reach the folly. Once there he would be safe. They wouldn't find him and Claire there.

He opened the door, steadied himself and started to walk. The red car he'd been escaping from sat at the entrance to the main road, waiting till the road was clear. The driver was not Willie. He was a prosperous farmer on his way home, and he kept muttering to himself that people who drove like that crazy fella shouldn't be allowed on the roads at all.

Frank kept the grey stone tower in sight, concentrating on it, fighting to stay on his feet and cross the field. Twice he fell and dragged himself upright. He had to get there. He had to escape them. If he didn't they'd capture his sister. She'd been so upset about the dead fox . . . He pulled his straying thoughts back to the present. Only a little further. The ditch ahead and then he was there. The ditch was steep and he slithered into the bottom of it and lay gasping. His eyes wanted to close. He wouldn't let them. Get up, on hands and knees. Crawl till you reach the top of it. Never mind the brambles. Pull free. Now, just a little further, there's the base of the wall. Oh, God, thank God . . . He was mumbling out loud.

Now, all you've got to do is get yourself up to that little window place. You can do it. Try. Try and you'll do it. He pulled himself up the first few feet, clung, almost fell backwards, and then found the final toe-hold.

He reached the dark sanctuary of the window, and slid through it on to the floor. He had got there. He would never be found now. He lost consciousness.

Two teenagers found the BMW with the keys in it. They crashed at ninety miles an hour near Swords. Both were killed and the BMW burnt out.

There was no sense of time. He heard his father talking to him, and he wasn't angry. He couldn't understand what was said because it was a murmur, like listening to people in another room. He thought he saw his mother. Young and pale, with the fine red hair in the photograph. She didn't speak to him because she was dead and he'd never heard her voice.

She faded, and it was his uncle Kevin in her place. He wanted Claire. They were going fishing and they'd be late. He called her, and she came dancing through the darkness to him, all legs and pigtails flying, and he smiled in his delirium. He felt no pain, no sense of dying. He drifted from waking dream to fitful sleep, immobile, unaware of cold or dampness. The stillness prolonged his life. The exertion in reaching Reynard's hide had caused an internal haemorrhage and massive shock.

At the moment when Billy Gorman died rather than betray Claire, her brother saw her in hallucination, blonde as the sunshine, smiling at him, planning a day's enjoyment. As Claire Fraser set out to find him from the opposite end of the estate, crossing fields and ditches, Frank was back in time, floating between dream and reality. He was out hunting, following hounds with Claire close behind.

'Let's go through there, I know a short cut,' she called to him.

He smiled and turned his horse to follow her. She wasn't Claudia's daughter for nothing.

She had been too bold. She fell off, the foolish girl,

and he had to pick her up, all muddy and swearing, and they rode home together.

Life was full of happy days. It was bright sunlight outside the narrow window. He opened his eyes and all the dreams had vanished. There was a marvellous sense of peace. He watched the bright blue sky and saw a powder puff of cloud scud past. Don't rain, he thought. It's such a grand day. And then he heard her. He heard her voice and knew it was no wandering in his mind. Clear and urgent, coming from below.

'Frank? Frank, are you there, Frank?'

He found the strength to answer. 'Clarry. I'm here. Come quickly.'

An articulated lorry had jacknifed on the Dundalk Road. It sat across the road like a stranded elephant, its German driver arguing hectically with two traffic policemen and a posse of infuriated motorists. A group of people watched the pantomime from the roadside. They were grinning and enjoying the spectacle.

Michael Harvey didn't waste time. He pulled up, leaped out of the car and went up to one of the uniformed Gardai.

'What's the quickest way to Kells? I've a job waiting an' I'll lose it if I'm stuck behind this fella for a good half-hour.'

'More like a good hour,' the officer said. 'He's got a puncture and all. Reverse back there and take the second to your right. Follow the signs to Clonkelty. It's a bit of a detour sure enough, but quicker than waitin' for this lot to clear.'

Michael Harvey grunted his thanks and sped back to the car. He was turning and twisting round the narrow side roads, watching his rear mirror out of habit, and cursing the delay. It had put a good forty minutes on to the journey. Gorman lay dead on the floor of his kitchen and if his killers were in front, then there was little hope of Harvey doing anything. They'd reach Claire Fraser and she'd be gone by the time he arrived. He was a man who'd learned to trust his instincts. On more than one occasion they had warned him and saved his life. They didn't warn him now. He felt somehow that luck was with him, and the pathetic old man had either not known, or died rather than disclose where Claire was heading.

It was crazy, no question about that. So crazy that only someone born and bred in the country would have taken it seriously. A man on the run for his life taking refuge in a fox's hide.

No crazier than the man who had built it as a refuge for himself in his reincarnated form. Harvey could just imagine what his superiors would make of a story like that. But he believed it. He knew the country and the people, and he knew that the Arbuthnot brother and sister would make use of it if need be.

He was back on the main road again. No doubt the lorry and its driver were still beached on the road, with a jam building up for miles behind them. He swung off to the east towards the ancient town of Kells, with its Celtic cross in the centre and the history of Ireland's greatest treasure, the monastic Book of Kells, the rarest survival of the golden age of Celtic culture before the Norsemen came to burn and ravage.

If he had guessed wrong, and that tale told by an English swimming pool in the heart of very English Gloucestershire was just a tale, then Harvey had come over for nothing. Claire Fraser could be anywhere, looking for the renegade brother. But once committed to a course, Harvey had been trained not to doubt. He put his foot down on the open road and swung round the last corner into the town of Kells itself. Cloncarrig was beyond the Headford estate, some six or so miles on the map. But he didn't know where the house would be. And he had to find the house before he could track down the folly Claire had described. He didn't risk going on through Kells and hoping to find it. He stopped, then sauntered into a seedy roadside lounge named Loughlin's. It was bare-floored and dim, with a stale sour smell of cigarettes and spilt drink. A man in shirt-sleeves and braces was reading the *Sporting Life* behind the bar. Two old women sipped Guinnesses in a far corner and raised their heads like turtles to look at him as he came in. He noticed a juke-box and space game in a corner. Progress had reached even here.

He bought twenty Carrolls cigarettes and a box of matches and asked where the old Reynard house might be. The man stared at him, nursing the sporting paper under one arm.

'It's over at Cloncarrig,' he said. 'It's empty.' He counted out Harvey's change. 'Been empty for years.'

'Can you see it from the road?' he asked, looking him boldly in the eye.

'No. It's set back up a drive. Nobody lives there,' he repeated, questioning why anyone should ask about it. 'It's fallen down by now, I'd think.'

Michael Harvey scooped up the coins. 'I'm lookin' for lead,' he said. 'To buy. Thanks a lot.'

The man watched him go, the lounge door swinging behind him. 'Buy is it?' he muttered.

One of the old women giggled; they'd been listening to the exchange. 'Buy me arse,' she chuckled. 'Divil a bit of lead he'll find. Our lads have had it all!'

Even the dour old barman joined in her laughter.

He passed the magnificent gates of the Marquis of Headford's estate. He drove on down the road, watching the miles on the clock, and almost missed the faded little signpost to Cloncarrig. It was a hamlet, a cluster of grey stone houses either side of the street, with a big ugly church at one end, and signs saying Kelly's Lounge Bar, and another Loughlin's, cheek by jowl with a mean little shop with a green post office sign outside it. A large, dirty dog with prominent ribs scoured the gutter for scraps and looked up briefly as the car passed. Two young girls, both wheeling prams, walked side by side in deep conversation. He wondered what the people did for work. The hamlet was gone like a dream blinked away, and the road was open before him, with fields and

309

belts of tall trees. Rooks nested in them; their clumsy flight and raucous calling reminded him of long ago when he walked the woods with his father and his first rifle. Pests, they were, killing off the nestlings of other birds. For all their clumsiness, they were clever and difficult to shoot.

He took his foot off and slowed down. Nothing following him, and nothing in front. Up a drive, the man in the lounge had said. That meant some kind of gates maybe, certainly an entrance. It would be overgrown, but still there. He saw something on the left, and slowed right down. There had been gates, but they'd gone. Only the tall stone piers were left; one was crumbled half away and both were robed in triumphant ivy. He turned the car in and found the remains of a drive. Pot-holed, muddy, carpeted with weeds. A wind had blown down some branches from the trees on either side. Light, twiggy things, the car passed over them. As another car had done, he noticed, seeing the broken branches. One, quite substantial, had been laid at the side. He saw the house at the end, revealed by a turn in the approach, and for a moment, just as Claire had done, he thought it was inhabited. But only for a moment. There was no roof, no window glass. The front door leant like a drunken man on two hinges, and the flight of steps leading to it was green with moss and sprouting couch grass through the cracked stone. It reared up in front of him, sightless and open to the air. He'd seen many houses like it before.

There was no point in stopping; he had to get his bearings and put his car out of sight. And where better than in the place designed for cars, if it still stood – round by the back, under a handsome archway, through the dripping trees and crowded bushes that had become a jungle, and there were the garages, and beyond was what had been the stable block, with a weathervane of a horse turning idly in the breeze on the skeleton of its roof. All the slates had gone, and the clock in the clock tower had been shattered by stones. He drove in under shelter; there was a door that actually closed if heaved by brute strength across the entrance.

He took the automatic rifle out of the boot, packed the ammunition in the pockets of his anorak, checked the gun and lodged it in his belt. Then with the car hidden, he skirted the old mansion and came out on the west side, facing a sheet of grey-green water that had once been a fine lake. Beyond it, like a pencil tip writing in the sky, Harvey saw the first of the follies, three long fields away. He set off at a slow, jogging run that covered the ground at a surprising rate.

From the windows of the empty house, the birds roosting in the ruins inside watched the figure of the man get smaller, and the danger to themselves diminish with him.

Marie Dempster stood by the window in the house. Pat, the professional from Cork, with the brutish Willie driving, had set off for Kells. And behind them, in a separate car, Hugh Macbride followed as back-up.

'Spy,' she said bitterly to Sean Filey. 'He's gone to spy and report back if something goes wrong.'

Filey shrugged. 'He can't do either of us any harm,' he said. 'We have our own council down here; they have theirs in the North.'

'He can make trouble for me,' she said. She touched her bruised face with a timid finger. 'He'll find a way to blame me if they don't find her.'

Sean knew that she was afraid.

'We know where the car is; the place is empty and derelict. She knows Arbuthnot better than anyone in the world. If she's gone there, it's because she expects to find him. We'll get them both.' He turned away from the window. He looked at his watch. The gesture made her want to scream. 'I have to look in on a patient at the Rotunda,' he said. 'Phone me there if anything comes up. Otherwise I'll go straight home.'

'And what about me?' she demanded.

'You wait here,' he said. 'Don't you want to be on the welcoming committee?'

She let the curtain drop and swung away from him. He couldn't help turning the knife. Maybe it was a reaction from the patient kindness he needed in his profession. It was difficult to imagine him being sympathetic, but she knew his reputation. She knew that he spent longer with the poor in the state mental hospitals than he did with the rich neurotics who could pay. He had a heart somewhere, but she had never seen evidence of it. Whoever said the Irish were all hot blood and impetuosity? Some of them were cold as charity. He left and she heard his car drive away.

She was alone, and she didn't know for how long. It might be many hours before the others came back. It might be soon. The suspense was tearing at her with sharp teeth. She couldn't sit still. She walked in and out of the few rooms on the ground floor, and then found herself drawn to mount the stairs and pass along the narrow passage. There was the room where he'd been kept. She opened the door and stood on the threshold. One hand reached out and switched on the light. The window had been whitewashed. There was the bed where he'd been confined. And the few drops of his blood staining the bare floor.

'Oh, God,' she said aloud. 'God, how I hate you. If you'd loved me, none of it would have happened. But it was her, you bastard. She was the one.' She leant against the door frame and began to cry. No tears came, only the anguished sobs of a woman suffering past endurance. And then the storm was over. Filey was right. She'd never be at peace till Arbuthnot was dead. Maybe then she would stop loving him.

She went back down the stairs to sit and wait.

Hugh Macbride followed the other car at a safe distance. He had lived with searches and road blocks most of his life. He knew the real meaning of living in the midst of a savage civil war. The Dublin heavy and the self-proclaimed hard man from Cork didn't impress him. They'd managed to kill the old fellow at Riverstown and got nothing out of him for their pains. He grunted and swore when he thought of that. He was following, and he'd be close enough when the action started to take over if it was necessary. He had his own gun, concealed in the car under the seat, and he wouldn't hesitate to use it on Mrs Fraser if she made any resistance. He knew how to disable without killing. The killing was the easy part. He'd leave that to Filey's men.

There was heavy traffic, unexpected at that time of the early afternoon. He scowled, moving a few yards at a time. Willie's grey Cortina was there ahead of him, likewise slowed to a crawl. He found the reason on the Dundalk road. A huge lorry had come to grief and been moved far enough over to allow one lane of traffic under the control of a policeman. Once past the obstacle, the cars picked up speed, as drivers vented their frustration and drove fast to make up lost time.

Turning down the main road into Kells he saw Willie's indicator flashing. The Cortina pulled into the side. The one called Pat got out and walked back to Macbride. He put his head through the open window.

'Willie's goin' to make sure of the road. The map doesn't show it.'

Willie had gone into Loughlin's lounge. The car with Gorman's number plate had been sighted under some trees on the old Reynard estate by a man out walking his dogs. But it was off the main road. Willie didn't buy cigarettes as Major Harvey had done. The same man was behind the bar, wiping it down with a wet cloth.

Willie said, 'I'm lookin' for a place off Cloncarrig Road. Mount Reynard. D'ye know it?'

The man nodded. 'I do,' he said. 'You're the second asking about it today.'

Willie stiffened. 'A woman, was it?'

'Not at all.' The barman dismissed the suggestion. 'A youngish fella. Lookin' for lead, he says. Lookin' to steal some, says I to meself. I told him the way. You wouldn't be after lead, would ye?'

'No,' Willie answered. 'Was he a dark sort of a fella?'

The barman put his rag below the counter. He didn't much like the type of a man, with his nasal Dublin way of speaking, and that nasty look in the eye.

'Not dark at all,' he said. 'More reddish. Is there anythin' you're wantin'?'

'Only what I asked,' said Willie. 'The best way to the place off the Cloncarrig Road.'

For a moment, Loughlin, who owned his own lounge and could heave a trouble-maker through the door if he had to, was tempted to tell him the wrong way. But he thought better of it. There was something about the man; he didn't like the look of him at all. He'd be the kind who'd come back. He gave directions, and watched Willie hurry out.

Macbride saw him coming towards the car.

'There's someone else gone ahead of us,' he said. 'A man, askin' the way.' He saw the question coming. 'Not *him*. Ginger-haired, the man says. Askin' about lead.'

'Why wouldn't it be true?' Macbride demanded.

Willie shook his head. 'Ye heard the Doctor say. It's been empty for years. There'd not be a slate or a lead pipe left be now.'

Macbride narrowed his eyes for a moment. 'Forewarned is forearmed,' he snapped. 'Let's get goin'.'

They set off, and now Macbride eased his gun out from under the passenger seat and slipped it into his pocket. Another man asking the way to a derelict house on the same day. Coincidence? Maybe. Macbride didn't like coincidences. They usually meant that things went wrong.

It was a quarter to three; Neil Fraser had just come back from a visit to the Prime Minister. It was brief but sympathetic. The Prime Minister had been informed by the security services and was keeping in close touch. Major Harvey was an expert, and had in fact rescued a hostage in similar circumstances in the North. Neil said thank you, and pretended that he was optimistic, but he left the building with his head bowed and little optimism in his heart. He went back to his office, because he could be alone there.

His appointments had been cut down, leaving only the most important business. It had helped him to work. But that was in the morning. As the hours passed, and he calculated mentally that Harvey had arrived, and still there was no news, he began to fear. It was a strange feeling, because he couldn't remember ever being frightened in that way before.

This was not an ordinary fear. It crept, like a paralysis, until he couldn't think coherently. It churned his stomach, until he could have vomited. He had been a target for assassination. The threat of a bomb that would blow him to bits or leave him maimed had been very real. The lurking killer in the grounds of his home, or on the street, had threatened him. He had been worried by it, even nervous, but never the prey of this sick fear. He kept seeing his wife helpless, hooded, captive. Memories of other terrorist victims all over the world tormented him with images of Claire, terrified, being mistreated. Or dead. He couldn't bear the silence and he rang through to his secretary.

'Any calls?'

She knew what he meant. 'I'm sorry, sir. Nothing yet. Is there anything you want? Some coffee – tea?'

'No thanks. No, wait a minute. I think there's some whiskey in Bertie's office. I think he keeps a bottle for visiting firemen. Could you bring it in if there is some?'

He'd never had a drink in his office in his career. He'd never admitted to such a human weakness, but suddenly he didn't care. He wanted a drink. He wanted something to help him pass the time until he heard his wife was safe.

When his secretary buzzed, he snapped down the intercom button. His hand shook so much that he slopped a little whiskey out of the glass on to his desk.

'Jean, yes?'

'Mr Brownlow is here, sir. He wondered if you were busy or if he could see you for a few minutes. It's nothing urgent, he says. He was just in the vicinity.'

He wasn't coming with any news. No news, either good or bad.

'Ask him to come through,' Neil said.

He shook hands with Brownlow.

'You're sure I'm not disturbing you, Minister? I was on my way to the office and I thought I'd look in.'

Brownlow thought, the man's a wreck. He's aged twenty years in the last few hours. He felt sorry for him for the first time. He sat down, and refused a drink; he was surprised to see Fraser with whiskey on the desk. It just proved you couldn't rely on first impressions.

'There's been no news so far,' he said. 'That's not a bad sign. Of course the trouble is we've so little to go on.' He paused. Brownlow had never dropped in on anyone like Neil Fraser in his life. It was his way of trying to get more information out of him.

'Yes,' Neil said, because he couldn't think of anything else to say. 'Are you sure you won't join me? I felt it was excusable under the circumstances.' He lifted the glass and sipped a little.

Brownlow decided it might make Fraser relax if he accepted. 'Well, why not? Just a small one, thanks.'

Jean had to come in with a glass. Neil smiled, unaware that it was more of a grimace.

'I've got a junior chap here who keeps a sort of cocktail cabinet in his room. He gets all the visiting firemen to look after . . .' He repeated the cliché for the second time. 'I must say, it's come in handy today. Brownlow, when are we going to get some news?'

'I wish I could predict,' was the answer. 'If we'd any idea where your brother-in-law might be hiding, we'd know where Major Harvey had gone. He seemed to think he had a clue, but he wasn't giving any details away. You've no idea, have you?' He watched the Minister, looking for some sign of reticence. Politicians were masters of evading the issue.

'I wish to God I had,' was the reply.

Brownlow cleared his throat, signalling a sensitive question. 'Is it possible your wife would have confided in Major Harvey? Were they . . . er, close in any way?'

Neil Fraser understood the meaning of the question that Brownlow hadn't asked.

'The answer's no. Harvey was more of a friend and confidant to me than he ever was to my wife. They did talk about Ireland quite a lot. Which I didn't, because, to be honest, I couldn't stand the place.'

He finished his drink, and poured a second. He leaned forward and Brownlow thought, 'He's going to talk to me. He's desperate to talk to someone and all I've got to do is sit here and listen and look sympathetic.'

'Bloody awful climate,' Neil went on. 'Always raining. So depressing. The flies in the summer reminded me of the Australian outback. Well,' he shrugged, admitting that he'd exaggerated. 'Maybe not quite so bad, but you couldn't sit out by the river or go for a walk . . . They didn't seem to notice. It's because of the cattle, or the horses. I found the pace was so slow. Nobody hurried about anything. Some English people love the life over there for that reason. I couldn't stand it.' He sighed. 'Trouble is, I like the rat race, Brownlow. It's what makes me tick.'

'That's true of most of us.'

Neil didn't notice any interruption. 'That's what got on my wife's nerves about living over here,' he went on. 'She used to say, I've been brought up where there's time to breathe. No wonder everyone's on pills and dope and Yoga classes. It annoyed me quite a lot. But she wasn't critical in the beginning.'

Brownlow prompted gently. 'She was very young, wasn't she? It must have been quite a change marrying you, sir. Going straight into being an MP's wife.'

Neil dismissed the idea. 'Oh, she didn't mind that. She was wonderful with people, and she wanted me to be a success. We were very happy together.' He stopped suddenly and Brownlow didn't break the silence. 'I thought I'd be enough to make her happy,' Neil said slowly. 'Everything went so well to start with. We had our first boy, and I got promoted off the back benches. We had a lovely house, and she had a free hand to do whatever she liked. You don't mind me talking like this, I hope? I know it's confidential.'

'You can be quite sure of that,' Brownlow said. 'Please say anything you feel might help. Anything at all.'

'There isn't anything to put your finger on why it went wrong,' he said. 'We used to go to Ireland twice a year; I went to please her, but it was a relief when I was advised not to go after I got a Junior Minister's job. I think she knew I found the whole Irish scene a bore. And then her father died, and I thought maybe her mother might come over here to live . . . she was born in England, actually. But she wouldn't hear of it. And then my brother-in-law broke cover, so to speak. That's what started it going haywire for us.'

'How do you mean, broke cover?'

Neil frowned. He looked angry as he remembered. 'He came out in open support of the IRA. After Bloody Sunday.'

'That did have quite an effect on people in the Republic,' Brownlow said.

'That's what everyone thought,' Neil said. 'But I never believed it. My father-in-law cut him out of his will. That's what tipped the balance. He went to America and addressed Noraid rallies. Nice publicity for me, at this point in my career. Just when I was made Minister of Agriculture. It could have ruined me.'

'But it didn't,' Brownlow pointed out. 'Seeing the job you have today.'

'My wife didn't seem to realize what it meant to me,' he went on. 'I thought she'd got that brother and his crackpot ideas out of her system. We had two lovely children and for God's sake, I was being talked about as a possible Prime Minister in a few years . . . She wouldn't hear a word against him. He used to come over to London to see her. By that time I was a target and she couldn't risk going to Ireland any more. Can you imagine what the press would have made of those meetings if they'd ever found out?'

'You couldn't stop her?' Brownlow asked.

Neil Fraser said bitterly, 'He came first with her always. I was second best, if you want the truth. Sometimes, I used to wonder about the children even . . .'

'I see,' Brownlow said. 'Everything you say reinforces my original view that Arbuthnot's disappearance is part of an IRA plot to seize your wife. If they're as close as you say, it would be widely known. It looks to me as if he's still alive and being held where she'll be sure to look for him.' And that close-mouthed soldier has a bloody good idea where that might be, he said to himself. He took off a damned sight too confidently for someone going into a shot-in-the-dark situation . . .

'Tell me something,' Neil Fraser said. 'What happens if Major Harvey finds Arbuthnot and my wife together?'

Brownlow's expression didn't alter. 'He's only instructed to bring out your wife.'

He had got up to go, when the buzzer sounded. There was a call for Chief Superintendent Brownlow.

Neil said, 'Put it through. At once.'

It was impossible to judge what was being said. He watched the policeman's impassive face register nothing, while he said only, 'Yes . . . Right : . . I'll tell him . . . Right.' He turned and Neil saw a flicker in his eye that was more telling than words.

He said, 'She's been found? She's dead?'

'No, nothing like that,' Brownlow answered. 'No news of Mrs Fraser at all. But the old gardener at her home was found murdered. A set of UK number plates was hidden in his garage and the plates from his own car had been taken off. His dogs were shot dead and the poor devil had been beaten up and then shot. It's an IRA execution job, according to the local Gardai. Your mother-in-law found him. She got on to your home to

319

tell Mrs Fraser. She spoke to one of our chaps up there. She's no idea her daughter's missing and nobody let on. Apparently she's very distressed and a bit hysterical. I think it might be a good idea to telephone her and calm her down. Say your wife'll call back later.'

'What does it mean?' Neil demanded. 'Why would they kill old Billy Gorman?'

'Because he's obviously sheltered your wife,' Brownlow answered. 'The number plates matched those on the car she hired to drive over. Obviously they tried to beat him into saying where she'd gone. Either he didn't know or he wouldn't tell them, so they killed him. From that point of view it's good news. The chances are they haven't found her, and that's in Major Harvey's favour. I'll get back to my office now.'

Neil said, 'How long are you going to give Harvey?'

'Until nine o'clock tonight,' Brownlow replied. 'He said if he wasn't back by then, he was in trouble.'

'Now just a minute,' Neil confronted him. 'This murder has brought the thing into the open. Why not enlist Dublin now? How can one man hope to cope in a situation like this?'

'He's coped before. If you insist, I'll release the news and ask for help. But I'll tell you this, Minister. It'll be a sentence of death for Major Harvey and your wife. Take my advice. Give it till nine o'clock tonight.' He decided to be brutal. 'If they're not out of there by then, the chances are it won't matter what we do.'

The doctor had been sent for and he was sitting with Mrs Arbuthnot in the little study. The maid, Sheena, had been called from her home in Sallins and come hurrying up on her bicycle, agog with horror and excitement at the terrible news. Old Billy murdered, and herself coming home unexpected and going down to see him and finding him dead as a doornail in a pool of his own blood. Sheena was followed post haste by Molly, who'd come on from being a dim-witted parlourmaid to a plump middle-aged widow who cooked for the missus.

They'd lit a fire in the study and made tea, and rung up Doctor Simons at the Garda's suggestion. The missus looked white as a winding sheet and shaking all over. Molly laced the tea with whiskey for her, and hovered round with Sheena trying to listen while she made a statement. Old Joe Burns' son, looking a picture in his uniform, in Sheena's eye at least, sat in the kitchen while the senior officers talked to herself. He kept saying what a terrible thing it was for poor old Billy to be murdered like that . . . and him a poor old fella that never did anyone any harm. He looked grey-faced himself, the women thought, but then he was only a bit of a lad, and this was his first sight of a murdered man. No word of Miss Claire, he asked them, wouldn't she be dead with the shock of it when she heard? They shook their heads and said, not a word yet, but the missus had been on the telephone to England and she was waiting for a call.

Young Burns drank his tea and handed round his cigarettes. The old mother hadn't seen her, that was sure. She knew nothing. He could report that back. He'd been on duty in the station since he'd left the others at the house on the airport road. He'd no way of knowing if they'd any news till he could get to a phone. He said to Molly might he make a quick call home and tell his mother he'd be late for his tea . . . If he got back for any tea at all! The phone was outside in the main hall. He slipped through and paused, listening to the deep men's voices and the faint woman's tones coming from behind the study door, as he dialled. The woman Dempster answered. He didn't like the way she spoke to him. Cold and brisk, like he was the dirt under her feet. Mixing too long with Arbuthnot, that was her trouble. Giving herself airs. He spoke low and fast.

'Gorman's been found. The old missus came back early. She's been trying to get the daughter in England. No, she doesn't know. Tell the doctor. They have? Jesus . . .'

She'd rung off in her peremptory way, leaving him with his stale news. The car had been sighted over at

Cloncarrig, and the lads were on their way. He felt a flush of pride. They'd strike a blow at the enemy's heart when they got that woman. He thought of Gorman without a qualm of pity. Dirty old scut, he said to himself. Arse-crawling to the end, when decent Irishmen were fighting and dying for their liberty across the border. He'd do it again, if he had to . . . He went back to the kitchen and sat down to another cup of tea and a cigarette. His hand was quite steady and he'd lost the grey look. He'd nothing to fear. He'd never be found out.

'Now, Mrs Arbuthnot, you be sensible and take two of these little yolks with a nice cup of hot tea, and stay in your bed. You've had a terrible shock, remember.'

Claudia reluctantly held out her palm for the yellow and red tranquillizers. Dr Simons was a dear and he'd looked after the family for twenty years, but she hadn't the slightest intention of swallowing any pill. Claudia considered taking more than two aspirins for a headache as little short of drug addiction. He was right about the shock, of course. She couldn't stop herself shaking. It was a continuous tremor, as if she were rattling inside. The tea and the stiff lacing of whiskey had helped her. It gave the illusion of warmth; she'd been hurt often enough out hunting to know that it was an illusion. She'd stopped feeling sick, which was a mercy. She had in fact been sick, outside Billy's cottage, holding on to the door and retching with horror after finding his body. And the poor dead dogs lying there in their pen, with their brains spattered everywhere.

The Gardai had been very considerate. Of course she knew them all so well. They were so kind, and protective. And so shocked and enraged at what had happened. There'd been tears in the eyes of the old Gardai who'd just left her, shaking her by the hand and saying over and over, 'Don't ye worry yerself, ma'am. We'll get the dirty bastards that did it . . . we'll get them . . .'

'I know you will,' she'd said.

'Curse o' God on them,' he muttered, and after all

322

these years there was still something that chilled the blood in that old Irish malediction.

'I can't believe it,' she said. 'I can't believe anyone would hurt Billy.' A tear welled up and trickled down her face.

Doctor Simons shook his head. 'It's terrible times we live in,' he said. 'First that unfortunate poor devil Donny, and now this. God knows what's happening to Ireland.'

He'd been called to that murder, since his surgery was within a hundred yards of the railway bridge where the Sallins idiot stood to watch the trains. There'd been eight deep knife wounds in the chest and lungs. It had taken him a long time to forget the face of the dead man. There was a half-eaten sweet still in his mouth. The pink, sticky kind sold to the local children at a penny each.

'They never caught them,' Claudia said. 'They won't catch whoever did this to Billy. He'd been beaten, the Gardai told me. I can't believe it. I can't believe he'd been mixed up in something, but they found these car number plates in the shed . . . It doesn't make sense. All he wanted to do was have his dogs and do a bit round the place here. I've been trying to get through to Claire, but I can't get hold of her. She'll be broken-hearted.'

Doctor Simons stood up. 'I'll call Sheena. Go on up to your bed now, and take two of those. Another two in the middle of the night if you wake. And don't hesitate; give me a call any time, never mind the hour. I'll come right over if you don't feel too grand.'

He went off and she let Sheena help her up the stairs. She had tossed the pills into the fire as soon as his back was turned. But she felt terribly unsteady and the shaking persisted. A hot-water bottle, she told Sheena, and a good hot toddy. That'll do the trick.

As the girl arranged her pillows and covered her against a chill, Claudia thought suddenly, they're the kindest people in the world. She couldn't be kinder if she were tending her own mother. Yet they can be so cruel, so wild. There are people in the two villages so close to us who know who killed old Gorman. People know who killed poor Donny – and why. But they'll never tell. If this child fussing over my comfort knew who'd shot that old man after knocking him about, she wouldn't tell either. That's the legacy of our long rule over them. She turned her head to watch Sheena go out closing the door very carefully behind her.

'I'll be downstairs, ma'am. If you want anything, just press on the bell.'

Macbride told them to spread out when they reached Cloncarrig. He sent Willie to scour the fields, the silent Pat stayed by the Fraser woman's hidden car, and he elected to search the ruined house and the buildings.

He moved through the ground floor, his gun in his hand, stepping carefully over the rubble that littered the rooms. He cursed the birds that took fright and flew calling in alarm as he disturbed them. A large notice had been nailed to the banisters by the local authority: 'This building is dangerous'. It was an old notice, defaced by time, weather and the graffiti of the local children. No one could go upstairs, because the staircase had collapsed before it reached the first landing. He made a slow, careful search of the kitchen quarters after he'd been through the reception rooms. No sign of anyone having been there. There were no footsteps in the dust but his own.

Then he made his way down to the fetid basement, sloshing in rain water and rubbish. He knew that she and Arbuthnot were not there. He had a nose for people in hiding. When he started to look round the outbuildings he opened the one door that was heaved shut, and through the gloom he saw the outline of Michael Harvey's car. They weren't in the house, or in the garages and stables. Willie was looking for them in the open, Pat poised to take them if they tried to reach her car in the coppice of trees. And he would stay by this new discovery and wait for the man who had gone ahead of them to Loughlin's lounge and asked the way to the same abandoned house. Macbride had a good idea what kind of a man he might be and what he was doing there. They weren't the only ones looking for the British Cabinet Minister's wife.

It was Willie who saw her. He stopped and stared at the little figure hurrying along the rise on the next field, too far away to identify, but clearly not a man. He gave a grunt of excitement, checked his gun and set off. He couldn't move very fast because he was a heavy man, with a Guinness belly on him. He could fight like a bull at close quarters, but he wasn't made for running. He was over the rise himself and scrambling through the muddy, overgrown ditch, when he saw the tower and the woman set on the side of it like a fly. Then she was gone, and he knew that all he had to do was get there, and he'd have the both of them.

It was dark and she could scarcely see her brother's face. It was a pale blur against her breast. She stroked his hair. His body was heavy in her arms.

'I knew you'd come,' he said. 'I wouldn't let go because I knew you'd find me.'

'I'll get help,' she promised. 'I'll get you out of here.' She was weeping and her tears fell on him.

'Don't be silly,' he smiled up at her. 'I'm not going anywhere. I was shot . . . I can't remember much about it. I think it was Marie . . . or maybe it was my own fault. It doesn't matter now.'

'Oh Frank, Oh God, what can I do? Does it hurt terribly?' He didn't hear the anguish in her voice because at times it faded. Only the last question was a murmur and he tried to reassure her.

'No, no, I don't feel anything. Just tired, Clarry. She was so jealous of you – that's what made her do it. She knew I loved you the best . . .' He was wandering, and Claire held him close and went on stroking the damp hair, her fingers brushing against his cold cheek.

'I loved you the best.'

'As I've loved you,' she whispered. 'Better than anyone in the world. And always will. If I could, I'd die here with you.'

He moved in sudden agitation, his mind clear. Fear for her had brought everything into focus again.

'You've got to get away, they mustn't find you . . . it was you they wanted. I was just the bait. You must go home where you'll be safe. Back to England.'

'I will, I will,' she promised, trying to soothe him.

'Go to the Garda,' he insisted. 'They'll protect you. Whatever you do, don't try to do anything on your own . . . You promise me, Claire?'

'I promise.' She bent and kissed him.' Just be quiet now, and don't worry.'

It was so tempting. But he mustn't. He mustn't let himself sleep, not yet. There was so much he wanted to say to her, and so little time left to him. 'I always worried about you,' he said. There was no sunlit sky in the opening now, just clouds bringing the darkness closer to him. 'It's funny . . . I kept dreaming about us when we were children. We had such happy times, didn't we?'

'The best times in my life,' Claire said.

His hand came up and groped for hers. Their fingers intertwined, and she felt how cold he was.

'I'm so glad you came,' she heard him whisper. 'I don't mind anything now. It was bad luck on us, right from the start . . .'

'Yes,' Claire answered, knowing it was their common blood tie that he meant. 'It was. Rotten luck. My darling brother.'

She held him close, waiting for the end. The pain of truth mingled with the pain of loss. She felt his spirit leave him with a little sigh. She stroked his hair once more and held on to the lifeless hand. She thought she saw a heap of whitened bones in the corner and remembered the fox of long ago.

And then she heard the savage shout below.

'Come on out of there! Come on down or I'll come up and blast the two of ye!'

She froze in terror. She held her breath. They'd found her. She eased away from her dead brother, and felt for the heavy revolver with its clip of ammunition that she'd brought from Riverstown. She lifted it and loaded it.

'Are ye comin' out?' the bellow came again.

Claire braced herself against the wall, holding the gun in both hands. Frank had taught her to shoot when they were children. She thought, I'm not going to shake, I'm going to pull the trigger.

She heard a scratching noise and animal grunts as the man began to pull himself up. He'd have a gun too. If she hesitated, there'd be no second chance. They'd killed Frank . . . As his head came above the level of the little opening she fired.

As Willie saw Claire, so Michael Harvey saw him. He could see the clumsy figure lumbering along the field, and his easy lope became a run. He eased the automatic off his shoulder. He gained rapidly on the slow-moving target. There was the last of the three towers looming ahead, bathed in brilliant sunshine, and the man was at the base of it. His shouts floated back to Harvey. Claire Fraser was inside the folly. He stopped. The man was climbing. He brought the automatic rifle up to his shoulder and took aim. The crack of a shot split the silence. But the man fell backwards before he had time to fire. The brother was there, Michael Harvey thought. And armed, thank God.

He ran. And as he came close he saw the dead man lying face upward, his head a bloody pulp, and Claire Fraser slid to the ground and stood for a moment. She had a heavy old-fashioned army revolver in her right hand. When she saw him she raised it.

He shouted, 'Claire – it's me! It's Michael Harvey!'

She lowered the gun and he caught up with her and stopped her falling over the ugly corpse lying at her feet.

Pat heard the distant gunshot. He lifted his head and sniffed like a dog scenting prey. He was hidden behind the hired car under the beech trees. The one with the Irish number plates the dirty old bastard had put instead of the English ones. He'd paid the price, so Willie told him. His orders were so precise he didn't dare to disobey and move out of cover to see what was happening. He didn't want to be in the wrong place with someone like Macbride. The shot pleased him. That would take care of Arbuthnot maybe. He didn't think of the man who'd asked directions in Kells. It was only Macbride who'd been bothered about him. Pat was too stupid to imagine anything for himself. He lived for his hatred and the expression of it in killing the enemy. In Sean Filey's judgement, he was the classic psychopath who had a compulsion to murder. He stayed at his post, hidden among the trees.

There wasn't time for Claire to feel faint or heave at the sight of the dead man. Harvey bundled her to the perimeter of the field, trying to keep in the shelter of the hedges. He asked one question only: 'Did you find your brother?' and heard her answer as they hurried, bent low, Claire stumbling under his relentless urging.

'Yes. He was there. He's dead.'

He saw the tears streaming down her face. He wouldn't let her stop, or rest.

'There's more than one of them,' he threatened. 'They'll have heard that shot . . . Keep going, come on.'

He was brutal. He pushed and dragged her, and swore when she faltered. Both their lives depended upon keeping the impetus going. If he let her collapse on him, they'd never get moving again. He knew how to use cover; it took longer than the direct way across the open fields, but no watcher would have seen them. He asked one other question. Where had she left her car? The answer made him decide to go back to where his car was hidden.

Her car was in a clump of trees, far over to the left, just off the road. No doubt it had been seen and reported. That was what had brought the pursuers there. If he knew the form there'd be a man waiting by that car in case she went back to it.

When they reached the house itself, he kept close to

the outside wall, hissing at her to keep flat in the shelter of it. He had his automatic rifle at the ready. They skirted the building. It was very quiet. The sun had gone behind a heavy rain cloud and a few spots fell on them. Harvey kept moving steadily, walking like a cat. Claire trod on some loose stones and he swung on her furiously. Then he moved on, rounding the rear of the old mansion. The stable block and garages were through the archway.

He caught her arm. 'Through there,' he whispered. 'So far so good. Watch your feet. Not a sound, remember!'

Macbride looked at his watch in the darkness. The dial glowed at him. He'd been an hour waiting in the dark beside the car. He'd checked it. A change of clothes in the back. English clothes. As he thought: they'd sent someone over to find her. He waited with his gun in his hand, ready when the door opened and the man was silhouetted against the light. If he had the woman with him, too bad. Macbride knew that breed. He wasn't taking any chances.

'Wait here,' Harvey said softly. 'Don't move. My car's in there.'

She shrank back in the shelter of the archway. Dust and ivy embraced her. She watched him creep towards the line of half-open doors, many of them loose on a broken hinge. And then he stopped. Without turning his head, he raised his left hand to warn her not to move. He'd pulled the door across to hide his car. The drag marks were on the ground, scored deep into the dirt. A second lot of marks overlapped them and ran on by a good foot. Someone else had pulled that heavy door across since he'd been there.

He knew, as he had known in other situations, that there was a human being hiding there, waiting for him to show himself. He made a decision in the next few seconds. He grabbed the door and pulled. It lurched, unbalanced by its own weight and lack of proper support. Harvey dropped flat as it fell off its hinge. The figure of Hugh Macbride crouched in the corner, his gun levelled in both hands, came into Harvey's view, He fired before Macbride loosed off a single shot. Macbride was dead before he fell.

They didn't drive to the airport. They drove to the centre of Dublin, where Harvey changed his car for another make and left Claire sitting in the car hire office with a cup of tea and a man who never spoke a word. When he came back, he'd changed his clothes to the corduroys and jacket he'd worn when he left England.

'All fixed. Thanks, Bob,' Michael Harvey said to the man behind the desk.

He got up, nodded to Claire and went out. Harvey's manner was brisk. He wasn't going to be sympathetic. She had to keep going.

'I've fixed a private plane,' he said. 'We'll drive straight out to the airport now. It's not very big. I hope you're not airsick. Right, come on.'

She was numb in mind and in body. It was as if she were being moved about like a counter in some nightmare game. She couldn't think or feel. She did what he told her because if she questioned anything it meant she had to think. They arrived at the airport and she followed him obediently, boarded the Piper Comanche, strapped herself into the seat and shut her eyes as they took off. Beside her, Harvey decided she would just about last the trip.

'How long before we get to London?' she asked.

'We're not going to London,' he said. 'We're going to Belfast. There's some decent transport waiting there.'

He put his hand on hers and squeezed it. She was freezing cold and her hand was shaking as if she had a high fever.

'It's all over,' he said. 'You were bloody good. You'll be home and safe with Neil and the kids in a few hours. Here, take a big swig of this.'

He gave her a half-bottle of brandy. He had to unscrew

the top for her. She couldn't stop her hands from trembling, and her body was shaking with them.

'I'm glad I killed him,' she said. 'I'm very glad I killed him.'

She wouldn't be so glad, he thought, when the shock wore off.

'I wish I hadn't seen his face,' she said.

No, she shouldn't have to bear that too.

'You didn't shoot him,' he said. 'I got him first. I saw him going up the tower wall. An Armalite bullet makes a fair mess, you know. Forget about it. It wasn't anything you did.'

The call from Belfast had come through to Neil's office. His secretary didn't even knock. She came bursting in to give him the message. Direct via the Army. Mrs Fraser was on her way home, and would be landing at RAF Highmore at six o'clock. She had been seen by an army doctor, but she was unharmed and Major Harvey was travelling with her.

She couldn't help herself. She said, 'Oh, Minister, thank God!' and blinked back tears. She couldn't be sure as she hurried out in embarrassment, but he looked as if he were doing the same.

Claire had been given a sedative. It was very mild, the doctor assured her. Just enough to take the edge off, after what she'd gone through. She was offered sandwiches, which she couldn't eat, and coffee. The coffee was a godsend. She was very thirsty. There was a terrible dragging emptiness inside which made it an effort to speak.

People were being kind and protective, fussing over her because she was Neil Fraser's wife. She'd seen her brother die and two men killed. They hovered round her. The doctor and a senior WRAC officer sat and kept an eye, in case she cracked up. She wished they'd go away and leave her alone. How many Irish women in the past few years of conflict had coped with violent death, Claire wondered. No VIP treatment for them.

331

In the end, she said, 'I'm quite all right. Please don't worry about me.'

'Of course you are.' The girl in her smart uniform was comforting. She repeated Michael Harvey's words, 'You'll be home with your family in no time, Mrs Fraser.'

They sat side by side in the army transport plane. Now he could be easy on her.

'Claire,' he said. 'I meant it, you were marvellous. Now you've got to put it all behind you and get on with your life.'

She turned and looked at him. 'I don't want to go home,' she said.

They were flying steadily above the clouds. Michael Harvey drew a deep breath. He was fond of her. He admired her courage and her loyalty. She had guts and integrity and intelligence. But suddenly he was very angry.

'What about Neil?' he demanded. 'He'll be there waiting for you. What are you going to do, walk away from him?'

'I don't know,' she answered. 'I don't know what to do or where to go now.' A slow tear seeped out and ran down her cheek.

Harvey said quietly, 'Then I'll tell you what you do and where you go. You go back to your poor bloody husband who loves you, and your two little children. Your brother's dead. You walk out now and you'll spend the rest of your life looking for him. But you'll never find him. There'll be another man and that won't work either. Nothing would have worked so long as he was alive. And you know it.'

She put her hands to her face. He didn't spare her. He was fighting harder for this marriage than he'd ever fought to save his own.

'That chapter's closed. Neil loves you, he's always loved you. The kids need you; especially Peter. Go back and make it up to them all, Claire. It's the only way you'll be happy in the end.'

She didn't answer. She had stopped the silent weeping and sat with her head turned away from him. Make it up to them. She didn't ask him what he meant by that because she knew. As they came in to land she said, 'I don't want Frank moved. I want him left where he is. I don't want anyone disturbing him.'

Harvey nodded. 'I said in my report that he was dead. I didn't say where. It's up to you.'

'Thank you, Michael,' Claire said simply. 'Thank you for everything. Not just for saving my life.'

The plane taxied to a halt. He stood up and held out his hand to help her out of her seat.

'If you want to thank me,' he answered, 'go out and meet your husband.'

He let her leave the aircraft first. He saw Neil Fraser waiting on the tarmac.

For a moment Claire stopped. She had seen him too. It seemed a very long pause to Michael Harvey. Then she began to walk towards him. Moments later she and Neil Fraser were locked together.

Harvey began to walk down the tarmac, taking his time. They were still holding tight to each other as he came up to them.

'So far, so good,' he said under his breath.

The bodies of Willie and Hugh Macbride were taken away by their own people and given a military funeral in a lonely graveyard far to the north in the wilds of County Tyrone. Shots were fired over their graves and the tricolour flag of Ireland draped their coffins. They were heroes who had died in the course of their duty.

Sean Filey was tipped off that he was being watched by the Dublin Special Branch. There wasn't enough evidence to bring him to trial on a charge of kidnapping Frank Arbuthnot, and Claire couldn't be involved. His name and Marie Dempster's were passed to the Irish government as dangerous subversives. Filey applied for a visa to visit the United States for a conference of psychiatrists in Cincinnatti. He decided to accept a two-year fellowship, and his practice in Dublin was closed down. Patients, rich and poor, grieved at the loss of him. He had been a gentle healer of sick minds.

Marie Dempster was shot dead as she drove back from a party to her flat in Howth. The catastrophe which cost the life of Hugh Macbride was not to go unpunished. The sentence was pronounced upon her in the North. It was generally agreed up there that she must have connived at Arbuthnot's escape. If they'd been fobbed off with his alibi and Filey's defence of her before, it didn't hold any water now. Macbride himself had been suspicious and said so. It was reported as a robbery because her jewellery was taken. It was broken up and sold. The money went into a fund for widows and orphans of men killed in the struggle in the North.

Joe Burns applied for and got a transfer to a Gardai station in Trim. The family couldn't understand why he wanted to go. A better chance of promotion, he explained. He wasn't a nervous man, and he didn't have a twinge of conscience, but he didn't like driving past old Gorman's empty cottage of an evening. Once or twice he thought he'd heard those dogs of his barking in the darkness.

'Mummy,' the little boy said. 'I'm looking forward to Christmas.'

Claire smiled down at him. He liked to sit beside her on the sofa in front of the big open fire when he came back from school.

'So am I, Peter. It'll be nice to have Granny with us, won't it?'

'Yes,' he nodded happily. Claudia had a brisk no-nonsense attitude to children which pained the modern school of parents. Children loved it. She was affectionate but firm, and they felt entirely secure with her. 'Is she coming for long?' he asked.

'Quite long,' Claire answered. 'She's going to look for a house near us. That'll be nice too.'

A year ago she would have been impatient and brushed

the questions aside. His dark eyes were always searching her face for reassurance. She could never have imagined that a child could be company. A lot had changed since her life ended that spring in Ireland and began again in the months that followed. Slowly and painfully sometimes, with an ache of sadness. It hadn't been easy for Neil or for her. But a new kind of love was growing between them and it started when he had held her on the windy tarmac of the military airfield.

'My darling, thank God, thank God . . .' was all he said.

And she had said simply, 'I'm so sorry, Neil.'

'Mummy, isn't Granny going back to Ireland any more?'

'I don't know, darling. I expect she will.'

Claudia didn't need persuading. 'I can't stay here,' she told them. 'I see poor old Billy walking those dogs by the river every time I look out of the window . . . I'd as soon sell up if you don't want the house yourself.'

And Claire hadn't hesitated either. Neil, waiting for the answer, heard her say, 'No, Mum. You put it on the market.'

Peter edged a little closer to his mother. 'Will Granny be with us when the new baby comes?'

'I'm sure she will,' Claire answered. 'It'll be nice to have a baby, won't it? Lucy's growing up so fast.'

He didn't say anything for a moment. He had very dark hair and she ran her hand gently over his head.

'You won't love it better than Lucy and me, will you?'

She turned him to look at her. He glanced downwards and away, so that her heart turned over in recognition. 'You'll never find him,' Michael Harvey had warned her. He was right about everything else, but wrong about that. The Arbuthnot genes were strong in her son.

'No,' Claire said firmly. 'I'll never love anyone better than you and Lucy. Now I think that's Daddy's car outside. Let's go and meet him, shall we?'

Snow fell in Ireland that winter. There was no hunting.

No foxes ran at Cloncarrig any more. The Flanagans had refused the hunt permission to cross their land for many years.

Snow fell at Riverstown and it was so cold that part of the river froze. There was a new bus stop put up on the Naas road, and two women waited there, huddled against the driving wind. Such a winter was unknown. Everybody talked about it. It was grand for the children, throwing snowballs.

One woman was old, the other young. They worked at a very grand stud about a mile up the road, cooking and house cleaning for the family. There was a large 'For Sale' sign nailed up beside the gates of Riverstown. The young woman looked at it, pulling her collar close round her neck.

'I heard the missus say she'd gone to England,' she remarked.

'She had so,' the old woman said. 'The trouble was too much for her.'

'They were here a long time,' the girl said. 'My auld dad said they came here after Wolfe Tone.'

'Maybe they did, so,' the old woman muttered. 'They come. But in the end they go. Thanks be to God, here comes the bus.'